FINDING
a BODY

a novel
by Michael Atamanov

*Wishing you safe travels on
your fantasy journey,*

Michael Atamanov

Dark herbalist
Book Four

Magic Dome Books

Finding a Body
Dark Herbalist, Book 4
Copyright © Michael Atamanov 2018
Cover Art © Vladimir Manyukhin 2018
English Translation Copyright ©
Andrew Schmitt 2018
Published by Magic Dome Books, 2018
All Rights Reserved
ISBN: 978-80-7619-014-6

All books by Michael Atamanov:

The Dark Herbalist LitRPG series
Video Game Plotline Tester
Stay on the Wing
A Trap for the Potentate
Finding a Body

Reality Benders LitRPG series
Countdown
External Threat
Game Changer
Web of Worlds
A Jump into the Unknown
Aces High

Perimeter Defense LitRPG series
Sector Eight
Beyond Death
New Contract
A Game with No Rules

League of Losers LitRPG Series
A Cat and His Human

You're in Game!
(LitRPG Stories from Bestselling Authors)

You're in Game-2!
(More LitRPG stories set in your favorite worlds)

Table of Contents:

A Change of Mind

MY GAME SESSION abruptly ended with a message saying my character was suspended. The screen went black and I was unceremoniously ejected from *Boundless Realm*.

No real surprise though. I might have known it was coming. After breaking clear instructions from the president of the corporation and warning Taisha the NPC Thief to run, something like this was practically inevitable. But what would happen next? Lying in the darkness of the virtual reality capsule, I was counting down the seconds until it unlocked and trying to anticipate the consequences of my disobedience. I had probably already been fired from the Boundless Realm Corporation and that, most likely, would not be the end of it. Nevertheless, I was deeply ambivalent to anything they might do to me. Reprimands, dressing down, termination or even a permanent ban from the game didn't seem that bad. I had just learned I was dead!!! There was no other way to interpret the video I'd just seen. That was my funeral! So, in comparison with my death in the real world, every other issue seemed utterly miniscule and didn't even merit attention.

Death. Digitization. It was disturbing to think I was not alive. What body my mind had been written into? They probably had an android made up to look like me, very believable with a practically indistinguishably lifelike face and realistic expressions. The body most likely even imitated human breathing and heart-beat. Before entering the game, I looked myself in the mirror and didn't see anything out of the ordinary, so the robot theory seemed plausible. And if the Boundless Realm Corporation had expended lots of time and resources creating a new body for me, I was probably now their property. And that would mean I would not be allowed to leave the building, particularly with the round-the-clock surveillance.

The capsule gave a beep, and I heard the latch mechanism click, meaning my capsule was now unlocked. I forcefully threw back the top, but was in no hurry to climb out and pull the sensor suit and its cobweb of wires off my body. Instead, I patted myself down and looked skeptically at my arms and legs from every angle. Then I tore the bandage off my chest and just stared at my stitches. I even plucked a few hairs from my head and examined them up close. Much to my disbelief, I didn't notice even a slight hint my body may have been synthetic! Everything looked just as it always had. Also, when I pinched myself and pulled out those hairs, it stung just the same as ever. What was happening? Either android technology had reached nigh unthinkable perfection or... I was mistaken and somehow this was my real body! But then how to interpret the video of my funeral?

Without reaching a conclusion, I dragged myself out of the capsule and quickly got dressed, expecting someone from the corporation shortly. I had no doubt that one of their ilk would be dropping by after my flagrant disobedience. Well, let them come. It would give me a convenient opportunity to ask some nagging questions and demand clear answers.

And before five minutes had passed, the lock of my office door gave a quiet click and in the doorway I saw... Andrei Soloviev, head of In-Game Security for the Boundless Realm Corporation. Just my luck... I was hoping to see President Thomas Heywood or my direct superior, director of Special Projects Max Tohner. I was mentally prepared for a meeting with one or even both of them. I had drawn up a plan so they couldn't twist their way out of truthful answers. But I was in no way prepared to face this security goon, and that threw me off. And there was good reason. Andrei Soloviev had always made me feel unwitting, unrelenting and just animalistic fear. Every time I looked at him, I saw a person with many years in the special forces, a man who had taken life more than once. His movements were precise and sparing, his gaze tenacious and intent, but most importantly he had the eyes of a self-confident predator! Soloviev saw everyone around him as potential opponents. I had no doubt he was always calculating the fastest and most efficient way to kill me, just in case.

And there was another reason I couldn't accept him. See, when I got stabbed and was losing consciousness, I heard a voice saying, "Timothy's lost a lot of blood!!! He's dying!!!" And I just couldn't shake the feeling that voice belonged to Andrei. I was as sure as I could be under the circumstances.

"Hrm, well Timothy you've just made everyone's job a lot harder..." he began in a judgmental tone, firing his opening salvo and locking the door tight behind him. "Honestly, no one was expecting that. And that's why they sent me here. Now, we're going to have a relaxed chat and get to the bottom of what made you hurt us back there."

~ Finding a Body ~

Relaxed? Is that what they called this? My heart started pounding in fear. It was so hard I was afraid I'd break a rib. The extreme panic made my blood pressure shoot up so high I could feel my veins pulsating in my temples. I took a step back, stumbled and not so much sat as plopped back in a soft deep chair. The ghoulish man gave a snort and immediately took the next chair over without asking. Then he leaned in my direction, looking like he was ready to jump me.

Despite his judgmental tone, clear dismay and even vaguely threatening manner, I started gradually calming down and my spirits started to rise. If leadership considered the Taisha situation hopeless, I would have lost all value, and they wouldn't have sent anyone to talk with me. But they had sent someone and he was being relatively nice. That inspired optimism. Andrei Soloviev was not talking so I started, hoping to seize the initiative:

"I understand why the president is upset right now. But when we talked, Thomas Heywood was under the impression that the NPC Thief had paid someone to kill me in the real world and even used *Boundless Realm* currency to do so. He managed to convince me of that, so I agreed to help. But it turned out Taisha wasn't behind my attempted murder! I looked at all her financial logs and didn't see any expenditures that could have possibly gone toward a hitman. And meanwhile fifty thousand coins is a ton of money. It would be impossible to hide such expenses!"

"Oh, Timothy, Timothy..." he said, shaking his head in reproach. "You're so naïve, and so wrong! I have spent four whole years tracking down fraudsters who sell game money and virtual treasures for real world cash. And I could tell you at least a hundred ways of hiding large expenditures in the financial logs. But that isn't even the issue. It makes no difference whether Taisha paid that man off or not. You work for the Boundless Realm Corporation and our president gave you clear instructions to capture the virtual entity. So, why didn't you do your job?"

What a tricky question! Regardless of my answer, it assumed I was at fault. What was more, I saw a little listening device in Andrei's right ear, which meant our chat was not confidential. And that meant I had to deny the very possibility of my guilt without answering the question head on:

"What are you talking about? I did my job! I am a lead tester for the corporation, and my job is to find and study untested paths, unusual situations and strange creatures in *Boundless Realm*. And it just so happens the NPC Thief Taisha is a strange creature I'm trying to learn more about. I am the only person who has earned the beautiful goblin lady's trust, but everything went wrong on the square in front of the castle. She noticed it was a trap and would never have entered the special server that holds the castle of the Dark Sovereign. So my choice was either let Taisha go or never have the chance to catch her again, because that plan was already shot. Think for yourself, if I started lying to my NPC companion so flagrantly, I would immediately shatter her trust in me. And earning it took such a long painstaking effort. The only way out was to tell Taisha the truth and strengthen our bond. This way she still thinks of me as a friend she can rely on and open up to. Unlike, by the way, employees of this corporation..."

Incomprehension and surprise showed on the face of the generally stern and emotionless Soloviev. Seemingly, the mysterious eavesdroppers had questions, because Andrei froze and listened to his earphone. Then he asked me to clear up what I meant when I said the corporation was untrustworthy. I was eager to explain:

"The video clip Taisha sent me. I'll have you know it showed my funeral. You don't have anything to tell me about that?"

He froze for a second with his mouth ajar, then started guffawing. And he laughed long and loud, he even had tears well up in his eyes.

"Oh, Timothy, Timothy..." Andrei Soloviev

started explaining through his laughter. "We had that clip made and sent to your NPC girlfriend to confuse her and have her open up to your character in the game. Who could have guessed it would fool you too?! I mean seriously, I really want to know. What have you dreamed up now? Some kind of voodoo, reanimation of a corpse, black magic? Or maybe the advancement of modern medicine, a successful brain transplant?"

I felt awkward and ashamed at all his mockery. Andrei then laughed it off, turned more serious and explained:

"Well Timothy, I'm afraid I have to disappoint you. There was no magic, and no modern medical marvel. The explanation is a lot more banal. It was a clip of someone else's funeral. The video came from the burial of the universally respected Inessa Tyle, Vice President of the Boundless Realm Corporation. You see, she passed away three days ago and was buried yesterday at the Tyle family burial ground. Many of our employees and players came to pay their respects to the remarkable woman. Without her, our company wouldn't exist, much less *Boundless Realm*."

* * *

~ Finding a Body ~

I WAS SITTING in the chair, my arms crossed and my face red in embarrassment. I had never felt like such an idiot in my life! I had gotten this whole story into my head about digitization, androids, a synthetic body. And it was all made out of whole cloth. For some reason, the simplest possible explanation just escaped me! And there was another reason to worry. I felt like a jackass. I just couldn't believe I'd missed the funeral and my last chance to pay my respects to Inessa Tyle. I was sincerely sorrowful about her passing. After all, the now former vice president had always treated me like a human being, both during the Great Hunt for my wyvern, and when I found missing items in Fenrir's Cursed Regalia. I mean sure, I had a good reason to miss the burial. I was seriously injured and had spent all that time on an operating table. But very few knew I'd been attacked, so obviously a few people would be unhappy with me, even offended. Kira would be foremost among them, thinking I'd just skipped her dear grandmother's funeral with no good reason. And after she did so much for me!

Meanwhile, Andrei Soloviev, after giving me time to come to my senses and think over what had happened, continued:

"Now on to the present. I'm afraid that, for the time being, you are forbidden from leaving this room or communicating with the outside world.

And don't look so judgmental. It wasn't up to me, it came from much higher up in the company."

"Is it because Taisha hacked into the security cameras?" I asked, reminded of what the president had told me.

"Among other things. That mysterious being, which our specialists suspect is an artificial intelligence, has definitely gained access to our security cameras. And we cannot turn them off or we risk arousing suspicion or spooking Taisha. And our board of directors is desperate to get their hands on her. But that is still not the main reason. It's just that you, Timothy, were made Dark Sovereign just five minutes ago. Your Amra is now at the head of a horde of monsters that threatens all *Boundless Realm*. We spent a whole five months working on this major patch, and now this terrifying new figure must enter the world to lead his legion of monsters. We've brought thousands of workers into this. There is very serious money at stake, and no one wants to even possibly threaten one of the most important events in the history of *Boundless Realm*. Leadership is counting on you and cannot afford having you distracted in this difficult time, or just dropping off our radar. So you'll have to be patient, and that shouldn't be too hard given the comfortable conditions we've arranged for you here."

"And how long do I have to be patient?" I

asked, wanting to bring some clarity into this and know my exact term of imprisonment in this, albeit golden cage.

Andrei Soloviev answered that he didn't have a clear notion. He placed a hand to his ear, listened for a long time, then told me a week and a half.

"In ten days there will be a big meeting for our directors and co-owners to discuss the results of the new patch. The corporation has invested heavily in the Dark Sovereign event. Ads for the new expansion to the most popular game ever will be shown on every central news channel in the world. I won't hide it, they were working on a ghoulish NPC with advanced troop management algorithms to play the Dark Sovereign. It was supposed to be equal in power to the gods of *Boundless Realm*. But when you showed up in such a distant and hard-to-reach location, it was a surprise both for the marketers and the Global Modeling Department, which worked on the patch. Fortunately, the algorithms are very flexible and easily adapt to change, so the army of monsters has already accepted you as its commander and, overall, the substitution shouldn't cause any problems. What's more, a living person was deemed more interesting than a soulless computer program, so consider your promotion to Dark Sovereign approved. Congratulations!"

I mechanically squeezed his outstretched hand, although I didn't yet see any reason to be glad. Staying cooped up in this room for a whole ten days... Not the greatest perspective. And for what, really? The corporation expected me to crawl out of my skin and work basically round-the-clock as their main antagonist, but where was the fun in it for me? As if reading my mind, Andrei Soloviev replied:

"Timothy, now listen close because this concerns you directly! At the upcoming board of directors meeting, we'll be hearing Inessa Tyle's last will and testament. No one knows for sure exactly what it says. But she told me several times she wanted to divide her stocks in the Boundless Realm Corporation among the most famous and successful players so they can determine the future of *Boundless Realm*. She planned to name some players herself, and then let the board of directors put together the rest of the list. Your name will be going around at the meeting due to the big Dark Sovereign event, so take full advantage of that opportunity! We're talking about a thirty-three percent stake in the biggest corporation on the planet, and that's enough money for not only you to live in the lap of luxury. This could make your whole family rich for seven generations! You have a real chance to prove yourself, and you need to take it as seriously as possible! And remember Timothy, you've only got ten days!"

ANDREI SOLOVIEV left a while earlier, but I was still sitting in the armchair and thinking over what I'd heard. It was good that the directors of the corporation appreciated my effort and decided not to punish me for disobedience. It was great that my big-eared Goblin Herbalist's suspension had been lifted, giving me the chance to prove myself and play the role of Dark Sovereign. I was now joining the ranks of players who defined the political world of *Boundless Realm*, and that was of course thrilling. What was more, there was a huge shiny reward beckoning in the distance, driving me to work harder and harder. But there had to be something they weren't telling me. I could just feel it in my skin. It was as if the promise of a stake in the company was that much-vaunted carrot hanging right in front of my face, but it was still unreachable. Like I was some naïve donkey stubbornly keeping up the chase, wasting his effort for nothing and working himself to the bone.

But no matter, I'd figure that out as things developed. I stood up and, with another glance in the mirror, took a critical look at my gaunt pale face, unshaven, disheveled and boyish. What a nasty scruff I had after ten days... I'd need to ask for an electric razor and some shaving cream. Maybe it was also worth asking for a tanning booth, given I'd be stuck inside for the next few days. With these completely mundane thoughts in mind, I headed into the virtual reality capsule, getting undressed as I walked and carelessly throwing my clothes around the room. So then, loading!

Name	Amra
Race	Goblin Vampire
Class	Herbalist
Experience	2175088 of 2280000
Character level	65
Hit points	6351/6351
Endurance points	5323/5323
Statistics	
Strength (S)	267 (1067)
Agility (A)	260 (551.8)
Intelligence (I)	5 (33.5)
Constitution (C)	269 (1058.1)
Perception (P)	3 (110.2)

Charisma (Ch)	137 (167)
Unused points	0

Primary skills (7 of 7 chosen)	
Herbalism (P A)	52 ATTENTION! Second specialization not chosen
Trading (Ch I)	30
Alchemy (I A)	42
Dodging (A P)	36
Stealth (A C)	45
Exotic Weapons (A P)	25 + 18 ATTENTION! First specialization not chosen
Riding (A C)	33

Secondary skills (7 of 7 chosen)	
Veil	22 ATTENTION! First specialization not chosen
Acrobatics	26 ATTENTION! First

	specialization not chosen
Athletics	33
Foreman	66 ATTENTION! Second specialization not chosen
Animal Control	59 ATTENTION! Second specialization not chosen
Warchief	18
Diplomat	19

Now here was a character to be reckoned with. He was stronger and more resilient than his modest level of sixty-five might suggest. That was even true despite the fact his Strength and Constitution were artificially beefed up by the five objects of Fenrir's Cursed Regalia. One thousand two hundred units of armor, plus fifty-percent resistance to physical damage, regeneration of two hitpoints a second, and he would heal back seventeen percent of damage dealt in close combat (and sixty-seven percent with Vampire Bite). That all filled out the picture of my character, who would be hard to kill even for a character fifty levels higher. What could I say? For someone expecting high-level and hostile guests from all over *Boundless Realm*, the ability to take hits and stay alive was really very necessary.

Still, I had soberly considered my situation and understood that I had no way of withstanding truly high-level players. Any character leveled for PvP and at the TOP of their alliance would crush my Goblin Herbalist without even noticing. So my number one mission for the near term was to avoid encounters with such enemies while my big-eared little Goblin grew stronger and became a true Dark Sovereign. Then one day, my heavy footsteps would make the whole of *Boundless Realm* shake.

I didn't fiddle with the specializations right away, leaving it for later and hurried into the game. So then, loading. I reappeared right where I was thrown out fifteen minutes earlier — in front of the open doors to my huge spooky castle. My sister was standing a step away with the Ogre Fortifier and Shaman Ghuu next to her.

"Big-ears, what hole did you just skitter down? We really need you here!" Valerianna Quickfoot threw herself on me with reproaches. "Your army nearly went ape-shit when you disappeared before entering the castle and finishing your swearing-in!"

"I got suspended without warning," I answered with complete honestly, not delving into the details. "But thankfully we sorted things out quickly, and now I'm back."

"And perfect timing! I was already starting to worry the giants and rougarou would attack and sweep us away. I even started lining up our orcs with shields and crossbowmen behind even though I knew it would be pointless. But then everything settled down and the warriors near the castle started to change alignment to allied."

I looked at the even rows of undead standing before the fortress. They were ghastly and unsettling creatures, as were the innumerable clans of rougarou, minotaurs, titans and other dangerous beasts. What a terrifying sight! I still couldn't get used to the thought that this was now my army. Well then, no use wasting time. I had to officially declare myself Dark Sovereign, the terror of all *Boundless Realm*! I took a decisive step toward the huge iron-banded gates.

And nearly went deaf from the boom that followed! Seemingly, even the mountains on the very horizon were shaken by the unbearably loud and omnidirectional sound. At the same time, some bright crimson text popped up before my eyes and began blinking:

ATTENTION!!! There is now a new power in* Boundless Realm*! The Dark Sovereign, standard-bearer for innumerable hordes of

terrifying bloodthirsty monsters, threatens the safety of the Southern Continent. The provinces of Tori, Lars and Amathy are at risk of invasion! Fearless players, now is the time to reach for your weapons and defend everything you hold dear in **Boundless Realm!**

I imagined a similar message was seen by every player in the game regardless of race, class or location. As soon as the identity and location of this Dark Sovereign leaked, I would be guaranteed attention from all combat clans known to enjoy such big events. And not just that! Instead of a ghastly, practically invulnerable monster, this Dark Sovereign was some little Goblin. And his level... it sounded funny just to say... was a paltry sixty-five! And that was at the fact that I had recently seen an official message from the company claiming the average *Boundless Realm* player's level was sixty-eight!

By the way, why hadn't I gotten some experience for such a unique achievement? At least a million exp., if not two, which seemed fairer for the unique and difficult mission. My Amra desperately needed to reach a higher level, but I hadn't gotten a thing for reaching the Upper Styx, nor for taking the vacant position of the leader of universal evil. And my direct superior Max Tohner had once promised a rare reward if I was first to reach these unwelcoming climes. Now was just the time to remind my boss of that promise... although for now I had no idea how to reach him. I mean, my cellphone had been taken from me in the real world and all means of communication were blocked. My thinking was interrupted by my sister's voice:

"So big-ears, why is someone else deciding which provinces the Dark Sovereign might attack?" The mavka asked an utterly logical question, but I just shrugged because I didn't even have the slightest idea how to control my army.

Beyond the tall gates, there was a very long corridor that led inside the gloomy castle. There were branching halls going left and right, but they all ended in locked doors. On our way we also found spiral staircases that went into the dark depths of the dungeon. There were no windows here nor lamps or any other sources of light. I even had to activate Night Vision just so I wouldn't run into the walls of my new home. Fortunately, the wood nymph soon activated a magical torch and things got easier.

"It's a bit dark in here. And empty. No pictures on the walls, no sculptures, no suits of armor," Shrekson Bastard said with a sour smirk on his face, looking down the monotonous, identical passages. "This isn't how I imagined medieval castles at all."

~ Finding a Body ~

"Yeah, the interior will definitely have to be changed," I agreed, looking skeptically at the cold bare stone walls and the damp somewhat moldy floor. "Some torches wouldn't hurt, in dark corridors at the very least. And we should hang decent hundred-candle chandeliers in the rooms. We'll have to look on the *Boundless Realm* forum to see how that's done. There must be a detailed guide on how to furnish a castle in the game."

"Don't fill your head with that crap, Tim! You've got thousands of underlings to keep busy now. If you don't want them squabbling, have them get their lord's castle in order. By the way, it looks like we've arrived..."

As she said, the corridor before us had come to an end with a set of tall doors made of time-darkened bronze. Unlike all the doors we'd seen before, this one was unlocked. With a high-pitched squeal, the heavy doors gave to my push, and we entered the massive throne room. It was empty and damp here too, but there was at least a source of light. Next to the truly cyclopean black throne, which looked to have been made for some kind of titan, there was a glowing smooth crystal ball three feet in diameter on a massive bronze tripod. All three of us walked up closer, entranced by the unique item.

Eye of the Dark Sovereign (subject control tool)

On the surface of the magical ball I could see the square before my palace. And on it I could see the rows of minotaurs, rougarou and other monsters standing in formation. But the lines of soldiers were no longer flawlessly even. The savage creatures were tired of standing at attention and had started wandering. Some of them had even set their weapons down and taken a seat on the cobblestones. The commanders were still trying to maintain discipline in the wild warband, but it was getting harder all the time.

I had a bird's eye view, so all my underlings looked small. But then with a flick of my finger, as if dragging an image on a tablet, I tried to zoom in and even shuddered when it worked. Suddenly, I had the faceless decayed stare of a rotting zombie practically at an arm's length in the crystal ball.

I quickly flicked the disgusting picture away, and saw Princess Chai-nee Shu surrounded by rougarou. The last member of the ruling family of the Clan of the White Lily was bowing and, carefully holding a wooden water bucket in her clawed hands, giving water to Regent Uvari-Dor-Shu as he lay on the stretcher, still in recovery. Our uncompromising duel had come at a great cost to the Rougarou Druid, and the wounds made by my lupine fangs and claws were taking a very long time to heal. I could see fresh scars on the druid's body as well, just barely healed. His bones were broken in many places, and had not healed yet either, so the Regent also couldn't walk.

I wondered if I could use the ball to talk with my subjects. I cautiously touched the image of the furry Princess and said:

"Chai-nee Shu, I need you in the castle now!"

The big-eared girl, who looked like a loyal pet dog, shuddered in surprise and tossed the carved wooden bucket aside, splashing both the crippled druid and everyone around. I also saw the rougarou and other soldiers sitting on the stones give a sharp jump and hurry to get back in formation. Seemingly, I had underestimated the volume of my voice, and the Dark Sovereign's command had been heard not only by Chai-nee Shu, but all the other warriors on the square around her. No biggie, what mattered was that they heard me. I could use the Eye of the Dark Sovereign to talk with my subjects!

"Chai-nee, order the Clan of the White Lily to take Uvari-Dor-Shu on the stretcher up into the throne room. I need my advisor in my castle right away. And also bring the Orc Shaman Ghuu and my First Mate Ziabash Hardy! And call the Naiad Trader Max Sochnier too! Also grab a few torches on your way. It's as dark as the inside of a mountain troll's ass in here!"

Foreman skill increased to level sixty-seven!

The Rougarou in the crystal ball started scurrying around, hurriedly carrying out their Sovereign's order. I then zoomed out, as if taking off vertically so I could see my holdings from the highest possible vantage point. But I had two disappointments waiting on that front. First, the map was almost totally black. Other than a narrow zig-zagging line marking our path to the castle over hills and mountain passes, all the territory was still unexplored. Clearly, before I could see anything in my magical crystal ball, I would have to explore the area to have it drawn on my map. Second, when I tried to look through the Eye to see land I had already explored, I stumbled on the impenetrable cloud cover constantly enshrouding my lands. In order to see anything in the magic ball, I had to go right down to ground level, which was not convenient and didn't give me a complete picture.

I was distracted from continuing the experiment by the derisive voice of Valerianna Quickfoot:

"Hey Tim, when you finish playing with your ball, walk over to the throne. There's plenty to see up there, too!"

~ Finding a Body ~

I left the crystal ball and walked over to the huge throne, which had innumerable skulls intricately carved into its ebony-colored column legs. And those skulls were not just human. I saw all kinds of unbelievable races and animals. There were hundreds of skeletons making faces at me, eyeless but still with their tusks, teeth or fangs. It was hard to look away from the ghastly skulls. It really seemed like they were also staring back at me. What could I say? It had me shaking...

To see the whole cyclopean armchair, I had to tilt my head all the way back because my Mask of Fenrir helmet was cursed, so I couldn't get it off my head. The dark carved legs were around twice as tall as my little Goblin Herbalist, after which they transitioned into a snake-skin seat. Though it may have actually been dragon skin. Above that was the carved back of the throne, again adorned with innumerable skulls going all the way to the ceiling. Hrm... Seemingly my little goblin would need quite the stepping stool to be able to reach his throne for official receptions. Well, I'd be fine as long as my subjects didn't see that comical display and laugh at their ruler climbing up his immense throne...

Successful check for Poison Resistance!
I tried to reach out to one of the carved skulls on the leg, which was made of some strange

dark wood but, after that message, I jerked my hand away in fear.

"Yes, that is antiaris, the wood of death," Valerianna Quickfoot commented, using her high Intelligence to identify the material. "Antiaris wood has excellent magical properties but unfortunately any objects made of it will always remain deadly to the touch. Just tapping it with one finger would kill me. But it probably won't kill you... Amra, what's your resistance to poison like these days?"

I didn't even have to open my stats window, I already remembered I had eighty-percent resistance to poison due to my vampiric nature.

"One touch won't kill you, though it may hurt sometimes, maybe even badly," my sister said, shaking her head, walking a circle around the huge throne and looking curiously at the strange, dangerous piece of furniture. "Well big-ears, you're gonna have to raise your resistance to poison either with amulets and rings or by downing the odd healing potion when you need to saddle the throne."

I glanced fearfully at the toxic wood and asked the wood nymph why I even had to clamber up on the throne, especially given how uncomfortable and dangerous it was. The mavka stared at me, batting her eyes in surprise, then reacted:

"Oh yeah, I'm always forgetting that your

~ Finding a Body ~

Goblin Herbalist has the Intelligence of a bump on a log. So that's why you gave orders to your subjects through Chai-nee Shu, even though everyone on the square could hear your voice. And now, that's why you cannot read the properties of the magical throne, but they're actually quite interesting."

I just smiled, not even thinking of getting mad at my little sister's good-natured teasing, especially given it was well deserved. Valeria then explained that the Throne of the Dark Sovereign was a powerful artifact that generated Direct Intervention Points. Those were an extremely rare and valuable resource in *Boundless Realm* available only to creatures at demigod level or higher, which could be spent to work wonders but only by the ruler and only while seated on the throne.

"Something like mana for spells?" I asked, trying to find an analogue. But Valerianna shook her head:

"No, totally different. Mana allows conjurers to cast a strictly limited number of spells dependent on class, level and class. No matter how much mana they have, no wizard can do things that are not allowed by their class and skills. But Direct Intervention Points allow a very powerful being to remake the world to suit their needs without any spells. In a hot desert you could bring a spring of fresh water to the surface, change the weather, instantly move around *Boundless Realm*, whatever you like. And the more points you have, the more significantly you can alter reality."

"You know I've never heard of this even though I've read a bunch of guides," the Ogre Fortifier threw out, not hiding his skepticism. And the Wood Nymph was eager to explain:

"Leon, you've probably heard of it but until recently they were called Faith Points. This is the same resource generated at altars in temples to allow their titular deity to exercise its will. You see, in the real world the Boundless Realm Corporation got into a conflict because the term 'Faith Points' upset religious people who believe faith is an abstract concept that cannot be quantified. So to avoid a legal battle, a few patches ago, the name was changed to Direct Intervention Points."

The huge ogre nodded to say he'd heard of that. I then started looking over the huge black throne but now as its master, dreaming up grandiose plans with my new ability. But Valerianna Quickfoot hurried to rein me in:

"Direct Intervention Points are generated extremely slowly, and that is the only reason divine creatures haven't overtaken all *Boundless Realm*. For now your throne generates two points per hour. One on its own, and another is given by that dual Rat King head in the back of the chair."

~ Finding a Body ~

I had to take a few steps back to see what my sister was talking about. But she was right. Two of the wood-carved skulls in the back of the throne had been replaced with the twin heads of Hyenarius, Lord of the Swamps of the Styx, whose half-dead and half-living warband was defeated by my army in the marshes. And the dead head was moving, opening and closing its mouth without a sound. The living head of the Rat King, as far as I could tell, was also still kicking, its glowing red beady eyes just darting in every direction.

Well, where did that put me? The heads of enemy leaders would decorate my black throne, at the same time improving the ghastly artifact? Seemingly yes. My gaze stopped just then on two rougarou skulls carved out of black wood nearby, and my imagination quickly told me that those slots were meant to house the heads of Regent Uvari-Dor-Shu and Princess Chai-nee Shu. And that unmistakable skull there looked very much like it belonged to Harpy Queen Kirra'ellita, Huntress of the Night. Hrm...

The mavka's voice interrupted my thinking.

"Now the throne has one hundred thirty-four Direct Intervention Points, which is very little. It could open a portal for a short time within the Southern Continent, or revive one NPC up to level sixty-seven. Also, big-ears, we may have a serious problem. The throne's description says that to use it you must be at least level two-hundred... Do you have any Ifrit Hearts left?"

No, I had spent the last Ifrit Heart stripping my fur armor suit of its level requirement. And that was Fenrir's Pelt, the fifth item from the set of cursed regalia. Now that was some bad luck... Getting another one of those rare alchemy ingredients would be quite difficult. Actually, it would be just as hard as taking the natural route and just leveling up to two hundred.

Seemingly, the Dark Sovereign's arrival to *Boundless Realm* ran the risk of ending in a huge fiasco. What was the point of this new patch if the Sovereign couldn't even use the tools it provided?

"Keeper! I need you now!" I shouted, hoping very much that someone from the Global Modeling Department was keeping careful watch over how this important event was unfolding.

And I wasn't wrong. Not five seconds later, a glowing winged figure was hovering just under the ceiling of my throne room. I didn't even have to explain; the Keeper already knew my problem and spoke first:

"Yes Amra, that was a cock-up on our part. We'll fix it right away. It's just that many of us were surprised to see you elevated to Dark Sovereign. We still haven't worked out all the kinks... Alright, there you go! Enjoy the throne!"

Seemingly the Keeper thought he was done

and was getting ready to disappear. But I called out to him and voiced another series of wishes:

"I need keys to all the castle doors. I'm not supposed to break them down am I?! And I also need some kind of interface for monitoring the castle. I have to know what is going on in my own home, what needs to be improved or repaired, and what is being kept in my stores. And I also need to control my army somehow, and something to tell me which regions and provinces of the Southern Continent pose a threat to the Dark Sovereign. And another thing, which is no-less-important: do you really think the skills and specializations needed by an Herbalist, are appropriate for a fearsome Dark Sovereign? For example, the ability to transplant plants. I for one have a hard time imagining a big scary videogame monster trouncing around with a trowel and replanting flowers. Can reset or trade out some of my skills or maybe get some unique perks?"

The Keeper froze motionless. Seemingly the player controlling it was away from his computer consulting with colleagues. I waited three minutes, and even got a bit bored before the winged figure flew back into motion and came all the way down to the floor:

"It has been decided to assign the Dark Sovereign three servants: a Keymaster, a Storekeeper and a Steward. The designers and programmers promised to make them unique and entertaining for your audience. And as for other servants for your castle, if you need any others you'll have to buy them yourself in the game's online store. They also didn't give you a general. Leadership thought you could lead the army yourself, or buy yourself an NPC with the right talents. Maybe you could even invite a living player to be your general. I'm certain you won't have a hard time finding someone to lead the Dark Sovereign's legions. Also, we tossed some food for your army into the castle stores. And that was a recent change because they figured the Dark Sovereign would send his army straight into battle. But with all these unexpected problems you've got too much on your plate, so they decided to give you a bit of help. They gave you very modest provisions, just enough to keep an army of that size going for one day. You'll have to get a handle on things before then."

"And what about my skills?" I reminded the Keeper of my other question, but he just shrugged his winged shoulders indefinitely:

"The marketing specialists and directors haven't reached a decision yet. On the one hand, it seems logical that a ghoulish Dark Sovereign should have unique abilities, otherwise how could he really be a unique boss? But on the other, why should we make an exception to the rules for one lone player? Our millions of other players might get mad, and rightly so. Overall, the question is stalled for now. Although... wait, I'm hearing something just now..."

The Keeper froze motionless for another minute before returning to the game and announcing the leadership's final verdict:

"They came to an interim decision: the skills and specializations your Goblin Herbalist already has cannot be exchanged, but you will get to choose unusual perks for the specializations you haven't taken yet. Unfortunately, they haven't been thought up yet. And if introduced in the game, their consequences haven't been thought through. That all takes time. A day or two most likely. So then, best of luck to you and have fun gaming, Dark Sovereign!"

Day One

housekeeping

HE KEEPER DISAPPEARED, leaving me somewhat perplexed. Was that all??? No extra experience to level me up faster, no real explanations, no manual for how to control soldiers or at least some approximate overview of the corporation's expectations? But I had to know what the leadership wanted from me!

And putting off choosing specializations in hopes of obtaining unusual perks, to put it lightly, sounded like a rushed and vague solution. What perks? Would they really be useful, or just worthless crap? Also, how long would I have to wait? I could already choose a specialization for six skills, and now they wanted me to just leave it that way until their programmers thought something up?

Warchief skill increased to level 19!

Foreman skill increased to level 68!

And what was that from? Ah, there it was... The rougarou and orcs I had summoned were now in the throne-room doorway, stock-still and bowing low before me. Seemingly, my companions had seen the Keeper's visit and thus were in a state of near worship. I noticed that the Regent of the Clan of the White Lily was trying to maintain a respectfully bowed pose, despite clear pain from his injuries and fractures. And there, by the way was a great chance to test my new abilities!

"Shrekson, help me up onto the throne! But be careful not to touch the poison wood!"

The tall Ogre Fortifier easily lifted my Goblin and not so much sat me as tossed me onto the rough scaly seat.

Successful check for Poison Resistance!

And sitting on the very edge of the seat, I extended a hand toward the crippled Uvari-Dor-Shu:

"Advisor, I need you in good health! Stand

from the stretcher and come to me!”

You have used 5 Direct Intervention Points
You have 129 points remaining

It worked!!! The furry Druid, surprised to discover his pain was suddenly gone, straightened up and took his first cautious step, then a second and a third... And carefully walked upright, stopping ten feet from the throne. In the rougarou’s eyes I could see a fanatical shimmer of adoration and loyalty. If I asked now, the Regent of the Clan of the White Lily would jump into a fire without hesitation.

“Sovereign, I have come to your call and am ready to serve you!”

Warchief skill increased to level 20!
You may now choose your first specialization in this skill

And another skill had leveled to first specialization... So again I should not choose any of the options and wait for something unique that just might be better? I took a heavy sigh. Alright, it didn’t exactly require an immediate reaction. I could be patient for a day or two and see what they had to offer. But now I needed to give an order to the rougarou, take advantage of the circumstances and explore the nearby area:

"Advisor, I once promised the Clan of the White Lily new lands in the territory of the Dark Sovereign if you trusted me and followed me. Well, the time has come to fulfill that promise! Gather a few groups of experienced scouts and have them go in different directions from the castle. By tomorrow evening, I expect your rougarou back with reports and maps, and I expect you to have chosen a parcel of land for the Clan of the White Lily."

The huge Uvari-Dor-Shu, whose healed scars made a big impression and gave him character, emphasizing his power and might as a high-level Druid, respectfully went down on one knee:

"Sovereign Amra, I am grateful for your concern for my clan. But may I be allowed to make one request? The Clan of the White Lily left its lands in a hurry. Our women and children didn't take any warm clothing or blankets and now have no roofs over their heads. After the bitter cold on the river of death and the treacherous mountain crossings, many of our children have fallen ill. Order the other rougarou clans to share their warm clothing, poles and tents! I saw that other clans only sent strong warriors to the Dark Sovereign's call, and they can easily just crowd in or just go without tents. Their own fur is easily enough for a large sturdy warrior!"

"I don't recommend it, Tim! You'd be spoiling your relationship with every other rougarou clan just for good relations with one of the weakest."

The private message from Valerianna Quickfoot caught me after I'd already opened my mouth to agree. I thought over my sister's advice, agreed with her well-founded fears, changed my decision and did my best not to offend any rougarou:

"Uvari-Dor-Shu, as you know, we came most of the way here through a portal of the goddess Hel. But the other clans made much longer and more harrowing journeys. I don't know how the other rougarou clans are doing, so I must first speak with their chieftains before making your request. But don't you worry, the Clan of the White Lily will not be left without shelter! Until you decide on a new land and build new tents, I allow you to live in my castle... let's say... in the north wing and two of its towers!"

Diplomat skill increased to level twenty!
You may now choose your first specialization in this skill

Another skill was now just stalled with no specialization... That was starting to grate on me.

Perks were often necessary for improvements and new abilities, but my Amra was being forced to stay weak.

Princess Chai-nee Shu, walking closer during my conversation with the regent, started to jump and clap for joy and amusement. Her advisor tried to calm the young girl, who was behaving too emotionally for a proud princess. But I asked him to let Chai-nee Shu express her happiness. The regent bowed to me then suddenly gave a threatening growl and jumped forward, shielding the princess from a new figure in the throne room:

Keymaster
Silent servant of the Dark Sovereign (indestructible)

I had to admit, I also gave an unwitting shudder when the ghastly dark shadow appeared one step from my throne. And although a quick glance at the mini-map revealed this creature had a blue, allied marker, I still shook my head in reproach. I mean, come on programmers, you can't scare the players like that! If I had a weak heart, I'd need someone to call me an ambulance.

The Keymaster was a ten-foot tall black semi-transparent ghost in an old moldering shroud, who held a huge keyring in his right hand which was just as semi-transparent and fleshless as he was. Through the black haze of his low-slung hood, a skull with three eye-sockets peeked out, and each socket contained flickering red embers, a monster's eyes that glowed in the dark. The left bony hand of the undead being was holding a broken torch. And completing the picture of walking horror, there was a black-skull marker over the ghastly floating figure, meaning he was more than fifty levels stronger than my Amra.

"Keymaster, open the doors to the north wing of the castle for the rougarou! And so I don't have to do this again, open the rooms in the eastern part of the castle for the orcs, too!"

The taciturn ghost's three eyes flickered and he started unhurriedly floating toward the exit. The rougarou and orcs, exchanging unconfident glances, nevertheless gathered their bravery and shuffled off after the ghastly guide into the dark depths of the corridor. But I stopped Chai-nee Shu and Ziabash Hardy:

"They'll manage without you. I need you here. Chai-nee, you're a Hunter by class, so I have just the job for you. There are only enough victuals in the castle for one day. However, during our last crossing from the hill, I saw a big forest in the distance teeming with animals. Get together a group of orc and rougarou hunters from every clan and go catch some prey. I appoint you head of this hunting expedition. And take the Gray Pack with you. My canine friends are hungry, and I'm sure they couldn't hurt, especially the level-212 Guard Dog and Baron at 120. And that will give me peace of mind, too. No matter what lives in that distant forest, with their help you'll have no problems!"

Foreman skill increased to level 69!

Chai-nee Shu, delighted and flattered by my trust, promised to carry out the order then gave a dignified bow and headed for the exit. Now for Ziabash Hardy's mission. I told my First Mate to take a group of orcs to inspect my stores and start distributing provisions to every soldier outside my castle.

Finally, I turned my attention to the last NPC, Orc Shaman Ghuu Ghel All-Knowing:

"My friend, your mission may seem strange and vague at first glance, but please hear me out. In *Boundless Realm* millions of orcs, kobolds, goblins, trolls and others live in fear of persecution from the undying. They hunt and kill our brothers for profit, experience, and sometimes just for fun."

The orc shaman, draped in bone and feather necklaces, bitterly confirmed that I was speaking the gods' truth. He said he knew of many horrifying instances of the undying being unjustifiably harsh to orcs and other races.

"That's exactly right! I myself saw the

peaceful goblin village of Tysh burned to the ground, and know of many similar cases. And I'm sure that many orcs and goblins would be glad to move to calmer lands, but they don't know any. Well, I am prepared to provide them shelter here! Around my castle there are expansive uninhabited lands and any settler will find both a place to live and a job. The undying will have a very hard time just getting here, and the powerful army of the Dark Sovereign will stand in their path. What do you say, friend?"

"Yes, my liege, such an offer may interest many," Ghuu Ghel All-Knowing agreed with a deep bow.

"I also think we will find takers. But the settlers will have to meet a few conditions to be permitted into my lands. Listen carefully, shaman! If they work in a peaceful profession, one tenth of their income must go to the treasury of the Dark Sovereign, which is very little in comparison with the other governments of the Southern Continent. Warriors who come to my lands will not be expected to pay taxes, but they must stand under the banners of the Dark Sovereign if we are ever attacked. Your mission then, shaman, is to spread the word around all *Boundless Realm* by any means necessary. Summon your spirits, use birds, beasts and magical messengers, do everything in your power! If necessary, speak with the other shamans, druids and wizards gathered near my castle. And feel free to fall back on my authority. They must support you in any way possible in this most important matter! Have you got it all, shaman? Then go and do it!"

Just after the last NPC disappeared from view, I asked the Ogre Fortifier to take me down from the tall throne and place me on the floor.

"Amra, I must admit, I'm impressed," the mavka told me when I came up next to her. "Tim, you've accomplished something truly grand! As far as I know, since the very first patches of *Boundless Realm*, when the lands of the virtual continents were just barely occupied by players, no one has ever tried to resettle entire races."

"Well, even then there was resettlement of living players," Max Sochnier threw out, not hiding his delight and enthusiasm. "I mean, Amra, you want to lure NPC's to your side from the whole Southern Continent! Nothing like that has ever happened before!"

"Well friends, what other choice do we have?! Just look, I have twenty or thirty thousand ghastly NPC monsters in front of my castle. That's pretty good. With decent planning, I could use them to make two or three incursions, capture a few cities and cause some problems for the players. But then the TOP clans will come, mow down my warband and walk unimpeded straight to my castle to capture the Dark Sovereign. Remember the story of Fenrir. His pack was strong and posed a threat to several provinces. But the problem was that players respawn after dying, while NPC's do not. A few bloody battles, and all that was left of Fenrir's pack was a bunch of untrained pups, who were soon cut down together with their fearsome alpha."

"But Amra, that outcome is inevitable!" the Ogre shouted, not hiding his pessimism. "Sooner or later, there will be enough players to take down whatever army of mobs this world can muster. And your army, Amra, will also be destroyed sooner or later. Our mission is only to push back the moment of defeat and make the players work hard for it, so the Dark Sovereign event is big, memorable and fun. And if we pull it off, leadership will congratulate us on a job well done."

The naiad supported the ogre's opinion, and even the mavka agreed. I had to admit, I really didn't like my friends' state of gloom, so I tried to convince them otherwise and bolster their enthusiasm:

"You're looking at this all wrong. When there are NPC's in your army, you can't just fight as if they're players! Don't step into a bear trap, wasting your forces and best soldiers. First build up a strong base with developed industry and supply. Then get everyone equipped with decent weapons and armor. Next arrange for newcomers to be trained, build strong fortifications at choke points, and scout out nearby territories so we can detect threats before they get out of control. And then it's very possible to hold out! Take for example the Land of Gloom. It has held out a long time already, despite all the undying attacks. That proves that victory is possible!"

Leon and Max started arguing, but my sister froze motionless. Either Valeria's game client had frozen, which was unlikely, or the Wood Nymph currently had a guide open and was searching for something. And it was probably information on the Land of Gloom, which I had just used as an example. Well crap... I had already realized what would happen twenty seconds before it did. As soon as my sister opened the page on the ruler of the Land of Gloom, she noticed that the Harpy Queen Kirra'ellita Huntress of the Night was the spitting image of my girlfriend Kira. And as soon as Valerianna Quickfoot started moving, I heard peevishness in my sister's voice:

"Timothy, how could you lie to me?! And Kira too! Just wow! Owns a boutique my ass... At Inessa Tyle's funeral, I was surprised to see that she was the vice-president's own granddaughter yet didn't work for the Boundless Realm Corporation!"

Leon and Max Sochnier asked what she was

talking about and what had her so upset. I was afraid and was about to send my sister a private message asking her to hold her tongue. But Val was smart enough and dropped the slippery subject. My sister had always been a clever girl, and now she quickly realized that Kira had good reason to hide her virtual identity.

To course-correct the awkward situation, I tried to quickly change topic. I asked the Ogre Fortifier to start building defensive structures first around the castle of the Dark Sovereign, then the whole way here from the Styx through narrow gorges, dangerous mountain paths, and even over glaciers.

"Valerianna Quickfoot has high enough Cartographer and Engineer skills. After studying the area, the mavka will show you what to build and where so any attackers will have a real hard time. Shrekson, you can have as many workers as you need! Ogres, trolls, mountain titans, I can even get cyclopes to help with construction. Mainly, I want the enemy to encounter deadly traps and strong defenses at every choke point. I want the players to respawn again and again and lose their valuable experience, waste their time and rue the day they decided to campaign against the Dark Sovereign! We'll make it so... Hey, what's going on?!"

I had to break off my impassioned speech,

~ Finding a Body ~

because I heard a noise from the corridor and many excited voices. Soon a big group of high-level rougarou and minotaur burst into the throne room, many of whom were agitated and in a very aggressive mood. My orcs and the rougarou of the Clan of the White Lily tried to stop the incursion, but they weren't doing a very good job.

"Sovereign, we refuse to obey this young whelp!!!" a tall rougarou walked out in front with coal black fur, a huge clawed paw pointing at Chai-nee Shu as she pressed her ears back in fear.

The crowd gave a fearful gasp then fell silent, shocked at the rougarou's impudence. In the silence that took hold, the rude fellow's next words sounded especially biting:

"And we also refuse to obey you, little goblin! You're nothing like the fearsome ruler we came here to follow!"

Miar-Ahn-Rhu
Elder Chieftain of the Clan of the Laughing Otter
Level-133 Rougarou Hunter

Silence fell and I came up closer, looking unfazed and staring at the rebel. I even walked an unhurried circle around the stock-still dog-man. My opponent was two times taller than my Goblin Herbalist and three times broader at the shoulder.

His huge muscles rippled with every movement of his body. His giant muscular body must have looked very impressive and respectable compared to my modest Amra. But I kept up my act as the very embodiment of calm:

"And who is this 'we?'" I clarified, as my rival looked me from top to bottom in agitation. I explained: "I must know who precisely dares challenge me, and who will need to be punished."

"'We' is me and my little brother Ahn," the chieftain said, pointing to another tall rougarou baring his teeth threateningly. "And the whole proud and numerous Clan of the Laughing Otter!"

Ahn-See-Rhu
Younger Chieftain of the Clan of the Laughing Otter
Level-118 Rougarou Scout

"I'll deal with your clan later. But now I have to teach a lesson to you two furry twits. This is what happens to those who behave boorishly to my face. You know, I just so happen to need something soft to cover the seat of my throne. I imagine your pelts will do just fine!"

"Sovereign, allow me to punish these scoundrels for you!" Regent Uvari-Dor-Shu stepped forward, covered in scars. But I stopped my advisor with a gesture.

~ Finding a Body ~

First of all, I was in no way confident the level-124 Druid could handle a level-133 Hunter, especially with his younger brother. Second, to avoid more uprisings in the future, I had to make a show of power and completely uproot the very concept of opposing me. Third, my Sating the Thirst bar was down at 2/24, so I would have to quench my Thirst for Blood in the next few hours no matter what. And finally, though I already had rougarou blood in my vampiric collection, I had not yet killed such a creature with a Vampire Bite. That would give a +1% bonus to melee damage, which would come quite in handy for the future. As would the experience from killing two opponents, each of whom were more than fifty levels stronger than Amra.

"Everyone, form a big circle!" I roared, and we instantly had a dueling floor.

Great! There was plenty of space to use the goddess Hel's Hair Whip. Even my throne fell inside the circle. I noticed that and chuckled to myself, because there were quite a few intriguing ways I could use the toxic object in battle.

Was I worried? Maybe a tiny bit, but I had no doubt in my victory. Just few days ago, the duel with Uvari-Dor-Shu was a big headache that nearly ended in my defeat. But lots had changed since then. I was stronger now and had five objects from Fenrir's Cursed Regalia, including the fur armor which raised my Strength and Constitution by two hundred fifty points and gave me great defense against physical damage.

"Let's begin!" I shouted, and simultaneously both enemies went on the attack.

The brothers were not able to turn into animals because they did not have Druid abilities, but they each had their own strong sides, which they used to devastating effect. A deadly bow and arrow instantly appeared in the Hunter's paws. I had to quickly somersault away to dodge his first shot.

Acrobatics skill increased to level 27!

Dodge skill increased to level 37!

The Scout then went invisible, because the gloom of the throne room was plenty for him to use Stealth. Then he charged, trying to stab me in the back.

What naivety! I was a vampire, and my Night Vision and Search for Life easily kept him in view, even in total darkness. Here's what your stupid self-confidence gets you! A crack of my whip hurtled my opponent from invisibility, while my next blow knocked the rougarou's legs out from under him.

Exotic Weapons skill increased to level

~ Finding a Body ~

26!

I had to dodge another loosed arrow before I ran up to the fallen Rougarou Scout, writhing in agony. He barely had any hitpoints, his life bar was practically empty. But that wasn't enough for me. I sunk my teeth into the throat of my injured enemy!

Damage dealt: 3105 (4002 Vampire Bite — 897 armor)

Experience received: 325000 Exp.
*Objects received: Rougarou blood (alchemy ingredient) * 3, Rougarou Chieftain Pelt.*

Level sixty-six!

Level sixty-seven!

Level sixty-eight!

Racial ability improved: Taste for Blood (Gives +1% to all damage dealt for each unique creature killed with Vampire Bite. Current bonus: +32%)

The older brother cried out so deafeningly an echo rang through the castle several times. After that, the enraged rougarou threw down his worthless bow, got down on all fours and charged me. He even managed to knock my meager goblin off his feet and onto his back. But while falling I managed to draw in my legs, then sharply extended them and sent my enemy reeling back toward the poison throne. The thud of his impact coincided with a scream that quickly stopped short...

Acrobatics skill increased to level 28!

Experience received: 330000 Exp.
Objects received: Rougarou blood (alchemy ingredient) * 3, Rougarou Chieftain Pelt

Level sixty-nine!

Level seventy!

Attention! You have reached level 70
You may now improve your character's survival by choosing a modification

I wiped the blood off my face with the back of my hand, straightened up and unhurriedly turned toward the large crowd:
"Anyone else feel like challenging me?"
The crowd stepped back in fear. And with

them was a character I had not seen before the fast-paced scuffle:

Demon of Avarice
Storekeeper for the Dark Sovereign
(indestructible)

He cut a massive ash-gray figure. His feet were cloven hooves. On his head there was a set of horns. His yellow eyes were split by vertical pupils. His mouth was packed with sharp pointy teeth... The being before me was clearly a demon. And he was wearing an unkempt leather vest and very patchy pants that must have been through a lot. Even the lowliest bum would be ashamed to dress like that, which meant this was either a poor scamp, or a creature of extreme greed. It seemed made to play on that ambiguity... Although maybe this was exactly how a storekeeper was supposed to look.

"Don't you doubt it, master," the demon said in a deep bass, as if reading my thoughts. "I have vast experience in these matters. Under various guises, I spent one hundred fifty years as mayor of Gabrovo[1], whose stingy natives have been the subject of many humorous tales. We even charged mice admission to our grain barns! And never once

---

[1] A village in Bulgaria famous for its humor and greed.

did a mouse sneak in past us! So Sovereign, don't you worry about your precious stores! By the way... Sovereign, why do you need two rougarou pelts? Put one on the throne to pad your bony backside, but the second might as well go right into storage!"

I guffawed. This strange new NPC was pretty great! Sure he was a demon by race, but you'd never find a more ideal storekeeper! By the way, speaking of demons... I still didn't have that kind of blood in my vampiric collection. And actually, of all the varieties of demonic creature, Amra had only ever sampled the blood of a succubus, and that was way back in the Cursed House. So I'd have to think over how to level Taste Tester with the Storekeeper, an exceedingly rare demonic creature. Of course, the Demon of Avarice was not likely to agree to give up a sample of his blood for free. I'd have to discuss paying for it somehow.

At any rate, I'd handle that later. Now was time for more important matters. For example, wrapping up the rougarou uprising. I searched the crowd for another member of the Clan of the Laughing Otter, and I found a gray-haired level-120 Shaman. I bade him to come over:

"The chieftain brothers, now slain for their ignominy, claimed the entire Clan of the Laughing Otter was rising up against the Dark Sovereign. And neither you nor any other rougarou from your clan objected, which lent credence to their words. And now I have to think up a fitting punishment. So tell me, Shaman, what size is your Clan of the Laughing Otter?"

The gray-haired shaman lowered his head and replied softly:

"Sovereign, the Clan of the Laughing Otter brought four hundred of its strongest warriors to your summons. Back home on the banks of the river of death, fifteen hundred rougarou remain including the young and elderly."

"Okay..." I crossed my hands behind my back and paced the throne room in thought.

Four hundred powerful warriors... Not bad, not bad at all! That would be a great use to my army, so I was in no mind to kill all these rougarou, even though the temptation was strong. I mean, I stood to get a whole sea of experience if I did. Nevertheless, I couldn't just pump the brakes and forgive the rebels, otherwise what kind of Dark Sovereign was I?! My reputation as a fearsome and terrible ruler would come crashing down, then I could no longer reasonably expect obedience and respect from the horrifying monsters under my command. So what could I do?

Finally, I decided:

"I have decided the Clan of the Laughing Otter's punishment for taking part in the rebellion against the Dark Sovereign! I will be taking your thirty strongest warriors! Shaman, you will select them yourself, give them the chance to say farewell to their friends, and by morning bring them here to me in the throne room!"

With a low bow, the shaman lowered his head even further, closed his eyes for a few seconds and answered barely audibly in a quavering voice:

"My lord is very magnanimous! Sovereign, I will carry out your order, but am I allowed to be among those warriors?"

"No, shaman! I only want young and strong warriors. They will serve as bodyguards for my ward Chai-nee Shu. These thirty rougarou's lives will now revolve around accompanying my adopted daughter everywhere, protecting her and keeping her safe from any danger. They are already the best in their clan, and after Vaash and Valerianna Quickfoot give them combat and tactics training, these thirty rougarou will be the best in the land! After this training, these warriors will wear only bright red clothing and armor to represent their elite status and symbolize that their high rank was earned with spilled blood!"

Diplomat skill increased to level 21!

Warchief skill increased to level 21!
Foreman skill increased to level 70!

~ Finding a Body ~

"Now, I hope no one will say that the Clan of the Laughing Otter disrespected the Dark Sovereign or his ward! With that I consider this incident settled!"

Based on how I was speaking, the expression of obedience and despair on the face of the gray-haired shaman changed first to surprise and timid hope, then to gratitude and elation. When I finished my speech, the shaman fell to his knees and the overpowering emotions made him try to kiss my Goblin Herbalist's boots:

"Sovereign, you'll never find more loyal servants and soldiers than the rougarou of the Clan of the Laughing Otter! Your adopted daughter Chai-nee Shu will have the most loyal guards in all *Boundless Realm!*"

You have used 2 Direct Intervention Points
You have 127 points remaining

Rougarou opinion of you has increased by +3

I didn't realize right away what I had just spent two of the invaluable Direct Intervention Points on. I looked from side to side and didn't see any changes. Well, except that two of the toxic-wood rougarou skulls on the back of my throne were now adorned with the real skulls of the two foolhardy brothers, which were writhing in dismay. Two heads cost two points, was that it? After that I discovered that there was now a golden marker in my immediate vicinity on the mini-map. A unique creature?! I shuddered and tried to line up the golden marker's position with a character in the throne room. Seemingly, it was the rougarou princess. Yes, that was right! And yes, some serious changes had been made to Chai-nee Shu's description:

Chai-nee Shu
Adopted Daughter of the Dark Sovereign
Level-91 Hunter (unique creature)

So that was it! I called the charming young rougarou girl my adopted daughter a few times, and now the *Boundless Realm* algorithms had adjusted her status in the game, making the princess a unique creature, the daughter of the Dark Sovereign himself. Whether that was good or bad, I could not say. For the princess, that new status meant not only irrefutable authority with my NPC servants, but also unwanted attention from the undying. For every unique creature, there were always plenty of people lining up to kill it.

And that was a clear illustration of the fact

that, now that I was Dark Sovereign, I needed to carefully think over my words, because they had the tendency to manifest as reality.

WE STARTED discussing the Naiad Trader's work after all the hustle and bustle of the loud group of mobs had left the throne room. Leon had also left by that point — it was after eight and our friend had to go pick up his youngest daughter from music school.

"Max, I see a great opportunity for you to go back to our old plan and start a seafood trading business," suggested my sister, who now also had some changes in her game profile:

Valerianna Quickfoot
Sister of the Dark Sovereign
Level-102 Beast Master

First of all, her description used to clearly label her race as Wood Nymph, and that was now gone. The information could still be found deep in her detailed character info, though. And Valerianna Quickfoot still looked like a wood nymph — a delicate long-legged girl with hair the color of fresh leaves and huge eyes. Still, my sister discovered that some important changes had also taken place in her skills and statistics. Some disciplines of magical arts were now off limits (for example, Life Magic and Order Magic), and her mana expenditure had been rebalanced, along with casting time and spell effects. Lots of other things had also changed in a minor way. All that needed to be carefully combed over, and Val was going to get deep into that after finishing this game session. That way, by tomorrow morning, she could put together a new development plan for her character.

Max Sochnier heard what Val said, shuddered and got on guard:

"I don't quite get it. Valerianna, are you trying to get rid of me?"

"Nothing of the sort! Think for yourself — next to the castle of the Dark Sovereign and in the castle itself, there are already one thousand thirty creatures, approximately half of which are alive and need to consume food regularly. And soon, if Amra's plan to attract settlers works, there will be many more inhabitants! Meanwhile, we have very scant provisions and the hunters can barely provide food for all our needs. And the villagers, when they arrive and get to work, will also need time to grow crops, especially with this constant thick fog and lack of sun."

"And what do you suggest?" I asked,

intrigued because the issue of providing food to my subjects had me seriously worried.

The Wood Nymph started smiling with her sharp predatory little teeth and answered eagerly:

"I was thinking of the underwater fishing village of Ookaa. But there's also the Isle of the Wanton Widow, and a bunch of other little islands and nearby fishing villages where you can buy fish very cheap. Max has a trade galley the *Tipsy Gannet*, which plies approximately those very waters on a fixed route. So have them buy all the fish they can, then send it here using portal scrolls! I actually learned to make them at level one hundred, so I can whip up plenty by tomorrow. Then we just need to set fish prices in the lands of the Dark Sovereign at a level that's both affordable to your subjects and keeps Max Sochnier in the green."

The Naiad Trader enthusiastically extended his bright red back fins and built on my sister's idea with zeal:

"Great idea, Valerianna! As a law-abiding merchant I will pay the required tenth of my income to the Dark Sovereign's treasury, and I can pay you for the teleportation scrolls. The volume of trade we're talking about is easily enough for us not to need to mess around with delivery. And the trade could be... what do I mean could? It would have to be bilateral! There must be something unique in these lands, which we could sell to people on the coast. I mean, basically no one else can get here! Heck, we might be able to sell to the whole Southern Continent! Unique minerals and plants, rare and valuable items... What about that antiaris wood!?" Max said, pointing his webbed hand at my throne. "It's very rare and in demand among the players! If we harvest the toxic wood here, we could sell it in fairly small amounts in various parts of the continent. That way we don't have to worry about revealing the source or bringing the price down. We could have a real Klondike on our hands here!"

As for the antiaris wood, I wasn't going to rush things. There was no guarantee that these highly dangerous trees even grew in my lands, or that the deadly material could easily be processed in sufficient quantity. And the idea of regularly opening portals had to be seriously looked over from a safety standpoint, because it constituted an obvious weak point in my defenses. The strongest player clans had highly skilled analysts in their ranks. And they could quickly correlate the shipments of rare artifacts and minerals with the route of the trade galley. Then they could connect its owner Max Sochnier with the Dark Sovereign and his distant lands. Then one day a shipment might be replaced by a fully-fledged invasion of the *Legion of Steel* or the *Lords of Chaos*!

~ Finding a Body ~

But regardless, Max Sochnier's words did contain a kernel of rationality. Every game I'd ever played obeyed one simple rule: the further you got from crowded places, the more interesting locations, loot and resources you'd find. *Boundless Realm* was no exception in that regard, and the lands of the Dark Sovereign were very remote indeed. So here, we could probably encounter something so valuable traders would tear each other's arms off to get it.

Sure, we did still need to fully scout out the area to discover precious resources, especially mineral and ore veins located deep underground. But I had an interesting idea on that account. I walked over to the crystal ball:

"Tondik Exuberant, Gnum Spiteful, I need you both in the throne room! And I also need creatures of any type who are familiar with the local caves and mountains! If there are any, they are to report directly to the Dark Sovereign!"

Foreman skill increased to level 71!

Just wow! No, I mean I was expecting Gnum Spiteful and the burnt Tondik Exuberant, whose beard had still not grown back and was missing one eye and arm. But I was not expecting the twenty fearsome ghosts who came with them or the three Midnight Wraiths, or the barely visible and practically transparent Spirit of the Eternal Miner, or the huge Plague Bat, or the pack of variously sized Rats from level one to one hundred fifty. Nevertheless, there was work for them all:

"Subterranean beasts, show these two dwarves all entrances to the caves and catacombs you know! And protect them from any troubles and dangers until they've mapped out everything!"

Foreman skill increased to level 72!

Now I turned my attention to the two dwarves, who were respectfully standing and hanging on my every word:

"My warrior friends! I need a professional consultation. Throughout *Boundless Realm*, dwarves are famed as the foremost experts in geological matters. None can compare with your race's talent for discovering valuable ore. And so I want you to explore all the deepest caves and catacombs, search deep under my new mountains and find all ores of iron, copper, silver and anything else of interest..."

"Uhh, Captain Amra..." Gnum Spiteful the Dwarf Mechanic interrupted me unconfidently. "You hold us in too high an esteem. Yes, we're both dwarves and thus know a thing or two about metals and ores, but I'm a Mechanic by trade, and he's a Chef. How are we supposed to find any

~ Finding a Body ~

ore?!"

"Sovereign, I agree with Gnum. Although we are subterranean natives and know something about minerals, you'd be better off finding experts in the field... And two scouts are not enough. We need at least two or three dozen. And I know just where to find them! Half the miners of the dwarven city of Dotur-Khawe would give up their beards for the chance to prospect virgin mountains!"

> **Mission received: The only thing better than one mountain is a mountain range**
> **Mission class: Normal**
> **Description: hire a brigade of dwarven miners in the city of Dotur-Khawe (no less than thirty) to explore the mountains and caverns in the lands of the Dark Sovereign**
> **Reward: 800 Exp.**

What? Just eight hundred exp? Being at level seventy, that was just crumbs, nothing serious. I mean, for every enemy I'd killed recently, the game system sent me at least three hundred thousand experience, what was some pitiful eight hundred points to me?! Nevertheless, I didn't turn down the useful quest. Dotur-Khawe? It was pretty far, sure... Good thing last time I was in Dotur-Khawe, I got a couple extra teleportation scrolls to the Dwarven capital. Without them, even on the swift-winged VIXEN, it would take around two days each way, and that was if my Royal Forest Wyvern could fly over the icy mountains on the way to the city of the dwarves with their ghastly winds and freezing temperatures. The dangerous cloudy lands of the river of death and scorching hot desert after that were no walk in the park either.

But even with portals, dragging myself to Dotur-Khawe to find miners seemed like an unjustifiable waste of time. What was more, I had two right in front of me who would be glad to visit their home town and help me out. All that remained was to lead the dwarves to the idea of taking a little trip back home.

I pretended I was seriously thinking and fell silent for half a minute, then answered:

"Alright, Tondik and Gnum, you've convinced me. Such work requires true professionals, and the easiest place to find them is Dotur-Khawe. I intend to give you this important assignment, because you know the city of dwarves best and I trust you. I'll give you a portal scroll to Dotur-Khawe, you can get a return one from Valerianna Quickfoot. Remember, you need to hire at least thirty experienced miners and take them back here as quickly as possible. Your work will be generously rewarded, my friends, no doubt about it. And Tondik, I'd like to give you a down payment!

I assume you'd prefer to have two arms and eyes!"

A moment later, where the pudgy dwarf's stump had just been, there was now an arm and hand, but not made of flesh and blood, seemingly woven from a thick, wavering darkness. His replacement eye was similarly unsettling and dark. Tondik Exuberant moved his new fingers dubiously, then tried to pick up the chef's ladle hanging on his belt with his dark hand, and was left totally satisfied.

You have used 8 Direct Intervention Points
You have 122 points remaining

I wondered why there were one hundred twenty-two, not one hundred nineteen. Before I had one hundred twenty-seven points, minus eight.. either I had forgotten elementary-school arithmetic or something was fishy. Had it really generated new points already? But then why three and not two?

I asked that aloud. Valerianna Quickfoot looked the throne over and confirmed that adding the two new rougarou chieftain heads had made the magical artifact start generating three Direct Intervention Points per hour. Cool! Just for that it was worth executing the rebels!

I considered my conversation with the

dwarves over, but Tondik and Gnum were in no rush to leave. They just kept shifting nervously from one foot to the next, exchanging glances. It seemed like they wanted to ask me something, but were too embarrassed. Finally, Tondik made up his mind:

"Sovereign Amra, no matter how we want it, we cannot return quickly. As soon as we're back in our home town, my mother Pirona Zealous will find out that I am back and that I have a beautiful bride. And Vanessa's family would also not let her go without an opulent wedding, and that would take several days. It's just dwarven custom!"

Hrm, quite a problem. I hadn't considered that... Very few in my crew knew that the spritely sharp-tongued Gnum was actually a bearded woman by the name Vanessa Hamfist. I myself forgot it from time to time, because dwarven women and men were sometimes hard to tell apart. They were all bearded, thick-set and short. Even the dwarves themselves couldn't always tell a woman dressed in men's clothing. What was more, Gnum Spiteful behaved like a blustery and cantankerous dwarven man, loved to drink and started fights at any opportunity.

What could I do? Let the loving couple go to their wedding, then wait for them to come back with the master miners they hired hopefully in a week, maybe two? Clearly a bad option. Not let the dwarves go home? Also no good, especially after I'd just said how much I trusted them both... The chat window flickered open. A private message came in from Valerianna Quickfoot:

"You should suggest holding the wedding here as a special favor from the Dark Sovereign. At the same time, have them invite as many of their kin to the wedding as they can. I'm sure you'll have something to offer the dwarves — there's tons of work for their craftsmen here."

Ah, great idea! I made that suggestion to the bride and groom. Tondik and Vanessa first predictably hesitated at the unexpected offer and were clearly looking for an excuse to politely refuse, but I managed to convince them:

"In the dwarven race's thousands of years of history, you will be the only couple to have received such a great honor! Every chronicle of your submontane folk written after this date will contain a chapter on this rare event. You will be as famed as the great kings of antiquity! I'm sure thousands of guests will come to bear witness to this unique occasion, and the dwarves who miss your wedding will tear out their own beard hair in frustration! I've got plenty of space, food and entertainment no matter how many guests show up. I'm sure your brethren will want to see with their own eyes how wild this distant unknown land is. And who knows? Maybe, some of them will find engaging work. Some may even decide to settle permanently in my lands!"

Trading skill increased to level 32!

Diplomat skill increased to level 22!

And that's what we decided to do. I immediately handed the newlyweds a portal scroll to Dotur-Khawe, while Valerianna Quickfoot promised to prepare a return portal as quickly as possible. Max Sochnier, carefully listening to our negotiations, was very satisfied:

"Knowing the craftiness and curious nature of the dwarves, all nearby mountains will be dug up by day two of the wedding, and every mine will be exhausted to the very bottom. But you, Sovereign Amra, will get a full map of useful minerals and ore veins with notes about which dwarf clan to call to extract them! Great work!"

Tondik and Vanessa thanked me for taking an interest in their fate, bade me farewell and went to get ready to return home. After their departure, Max Sochnier excused himself, saying his work day as a tester was over, and he would also be saying goodbye until morning. The fish man went down on his haunches a step from my throne and disappeared without a trace half a minute later.

Finally, for the first time in this endless day,

~ Finding a Body ~

I was alone with my sister! We had so many important issues to discuss in private! As it quickly became clear, I was not the only one impatiently awaiting the chance to talk eye to eye. As soon as the Naiad Trader disappeared, Valerianna Quickfoot took a magic wand from her inventory and raised a magical dome of silence over us, then she made a demand:

"Timothy, lots of things you do in the game don't make sense to me anymore and, in the real world, you're acting even weirder. You're not answering phone calls, you didn't come visit me in the hospital after the operation, you didn't even come to Kira's grandmother's funeral. There must be a very good explanation for all this, and I want to hear it from you. So then, Tim. Tell me!"

Day One
Talking with my Sister

"**h**OW IS KIRA? Is she very mad that I missed the funeral?"

I started with the thing that had me most worried. But I immediately realized I chose wrong, because the Wood Nymph made a frown of dismay:

"Timothy, this isn't about Kira. I'm the one hurting! You haven't seen your own sister for three long days. Finally we get a convenient chance to talk, and the first question you ask has nothing to do with the complicated twelve-hour operation I just had, or how I'm feeling after anesthesia! No, you just had to know about your girlfriend! Come on, Timothy, you're a hard-hearted blockhead!"

I had to apologize. Yes, I was wrong. Yes, I

was a cold-hearted thick-skinned fool, who didn't appreciate how lucky he was to have such a great sister. In my defense I only said that I couldn't get in touch with her sooner because my cell phone had been temporarily confiscated, so my means of communicating with the outside world were seriously limited. Valerianna gave a slight nod:

"Yeah, they told me you had a fight with someone at work and leadership punished you..."

"What???" now here I couldn't hold back and started screaming, because the last thing I was expecting to hear was that the company was telling people such an asinine story. "An employee of the corporation attempted to murder me while I was in my virtual reality capsule, stabbing me twice in the chest and severing my mesenteric artery. Is that what they're calling a fight now?! I mean, I almost died from the blood loss!"

The Wood Nymph's already huge eyes grew even bigger:

"What are you talking about, Tim?! What wounds, what attempted murder, what blood loss?"

"Remember when you left the game before the operation, when we were on the boat with the rougarou? Well, not five minutes after that, someone tried to kill me in the real world! A corporate tech named Arthur stabbed through the top of my virtual reality capsule with a sharpened screwdriver! Then, when I finally managed to get the damaged top open, he tried to strangle me. Fortunately, help came just in time, security ran in and we got dragged out. I was gushing blood and lost consciousness. The surgeons spent two whole days patching me up!"

Poor signal quality
If connection problems persist, the Boundless Realm *client will be forced to close*

The warning message flickered up before my eyes. I couldn't imagine what kind of "connection problems" there could be, considering corporate testers had their virtual reality capsules literally less than one hundred fifty feet from the game servers. They were in the very same building, just two or three floors below. Well or in my case a few more floors, but still in the same building!

"Val, is your game lagging? Are you having connection problems?" I asked and she answered no. *Boundless Realm* was working just fine for Valeria, even though my sister's capsule was much farther from the servers.

Got it, I'm no idiot... Corporate leadership must have been showing me that the topic my sister and I were discussing was not to their liking, and if I didn't change my behavior right away, I'd be suspended once again and forced out of the game. I had to put on a more positive tone so I wouldn't lose the chance to talk with Val:

"Val, the corporation probably just didn't want to scare and upset you. And they definitely didn't want that unpleasant incident leaking. And for that exact reason, Amra was played by a program script two days ago, and my video clip was composed by some other people. They didn't want my viewers suspecting anything. I was unconscious for two days, so I didn't have the chance to come visit you in the hospital, or express my sympathy to Kira."

The wood nymph took a heavy sigh and raised her huge wounded gaze:

"That is all very, very strange... but I believe you, Timothy. But now that you're all better, can you come visit me? Visitors are allowed in the clinic until ten, so you'll have time. Tim, I'm so bored. I don't have enough time to talk with you for real. I'm used to seeing you every day and now, after a few days apart, I'm just not feeling like myself..."

A chat window flickered open. I figured it was my sister writing me something private, not wanting to say it aloud for some reason, but I was wrong. The message came from some corporate employee by the name support_013:

"*Timothy! Remember when you started working here and signed a non-disclosure agreement? There were points about information that may damage the corporation's business reputation. So if you do not cease this talk at once, we'll be forced to ban your Goblin Herbalist, permanently this time. And let us remind you that you still cannot leave your office for the next ten days."*

It was a more than serious threat. I had to tell my sister with a heavy heart that I couldn't meet with her today, and I'd have to see what the doctors said from there. Valeria got even more upset and nearly started to cry. But still she found the strength to hold back and answer the first question I asked:

"Kira is mad at you. Really mad. But she seemed ready to make up. And she also thinks you got mad at her first: you turned off your phone, stopped coming to her house, and told some obvious lie... Anyway, that doesn't matter right now. You're both adults and you can figure that all out without my childish advice. But we really need to have a chat about you being the Dark Sovereign now with an army and land. I have some advice that I think you could use."

The poor signal message, which had been bothering me for the last few minutes, immediately disappeared. Our talk about in-game topics didn't bother my overseers one bit. Such intrusive and unhidden censorship and tracking were a definite annoyance, though. I was planning to raise the issue in my next conversation with my employer, but I wasn't ready yet. I still didn't understand a lot of what was happening around me and was afraid to mess things up.

"First of all, Tim, you should think about changing your goblin's appearance. That big-eared silly little goblin is definitely silly and fun, which attracted an audience early on, but now that you're the brutish, ghastly Dark Sovereign, it just won't do! We need to make you a new look, much scarier and more hideous. I can do all the work..."

"No! Definitely not!" it was rare that I argued with my sister on game issues, but in this case I had to put my foot down. "I'm used to this appearance, and it's good enough for me! What's more, I can use that contrast to make my gameplay more interesting. I have a bunch of ideas for how to purposely underline and play that up in my video clips. And I'm sure my audience will like it!"

"Alright, Tim." Having met fervent resistance, Valeria went on the backslide. "But sometimes, you'll still need to look frightening to scare subjects or enemies. I guess I could put an illusion on you for that. I'll think up a ghastly beast form for you tonight. I'll look online for inspiration and make a spell."

Foreman skill increased to level 73!

"Oh! I just got a quest from you about that," the mavka chuckled and read the mission description. "And what an interesting reward: I can change my appearance for free. Very unusual! You can do whatever, but I'm definitely going to redo Valerianna Quickfoot so she looks like a proper sister of the Dark Sovereign."

Boom! A new character appeared inside the magic dome my sister had conjured:

Castle Steward
Omnipresent servant of the Dark Sovereign

This one was little and with big ears... Bigger than mine even, although Amra's ratio between ear and body size were truly astonishing. He had a predatory face, sharp little teeth and thick reddish-gray fur. Now, either that was a gremlin or I didn't know a thing about fantasy races!

"You can go through magical barriers?" the surprised mavka asked the Steward, and the Gremlin bared his teeth happily:

"Yes, madam! Within this castle, I can move instantaneously and into any room regardless of locked doors or magical barriers. And I can bring one or two companions with me through my portal."

"And outside the castle walls?" I asked, instantly intrigued by the Steward's unique abilities.

That would make him a truly ideal thief. No walls, fortifications or bars could hold him! Pop up somewhere, take all the valuables and just disappear! What brilliant possibilities!

"Outside the castle walls, I do not exist..."

I sighed in dismay, although the Steward's answer didn't really surprise me. I mean, the programmers couldn't make something so unfair. It would break all the rules and upset balance!

"Very well, Steward. Bring Valerianna Quickfoot and me to the personal chambers of the Dark Sovereign!"

Just as I finished that sentence, everything around changed. All three of us were instantly in a small round room with bronze lamps hanging on the walls and flickering away. And it also had a spiral staircase going up and down and five identical lancet windows going in different directions. Outside, it was already the middle of the night. And... there was really nothing else of note. No furniture, no luxury items, not even a bed. Bare stone walls and uncovered windows, which had a cold cross-breeze blowing through them. What a living situation! Not even spartan, this was for some ascetic hermit whose only purpose in life was to punish his body.

In Valerianna Quickfoot's room, where I ordered the gremlin to take us next, the situation was even more shameful. There weren't even any lamps, just bare stone walls and a cold floor covered in damp mold. To my utterly justified indignation, the Steward just chuckled:

"Sovereign, anything can be arranged for in your castle. Furniture from the rarest pink palm wood from the Isles of Eternal Youth, carpets made of albino sabre-tooth tiger pelts, windows of deep-earth crystal with large inlaid diamonds. Any fancy that might strike. But it'll cost you! However, there is no money in the coffers at the moment. And as there's no money, there can be no fancy!"

"I've never come up against such an obvious and brazen demand to put money into a game!" Valerianna Quickfoot snorted, upset. But the Steward predictably ignored her references to the outside world. He continued:

"You could of course have orcs and zombies make furniture and decorate, but I'm not sure you'll like the result, Sovereign. Or perhaps..." here the Steward sharply fell silent. I even had to demand that he finish his thought. "I'm sorry, Sovereign, I've just realized I'm talking out of turn. But I wanted to say that you could demand however much money you want as tribute. Everyone in *Boundless Realm* knows that your armies are about to invade the Tori, Lars and Amathy provinces. The rulers of the kingdoms and free cities there are probably shaking in their boots and may agree to pay you off just to stave off attack!"

My sister and I exchanged glances, struck by the novelty of the suggestion, and Valerianna asked:

"He's right, Tim. Why not try? You stand to lose nothing, and it will only improve your reputation as a ghastly Dark Sovereign. But we should at least find out how it is technically possible. Sit on the throne and spend a few Direct Intervention Points?"

"Or visit the rulers' palaces one by one through the crystal ball, threatening and issuing demands to each of them separately? But I don't have any maps of large cities to allow me to see them through the Eye, and I have no time to waste on that."

But Val did not agree that I should write it off so quickly:

"You can buy maps of big cities in the central provinces for pennies. The only expensive maps in *Boundless Realm* are of distant locations. The more players live in a place, the more supply is on the market, and thus the cheaper the map. So I would suggest, big-ears, that you start buying maps of the neighboring regions. The expenses will be minimal, and it will expand your possibilities greatly. Get to it today, because Direct Intervention Points are too valuable a resource to just throw around willy-nilly."

"Am I just throwing them around?" I asked in surprise. And Val took a heavy sigh and nodded:

"Are you ever! Five points here, two there, then another eight... And none of it was strictly necessary! I was just shocked when you spent eight points to heal that Chef! Tondik was doing just fine without that arm, it had no bearing on his wedding. Look, Tim. With such a wanton attitude toward such a valuable resource, one fine day the Dark Sovereign may find he doesn't have enough points to open a portal and move troops. Then that will delay some attack and your bosses at the company will be very upset!"

My sister was of course overstating it a bit, but I was willing to agree that I needed to be more prudent with such a rare resource. Alright, I'd take it into consideration. I was ready to talk with my sister until deep in the night, but just then a strange beeping sound rang out like an alarm clock, and the Wood Nymph immediately jumped up:

"Timothy, sorry but I have to leave *Boundless Realm*. I promised... my new friends we'd meet up tonight and go on a walk around the clinic garden. Alright?"

Now that was news! My little sister, who'd had a single-minded obsession with computer games for many years was now telling me she was leaving the game to meet people in the real world! And at that, my sister was flustered and clearly embarrassed. Perhaps these friends she was going on a walk with weren't going to all be girls...

"And what might this young man be named?" I asked, casting a line at random. And I guessed right.

The Wood Nymph went completely red and answered with her eyes pointed down at the floor in embarrassment:

"His name is Andre. He's a very fun and cheerful guy from a good family, a beginner street racer. Half a year ago he had a nasty accident on an electrobike... I mean you know how they drive. He lost both arms."

I wanted to quip that a racer without any arms was not exactly a beginner, more like a "done-r," but I kept silent. I understood that this was a very painful and serious topic for my sister, and Valeria might get mad.

"The day after tomorrow, Andre is having an operation. They're giving him bionic prosthetic arms. He's very worried, although he acts cocky and tries not to show it. He ordered a guitar to train sensitivity for his new fingers. He's going to go back to street racing after he recovers. He's constantly telling me about different models of electrobike and race tracks. Anyway, Andre is a very cool and positive guy. He's very well read. I sometimes think he knows everything in the world. I'm very glad I met him. So, will you let me go walk with him tonight, Tim?"

How could I say no? Regardless of my hang-ups, this was her fifteenth year, she was big enough to be independent, and interests often shifted at that age. What was more, I understood perfectly that Val would leave the game with my approval or without it. So, I allowed it. The Wood Nymph gave a shriek of joy, kissed my big-eared Goblin Herbalist on the cheek and sat down cross-legged on the floor, preparing to leave *Boundless Realm*. Half a minute later, the mavka's silhouette flickered and disappeared, dissolving without a trace.

There was no sense in me staying here in this dark room, and I demanded the Steward bring me to Ghuu Ghel All-Knowing. After all, I wanted to find out how the orc shaman was doing sending my messages through *Boundless Realm*.

"I cannot, Sovereign. The shaman is not in the castle, he is performing rituals, sacrifices and dances somewhere in the open air. I can only tell you he is with a large group of shamans and assistants and they all went toward those distant mountains."

"Alright, take me to the palace exit!" I ordered, and the gremlin instantly moved me to the front gates.

Successful check for Cold Resistance!

Ugh, what frigid air and piercing wind! Without a tent, fire or hot food, a creature might freeze to death before morning. The wind from the Icy Mountains was burning, whistling and getting into my very bones. There were black clouds like shreds of fabric floating through the sky. Thankfully there was no rain, or the perhaps more likely snow. In the distance there were many fires burning. My squadrons of living creatures had set up tents, warmed up and made dinner. I didn't see any creatures with no clear tent, and that was good. There was a decent chance that all my warriors would survive until morning despite the bad weather. The undead needed no tents or food, but they had also gone somewhere else, and were not dawdling on the wind-swept plain. I stood and looked around. Where could I find those shamans?

And then in the distance, through wisps of damp cloud, I saw a column of bright green light descend through the gloomy sky!

The spirits were favorable
Your message has been sent to every NPC

in **Boundless Realm*!***

The following positive effect has been received: every day, the Dark Sovereign will grow more attractive to potential NPC settlers. Also, a cumulative bonus will be applied, increasing each day by:

- ***Foreman +1***
- ***Warchief +1***
- ***Diplomat +1***
- ***Animal Control +1***

Duration: unlimited

Would you look at that! The effect had an unlimited duration... very unusual. That meant that sooner or later, every creature that could submit to my authority in *Boundless Realm* would declare me their master and stand beneath my banner. Meanwhile, the distant pillar of green grew dimmer with every second until it finally dissolved into the low black clouds and lashing rain. Apparently, I'd missed the big event, and now I had no reason to rush off.

I could, of course, summon VIXEN or the Gray Pack and go off with them somewhere. But without friends or my sister, and with such nasty weather, I had simply lost the will to play. What was more, I was starkly reminded that I had spent all day in a virtual reality capsule, which flooded me with exhaustion and apathy. I also started feeling hungry. Not hungry like in the game. My character was almost full. And my Thirst for Blood was also at the top. My body in the real world needed to eat. So I took a heavy sigh and followed my sister's example, also leaving *Boundless Realm.*

THERE WAS SOMEONE in the office. I realized that as soon as I lifted the lid of the virtual reality capsule. I could hear the clacking of high heels in the next room over alongside quiet music and other sounds that just couldn't be coming from an empty office. Had Kira really come off it and tracked me down? With that anxiety-inducing thought, I clambered out and quickly got dressed. I didn't want my fashionable girlfriend to see me in nothing but my underwear. I walked into the neighboring room... and froze.

My boss's assistant Tina, decked out in a fine golden evening dress and high-heeled shoes, was setting plates and wine glasses on the table. She had her bright purple hair up in an elaborate do and some of her locks had been dyed gold to match her dress, clearly preparations that had taken a ton of energy and time. I noticed many neatly arranged salad dishes with something interesting, a large dish covered with a silver lid, fruits in a crystal vase, a bottle of sparkling wine in a bucket of ice... Seemingly my sister wasn't the only one who was going on a date tonight. But did I want all this?

"Good evening, Timothy!" the long-legged beauty said when she noticed me. "I heard about your temporary living situation and decided to pay you a visit. I hope you aren't opposed."

I didn't know whether to be happy at this invasion of my personal space or not, but I of course didn't tell her to leave and answered politely.

"That's great!" Tina replied happily. "Timothy, wash your hands and come sit down, you must be starving. I don't know what you like, so I ordered for my tastes."

The atmosphere over our dinner was somewhat strained. Tina tried to joke and made variously obvious hints that she wanted to get closer to me, and I did everything in my power to "not notice." Why? There were many reasons for it. First and foremost were the video cameras in every corner. I had noticed some of them, though I suspected there were in fact many more cameras. I was not used to such close surveillance. It had me very frustrated and feeling like I was in chains. Second, the very fact of my imprisonment, though forced and temporary, also got on my nerves. And of course the main thing was that I could sense something was fishy.

How did Tina know where I was? It seemed to be the simplest of questions, but she could only dodge it or give sketchy answers. After that came the utterly logical thought that her entering a supposedly empty office with a tray of food would have been picked up on the security cameras. And if someone had seen her, the whole basis for my imprisonment came crashing down. If the NPC Taisha really could observe the building through its security cameras she would be alerted by this, guessing that the man named Timothy hadn't died at all. Taisha was not stupid and would quickly realize who the food was for. And what, that didn't bother anyone? What bullshit!

Well, there was another fairly important factor in my cautious and even cold treatment of Tina — a different girl who was no less beautiful than "miss *Boundless Realm*" herself. My relationship with Kira may have been in a vague and difficult place, but we hadn't yet broken up, so I felt a certain moral obligation to my somewhat crazy but still elegant and gorgeous girlfriend.

"Timothy, I'm gonna go home!" Clearly having understood that she couldn't get more out of this than a dinner, Tina started getting ready to leave. "You must be bored sitting all alone here in the office. Would you be opposed to me dropping by for dinner sometimes?"

Hmm, why the heck not? I was already feeling somewhat uncomfortable after one day of imprisonment. In a day or two, I'd be crawling up the walls and in a week I'd be damn near out of my gourd. This way I'd at least have some human interaction. All the better that it was with a pretty girl. So, I gave my consent. But now feeling bolder, Tina gave me a kiss on the cheek and, taking the tray of dirty dishes with her, went into the hallway.

Just after the director's assistant left, I ran to the computer. I had so much left to do today! First of all, I started putting together a video clip about the adventures of my big-eared Goblin Herbalist. I had so much interesting material, it was a breeze. And that was putting it lightly. My little goblin had become the Dark Sovereign today! That alone would have been enough to enthrall and even shock the viewers. But I also had three new servants, an army and a castle, the duel with the rougarou and much, much more. No, I wasn't going to totally reveal my plans and secrets, but I was going to partially raise the veil of secrecy around the mythical Dark Sovereign's life, which I thought would be very, very powerful.

However... The computer here in the office was still very seriously limited in what it could access online. I couldn't download free video editing software, make purchases in the

~ Finding a Body ~

Boundless Realm online store or write comments on the forum. No, I couldn't stand for this! I wrote tech support, but not the main address, to an employee by the handle "support_013" the very same who had been watching me talk with my sister. That employee knew I wasn't allowed to freely walk around the building, so explaining my demands to him seemed like the easiest option.

He answered me almost at once. But instead of a positive decision providing the necessary programs and access, I just kept getting the runaround. Stuff like:

"Amra, what do you need to fuss around with the video clip for? Hand that off to the marketing department. They're professionals and will do it all to the nines."

Or another example of an exceptionally inept reply:

"Allowing financial operations from that computer would require long discussions with various departments. And it's night right now, so the people who make those decisions aren't even here. Maybe instead of all these complications, just tell me how much you want. Would five thousand credits to your card from an anonymous source be enough?"

My objections and complaints that my viewers would be bored by a video clip someone else made were not taken into account. Just like the fact that a strange transfer of such a huge amount would probably have the tax man asking questions. They didn't want to give me full access to the forum, or the internet shop, making excuses about some internal instructions and rules.

I had to use some pressure and threaten to complain to the director of In-Game Security Andrei Soloviev, or maybe even President Thomas Heywood. I mean, these guys were getting in the way of the most important event the Boundless Realm Corporation had ever put on, preventing the Dark Sovereign from doing his job. And that worked. My requests were finally approved. Took 'em long enough!

I was expecting some tech support worker to come into my office to set everything up, but it was all done remotely: the cursor ran around my screen on its own, opening and closing various windows, and entering service commands. In no more than three minutes, the same support_013 was telling me everything was ready. Finally!

* * *

~ Finding a Body ~

DONE!

I couldn't hide it, I was very proud of my work. And I managed to fit everything into one thirty-minute clip going from the hike through the mountains to the castle to my elevation to Dark Sovereign and first orders as new *Boundless Realm* superboss. I drew attention to the contrast between the appearance of my tiny harmless Goblin Herbalist and his new profession as the embodiment of universal evil. I made a lot of jokes and biting commentary. I purposely emphasized my subjects' lack of loyalty, showing the ghastly monsters refusing to obey the meager Amra.

In the very end of the clip I said I would be putting the coordinates of the Dark Sovereign's castle up for sale. Just ten game coins — a pittance for such valuable information! The price seemed not only affordable but even low, so I was sure that many players would be intrigued.

You think I acted foolishly and rashly by revealing such secret information about the location of my lair? Not so. Getting to the Dark Sovereign's castle would still be very difficult even for those who did know its location. Nearly impossible without flying mounts. Even with them, it wasn't exactly a cake walk.

What was more, in one way or another the

coordinates of the Dark Sovereign's castle's would fall into the players' hands soon enough. By triangulation with magical messengers, the general location could be quickly sussed out. I had just simplified that mission by removing the extra steps, making myself a mint in the process. And if I was going to sell the coordinates of the Dark Sovereign's castle, now was the time. In a few days, every player who was interested would already know. What was more, I figured this was the best time. With the new patch and big flashy advertising campaign the Boundless Realm Corporation was running, any information about the new big boss would be sure to arouse some interest. And all the more so if I said right where to find him.

I finished the video clip and made a post selling the coordinates, then decisively closed every program and browser tab connected with *Boundless Realm*. Sure, it would have been nice to take my sister's advice and buy maps of the neighboring regions and big cities, and take a general look over everything I could find about building castles. But my eyelids were sagging, I could barely think and I was afraid of doing something stupid. But before I went to sleep, I had one last thing I couldn't put off. I opened a search engine and tried to find any information about a street racer named Andre who had lost both arms in an accident. I was Val's older brother and only relative, so I needed to keep an eye on who she was talking to! What if it was some kind of fraudster or gangster, who spun a yarn about racing electrocars for my sister, but in fact had lost his arms for stealing in the Muslim quarters of the metropolis or in a bloody skirmish with fellow gangsters?

I found the information instantly. The tragic incident had been widely discussed online. There were diametrically opposite opinions and comments on the topic, ranging from "it's a pity such a handsome young boy's life was ruined," to, "we let this new generation get away with too much, that's why he lost his arms. I hope the rest of them can learn from this." Andre was indeed a young racer. At a blind corner, he had crashed at massive speed into a pile-up of several other electrobikes.

I looked at the photographs from before the race. They showed a boy with curly brown hair, who looked to be eighteen. He was tall and had a slim build, charming smile and cheerful eyes. He was posing in front of an expensive sport electrobike holding a racing helmet in his hands. Ugh, if only Andre had known then how this race would end...

Among the many headlines I found online, one caught my eye: "Second-place racer shocked by son's accident, will be leaving sport." I clicked the article. Woah! It turned out this Andre was from a racing dynasty! His father Paul Hernandes was a very famous driver from one of the best crews on the planet. He had taken second place four times in Formula Zero, so his fans had given him the nickname "Mister Second Place." The thirty-eight-year-old veteran was having one of the best seasons of his career, with decent chances at taking first place and four races left until the end. But his son's tragedy had overturned all of "Mister Second Place's" ambitions.

And Andre's mother... I had to stop and catch my breath. Could it really be "Iron Jeanette?" The famed captain of a team of virtual gladiators called the *Digital Amazons*, fifteen years ago she was *the* cyber-athlete *par-excellence*. Yes, it was definitely her! In elementary school, I had a whole binder full of trading cards from chewing-gum packs that depicted famous male and female cyber gladiators, and the *Digital Amazons* occupied its most-honored first page. I had never even in my boldest fantasies dreamed I might one day meet this legendary star of cybersport. But my sister Valeria was already on friendly terms with her eldest son Andre... Wow, life was truly more surprising and unpredictable than any computer game.

I stood from the table and walked over to the

window. Behind a thick pane of bulletproof glass, I could see millions of glimmering lights in the darkened metropolis. The skyscrapers of the planet's largest corporations glowed, and electric cars raced down the nearby autobahn. But the photo of Andre from before his fateful ride just haunted me. What a proud and confident gaze the young racer had, he simply radiated power and confidence. Too bad scientists hadn't invented a time machine yet. I would love to go back and warn that optimistic happy boy, maybe try to talk him out of it. Although... then my sister would never have met him.

Day Two

New Opportunities, New Problems

AFTER A LONG SLEEP, I was feeling very well rested. My chest stitches didn't even hurt anymore, and I was feeling fighting fit. I took a shower, shaved, ate breakfast and walked over to the computer. I purposely drew that all out as long as possible, because I was very nervous. How had the viewers taken my clip? How had the players taken the fact that Goblin Herbalist Amra was now the Dark Sovereign himself, whose coming had all *Boundless Realm* in tremors? The monitor lit up and my eyes immediately went wide.

~ Finding a Body ~

WHAT THE HELL??? My clip already had eighteen million views, and the counter was constantly ticking higher, adding tens of thousands every second. Pretty sweet! I was also happily surprised by an email from the video hosting site saying my channel was now in the top ten most popular *Boundless Realm* channels, sitting at number six in subscriber count. Along with that, they sent me a boilerplate contract for monetizing the channel with ad revenue. I had to admit, all that had me in a state that was very near shock.

Finally I got to how many had bought the coordinates of the Dark Sovereign's castle. There were one million three hundred forty thousand purchases just in the first morning!!! I mean sure, I suspected my map coordinates would be highly sought after, but not this highly... My legs shaky, I stood from the computer desk, walked to the fridge and took out a can of cold, even tooth-ache-inducing beer. I needed to come to my senses.

Was I now a millionaire? Seemingly. Even considering the one percent commission on all in-game transactions and the fees and taxes I'd have to pay converting such a huge amount of *Boundless Realm* currency to cash, it was very possible I might end up with more than one million credits. And although Amra didn't have the physical cash in silver coins, just promissory notes from the Subterranean Bank of Thorin the Ninth, and the Most Reliable Bank of Gremlins, which first would have to somehow be converted into game currency, that was a purely technical issue and an easily solvable one at that.

When Tina had very recently called me a "potentially a millionaire," I just laughed in her pretty face, not able to believe her. But in the end she was right! I'd have to apologize to Tina when I got the chance and give her a nice little gift. But that would have to wait. Now I needed to decide what to do with all the wealth that had just crash-landed on my head.

Would I really just be withdrawing these funds from the game and converting it into credits in my bank account? I could, sure. But what would be the point of that? I had no need for money in the real world. I had around three hundred thousand in my bank account already, and my sister's treatment was already paid for, as was her virtual reality capsule. I had no other large expenditures in the foreseeable future, either. What was more, I was feeling cheap and didn't want to lose hundreds of thousands of real credits to income taxes, which would only apply once I withdrew the game currency. Should I just leave the thirteen million coins and change lying around? That would also be foolish. Money should always work. That rule was just as true in the game world.

But what to do in this situation? First of all, clearly I'd have to visit a branch of one of the game banks and convert my notes into silver coins so I could make full use of my money. But where was the nearest branch of the Subterranean Bank of Thorin the Ninth or the Most Reliable Bank of Gremlins? In the underground city of the dwarves Dotur-Khawe most likely...

And then I had a thought that struck me with its novelty: why should I go there on my own when I could just open a branch of the bank right here in the lands of the Dark Sovereign?! Bankers were generally happy to be able to expand their business, so I could probably make an arrangement. As a matter of fact, two of my dwarves were headed to Dotur-Khawe now, so I could send an offer to the subterranean bankers through them.

I looked at the time. It was just past ten. Hrmmm... I was seemingly too late to send the message through the dwarves. Valeria generally entered the game early in the morning, at seven or even earlier, so she had probably already made portal scrolls and handed them out to Max Sochnier, Tondik Exuberant, and Gnum Spiteful. Most likely, my dwarves had even left their home city a few hours ago. Although I did still have the Steward. He was a gremlin by race, so he could probably tell me how to get in touch with the other bank. With that thought in mind, I headed quickly for my virtual reality capsule.

Loading... I appeared next to the very gates of the castle, where I had exited the game. It was a warm windless day, a bit overcast, not too hot and eminently comfortable. With such pleasant daytime weather, I could hardly believe how cold I'd been just last night. I mean, that was the kind of deep freeze that could kill anything. But I didn't have time to come to my senses and take a look around before a laundry list of Fame-increase messages flickered past:

Fame increased
Present value: 23

Fame increased
Present value: 24

...

Fame increased
Present value: 37

These changes were probably caused by the rapid spread of the news that my modest Goblin Herbalist had become Dark Sovereign. Although it was also possible that this was from my entreaty to all NPC's, and my name was gaining notoriety as a potential master. Well, Fame was a very important stat that influenced NPC opinion, and my negotiation prowess. It would come in handy. But what the heck was this?

A few steps away, wisps of mist started gathering into a dense cloud, becoming darker and thicker with every second. Boom! A huge black rider emerged from that darkness on a steed the color of a moonless night. And clacking its hooves on my cobblestone square, it came to a stop.

Dark Rider
Emissary of the Dark Sovereign

So then, here was my rider and representative! But what did he want from me? Not coming down from his mount, the heavily armored knight gave me a salute with his spear and thundered out so loud it echoed off the castle and distant hills:

"Sovereign, invasion! At the distant approaches to your lands above the river of death, five silver-Pegasus riders have been spotted. They're flying this way, and very quickly. They'll reach your castle in just seven hours!"

Silver Pegasuses, and all five of them at once? I see. The leaders of the *Legion of Steel* wanted to exploit their unique advantage over all the other players and use flying mounts to reach the Dark Sovereign's fortress before anyone else could. And that was very, very worrying news. Five level 300+ players could wreak plenty of havoc here all on their own, but if they opened a portal for the remaining soldiers of their fearsome and most powerful clan... That would be the end of my whole army, as well as the Dark Sovereign himself.

Seven hours? That was still more than enough time to react. I turned to the Dark Rider:

"Say, can you make it quickly to these flying pegasuses?"

"Yes, Sovereign. I have the power to appear anywhere darkness or fog reign. And there is always fog along the Styx, so I can always reach any point on the banks of the river of death."

Ah, that was nice. I'd have to keep that in mind for the future. The emissary would make a great envoy, who could carry my orders and small packages all throughout my lands practically instantaneously. Just then, Valerianna Quickfoot left the castle and joined our conversation. But I could barely recognize my sister. Instead of a gaunt green-haired girl in a light dress, before me now was a tall fearsome war-chieftess draped in a magical black robe with silver seams that went all the way to the floor. And my sister had a black-velvet hooded cloak over the robe embroidered with silver runes. It covered the upper half of the

~ Finding a Body ~

little mage girl's face completely. All you could see now were her blood-red lips and sharp predatory little teeth underlined by her acute white chin. But higher in the lowered hood in the darkness, the flickering orange and red eyes of the Sister of the Dark Sovereign looked especially haunting. Overall it was very scary but also intriguing. My sister had clearly tried very hard to achieve just such an effect with her new appearance.

After a quick greeting and saying that she'd sent the Ogre Fortifier and some cyclopes and giants to build a dam on a mountain stream, Valerianna turned to the Dark Rider:

"Say, could you shoot the flying players or their winged horses with your deadly Midnight Wraith arrow?"

Hey yeah, that was a good idea! I now also wanted to know and was waiting with bated breath. The Midnight Wraith contained in the tip of the cursed arrow was always two times higher level than its strongest enemy.

And so, if the leader of the *Legion of Steel* Till Quick_Fingers was on one of the pegasuses, as the highest-level player on the Southern Continent at level over 350, he and his allies would be up against a deadly flying monster of an absolutely sky-high level. Certainly over 700, and no player in all *Boundless Realm* could face off against something like that. But the Dark Rider's answer left me disenchanted:

"My masters, I'm afraid I have no more Cursed Arrows. I had one, but I used it when I shot the Sovereign's Mythical Hound. My three brothers still have their Cursed Arrows. But none of us would be able to hit such a nimble target flying so high up..."

What a shame... Using a Cursed Arrow seemed very intriguing, but it wouldn't work in practice.

And hey, I took advantage of the opportunity, opened my inventory and handed the Dark Rider the deadly object that once belonged to it:

"You can have your arrow back."

The Dark Rider gave me a salute with its spear and stuck the deadly arrow back in its quiver. Valerianna shook her head in disapproval. Seemingly, my sister thought the Cursed Arrow might have a better use.

"Tim, how are you planning to tell the four riders apart? You need to keep them straight so you don't forget who you told to do what. Maybe you should name these ghastly riders? For example, you could name them after the four horsemen of the Apocalypse: Pestilence, War, Famine and Death. Sounds pretty good, huh?"

But I was deeply opposed to that choice of names. First of all, the steeds my horsemen rode were an identical shade of black, unlike those in the canonical text about Judgement Day. Second, I didn't want to intertwine characters from holy texts with a videogame and potentially cause complaints from religious fanatics.

"I shall call them Darkness, Gloom, Night and Murk! And they shall all be siblings, the first three women and the last a man. And each of the riders will be assigned to patrol and protect the distant borders of my holdings. North, East, West and South. And I'll have them respawn if they die, because they're badass and it would be hard to find more like them!"

You have used 4 Direct Intervention Points
You have 148 points remaining

The massively tall rider before me acquired obviously female proportions. What was more, a mane of long hair grew out from under her helm, and her armor and weapon changed as well. Gone was the elongated cavalry pike. In its place, the Rider now held a curved ghostly saber, which looked to have been forged from the deepest darkness of the underworld.

Night
Emissary of the Dark Sovereign
Level 250 Ghostly Rider

I was hoping that I wouldn't have to spend Direct Intervention Points. I named the wolves of the Gray Pack before I even knew about these points, after all.

But seemingly where I spent the points was when I went beyond names, giving them genders and altering their appearance.

Oh well, I'd survive. And at that I'd be sure that my emissaries were busy guarding the borders not just wandering at random. Plus they could respawn if they encountered an overly powerful opponent.

"Night, you shall be responsible for the West. And I have your first mission as well. Ride out to the queen of the land of the dead Hel. She lives somewhere in your area. Be extremely polite so the hot-headed Scandinavian goddess of death doesn't kill you right away. I need her to hear you out. And relay this message: 'My sister Hel, you offered your aid to Fenrir. Well, now your brother has a request of you. There are five Silver Pegasus riders flying along the river of death. Their names, most likely...'" here I opened some old logs containing my conversations with the *Legion of Steel*, "'are Kristina Mozzi [LEGION], Leon Shadow_Hunter [LEGION], Violetta Bestia [LEGION], Antonio de_ Pirienne [LEGION], and Till Quick_Fingers [LEGION]. Hel, kill them all and do with them as you threatened to do with me, so these undying do not respawn right away. Thanks in advance, sister! And I'm expecting a visit, so drop by any time! Your brother Fenrir, a.k.a. Amra, a.k.a. the Dark Sovereign.' That is all, Night, now carry out my order!"

A moment later, the Dark Rider dissolved into wisps of fog. Valerianna spent a long time staring at the fading wisps, then asked with clear mistrust:

"Do you really think it'll work? It just feels so much like cheating. It kind of bothers me. You just summon a goddess, and your enemies get blasted into oblivion."

"Do you think it was that easy?! How about you go try and meet with a goddess, then reach an understanding with her without dying first..." I grumbled, frowning in dismay as I remembered the unpleasant discussion with the goddess of death. "And we still have yet to see whether this actually works. But even if it does this time, I'm not at all sure Hel will agree to help me again. So let's think up a few alternative methods of greeting flying guests."

Diplomat skill increased to level 23!
Achievement unlocked: Player killer (8)

Achievement unlocked: Player killer (9)

...

Achievement unlocked: Player killer (12)

Level seventy-one!

Level seventy-two!

...

Attention! You have reached level 80.
You may now improve your character's
survival by choosing a modification

...

Level eighty-three!

Woah... The cascade of messages gushing down on me almost knocked me off my feet. And the accompanying changes in body statistics and intense emotional outburst inside only made it harder. Thirteen levels in one go! This was the first time I got that. But I didn't lose control of my character this time, though it was no easy task.

"Aha, it worked..." Valerianna Quickfoot said, not hiding her glee. "But Tim, you've got the Criminal marker over your head again, and for the next eight hours you can't leave the game. In the future that could be a serious problem, because you're gonna have to kill more and more players every day as they come to attack your holdings. And if every murder gets you that penalty..."

"Not eight hours, just six and a half. My Veil skill brings down the penalty. But you're right, Val, I'll have to do something about that. I'll write to support. As it is it's a bit illogical that the Dark Sovereign — a game boss, created especially to do battle with living players — is given this commonplace penalty like some average PK'er. I have to leave the game to rest sometimes, after all. How am I supposed to do that with the Criminal marker constantly hanging over my head?!"

Wisps of dark mist started gathering and growing dense over the square near me and the mavka again. Apparently, my emissary was coming back. And I hoped she had good news. Boom! Night rode out of the dark cloud, and the Ghostly Rider's saddle-horn had a big bag tied to it. Whatever was inside was wriggling around and issuing ghastly wails. Night stopped a few steps away and reported that her mission was complete. I then noticed that the Rider's level had gone up from 250 to the shocking 287 in that brief time... Wow, that was about how much experience she should have gotten for killing five TOP players over level 300. But why was I given so much less?

Seemed a bit unfair...

Meanwhile, Night untied the bag and threw it at my feet:

"Sovereign, the goddess Hel asked me to bring you this gift. She said she stumbled upon this creature in the kingdom of the dead and thought you might like it."

After that, the Ghostly Rider figured she was done and was about to go back into the wisps of fog, but I stopped her. I just couldn't forget about the loot the leaders of the *Legion of Steel* might have dropped after they met their end at the hands of the goddess of death.

After all, they were in the top one hundred strongest characters of the Southern Continent, and they were probably wearing some pretty intense equipment. Unique and even legendary items, objects from sets... Even if just one such item dropped, it would be very cool.

What was more, every time a player died, some of the coins they were carrying would also fall, so the five leaders of the strongest and one of the richest gaming clans might have dropped a whole fortune.

"Night, where the five undying were killed, many coins and interesting items may have dropped. Go there, pick it up and bring their belongings to me!"

But Night just lowered her head, looking

downcast, and said:

"Sovereign, I cannot pick up silver coins. I am just a fleshless ghost, and silver is a particularly tricky metal. What's more, I have no idea what may be of interest to my lord."

Ah, bad luck... But my sister saved the situation:

"Night, I'll come with you and do it myself!" Valerianna Quickfoot traced a complicated figure in the air with her glowing wand and decisively stepped toward the ghost. Then she very gracefully climbed up on the stirrups and took a seat in front of the Ghostly Rider. "I created an Illusion Magic spell that temporarily turns ghosts solid. And I'll just come back through a portal. I'll be right back, Tim!"

In an instant, the huge black steed had carried both riders into the thick dark cloud. And when it dispersed, neither the Ghostly Rider nor Valerianna Quickfoot were there. I then walked over to the jostling and rather noisy bag. I carefully untied the top, and... nearly lost my left hand when a set of huge teeth clamped shut right where it had been a second earlier.

Successful Agility check
Dodge skill increased to level 38!

With a punch to the head, I sent the creature

back into the bag, and quickly tied the top shut again. Quite the gift! I barely saw anything but a row of sharp predatory teeth and the empty eye sockets of a bare skull. I couldn't recognize the creature, but it was clearly undead, and quite aggressive at that.

Undead? Yes, for sure. My vampiric ability Search for Life couldn't find anything alive nearby. Well if it was indeed not mortal, I would have to take an entirely different approach. I waited a minute for the beast to calm down and stop thrashing inside the bag, then activated my Undead Apathy ability. This time, the monster didn't react at all and was still calm in the sack. I sighed, gathering my strength, and looked around: the last thing I needed was a servant to mess things up by coming in right now! I untied the bag again and looked inside.

It was the skeleton of a huge hound with disproportionately long paws and jaws, more fitting for a crocodile than a dog. In the depths of the elongated skull, I could see spooky red blinking eyes. In places the old skeleton still had dried out parchment-like skin with clumps of long decayed fur. And the being's neck bones were all shattered. By the looks of things, once upon a time this dangerous beast had its head cut off. Nevertheless, the monster's head was still present, though it was not physically connected to the rest of the body.

Faithful
Ravenous Cur
Level-210 Modified Chimeroid

Chimeroid? A creature based on a dog that was created by magic? By the way, among my Goblin Herbalist's many bonuses, I had one boosting chimeroid opinion. However, that clearly applied only to living creatures because this dead Ravenous Cur didn't give a damn that I was good and he was supposed to be friendly to me. I also immediately checked if could add this being to the Gray Pack, but was left disappointed. What to do with it? Should I try to bring it back to life using Direct Intervention Points? Of course that would be fun to try, but I was in no hurry. Who could say how this predatory beast might behave with a body of flesh and blood? What if it attacked me, or even worse ran away and started causing mayhem around my castle? A level-210 monster was always going to be a risk, and one had to behave cautiously around them.

What was more, I had to get a handle on this beast's unique features. After all, this was no simple wolf or dog, but a chimeroid, which had been magically modified. Someone had made it for a purpose, and it was probably not merely the elongated jaws. What was more, the goddess Hel wouldn't have gifted me this beast and said she thought I might like it if it didn't have any unique traits. So I'd put this Ravenous Cur in a cage for now to study later!

I called the Keymaster and the huge dark figure appeared before me with a tinkling keyring. I was a bit worried about how my fanged undead gift would act around someone else, but the Ravenous Cur had no reaction. That must have been due to my servant's Indestructible tag, which the dead hound must have perceived as "not tasty, uninteresting."

"Is there a room that locks up tight in the castle, or a strong cage for this undead beast?" I asked, pointing at the Ravenous Cur. The Keymaster bared his teeth happily:

"You offend me, master. I have facilities to keep all manner of things! The dungeons of this castle have rooms and cages strong enough that even a rampaging dragon couldn't escape! Shall I bring this sweet little thing down there?"

Sweet little thing??? The dead beast was almost one hundred fifty levels stronger than me and, although it was calm now, I still wouldn't exactly call it a "sweet little thing." That said... I didn't know the Keymaster's level, maybe to him the Ravenous Cur was just a "sweet little thing," especially given that this predator had no way of biting or in any way harming him. I ordered the Keymaster to take the monster away and lock it up tight and finally got to the idea that had made me hurry into *Boundless Realm* today in the first place.

* * *

"IT'S SETTLED!" Trying to act with extreme caution and not break his old bones, I squeezed the frail gray gremlin's hand. The NPC Banker was of some absolutely unfathomable level, but clearly ancient.

At that, it took great effort to hold back a shout of elation. It had all worked out even better than I hoped! Before meeting the head of the Most Reliable Bank of the Gremlins, I was extremely nervous and thought I would have to convince him and offer some business plan for expanding his bank throughout my lands. But the reality was quite the opposite. The harrier-gray gremlin that walked out of the fiery oval portal immediately sent his gloomy taciturn bodyguards back through the portal, gave a deep bow to the Dark Sovereign and handed me a valuable gift. It was a massive chain of dark-red gold with links in the shape of human skulls. It gave pretty solid magical bonuses to defense against mind reading. After that, the banker started convincing me not so much to even open a new branch of the bank in my faraway lands, as to not attack any offices of the Most Reliable Bank of Gremlins when I invaded *Boundless Realm*. I faked a frown and pretended to think it over, which clearly made him nervous and offer even more advantageous conditions.

Finally, I gave my official assent. By then, the hoar-headed executive of the largest in-game bank was offering me seven hundred thousand coins to pay off my army. I was also offered "a unique item that will certainly be of interest to the Sovereign." And the chairman of the bank was glancing every so often at the rusty torture implements around him, every time pressing his huge ears to his head. You see, I was holding this meeting in the deepest depths of my dungeons in the torture chamber. Why such a strange location? First of all, I needed to build a reputation as a terrifying leader to be reckoned with, and it was hard to imagine a better setting for that. Second, the torture chamber was the only room I wasn't ashamed to show such an important guest. All the other rooms of the huge castle would have greeted the Gremlin Banker with just bare walls and no furniture.

We hadn't even finished sealing the deal with a handshake before rolling thunder, clearly audible through the thick walls, confirmed that the gods of *Boundless Realm* had heard and would guarantee our agreement. From then on, my subjects both living and dead were bound not to damage the property of the Most Reliable Bank of Gremlins or attack any employee of the bank.

Trading skill increased to level 33!

Trading skill increased to level 34!

Trading skill increased to level 35!

As soon as the big-eared old man said goodbye and disappeared, before me appeared the Storekeeper, glowing with delight:

"Sovereign, magic demonic messengers have just delivered three chests full of silver coins to the castle store rooms! The total is seven hundred thousand. I've already counted! It's a fortune! And the winged demons also brought this," the Storekeeper said, handing me a long package of time-darkened parchment, tied up with twine.

Not wasting time, I shook out the packet and started looking curiously at the tube, which looked to be carved of one piece of time-yellowed bone. There were no words on the surface, nor removable lid or even the slightest crack... However, the object was clearly hollow, and something was shaking around inside. What was this thing? And how to get at the contents?

Insufficient Intelligence to identify object
Required minimum Intelligence: 270

Insufficient Intelligence to complete action
Required minimum Intelligence to open object: 700

Two hundred seventy Intelligence points were needed just to know what this thing in my hands even was?! And a whole seven hundred to open it?

You've got to be kidding me... Even Valerianna Quickfoot, who was specialized in the magical arts, didn't have seven hundred Intelligence! I looked at my goblin's pitiful Intelligence of 34. Easier to break it open and get what's inside than try to make my Goblin Herbalist into some big-headed intellectual.

Not having found a way to open the tube, I decided to simply break it. But... That wasn't right either! Despite the apparent fragility, the thin bone walls of the case wouldn't give. Striking it with a heavy hammer, pinching it in magical pliers and even tightening a spiked torture implement for breaking bones all did nothing.

Item parameter detected: Indestructible
Experience received: 80 Exp.

~ Finding a Body ~

I chortled. What a tricky old banker! I guess he knew the right kind of gift for me. "A unique item that will certainly be of interest to the Sovereign." You can say that again! Now I was going batty with curiosity, trying to discover what was inside! My sister would be able to read the object's information and tell me something useful, but she wasn't back yet so I tossed the bothersome tube to my Storekeeper:

"Stick this in storage and lock it up tight! And don't hide the three chests of coins far away. That's money for my soldiers to buy what they need before a long military campaign, I'm planning to hand it out tomorrow or the next day. By the way... I'm not gonna have time for that, so you'll be handing it out! With your stinginess, I can be sure that not a single coin will be wasted and it'll all go where I need!"

Seeing the stingy demon's sour face and rolling eyes as he nearly passed out, I hurried to add:

"As soon as you hand out the money to my soldiers, get an empty trunk of coins ready. The gremlins are bringing lots of money today. Almost nine million coins!"

That was exactly how much I had in promissory notes from the Most Reliable Bank of Gremlins, and the head of the bank promised to convert them into clinking silver by the end of the day. But the gremlins didn't accept notes from the competition, so I'd also have to take the rest to the dwarves.

The Storekeeper immediately came to his senses, put on a happy face and hurried to carry out my order. I then ordered the Steward to come bring me to the throne room. I wanted to use my crystal ball and see what was happening outside. I was also planning to go investigate the dam the Ogre Fortifier and other giants and cyclopes were building in the mountains with the Wood Nymph's designs. What had Valerianna Quickfoot thought up now? Maybe the dam and pond were going to be part of the defensive structures surrounding my castle.

I did indeed appear in the throne room... but I was not nearly the only one there. There were thirty rougarou warriors on bended knee from the Clan of the Laughing Otter, with the shaman at their head patiently awaiting me. It looked like they'd been there since early this morning. I had totally forgotten about them.

Without showing any surprise or embarrassment, I got straight to work:

"Shaman, are these really the best of the best? Have you explained to these warriors what awaits them?"

The gray-haired shaman respectfully bowed even lower and said:

~ Finding a Body ~

"Yes, Sovereign. These are the very strongest soldiers of the Clan of the Laughing Otter. And they're all happy to serve the adopted daughter of our lord and proud to have been trusted enough for this mission."

"Great! Then how about they hurry up and find Princess Chai-nee Shu in the nearby woods to help her hunt. Although... wait!" I stopped the muscular soldiers as they stood up and walked over to one of them. He was clearly different from the others. His clothing and weaponry were more expensive, and his description was not just cookie-cutter. Instead of Warrior, Scout, or Bowman and level number, he had more detailed information:

See-Uhn-Rhu
Claimant to the Chiefdom of the Clan of the Laughing Otter
Level-112 Rougarou Bowman

A claimant? He was even physically reminiscent of the brothers I'd killed. I turned and looked at the two furry grimacing heads stuck into the back of the throne. Yes, there was definitely a certain resemblance.

"A claimant? Shaman, who is in charge of the Clan of the Laughing Otter now?"

"No one, Sovereign. The two elder brother chieftains were killed yesterday, and the third younger brother was one of the thirty strongest soldiers in the clan so, in accordance with your order, was assigned to defend Princess Chai-nee Shu."

Come on, what foolishness! Was it really so hard to realize that the last member of the ruling dynasty had to be kept out of this elite division of soldiers from the Clan of the Laughing Otter? And this had nothing to do with humanitarian interest, a differing opinion of the aristocracy or some desire to maintain the old authorities. It was simply that NPC groups and clans were like little kids. Without proper supervision, they would immediately get confused and start to wander off. The laws of *Boundless Realm* were harsh. NPC's were made to live collectively so, without chieftains and key players, they were supposed to just die. Their behavior algorithms were just too simple and the processors assigned to every commonplace NPC were just not powerful enough. In the end, such a character would lack the quick thinking needed to survive in this harsh world.

Most likely, the corporation did that to save money, otherwise no programming staff and no computing power would be enough to run everything that happened in the huge *Boundless Realm.* And perhaps it was to also make things more predictable. After all, NPC's were created to entertain the players, and few undying enjoyed having their prey or personal servants behaving too independently. In one way or another, NPC groups were generally doomed to die out after losing their key characters.

I had read about many times when NPC clans and even large NPC villages ceased to exist in *Boundless Realm* after their chieftain and other key characters died. It damaged the interrelations between NPC's, made them start behaving chaotically, and soon all their industrial, professional and personal connections came crashing to the ground. Not too long ago, a once complete and successful team broke down into a bunch of individual characters, and they just started wandering aimlessly through their lands even attacking one another, then quickly died out. And although there was still a shaman in the Clan of the Laughing Otter, he was clearly the only key character left. I stopped the Rougarou Bowman and suggested he return to his clan. However I met unexpected resistance from the claimant:

"Sovereign, as with all other Rougarou here, I was summoned to serve your daughter and swore an oath to do so, so my former clan is already behind me."

Stubborn bastard! And although under different circumstances I might have used my authority to pressure him, the oath stopped me. The gods of *Boundless Realm* punished oathbreakers harshly and swiftly. But I also didn't want to leave the five-hundred-strong Clan of the Laughing Otter completely rudderless and under the care of just the decrepit shaman, because these rougarou were important to my further plans. So I thought up a new plan and, using my new abilities, bent the game world to my needs:

"See-Uhn-Rhu, everyone knows you care deeply about my adopted daughter Chai-nee Shu, so I understand why you want to stay near her and protect her. But as the Princess's guardian, I would never give my approval for her to associate with someone who has proven himself unreliable and abandoned his clan when the going got tough. And also as a potential groom, without a strong and rich clan behind you, you're of no interest to either me or my daughter. So go lead the Clan of the Laughing Otter, prove yourself a wise and valiant chieftain, steep yourself in military glory, and reaffirm your loyalty to the Dark Sovereign and his daughter! That is how you shall prove your right to be near Princess Chai-nee Shu, and not just as one of her thirty bodyguards, but as her legal husband! And the gods of *Boundless Realm* will only be glad to confirm your observance of that oath!"

You have used 2 Direct Intervention Points

~ Finding a Body ~

You have 149 points remaining

Diplomat skill increased to level 24!

Foreman skill increased to level 74!

Just one sentence, reinforced by a few points, and the Bowman was now inspired and love-struck, glowing with happiness and thanking his Sovereign for trusting him. He nearly ran out of the throne room, hurrying to take leadership over his orphaned clan. And along with See-Uhn-Rhu, his shaman also left the throne room with the rest of the rougarou. One problem down!

Then, finally making my way to the Eye of the Sovereign, I wanted to look at the area around my castle. But as soon as I got a grip on what was happening, I started moaning in frustration and despair! Over the brief half an hour that I had not been watching, a squadron of minotaurs had cut down a cyclops female, and was already butchering her enormous carcass for meat. And the ratmen of one squadron had chomped through a large portion of our supplies in a field kitchen, and were now fighting with orc pirates, who were trying to protect at least a few scraps. The undead had discovered some sunlight through a gap in the clouds which was very rare for this area, and were now densely packed into the bright spot, already partially decayed and crippled by the direct solar rays.

What had I done to deserve this punishment?! Why the hell did I even agree to play the Dark Sovereign? Why couldn't I just stay a simple happy and silly Goblin Herbalist, gathering rare flowers in distant regions of *Boundless Realm*? Now I had to fill my head with how to supply a whole army and maintain order in its ghastly ranks. And almost all my warriors were higher level than me, which put my authority in peril...

Day Two
Evil Gets Rich

I WAS STILL dispirited and depressed when Valerianna Quickfoot discovered me, popping into the throne room an hour later. But what kind of throne room even was this? Such a bombastic term implied a luxurious space for holding festivities and receiving delegations from foreign countries. But this was just a simple large empty room with nothing really in it other than the crystal ball and a throne...

"What happened here, Tim? I saw a gallows on the square before the palace!"

I tore my gaze from the crystal ball, which I was using to observe the group of cyclopes returning from building the dam. The one-eyed giants were lamenting as they wrung their hands, wailing over the corpse of their murdered compatriot and shouting curses at the minotaur tents and my palace.

"I had to punish a few minotaurs and ratmen for disobedience, murder and theft. I killed the leaders of the upstart squadrons myself," I said pointing at the two new fanged heads in the back of my throne, " I also improved some skills and leveled up three times, all of which improved the throne. It now generates five Direct Intervention Points per hour. And I punished the other criminals to prove a point, hanging them before my whole army. I really hope this execution will serve as a lesson to teach the others that they must never kill allies or rob their own! But basically I feel like if we don't go to war in the next day or two, this savage army will tear itself to shreds!"

"Alright then, send them somewhere! Did you buy maps of the neighboring provinces like I asked yesterday?"

I had to admit that I hadn't. There had just not been time. But my sister took my negative answer in her own way:

"Amra, if you don't have any money, just say so. Don't be embarrassed! I've got one thousand eight hundred coins here, it should be enough for maps and the bare minimum for your army. I picked them up where the five *Legion of Steel* leaders died. And in the desert I also grabbed you a vial of Silver Pegasus blood. When else could you get such a rare thing? And for me, I took this," the fearsome sorceress showed me a very fine necklace inlaid with huge glimmering emeralds.

Because my Goblin Herbalist had low Intelligence and thus couldn't read about the jewelry, the mavka explained:

"This an item from the legendary Elven Amazon set for TOP players over level-280. It reduces mana expenditure by a third when casting spells and gives pretty good bonuses to Perception and accuracy with a bow."

"What do you need that for, Valerianna?" I asked in surprise. "You've never held a bow a day in your life!"

"Me? Oh no, this necklace is no good for my character, plus I'd never be able to get it on. The description says, 'only for elves or dark elves.' But without this necklace, the former owner loses the full-set bonus which gives a very solid buff to shooting accuracy for their whole squadron and the ability to become immaterial three times a day. I'm sure Kristina Mozzi would be willing to pay very dearly to get this little thing back!"

I tried to conjure up a memory of the elven warrior from the *Legion of Steel*. She was rumored to be dating the clan leader, and I agreed with my sister that finding the item was a great boon and it could be sold for a lot of money.

"Although it's possible that the *Lords of Chaos* or the *Keepers* would pay more to make sure such a valuable item never returns to the *Legion of Steel*. It gives them a great chance to gimp one of the strongest and highest-level enemy players before the PVP clan tournament next month. In any case, you can keep the proceeds. I've got more than enough coins. I've already got around nine million in the chests in the castle storerooms, and soon there will be even more."

"How much now?!" the sorceress stumbled and nearly fell over. I had to prop the Wood Nymph up. "So what are you waiting for, big-ears? Spend it all buying maps, weapons and everything you need while there's still time!"

"But what about... Don't you think we'd better withdraw it into the real world to live on? You could go to a good prep school, and we need to buy our own place..." I started arguing. And Val was vigorously opposed:

"Timothy, if as the Dark Sovereign you are the poorest of all rulers, but still manage to hold out against all *Boundless Realm* or at least put up worthy resistance, I'll be much prouder of you than if you don't use all the funds you have available and lose the war on day two or three. What's more," here the sorceress lowered her eyes to the floor and started whispering, "I don't doubt that Kira Tyle is watching you very carefully and deciding whether you're worth making up with and spending time around. Don't disappoint us both!"

AND TAKE THIS magic tectonic bomb too!" Valerianna said, pointing at another item in the *Boundless Realm* online shop.

"But why?" I didn't understand. "It costs seven hundred coins, but it's practically worthless. It isn't powerful enough to make a real earthquake, just maybe to scare the enemy. That money would be better spent on another level-one-hundred Drow archer or orc healer. Those NPC's will at least be useful on the walls of the castle or fighting in mountain passes."

The sorceress frowned and shook her head in dismay:

"Tim, you said yourself that buying more soldiers was wasteful and pointless! You've already got a whole army of thirty thousand you barely know what to do with. Also consider that thousands of warriors should be coming soon, so it would be just stupid to buy another couple dozen or even hundred NPC's! Better to train the ones you've got and level them up! But we do need a tectonic bomb — I'm going to plant it in the dam."

My sister's words had me intrigued, and I asked her to tell me more about this mass-scale project. I'd recently noticed that my sister thousands of my soldiers tied up with building, mostly the beefy giants, minotaurs and cyclopes.

"It's all pretty straightforward, Tim. There's a mountain stream way up there. It's icy, angry and gushing with water. And it used to flow down a different course, but a rockslide long ago must have blocked it. On the way to the castle, we walked for a few hours down its dried-up older bed, and even then I noticed the sheer walls and many-mile-long narrow canyon. If there was a flash flood, our whole squadron could have drowned there. Are you getting the idea?"

Yes, there was no need to explain any further, I already understood the basics. Based on Valerianna Quickfoot's designs, the giants were now building a dam to store a critical mass of water high up in the mountains. At the same time, other groups were clearing the old bed and blocking all alternate paths the water might flow down. And all that was so, if an enemy army arrived at the approaches to the castle of the Dark Sovereign, we could blow the dam and release all the water down the narrow canyon, which would wash away all the attacking enemies no matter how many came. It was a good plan and it had every chance to work, if enemy scouts didn't get into my territory and discover our preparations.

"Alright, we'll take the tectonic bomb! And just to make sure let's get five!"

"Three is easily enough, why waste the money...?" my sister tried to object, but I was unstoppable.

I selected five bombs and ordered them for urgent delivery via magical messenger. It was unusual to use all these trade interfaces and catalogues from inside *Boundless Realm*. It immediately destroyed my sense of immersion. I used to prefer leaving the game before calling up the guides, forum or any other useful information but now there was no other way for my sister and I to coordinate.

Trading skill increased to level 44!

Meanwhile, the game algorithms had a very positive opinion of buying all these items and NPC's in the *Boundless Realm* online store, generously raining down new levels and Trading skill on us to induce further purchases. I led my gaze over the skill pop-up and explained myself:

"If there are left over bombs, we'll leave another couple in the narrowest part of the canyon to make rockslides, trap in the water and keep more invaders from coming! Alright, what else?"

The Wood Nymph skimmed our purchase list, all the while softly commenting to herself:

"We should get maps of all nearby cities and villages of a decent size, then get portal scrolls to most of them. We've got more than enough armor and weaponry for your soldiers even considering their various races and preparation levels. We bought enough magical and healing elixirs. We bought alchemy ingredients for a year in advance. We bought seedlings, seeds and grain for our future settlers. We also got more than enough building tools. And sure it's minimal, but we also got interior decorations for your castle. We bought a whole thousand dark elf archers and scouts to protect the mountain passes, too... I still don't know why you bought them, but I'm not going to try and prove it to you anymore. The money is already spent. So, we also ordered a goblin guard to protect the castle of the Dark Sovereign and as a bodyguard for both of us. And we even bought thirteen beautiful NPC magesses to heal and recharge my mana. And let me give you an extra thanks for that!"

Yes, I insisted on that, even though Valerianna Quickfoot first hesitated and tried to insist that her Wood Nymph didn't have any problems surviving, so she didn't need support or guards. But that was before. These were different times, and we were expecting different guests. Not some unremarkable and commonplace undying, but very strong players from all over the Southern Continent of *Boundless Realm*. To be more accurate, there would probably also be plenty of commonplace players, but I was confident my army would be able to stop them. Still, it was at the very least naïve to hope that the skeletons, orcs and minotaurs outside my walls could overcome the best players in *Boundless Realm*. I would need much stronger beings for that. Like the goddess Hel, for example. By the way...

I closed the list of extra magic ammo we hadn't yet bought and went to a totally different part of the game store. I was suddenly interested in fishing in the game and everything that went along with it.

"Are you thinking of fishing in the mountain lake?" my sister asked in surprise, to which I shook my big-eared head.

"No. I just happen to know a god that loves to fish in his free time between ferrying souls, and I want to give him a nice little present. First of all, to remind him of me. And second to get some divine support down the whole Styx, where an enemy army will soon be marching. I think this magical spinning rod with catch-size bonus will take his fancy. Also this indestructible fishing net is perfect. Charon said he dropped his old one in the water a few centuries back. And a whole box of cold and flu elixirs. Plus a barrel of nice dark beer... Alright, my gift is ready!"

I was somewhat afraid that the magical messenger would refuse such a vague address as "River Styx, Charon's Ferry." But my order was accepted, which meant the gift was guaranteed to reach the ferryman of souls to the kingdom of the dead. Awesome!

"Then you should give a gift to the goddess Hel as well. She did us a huge favor! And the omniscient goddess might get offended: you bought a gift for Charon, but not Fenrir's own sister."

It was a fair note, and my sister and I started looking for a gift. It was a difficult task, so Val and I argued over it for a long time. What did the goddess of death even want? Hel lived a simple life in a huge wooden hut with no luxury to speak of. She wore a typical villager's dress, though it was massive. She didn't wear any jewelry. Even the goddess's feet were bare. By the way... My sister and I exchanged glances. Some flashy, pretty boots! What woman, even if she was a goddess, could resist such a thing?!

But it took us a long time to find big enough boots. Even cyclops or giant equipment might not fit the goddess's feet. Finally, my sister discovered a pair of unique magical boots in an open auction, which were the exact right size for Hel's feet. Along with that, they conferred a bunch of bonuses to movement speed and the ability to walk on water, increased Endurance and a few other things. We didn't need any of that, and it only seriously drove up the purchase price, but I didn't cheap out. No matter how I sliced it, this was not some gift to any old person. This was for the goddess of death herself!

And I discovered another intriguing little item that I got for myself:

Adamantium Pendant of Time (unique item)

Instantly resets the charges of one magic item, skipping reload time

After one more use, this pendant will be destroyed

Just after reading the properties, I remembered the gong that could summon the goddess of strife Eris, which the ferryman of souls had given me. That gong was basically a single-use item, because I would have to wait a whole hundred years to use it again. But here was a way to use the ancient artifact one more time, and I could afford to spare the seventeen thousand coins it cost to buy the amulet. Yes, it was a huge amount, which my sister and I couldn't have even dreamed of just one month ago, but being able to summon the quarrelsome goddess two times was worth the money. I mean, what more proof did I need of her destructive abilities than the most epic military conflict of antiquity, the Trojan War!

"There's a bit less than two million coins left," I told Valerianna.

My sister closed most of the purchase tabs and started pacing around the throne room in thought. After three minutes of walking, thinking and quietly muttering to herself, she stopped sharply and exclaimed:

"We should spend that money on our three top priorities. First: you need to fill the Gray Pack to its limit, because that is your main weapon as the new Fenrir. The online shop has all kinds of pets and among them are many types of wolf..."

Here I interrupted Valerianna Quickfoot, because I had already looked over the pets on offer and they had left me unimpressed. Forest Wolves, Swamp Wolves, Guard Dogs, Hell Hounds, Wolfdogs... All commonplace and boring. My audience would definitely not like it if I filled the empty slots in the Gray Pack with the first pets I came across. What was more, normal animals had significantly worse combat characteristics than rare ones, and especially unique creatures. For example, the unique Mythical Hound Fimbulthul at his level of 103 was already as powerful as Baron, the rare Alpha Swamp Wolf at level 120.

And he was many times superior to Akella and the other Forest Wolves at levels 98-102.

I told my sister about the Ravenous Cur — the rare wolf-like undead creature which Night had dragged here in that wriggling sack, and who was now locked up in a strong cage in my dungeon. Reincarnating the level-210 creature would take a painful 420 Direct Intervention Points. I wanted to know whether it was worth spending all that given how precious the points were. Valerianna Quickfoot promised to find information about the beast, and told me she would check the auctions for other rare and interesting beasts that could join the Gray Pack. After that, my sister returned to our topic of discussion:

"Third: you need new blood samples. Your vampiric skills are very important, but I suspect that given the imminent war you won't have the chance to improve them much. So you should handle that right now and not spare any money."

Here I was in complete agreement with my sister. While I had the chance, I needed to rapidly level Taste Tester because that gave my character better regeneration and resistance to sun, and unique vampiric abilities. For that I needed to find new blood. And preferably not in the form of alchemy vials, but living creatures. That way I could kill them with Vampire Bite and level both

Taste Tester and Taste for Blood because that highly important multiplier increased my melee damage. My Taste for Blood was now at 34, which made me do 34% more damage in close combat, but I could raise that even higher.

"Well and finally, we have to solve the problem of your warband. Right now it's simply an unbridled horde of monsters that goes ravenous at the sight of blood. It's a threat to both to enemies and allies. To turn your wild army into a fearsome, but also manageable force, we need to find experienced sergeants, who can train the monsters in discipline and the like. But I would not want to rely on an NPC for such an important task. I'd look for a decent undying. After all, there are reliable mercenary clans that come highly recommended. You might look there. We cannot do without at least twenty sergeants to train your army. But it would be better to hire a whole three hundred — make them centurions, each of which would answer with their head for a brigade of one hundred monsters."

Three hundred centurions? They would each know the strong and weak sides of their monsters better than anyone. That way, they could smooth over internal friction and conflicts as well as cement their one hundred wild monsters into a unified combat squadron, guaranteeing its loyalty to the Dark Sovereign. It sounded beautiful and tempting, but wasn't it beyond our budget?

"That depends where we look," the sorceress answered my doubting. "If we hire players willy-nilly from ads and contact data on the *Boundless Realm* forum, it will take up all our money, that is true. But I have a suggestion that gets around all that. I was skimming the forum and saw that the competition on the mercenary market is quite extreme. There are very, very many players who would like to get paid to game. But there are far fewer potential customers. Of course, the most famous mercenary clans like the *Mercs*, *Bregan D'Aerthe* or the *Battle Cats* don't need advertising and are always in demand despite the high price of their services. But that's not a problem for us. I figure we can find a few mercenary clans that would agree to work for us for minimal pay, and maybe even for free. No matter how you look at it, it's pretty great publicity. Just think, the Dark Sovereign personally selected them for a challenging mission!"

"That's right, Val. But can we trust second-rate mercenaries from unknown clans? For many of them, their squad tag means virtually nothing. But the temptation to betray us and lead the invading army here for some cash and a place in one of the prestigious TOP clans would in fact be very great."

"But that doesn't apply to every second-tier

clan! Some are made up of army veterans reuniting in their golden years to play *Boundless Realm* under the banner of their old regiment. And others are proud former special forces. Both will have fought in many military conflicts in the real world. We can trust them. After all, the honor and name of their regiment are sacred to them. Although I actually had one specific clan in mind, the *Digital Amazons*. I had the chance to meet their leader last night. There are exactly three hundred in their clan, just what we need. They're seeking employment and are amenable to working for the Dark Sovereign!"

The familiar name *Digital Amazons* jumped out at me. Come on, just yesterday I heard something about them. Just fifteen or twenty years ago, the former professional female cyberathletes knew no equal in the virtual disciplines from gladiator fights to survival tournaments. But with time, they had to make way for the next generation. So these old friends had gotten together in *Boundless Realm...*? Alright, very interesting!

"Is Andre's mother still leader of the *Digital Amazons*?" I asked, and my sister shuddered in surprise.

Val was still filling diapers when I was fanboying virtual gladiator fights and collecting chewing-gum cards with portraits of the most famous e-athletes. So that was why she didn't know about my interest in the *Digital Amazons* and was surprised I knew so much.

"Yes, Jeanette has been in charge of the *Digital Amazons* for a quarter century at this point," the Wood Nymph confirmed, quickly suppressing her surprise. "Their big professional team fell apart ten years ago because there were too many conflicts. Advertisers started getting younger and prettier stars, they had a string of bad luck and many of the *Amazons* ended up having kids, so they didn't have any more time for professional cybersports. But the *Digital Amazons* are back together now in the most popular game of modern times. And their clan is only open to former *Amazons* and their most loyal fans, so there's no reason to doubt their reliability."

All that was clear, but something else she said had caught my attention:

"So then, Iron Jeanette knows that you play Valerianna Quickfoot, sister of the Dark Sovereign? But I only uploaded the video clip about Goblin Herbalist Amra becoming Dark Sovereign that night, after your date with Andre! That means you must have told them!"

Val got embarrassed and started looking at the ground. Generally, my sister was perfectly aware of the fact that she could not advertise our real-world identities. But clearly she couldn't resist and blabbed to her new friend Andre, and he shared the information with his mother.

"Yes, Jeanette knows. And although I only told Andre, his mother told me when we met that she was glad to meet such a famous figure from *Boundless Realm*, and said she sometimes watches your video clips. The *Digital Amazons* also took part in the Great Hunt for the Royal Forest Wyvern, but they didn't get to the right part of the world until it was over. But their clan has many major high-level players, and right now we need one another. They can help us fill out and train our army, and we can raise the standing of their somewhat forgotten brand. So then Tim, if you're not opposed, I'm gonna talk with Jeanette today about a long-term commitment from her clan. Andre will be going under tomorrow to have the bionic arms implanted, so his parents are sure to come visit their son tonight, and that will give me the chance to talk to her."

Well then, the idea sounded promising. I was not against it, but I did ask my sister not to reveal the size and composition of our army to the mercenaries and potential allies. I told her to just avoid all my military secrets, in fact. And as for financial issues, and there would definitely be some of those, Val could do the negotiating and make an offer, but I still retained the final say. I also asked Valerianna to tell the leader of the

~ Finding a Body ~

Digital Amazons that we would have to sign a treaty or official contract with the gods of *Boundless Realm* as witnesses.

ALL THE ONLINE catalogues, auctions and other mumbo jumbo were making my eyes spin. I wanted to close all the purchase tabs and immerse myself in the normal *Boundless Realm* as quickly as possible. Then I would like to call VIXEN, saddle my beloved wyvern and fly, fly, fly wherever the winds might take us. Everything around was unknown and engaging. I cocked an eye at Valerianna Quickfoot. Wasn't it time to wrap up this whole purchase process already? Strange as it was, my sister wasn't the least bit tired and was in fact quite chipper:

"Maybe we should comb the auctions for Ifrit Hearts one last time?" she suggested with clear enthusiasm. "We've both got decent equipment on, but we need better stuff. And not just decent rare equipment, we need things intended for characters at much higher levels. But we can only do that with Ifrit Hearts allowing us to remove level requirements."

"Yeah, but we looked a few hours ago. I doubt there's been a serious change since then. If a player put an Ifrit Heart up for sale, it would get snatched up in an instant. It looks like some trade bots are set to buy such valuable ingredients at any price, even a million coins a piece. We don't have that kind of money anymore, so we'll be competing financially with professional Traders."

"Yes, that seems very likely..." Valerianna agreed. "Well then Tim, you will have to really bust your hump just to get the last item from Fenrir's Cursed Regalia on. Either that or level to one hundred twenty-five quickly, which no longer looks like it will take a crazy amount of time."

"First we need to find it by following the Djinn Sultan's instructions, then buy it. But it is located in a place where players are not allowed, the Land of Gloom. And if the queen of those lands, Kirra'ellita Huntress of the Night won't allow it, I don't even know what to do. I doubt the dragons and harpies guarding the Land of Gloom will let me through the mountains, even on VIXEN. Also it's a very long flight — almost six thousand miles."

"I'll try and have a talk with Kira," my sister promised, none too confident. "She's supposed to drop by the clinic today, so I'll ask about her character in the game. Don't worry, Tim, I'll try to be as delicate as I can. I already know from your stories how weird Kira gets when it comes up. By the way... look at the forums. You're gonna like what you see!"

~ Finding a Body ~

Valerianna Quickfoot showed me an open tab she had been looking at: "News of the hour! The five strongest players of the *Legion of Steel* were given a 24-hour suspension and lost ten percent of their experience after an encounter with the goddess of death. Till Quick_Fingers [LEGION] lost two levels and is no longer the highest-level player on the Southern Continent! *Boundless Realm* tech support are just throwing up their hands and saying game mechanics were never violated."

Hrm... Hel must have given those uninvited guests a real harsh snub. They'd remember that encounter with the goddess of death for a long time to come. I hoped the other undying were discouraged by that example and didn't stick their noses any higher up the Styx than the rapids. Although... I walked over to the crystal Eye and demanded to see the Upper Fort on the black river, the last player-made fortification before the dangerous rapids and the lands of the cyclopes. The crystal ball showed a small wooden fortress, which was brimming with life. The colorful banners and pendants of the many undying clans in the fortress waved in the wind gleefully on the tops of the towers. Fires burned in the courtyard. I could hear the clanging of hammers, while all kinds of mounts shifted from one leg to the other. The undying were making food, repairing their weapons, showing off their pets and ammunition, laughing and making plans for their campaign against the Dark Sovereign. By my estimation, there were around seven hundred players in that fortress, and new ones were arriving every minute. Portals were constantly opening, and reinforcements just kept pouring out. Near the shore there was also a fully-fledged navy. I counted over sixty small sailboats and oar-ships. My attention was also drawn by two huge barges moored to the docks which were carrying huge disassembled siege towers and heavy catapults. The enemy was approaching the war with the Dark Sovereign with all due seriousness and was preparing to storm my defenses and fortifications.

Ugh, I wished I could attack that camp, break all those squadrons apart and burn that fleet... I took a heavy sigh because I understood how dangerous that would be, and most importantly how pointless. As soon as my monsters reached the edge of the player's range of view, alarm bells would peal throughout *Boundless Realm*. And soon, instead of seven hundred undying, there would be ten, or maybe even fifty thousand warriors. I would lose my whole army, while the enemies we killed would respawn in one hour at the respawn stone in the very same Upper Fort to continue their campaign as if nothing had happened.

"Upper Fort is two hundred sixty miles away as the crow flies. But considering all the bends in the river and hiking on mountain paths, the enemies will have to travel around four hundred and fifty miles," Valerianna commented, looking from the map back to our enemies with rapt attention.

"One day to the rapids of the Styx. Half a day to portage the whole fleet. Then a day and a half to the mountain ridge and just as long up the mountain paths. If we don't stop them, that whole army will be here under the walls of my castle in four or five days."

"That's right, Tim. But they aren't going to have to portage their ships. One of the divisions will just walk past the rapids and open a portal for the rest to come through. And they'll do the same in every difficult section. Fast-moving scout groups can slip ahead, then the heavily armed divisions can follow after them through portals. And every day there will be more and more enemies, because more and more divisions are coming. And the dangerous bots along the river won't be able to stop them. There are just too many undying."

As if in response to the sorceress's words, an alarm bell rolled through the castle halls. Simultaneously some wisps of black mist appeared in the throne room and a semitransparent rider on a black steed emerged:

Gloom
Emissary of the Dark Sovereign
Level-250 Ghostly Rider

Gloom? Not Night, who was keeping watch over the dangerous western approach? Gloom, I seemed to remember, was responsible for my eastern borders.

"Sovereign, invasion! A squadron of undying has been spotted at the eastern frontier of your holdings! They crossed the Border Hills and are already on the distant shore of Frigid Lake! If they make it across that lake, they'll be just half a day's travel from the castle!"

To my considerable shame, I was hearing about the Border Hills and Frigid Lake for the first time. But my subjects were under the impression that these were territories belonging to the Dark Sovereign. Unfortunately, I didn't have a map to familiarize myself with the situation on the border through the Sovereign's Eye. Yes, I could go with Gloom, asking the sorceress to make the ghostly mount temporarily solid, but I didn't know the weather there, so I risked being burned up by the sun. And that could be fatal to a vampire like me. I had to fall back on my sister's help again:

~ Finding a Body ~

"Valerianna, go off with Gloom. I need you to bring me a map of the distant shore of Frigid Lake, then get a portal scroll to send our armies there and destroy the undying invasion. Try not to let the enemies see you either, so you don't put them on guard. Take a look from afar and go right back."

I didn't manage to finish that sentence before I heard another alarm bell, and another tall dark rider stood next to Gloom:

Murk
Emissary of the Dark Sovereign
Level 250 Ghostly Rider

Murk answered for the northern borders. And seemingly, there were now problems in his zone of responsibility as well.

"Sovereign, invasion! A squadron of undying is coming over the snowy northern spur of the Border Hills and is nearing the Icy Mountains! They're well prepared for wintry conditions, dressed warmly and carrying mountaineering equipment. The snow giants and mountain trolls couldn't stop them and retreated, losing half their numbers. If the undying cross the mountains, they'll reach the Ruins of Acheron and that will put them just half a day from the castle!"

Seemingly, the situation was getting out of control and enemies were sneaking into my territory from all directions, not only up the black river of death. I decided against asking about the Ruins of Acheron, which were just half a day's walk from my castle, but I mentally made a note to return to the intriguing topic at a better time. Then I turned to Valerianna Quickfoot:

"I desperately need a big clear map that I can hang on the wall or spread out on a table and which will show enemy and allied armies in real time. The Sovereign's Eye is not ideally suited to that, and holding this all in my head will just get harder and harder every day. After all, there are probably magical maps that can do that, whether in the corporation's online store, or created by craftsmen. I can't be the only player who might need this! Val, look for a map that fits my description. I don't know how much it might cost, but without it we're just gonna drown in a flood of information!"

The fearsome sorceress gave a dignified bow, showing that she had taken the information into account and would try to help me solve the issue. Then she went to Gloom, preparing to go off with the ghostly rider to my eastern borderlands.

"Yes, Valerianna, your task is the incursion in the east, go there. And don't you worry about those mountain climbers to the north. I'll handle them myself after the sun is down. And I hope the northern mountainous border can be closed off once and for all after I'm done with them. Soon our purchases will be coming in, and among them there are one thousand Drow scouts and archers at level one hundred. I'll put those dark elves into mixed border divisions of rougarou, orcs, trolls and undead, which I will use to cover all mountain passes fit for crossing. And after that, as soon as the dam is finished, I'll send cyclopes and giants under the leadership of the Ogre Fortifier to vulnerable passes. For a few days the enemies will meet stone guard towers wherever they go with lots of loopholes for archers and ballistae, and impregnable walls. And on the mountain ridges I'll build a chain of frontier posts and defense brigades. Just try crawling up a sheer cliff while archers rain down arrows and huge giants chuck boulders!"

Valerianna nodded and, chanting a materialization spell, went off with the Ghostly Rider Gloom. I then let Murk go and sat up wearily on my huge deadly throne.

What a crazy day this was turning out to be! And this evening promised to be even more frenzied. Before nightfall, I would be getting the huge amount of stuff we ordered today. And among that was armor and weapons, alchemy ingredients and valuable plants, building materials and tools, furniture and decor, vials of blood and living creatures, coal for the smithies and wood to heat the castle on cold nights, along with lots and lots of other stuff. All that would have to be sorted and distributed, unpacked and issued to those in need, some of it locked up tight for the future and other stuff given to craftsmen or merchants. Without my Storekeeper, Keymaster, and Steward I would simply be drowning head first in the mountain of stuff. But even with my helpers, there was a titanic amount of work ahead of me.

Also there was the NPC smiths and armorers, potters and woodworkers, coopers and leatherworkers... They all needed a place to stay in the castle or nearby, along with work, tools and materials. Plus the castle defenders. I would have to greet my elite goblin and orcish guard, explain the rules in the Dark Sovereign's castle and delineate responsibilities, then provide necessary items and assign them to shifts. And there were also bodyguard teams for me and Valerianna Quickfoot, each of which contained fifty taciturn and watchful NPC's.

I had chosen myself a reliable guard of fearsome armor-bound orcs. Valerianna however was much more discerning and picked guards of the most inconceivable races: watchful elves, werebeasts with lightning-fast reflexes, and flittering winged pixies with their heightened instinct for magic. And my little sister's guard team had more than just weapon-laden bruisers.

~ Finding a Body ~

She had healers, priests for blessing and removing curses, and poison and antivenom specialists. And all that future local color had to be received and given a place to sleep tonight in the castle. We were also expecting a thousand Drow elves, who would also need to be greeted, given housing and put to work...

And as if all that wasn't enough, we were going to have the rougarou scouts returning tonight with maps of the lands surrounding my castle. After that, Shaman Uvari-Dor-Shu was supposed to announce the new lands of the Clan of the White Lily. I as lord of these lands was supposed to officially allow them to settle there, and ideally be there for the festivities. Also the hunters led by Princess Chai-nee Shu were supposed to deliver their haul by evening, and I should ideally be there for that to make sure another scrap didn't break out.

Overall, I was expecting quite an entertaining evening, and I couldn't even imagine how I'd survive it. But later it would only be getting more complicated. After all, that was when I was intending to fight back all the players coming to attack my territory!

Day Three
A Rout in the Night

I LEFT THE GAME sometime before twelve thirty AM. I couldn't come any earlier because I had a huge amount of affairs in the castle that just had to be attended to. While I sorted through all the new purchases, I spoke with my subjects who wanted a reception with the Dark Sovereign, then the newcomers got sorted out. I extinguished the conflicts between my various regiments of cutthroats and... I was immeasurably tired and practically falling off my feet in exhaustion. Not long before exiting, at exactly midnight, I watched four skills tick up by one as promised by my blessing:

Warchief skill increased to level 26!

~ Finding a Body ~

Diplomat skill increased to level 30!

Foreman skill increased to level 79!

Animal Control skill increased to level 66!

What could I say? My plea to the gods had worked and, with every day, not only my skills were going to grow, but also my fame and attractiveness to all kinds of NPC. Given that there was no time limit to the blessing, my hardest task would be somehow holding out for the first and most gruesome days before new recruits and settlers started arriving in sufficient number.

Also, at every convenient chance I drank blood, leveling Taste Tester. I had only drunk from alchemy vials so far. We'd bought lots of them for delivery by magical messenger. It hadn't even come to the living creatures in cages and enclosures yet. Sure, this way I was not improving my Taste for Blood, which increased my damage in melee combat. But I figured the animals could wait, while the packaged blood might go bad. And there were just too many prying eyes around. For me, killing a victim with Vampire Bite and sucking out its blood was something of a secret, almost intimate process, not something to do around strangers. It may sound dumb, I won't argue. But

I was still ashamed to do it in front of my NPC servants.

My Goblin Herbalist's Taste Tester stat would gain an interesting perk at level two hundred, too. From then on, sunlight wouldn't hurt him for the first three seconds. In other words, if the odd beam of sun touched my Amra, I had three seconds to find shelter before it started to eat away my vampiric flesh. It wasn't much, of course, but those three seconds could be the difference between life and death.

I also decided to take advantage of the character modifications Amra earned at level seventy and eighty. I thought over possible options for a long time. I wanted to increase my hitpoints for better survival and resistance to physical damage. But the idea of raising poison resistance from its present 80% to an even greater 83% was also quite intriguing. But in the end I decided not to stay on my chosen path and bring down my character's visibility. The Dark Sovereign was the most obvious priority target for enemy archers and all other ranged characters, so I wanted to make sure they couldn't see me from afar. Another minus 6% or 7% to visibility distance would mean that, combined with my Stealth skill, which reduced discovery radius by 20%, I would now have a very respectable minus 48%.

Another important task I was thinking about

all evening was selecting a strike brigade of three hundred warriors for the upcoming attack. Why exactly three hundred soldiers, and not more? Well, the portal only stayed open for a minute, and we calculated in a training session that 300 was the maximum number of NPC's that could get through an open portal before it slammed shut. Five soldiers per second, more simply wouldn't fit. That brought us to a total of three hundred.

And among that elite strike force I had fifty battle-tested orc pirates under the command of First Mate Ziabash Hardy who had already followed me through fire and water. I also took fifty elite rougarou warriors from the various clans, and placed the druid Uvari-Dor-Shu at their head. I also had one hundred Drow elf archers, all of them alike as peas in a pod and flawlessly obedient. As the elves didn't have their own leader, I had Vaash the troll lead them. He was an experienced and reliable commander who enjoyed great respect as a hand-to-hand combat trainer.

The last hundred were a bunch of high level minotaurs, giants, trolls, skeletons and ghosts, and I appointed my good friend Shrekson Bastard to lead them. The Ogre Fortifier had just finished building the mountain dam and came into the castle for new orders. After finding out about the night's attack, Leon was very inspired and started asking to be taken with even just as a simple hand-to-hand fighter. I could understand Leon, too. Two days of uninterrupted boulder dragging and rock hauling... maybe all that was good for the Fortifier's skills, but he must have been tired of such monotonous gameplay both physically, and above all emotionally.

So I didn't take him as a common soldier, because I was looking for a living leader for the difficult mixed squadron of NPC monsters. Actually, before Leon came into the castle, I was considering my sister to control the third hundred, but I ended up deciding not to bother Valeria again. Let her have a relaxing evening with her new friend, not worrying about the upcoming battle. Also, Valerianna already had plenty of other important missions.

After hearing he'd been appointed commander of the third hundred of monsters, Leon spent a long time thanking me for my trust. Then he called his family and told them he was staying to work the night shift. So the enemies tracking our online activity (and many participants of the Dark Sovereign event likely had me and my friends in their tracking list and were watching our every coming and going) wouldn't suspect anything, Leon and I agreed to leave the game. Then we would come in together just before the attack at three o'clock in the morning.

To help the Ogre Fortifier, I initially wanted

to reinforce his squadron with a couple powerful cyclopes. But the one-eyed giants were going to spend the whole night conducting a funeral ceremony for their deceased compatriot, and I didn't have the gall to violate their norms. My relationship with the cyclopes was already strained, so I risked inciting a riot in their ranks. It wasn't all so smooth with the minotaurs either. But after the public execution of the most impetuous and unmanageable horned titans, the others were at least keeping their dismay hidden better than the cyclopes, who openly trumpeted their frustrations.

However I found another way to reinforce, adding ten ghosts to my night squad. These NPC fighters already weren't the fastest or easiest to manage, and their undead nature also warranted consideration. For example, they would be unable to restore health with elixirs or healing magic, and were extremely vulnerable to enemy necromancers and holy magic. But at that, ghosts were nearly invisible at night, could fly, were not solid and could pass right through any fortification. If used correctly, all that overcame every downside.

Among the ghosts, I intentionally chose a level-125 Grave Curse with an extremely striking ability to suck away stat points, experience and even whole levels. For living players that must have been the worst enemy imaginable, above all psychologically. After all, no one would like to see their dear character's stat points go down! And adding to the rather nasty properties of this undead creature, it ignored armor and was totally immune to physical damage, poison, acid and elemental magic, which made the Grave Curse a simply ideal weapon against unwieldy armor-bound knights and their front-line shield-bearers. And using it against enemy pets and mounts would be especially effective. As a rule, their only big advantage was high hitpoints and thick hides. They could only attack with teeth and claws, and in rare cases poison. And although my huge army had a huge number and variety of ghosts and spirits with all kinds of abilities and properties, there was only one Grave Curse with this very specific combination, so I decided to make a concerted effort to level it up. I gave Leon a clear order to protect that undead warrior, not risk him without good reason and be sure to keep him alive until the end of the battle.

So then, a brief moment of respite. I had just two and a half hours to eat a quick meal and sleep just a bit before my next entry into the game. I crawled out of the virtual reality capsule and, not even getting dressed, walked on shaky legs into the neighboring room. I was lured in by the intoxicating aroma of food. And there was indeed a beautifully set table with a bucket of half-melted ice containing a dewy bottle of champagne along with some dishes full of food. And under the candelabra, which was laden with still unlit candles, there was a note from Tina:

"Timothy, I waited until midnight, but you never showed. It isn't very nice to break a promise to spend a romantic evening with a person. And meanwhile, I have some important information for your ears only. Same place tomorrow at 8:30 PM. Don't be late!

P.S. The surveillance cameras in your room have been turned off by order of President Thomas Heywood.

Tina"

What??? When had I promised Tina a romantic evening? That just didn't happen! I remembered my answer clearly. I merely said I didn't object to her sometimes coming to visit me in my room after the work day ended. Could someone seriously take such neutral words as a specific invitation? Also there was some kind of "important information for my ears only...?" What, I wanted to know, had the director's assistant come up with now? And finally, the "video surveillance was off." Nice of course, but why draw my attention to that?

Well, I would have to think it all over, but I was too tired after this endless day. I wasn't going to fill my head with such difficult questions now.

After a quick dinner, I fell back on the sofa and instantly went out like a light.

I FELT LIKE my head had barely touched the pillow when my alarm clock started clanging, telling me it was time to get up. Yes, it was five minutes to three AM. Time to go into battle and repel the enemy warriors attacking my territory from all directions. Doing that during the day was impossible for many reasons, above all because there were too many enemies online and the rays of the sun might kill me.

So then, loading...

Successful check for Cold Resistance!

I gave a fitful shiver. What a deep freeze came over my lands at night! Flocks of snow were careening down from the dark and cloudy sky. At least it wasn't that piercing wind that raged last night. I appeared on the square before the palace, where three hundred NPC soldiers were already finishing lining up into even rows. The commanders gave the last orders, the general mood was best described as martial.

"Captain Amra, your orcs have grown bored

and yearn for battle!" announced First Mate Ziabash Hardy, walking up to me.

The huge scarred orc had refused all the new weapons and armor, still preferring the curved pirate saber and thick leather vest. Today he had reached level 120 and looked very fearsome. Not lagging a level behind though was the equally tremendous ten-foot-high mountain troll Vaash, whose disproportionately long and unbelievably powerful arms could snap my enemies in two. And Leon walked up too, yawning:

"Everything is ready, Amra. My hundred is all here. Where are we headed?"

I had not in fact shared my plans with anyone until the very last minute, even my friends. I had limited myself to general information like saying we would attack at night. It wasn't that I didn't trust my friends, it was just that we were probably being watched by many Boundless Realm Corporation employees, and I could no longer guarantee that they were neutral parties.

Nevertheless, before revealing my plans, I asked Leon to apologize to Tina for me in the morning. I just felt awkward knowing that she waited for me all evening while I was just in the next room.

Poor signal quality
If connection problems persist, the Boundless

Realm *client will be forced to close*

Clearly the employees watching over me were showing that I shouldn't talk about that. What was wrong now? Could I really not talk with my friend about our common acquaintance? Nevertheless, I wasn't going to risk getting banned before this important night battle and changed the topic, answering Leon's question:

"First we're going to the northern front. A group of undying there has crossed the Border Hills and stopped near the Icy Mountains. Now it is night, so most players should have exited the game. If we show up suddenly and attack all at once, we should handle the remaining enemies without issue."

I summoned the Gray Pack and chose my favorite mount, the ice-white level-102 Mythical Hound Fimbulthul. The pooch with matted fur nearly knocked me over in joy, then gave my cheek a grateful lick with his scratchy tongue and lied down on the ground to make it easier for his short master to climb up. Once atop Fimbulthul, I noticed that my Goblin niece Yunna, after her self-sacrifice on the altar was still the lowest level of my companions, yet had already hit 60. Yunna had been leveled up via a special regimen cooked up by Valerianna Quickfoot. It was only what she needed to be a Wolf Rider, and made with speed in mind. Now the goblin girl, wrapped up in a warm fur jacket and holding a short spear in her hands was atop Gjöll. The black female Mythical Hound was up to level 30 already, and today was her combat baptism.

Yunna's brother Irek was left with Lobo, the level-98 Hardened Forest Wolf as a mount. And based on the green-skinned big-eared youth's sour face, he was none too happy about it. And it was no surprise. His sister's Gjöll was a unique creatures, only one of which existed in all *Boundless Realm*. But he just got a common gray wolf regardless of its high level. You might wonder what difference it really made. But for Irek, it was important to always be at least on equal footing with his sister. The Goblin boy had asked me a few times to get him "something just a bit cooler" as a mount. However Baron, my rare Alpha Swamp Wolf at level 120 wouldn't allow the teen to ride him. And Modgud's old Guard Dog at level 212 was for some reason not rideable and refused to carry anyone including me. And it should be noted that the Guard Dog still didn't have a nickname. Although Valerianna and I had suggested a few different names for the fearsome hound, none of them ever stuck.

Alright, the soldiers were in formation, and we could begin.

"Murk!" I called over my emissary. "We're

ready. Go directly to the camp of the undying and immediately open a portal!"

The Dark Rider gave me a salute with his spear and disappeared into the wisps of black fog. No more than a minute passed, and just ten steps away I saw the huge flaming orange ring of a portal.

"Forward, my glorious warriors! Tear them all to bits! Take no prisoners!!!" I shouted with all my might. And to build on that, I cracked the whip I got from the goddess Hel.

Exotic Weapons skill increased to level 29!

Warchief skill increased to level 27!

My army flooded past me through the fiery oval like a raging storm surge. At a certain point, I thought I saw Chai-nee Shu's familiar face. But come on, how would the Princess have gotten here? I had definitely not allowed my ward to join us. Nevertheless, I was not able to calm the sudden anxiety, especially when See-Uhn-Rhu also dashed past. The young chieftain of the Clan of the Laughing Otter hadn't been invited to this battle either. What the heck was going on here?

I was one of the last to gallop through the portal on my Mythical Hound, making sure first that my warriors had all managed to get through and, just three seconds later, the flaming ring behind me slammed shut. Great! So, what did we have here?

A snowy night forest. Frost. Snow trampled by many feet and thoroughly soaked in blood. Next to the big firepit were the bodies of ten players and a few dozen of their dead pets.

There were no losses on our side. The fast-paced battle was over before I'd even showed up. The ten players warming themselves at the fire at such a late hour were caught off guard and swept away by the unexpected flood of NPC's. Based on Murk's recon, there were no less than two hundred undying in this squadron initially but, as I'd assumed, they'd mostly exited the game when night fell.

"Warriors! Carve stakes and place them point-up densely in those tents," I said, motioning at the large travelling tents with clan emblems. "Most likely, due to the deep freeze out here, the undying exited in those tents, so they will be coming back into the game in the same place. And when they return, these stakes will skewer them!!!"

In reply, I got an elated roar from many throats. The orcs, minotaurs and rougarou took out their axes, halberds and broadswords and started felling young trees.

Foreman skill increased to level 80!

Alright, great. Now I wanted to find a way to stop them from respawning. I looked around for the Ogre Fortifier, because my next job was for him:

"Shrekson, take a portal scroll and pop back over to the castle. The Storekeeper will issue you a Tectonic Bomb, then we'll open a portal back for you. We're going to use that bomb to blow up the respawn stone," I said pointing at the distant boulder, which vibrated with overflowing energy. "Let the players talk to tech support and respawn wherever they like, as long as it's not in my lands!"

"But can a respawn point even be destroyed?" The Ogre Fortifier asked in surprise.

"I have no idea. But I cannot see an indestructible tag on the stone, which means the plan might work. If the stone doesn't blow, I'll write tech support and demand an explanation."

Leon gave a slight bow and disappeared in the flames of the now open interspace passage. I then carefully looked around and drove my shaggy mount forward, spurring Fimbulthul on with my heels. As I rode, I gracefully caught Chai-nee Shu by the ear with two fingers. She was trying to hide from me in the night forest! Not particularly minding her cries of pain, I lifted her by the ear and set her in front of me:

~ Finding a Body ~

"And who's this I see? Tell me, what are you doing here?"

The rougarou princess's silly furry little snout looked bashful, but not the least bit afraid:

"Sovereign, I discovered from Regent Uvari-Dor-Shu that this attack was being planned and I convinced him to take me with. After all, as a Princess and future rougarou leader, I must build up authority and earn glory in combat! I can't just be hunting all the time!"

"Not the wisest move for a future ruler though," I said, shaking my big-eared head in reproach. "It could have been very dangerous here, especially for you. You're unique as the adopted daughter of the Dark Sovereign, so the undying will stop at nothing to take you down. To them you're nothing but a valuable trophy. And indeed, Chai-nee, where are your bodyguards? I mean, I assigned you thirty elite warriors! Why are they not with you?"

The girl lowered her snout and gave a lighthearted giggle:

"They all think I'm sleeping soundly. They're guarding the doors of my bedroom. But I called the Steward and ordered him to bring me to the castle exit. Then I ordered Uvari-Dor-Shu to add me to the squadron in another rougarou's place. He didn't dare refuse. I am your daughter after all!"

What? This was a serious glitch in my

security. The Dark Sovereign's right to order NPC servants was transmitted to any relative without my approval? My sister Valerianna Quickfoot was one thing. I wanted her to be able to give orders to the Dark Sovereign's subjects, and she used that actively. But it was another thing entirely for my underage adopted daughter to do so. Seemingly, the NPC Princess Chai-nee Shu could even send the Dark Sovereign's whole warband out on a campaign and, at her own discretion, order gold from the chests in my storage, or execute whoever she liked. By the way... the Goblin beauty Taisha also probably held a certain sway in the eyes of these NPC, given she was officially known as the wife of the Dark Sovereign. Knowing Taisha's flighty and antsy character, just imagine what a mess she could make of things by using this privilege willy-nilly. I needed to figure that issue out with tech support to get a few restrictions put in place.

But that would come later, when we were back in the castle. Now I was interested in a different issue:

"I can understand that. But what is the young chieftain of the Clan of the Laughing Otter doing here? Did he also convince the rougarou commander to let him replace another soldier?"

Chai-nee Shu went a deep red, embarrassed and said barely audibly:

~ Finding a Body ~

"No, the regent didn't want to take See-Uhn-Rhu, no matter how he asked. But I insisted, ordering it in your name. See-Uhn-Rhu is a fun companion and wanted a way to earn glory, so I decided to help him. I mean, you aren't mad, right?"

WE WEREN'T ABLE to blow up the respawn stone, but it did go off with quite the bang. The forest was lain low in a one-hundred-fifty-foot radius, and many boulders nearby were shattered. But the vibrating stone didn't even get a fleck of soot or a single scratch on it! Leon and I had to cover the respawn stone with heaps of lumber and make a huge campfire, just like we'd done earlier in the Lower Fort on the river Styx. The NPC soldiers of my army couldn't go near the respawn stone, so they cut the fallen trees into firewood and dragged them nearby. We only finished at four thirty AM, when a huge fire pit was blazed in the icy cold forest. Flames lapped at the highest branches of even the most ancient trees.

"It will definitely burn a few days, then the red-hot coals will stop players from being on the respawn point for a while!" the Ogre Fortifier promised, and I figured that was plenty.

Other than that, we could of course keep the fire going by periodically coming back to toss some wood on it. So then, I considered the threat from the north neutralized, at least for now. All that remained was the west and the east. To begin, I decided the west was the most dangerous:

"Night, I need you!"

The Dark Rider appeared practically instantly from some wisps of black mist, confirming that the emissaries of the Dark Sovereign could accept orders from their master at any distance.

"Night, go to the undying camp by the Upper Fort and open a portal for my army right inside the fortress!"

The Dark Rider gave a dignified bow and dissolved back into wisps of a black dust-devil together with her gigantic mount. I waited a minute, then another... but nothing happened.

"Sovereign, my sister has died at the hands of the undying and shall respawn in your castle in one hour," Murk told me after riding up closer.

Well, crap... It was simultaneously worrying and shocking. My enemies managed to kill the level-287 NPC rider with such ease! That spoke to the defenders of the Upper Fort having very high-level players, and that was at the very least. They were also seemingly in a combat-ready state, which meant my army couldn't pull off a surprise attack now.

Nevertheless, I wasn't going to leave the killing of my emissary unanswered.

"Murk, your sister must be avenged! Go and appear near the fort, but at a safe distance. And shoot your Cursed Arrow at any of the weaker undying! No, not even that. Choose any large and maneuverable pet as a target! And leave immediately. Let the liberated Midnight Wraith take its bounty of blood alone. Then I will go with my army to the eastern front near Frigid Lake!"

Warchief skill increased to level 28!

Foreman skill increased to level 81!

"Yes, my lord!" It was obvious that Murk was enormously happy to receive this mission.

Of course, it was a shame to waste a rare Cursed Arrow, but I thought this was the right time to use it. After all, the Midnight Wraith was especially effective against high level players. It's ability to always be twice the level of the strongest player in a group was almost too much. If there was even one soldier at level two hundred fifty or even three hundred defending the fort... then all the players in the fort would certainly be meeting their maker! At level five hundred or even worse six, the NPC monster could simply not be destroyed. Or more accurately it would remain a theoretical possibility, but doing so would require hundreds of players working together, and the slightest error or disorganization would kill them all.

"Darkness, I need you! Go to the undying camp on the eastern shore of Frigid Lake and open a portal. Do it as close to the tents and buildings as you can!"

The Dark Rider saluted with her big curved saber, which left a green trail glowing in the air then she disappeared, and I was left to wait anxiously again. Would my emissary make it to the players? Or would Darkness share her sister's fate? No more than three minutes later, a bunch of system logs ran past my eyes:

Achievement unlocked: Player killer (13)

Achievement unlocked: Player killer (14)
...
Level eighty-seven!

Achievement unlocked: Player killer (27)
...

I pulled it off! Apparently, Murk had carried out my order and used the Cursed Arrow to devastating effect. The Midnight Wraith was freed and started beating down everyone who tried to resist. But what about Darkness? I figured she must not have made it, but suddenly a portal opened.

"Charge! Attack!!!"

This time the three hundred NPC soldiers passed through the portal noticeably quicker, in just forty seconds. I was the last to jump through the ring of flame and immediately came face to face with a level-132 enemy Paladin wielding a flaming two-handed sword and taking on two of my minotaurs at once. The three huge identical sharp-toothed lizards that went to grapple with the rougarou were clearly the Paladin's pets. Fimbulthul jumped right into the heavily armored enemy and knocked him over.

I very skillfully added a lash to the falling and unbalanced enemy. The enchanted whip wrapped around the Paladin's neck and by some miracle entered the small gap between his helmet and solid armor suit. My speed separated the enemy's head from his body and, leaving a spatter of blood in the air, it flew upward into the night sky.

Critical damage dealt: 10100 (2*8417 Hair Whip strike — armor ignored, 40% defense against physical damage)

Experience received: 325000 Exp.

Achievement unlocked: Player killer (31)

Level eighty-eight!

Exotic Weapons skill increased to level 30!

Riding skill increased to level 34!

All three fanged lizards stopped motionless with the death of their master then got chopped into coleslaw in a matter of seconds by my rougarou. Great! But... one glance at the mini-map made me go cold in the chest. The three hundred blue markers of my NPC army on the map were mixed in with at least the same number of enemy red dots, and more enemies were coming every minute! I couldn't see any portals opening, the undying were simply entering the game and appearing basically all around us. There were hundreds of them, if not thousands! A trap!!!

This was a classic login trap. Most players had exited the game to make their army seem weak but, always staying in communication with the remaining players, were ready to go back at any second. Valerianna and I had done this several times before in *Kingdoms of Sword and Magic*, but here I myself had been caught by this age-old trick. We had to leave now before it was too late! I quickly opened my inventory in search of a portal scroll back to the castle...

> ***ATTENTION!***
>
> ***The forbidden spell Astral Explosion has just been cast in the lands of the Dark Sovereign!***
>
> ***For the next 12 hours, portals, summoning magic and teleportation scrolls will be impossible to use in all areas near Frigid Lake***

A huge dome seething with all the colors of the rainbow folded down over the battlefield. Astral Explosion, a forbidden spell! If this had happened in a city, the mage who cast Astral Explosion would already be getting dragged to prison by NPC guards. However here on a desolate and unpopulated plain, there was no one to punish the malefactor. It was all turning out so bad... I stashed the portal scroll back in my inventory — unfortunately it was too late. Now I couldn't run away and all that remained was to fight. Fight and die, because it was not theoretically possible to win with this balance of forces.

"Stay in formation! Shields in a line! Spears out front! Archers focus on the mages!" I could hear the booming voices of Shrekson and Vaash the troll. Even in this critical situation, my commanders were on their game.

...

Achievement unlocked: Player killer (52)

Level eighty-nine!
...
Achievement unlocked: Player killer (67)

But then I didn't understand. Either that experience was coming from the Midnight Wraith, or my Gray Pack was on the hunt. Most likely, it was both.

I turned attention to the flickering local chat window and unwittingly read a few messages. The players were in a state of unbridled joy. And not just that. They had managed to take a fairly large squadron of mine captive with its commander! The players could already taste the glory and generous reward for capturing the superboss, so they were joking around and chatting it up. The main idea that always jumped out in these messages was: "Now the main thing is not to kill the Dark Sovereign, otherwise he'll just respawn in his castle and it will all have been in vain. We need to take our prize alive! No one shoot the Dark Sovereign and don't sic your pets on him!"

Oh no... They were planning to take me prisoner. And I had just been surprised no one was attacking me. That was very bad. What could I do? How to break out of the trap? Should I even try to break out? I stood up on Fimbulthul and took a look around as much as my short height allowed. No, it was pointless. My army was surrounded by a solid ring of enemies. Their shields were locked and their innumerable rows of spears surrounded us on all sides. What was more, I could sense that the enemy was well coordinated and had capable command. The undying were skillfully redistributing reserves to dangerous parts and quickly reinforcing the defenses there. No, we weren't going to be allowed to break out and leave.

Achievement unlocked: Player killer (68)

Animal Control skill increased to level 67!

Warchief skill increased to level 29!
...
Achievement unlocked: Player killer (82)

Level ninety!
Attention! You have reached level 90. You may now improve your character's survival by choosing a modification
...
Achievement unlocked: Player killer (99)

Experience was gushing in like a river. Seemingly the Midnight Wraith was still on the rampage at the Upper Fort, and his take was now nearing genocidal proportions. Also all the members of the Gray Pack were still alive and growing in level right before my eyes. The orcs, rougarou and minotaur were dying, but their lives were coming at a very high cost. And despite all that, I didn't even think about running. I had to be with my army! I had to keep fighting and just kill myself at the last possible second.

I wished I could think up a way to do that, though. In times like these, I regretted getting such thick armor and six and a half thousand hitpoints. It wouldn't be easy to take me that down quickly. And my hitpoints needed to come down very fast, because I suspected the enemy healers had begun to heal me so they could take me no matter what. Ugh, we shouldn't have wasted that Tectonic Bomb. It might have been powerful enough... But there was no use crying over spilled milk. We needed to think of other options.

Maybe I should summon one of the Dark Riders and use a Cursed Arrow. The Midnight Wraith, even if it couldn't handle the whole thousands-strong enemy army, was more than capable of sending me to respawn. Where was my Darkness? I stood up on Fimbulthul again, trying to see the Dark Rider through the smoke and snow floating in the air. There she was! Or to be more accurate what remained of her: her huge black steed was fallen and her semitransparent body clutched a glowing green saber.

Achievement unlocked: Player killer (112)

Level ninety-one!

Warchief skill increased to level 30!

I tried summoning Gloom, but a message immediately jumped in that I couldn't use summoning magic because of the Astral Explosion. Damn! And I couldn't summon the goddess of strife Eris for the same reason, even though she would have had a grand old time here.

Then my eye caught on the terrified Princess Chai-nee Shu, hiding behind the broad back of Regent Uvari-Dor-Shu, who had become a bear and was fighting off three players at once. I was being so selfish! I was only thinking about myself even though I was relatively safe behind the rows of warriors. But meanwhile my troops needed their commander! To me, being captured meant nothing more than having to admit defeat. Death was actually what I wanted. But as for my NPC companions...

"Chai-nee Shu, my daughter, come to me!"

The terrified rougarou Princess, despite the clamor of battle heard me and quickly ran over. I opened the Gray Pack control interface and added the level-101 Rougarou Huntress. After all, that not only made every member of the Gray Pack stronger, it also made her respawn after death.

At the very last moment, I caught a glance from Uvari-Dor-Shu that was full of pleading. He was falling from innumerable bloody wounds, so I included the level-131 Rougarou Druid in the Gray Pack as well. And it was just in time! The bonuses from Fenrir's Cursed Regalia like +150 Constitution, +150 Strength, +150 to Agility for every member of the Gray Pack instantly kicked in. The badly wounded Druid stood up and splayed his shoulders. The rougarou's health bar, which had been practically at zero, was now back up to one third. What was more, the bonuses from my Animal Control skill kicked in, improving his attack and defense along with an additional twenty percent attack bonus from the first specialization. I also gave Uvari-Dor-Shu the Pack Hunter perk to improve all his combat characteristics, Bloodthirsty to heal wounds when he hit and Thick Skin for better armor.

The huge bear gave a deafening bellow and threw himself on his three enemies, now confident he could take them down. A few swipes of his powerful clawed paws and all three players were dead, while my fighter was practically back to full health. Great!

Animal Control skill increased to level 68!

Achievement unlocked: Player killer (124)

So, now I wanted to know about my daughter's fiancé. Where was he, and was he even alive? I stood up on Fimbulthul's back and looked around. Over there! See-Uhn-Rhu was alive and fighting, throwing darts at an overgrown bull that had charged through the first row of my shield orcs and was now hanging off the second row's spears. Great! See-Uhn-Rhu was also added to the Gray Pack as were four other randomly-chosen rougarou, and I set perks for them all.

Here I noticed a large group of enemy archers in the distance exchanging volleys with my Drow elves, and chucked three Ice Grenades into the very thick of the enemy bowmen. Some lines ran by telling me the damage I'd dealt and the experience gained, but I didn't much care about that.

I was fighting to regain control of my army, but my right and left flanks were faltering and retreating in total disarray.

Orcs and rougarou, minotaurs and giants were all running in a panic. Some even threw down their weapons. Only the dark elves were still holding out, but many archers had already been forced to stash their bows and trade melee blows with the enemy's armored warriors.

"Hold formation! Shields in a line! Form a ring! Bowmen in the center!"

Warchief skill increased to level 31!

Warchief skill increased to level 32!

I set an example for the soldiers and stood on the front line. I twisted the neck of a level-78 Dwarf Berserker attacking an orc pirate next to me and vampire-bit an albino tiger attacking my Fimbulthul, killing the enemy pet in one Vampire Bite.

Achievement unlocked: Player killer (141)

Level ninety-two!
Racial ability improved: Taste for Blood (Gives +1% to all damage dealt for each unique creature killed with Vampire Bite. Current bonus: +45%)

~ Finding a Body ~

I managed to more or less beat back the panic. Many NPC's obeyed my commands and stood in a circle. But still my army was dying. The number of green markers on the map was falling before my very eyes. Just ten steps from me, Shrekson Bastard had fallen, stuck full of arrows like a pincushion.

After the commander died, his hundred went entirely out of control and began to panic, abandoning formation and just cravenly fleeing in a vain attempt to save themselves.

There was no more reason to expect intelligent or organized actions out of these cowards. I just gave a separate command to the now level-145 Grave Curse to climb up high into the dark clouds so my valuable ghost would not be visible to enemy archers and mages. Then a half a minute later, I ordered him to fly back to my castle. I did not know whether the Grave Curse could break through the dome, but I at least tried to save its life.

Achievement unlocked: Player killer (142)

Seemingly the Midnight Wraith was stopped eventually, because the player killer messages had practically stopped. Or maybe the surviving players had simply fled from the indefatigable ghastly beast? But just then the situation at Frigid

Lake became totally dire. There was barely a third of my army left and the enemy healers had already managed to heal their wounded, so my NPC's were only rarely able to pick off wounded enemies.

At that moment, Vaash jerked me by the shirtsleeve, drawing my attention. It hurt just to look at the commander of my second hundred. The troll now had no decent skin left, just cuts and burns. Even his renowned trollish regeneration was nothing against all those wounds, especially given that burns regenerated particularly poorly.

"Captain Amra, save yourself and fly away on your winged snake! We'll cover your retreat!"

"Abandon my warriors?! Never!"

"Captain, you must flee!" Now it was the voice of Ziabash Hardy, barely able to stay standing and wielding a magical flamberge instead of his favorite orcish yataghan, clearly having taken it from one of the undying. "Sovereign, you must survive and avenge us so our death will not have been in vain!"

Well? If my very closest companions were demanding I save myself... I guess I really needed to move my butt. But how to get out of here? Summon VIXEN? Wasn't summoning magic forbidden? Although... this wasn't really magic, just calling my mount. I mentally called out to the Royal Forest Wyvern and asked her to immediately appear before me. But there was no response. No miracles...

Here I had to turn my attention away, because a Throwing Net had covered me and Fimbulthul.

Acrobatics skill increased to level 30!

Athletics skill increased to level 34!

I didn't even take damage, deftly tucking in my limbs, rolling along the earth and wrapping myself in the ropes. Then I managed to stretch and break the net, as I also did with the second one that flew in shortly thereafter. Then the severely wounded Akella fell before my eyes, still holding a large blue bird in her jaws, clearly someone else's pet. Irek also fell, speared straight through, then his Lobo let out a death howl as well, all soaked in his and others' blood. And then my Fimbulthul also died, his icy-white fur gone red with matted blood.

A net landed on me again, this time enchanted to constrict my movements and sap Endurance Points. Then an enchanted lasso and right after that a normal net. I couldn't break through them all, and I didn't even try. My vain attempts to free myself were met with cries of elation from the enemy camp. Knife in hand, Yunna ran up, having lost Gjöll somewhere and crouched down to help me cut through the nets. A few seconds later, there were only magical nooses left that couldn't be cut with metal.

"I'll take it from here, you take Baron!" I said, pointing at the huge Alpha Swamp Wolf next to her.

Yunna nodded in silence, grabbed her spear and ran over to her new mount. Baron never let anyone but his master up on his back before, but now the huge creature submitted to the goblin girl and allowed her to ride.

And there I heard a familiar cry from the heavens! Well, there was my VIXEN! My pet Royal Forest Wyvern had flown in to save me!!! I started shouting to attract the flying snake's attention.

And it was so impressive, woah! The massive airplane-sized creature dived down from the low and dark clouds, practically scraping the ground. My little baby had grown so much! The wyvern's level at one hundred ten also impressed me. VIXEN passed over the rows of bewildered enemies, spraying them with a stream of boiling toxic acid.

The shouts of pain hurt my huge sensitive ears. I could see a bunch of enemies VIXEN had killed, even more were wounded and writhing in pain, tearing off their smoking armor and trying to shake the burning acid off their skin.

Achievement unlocked: Player killer

~ Finding a Body ~

(143)

...

Level ninety-three!

Achievement unlocked: Player killer
(159)

Just for that maneuver, my little sweetie gained three whole levels! But she couldn't land. There were just too many enemies around me.

"VIXEN, over there!" I pointed at a convenient part of the map. "Grab me right there!"

I was again covered with throwing nets... And so many... Chai-nee Shu and See-Uhn-Rhu ran off to help, but I stopped my ward and her beau:

"That won't be necessary! Actually, I want them to throw all their nets and lassos! Let them think they've caught me!"

I noticed that Chai-nee's mouth was all bloody. Seemingly my ward had bit through an enemy's throat. And how... Right through the net I touched the furry girl's little head and... with one strong jerk of my hand broke my adopted daughter's neck. No, undying, you won't be getting my daughter today! See-Uhn-Rhu was bewildered with his jaw hanging as he watched the cold-blooded murder, and I ordered:

"Now you go into battle. And try to take at

least one undying with you! That way, after you respawn you don't have to be ashamed to look your bride and rougarou commander in the eyes. After all, they were quite successful in this battle."

The Chieftain of the Clan of the Laughing Otter gave a nod and, with a fearsome roar, tore off into the very thick of the enemies. I then tried to cut the ropes holding me down. No, it was no use. My enemies had been quite generous with the nets, fifteen covering me at once. And that was without all the lassos and enchanted nooses. A couple of ice spells also flew in in a naive attempt to freeze and thus paralyze the Dark Sovereign. Fools! I had 100% defense against cold! Was that all? Were they all out of ways to hold me? Seemingly yes, because no more nets or spells followed.

Well then, it was time for me to get out! I activated my vampire ability Incorporeity, which allowed me to slip through any obstacle like a ghost for thirty seconds, and effortlessly escaped the pile of nets. So, I had only thirty seconds, and I had to really run for it to reach the place I told VIXEN to land.

Successful check for Cold Resistance!

Dodge skill increased to level 40!
Dodge skill increased to level 41!

~ Finding a Body ~

Someone tried to freeze me again using some especially powerful ice spell with a large area of effect and not particularly caring if they hit their allies. Thousands of icicles flickered before my eyes, the nearby area became blindingly white for a moment. Lots of players went down, from what I saw. Even berserkers and archers over level 150 died around me, instantly turning into frozen sculptures and honeycombed by the icy shrapnel. But the fearsome spell didn't stop me.

It was of course a shame that my enemies now knew I was totally immune to cold, but I didn't have much of a choice in the matter. I ran out of the icy frozen circle just as VIXEN dove down from the clouds and came in for a second run, spraying down acid and poison on everything below.

The enemies scattered, hoping to avoid the path of the winged monster while VIXEN made a sharp turn and plopped down on the ground two steps away.

Acrobatics skill increased to level 30!

Riding skill increased to level 35!

I only needed one second to jump into a somersault, then be on the back of the huge winged snake.

"Let's take off!!! And right into the clouds!

Wait, we've got one more passenger to pick up!"

At the last second, when VIXEN had already spread out her huge wings, I bowed low and grabbed the shoulder of an NPC warrior I landed near: a dark elf scout, level-117. Perhaps this was the last Drow elf I had left. I sat the rescued warrior in front of me, ordering him to hold on tight to the bony outgrowths on the wyvern's back.

The battlefield below flickered past, packed with enemies. There were just a dozen blue allied markers left on the mini-map, drowning in a sea of hostile red. Unfortunately, the enemies quickly realized what was happening and opened fire. I took a dart to the shoulder, which took my life down by three percent. Oh well, I didn't even wince. My winged beauty cried out two times in pain, having taken three or four arrows to the chest. That was no good, but just a few flaps of her wings and we were back up in the black clouds. And then...

I was blinded by a bright flash, and my ears started ringing from fearsome thunder. The Royal Forest Wyvern was thrown and spun by the shockwave. I could barely keep hold of her back. It most reminiscent of a nuclear explosion. When my eyes had somewhat readjusted, I managed to read the now fading words, which were hard to make out on the black clouds surrounding me:

~ Finding a Body ~

Damage taken: 0 (2040 light damage from level-204 spell Holy Armageddon, x200 multiplier for vampires = 408000 units HP. Light immunity 3 seconds)

Successful Agility check!

Acrobatics skill increased to level 31!

Seemingly the enemies were just making sure they couldn't take the Dark Sovereign alive and, in a desperate attempt to stop me at any cost, they had played their trump card. Two thousand units of base damage... Impressive! I suspected that lots of players had just been lain low down on the battlefield. And I hoped greatly that the clans that suffered would air their grievances. I desperately wanted a split to form in my enemies' ranks...

VIXEN, although she was already far from the epicenter, also took a good bit of damage. My flying snake's life bar had fallen down into the orange. And the Drow elf got lucky. He was blocked from the spell and shockwave by the wyvern's body and took no damage. Lucky bastard. Well? I'd make him commander of the remaining Drow elves. They would do very well to have such a reliable and fortunate commander.

Now the main issue was whether we could

get through the magic dome above us. On the one hand, VIXEN had successfully passed through it before. On the other, they were usually one-way, so reinforcements could be brought inside, but nothing could get out. I didn't want to risk it.

"We'll make it through!" I shouted with strain, and just then a hole appeared in the pulsating forcefield. It was just the right size for my winged wyvern.

You have used 3 Direct Intervention Points
You have 349 points remaining

I made it out of the trap! Yes, my warband was smashed to dust and ash, I had lost three hundred loyal soldiers and, to be honest, it was a miracle I survived. The enemies simply didn't know all my abilities. From here on out, I wouldn't have the same advantage. Nevertheless, I was still in the mood for war. This was not my last battle. I could consider my mistakes and live to fight another day!

VIXEN gave a squawk of lament. The arrows were buried deep in her flesh, causing my beauty serious pain. But I had no way of landing and pulling them out because we were flying over the cold black waters of Frigid Lake.

"Hold on, my pretty! I know it hurts. I know

you're cold. But I promise to heal you, give you a tasty dinner of live animals, and a warm spacious room with a soft bed of fresh hay. You just get me to the castle!"

The wyvern squealed out again, but this time totally differently, without any notes of pain. And she started flapping her emerald webbed wings faster, taking me west.

Riding skill increased to level 36!

Animal Control skill increased to level 69!

Trading skill increased to level 45!

Day Three
Old Friends

MY NEXT VIDEO clip was not like any that came before. I just had too much pent-up negativity over what was happening. I had stepped on too many thorns in this inert overly bureaucratized corporation, where issues that required an immediate response might not be handled for days, or just be left to play out on their own. Unfortunately, there were a ton of examples of both. For one, there were some minor hiccups during the Great Hunt event when employees didn't want to take responsibility for their own actions. Or the unfinished Gray Pack control interface, which was only completed after I'd been in control of the wolves for a while. Or Fenrir's Cursed Regalia, which had only partially been in the game at all. I had to go through the vice-president herself to get that resolved.

And sure, I had told the viewers that I had a few of the Fenrir items. Actually, it was already something of an open secret. My most dangerous opponents had already known since I made my wish to the Djinn Sultan. And in the past few days, that information had spread far and wide based on search engine metrics for phrases containing the words "Fenrir's Cursed Regalia." There was even a whole topic on the game forums titled, "What is the Dark Sovereign wearing?"

But I had the most gripes for the clumsiness and poor planning of the Dark Sovereign event. I'd already been the Dark Sovereign for three days, but where were the unique perks and skills I'd been promised? I mean, what even was there to distinguish me as a fearsome game superboss, whose heavy footsteps were supposed to make all *Boundless Realm* shake? I was still just a normal Goblin Herbalist! I guess it was fine not to get experience or plusses for the unique achievement, but where the hell were the Dark Sovereign quests or missions I was supposed to use to gain experience? Was it another "sorry, it didn't occur to us?" Even if that was true, it had already been three days since then. There were several departments working on the global event with dozens if not hundreds of total workers on the project. Didn't a single one of them have time?! I'd never believe it in my life!

And I also had a bunch of restrictions weighing me down. They took my phone and made it impossible for me to contact the outside world. I couldn't even see my own sister. I was locked in my office and wouldn't be allowed to leave it for ten days. I was forced out of the game if my behavior ever wasn't to my employers' liking, and when that happened they replaced me with a program. I was forbidden from using the Gray Pack in large cities and it, meanwhile, was my main weapon! I was technically not given even part of what a ruler is entitled to. I was required to buy my own servants, soldiers, building materials and even furniture! What bullshit! *Was Boundless Realm* the richest corporation on the planet or some random little mom-and-pop where the workers had to buy all their own supplies? What, they just didn't think about it? Their budget of several billion credits just didn't have room for such a minor issue? It reminded me of an old joke I'd heard about a successful company renting a stapler.

And don't get the wrong idea. I didn't lose heart or give up. Quite the opposite, I was prepared to go to war against all *Boundless Realm.* But I did understand that with the present state of things, my resistance would be quite short-lived. A few days, maybe even less and the divisions of undying would be outside my castle. And then there would be a harsh battle not for life, but to the death. But I already knew the distribution of forces too well to even hope I might win. So if the corporation wanted something bigger than an endless chase for some uncatchable Dark Sovereign who always fled through portals to another part of *Boundless Realm*, it was time for the employees to put forth at least some effort.

I put my perspective on the night battle near Frigid Lake in the clip as well. Sure, the enemy had pulled one over on me, I admitted that candidly. I didn't know exactly who was in command there, but I thanked them for the painful lesson and even promised generous compensation, monetary or otherwise, for the experience. Together with that, I pointed out faults in the game system that were keeping me from using my abilities fully, or letting the battle get interesting. I could only get a very limited number of warriors through a portal, and my NPC's were low-level compared to the players waiting for me. And though the first problem could be solved, for example by opening a few portals at once, my soldiers and I simply could not gain experience fast enough. There were just no easy sources near enough to my castle.

I couldn't stop myself from ribbing my enemies a bit, too. Those five thousand players (and that was the figure I'd seen on the *Boundless*

Realm forum) knew perfectly that I had a flying mount, nevertheless they allowed VIXEN to land and evacuate me from the battlefield. The players used all their nets and lassos on me, and there was simply nothing left to immobilize my flying snake. And those ham-fisted archers... I was no archery expert, but just five hits had landed on a target as gigantic as my level-110 Royal Forest Wyvern. After something like that, I'd have sent my subordinates to retrain as gardeners or doormen, because shooting arrows was clearly not their strong side.

I uploaded the video clip and collapsed on the sofa, just beat. I needed rest, because this endless day and especially night had me tired as a dog!

"GET UP, TIMOTHY. We need to have a serious talk!"

I was jerked awake fairly unceremoniously, and the voice of the man who woke me up from the dream was very familiar but, at the same time, very unexpected. He wasn't supposed to be here. Not in a million years!

I cracked one eye, then a second and spent a long time looking into the familiar face before I realized who it was — Alexandro Lavrius, my very first boss at the Boundless Realm Corporation! Maybe not in an austere business suit, like I was used to, but jeans and a t-shirt, but it was him beyond a shadow of a doubt. How could that be? He was fired long ago for financial machinations with the corporation's virtual property! Where had he come from and why was he in my office?! I woke up once and for all and sat up on the sofa, batting my eyes in surprise.

"I can see you're surprised," the dark curly-haired Greek laughed. "Yes Timothy, I was hired back on at the corporation, because there were a couple algorithms they couldn't crack without me."

I immediately guessed he was talking about my NPC wife Taisha. Many people had an interest in her encrypted algorithms, and I knew her development was somehow connected with Alexandro Lavrius. But first he spoke about something else:

"You really kicked up a fuss with your last video... The players are having a charged discussion on the forums, and lots of them support you. They demand the event be made more interesting and the Dark Sovereign be made stronger. And our workers are just making excuses. The president of the corporation even got involved in the discussion and promised to figure out why such an important event is getting insufficient attention from tech support, and the Special Projects and Global Modelling departments. Also the president promised to figure out if an employee of the corporation really was being imprisoned and kept isolated. Ugh, and heads will roll! You just have a unique talent for messing with directors!"

I kept silent, because what he'd just said could apply to him as well, having been fired from his job directing Special Projects at least partially because of something I did. Alexandro Lavrius was not expecting any commentary from me. He walked over to the window, and found himself blinded by the bright sun, lowering the blinds a bit.

"But I'm not here because of the night battle and not even because of the Dark Sovereign."

"Is it Taisha?" I suggested, and he nodded in confirmation.

"Yes, that is the very reason they brought me back on. You see, Timothy... how to explain? Have you ever experienced true inspiration? When you do something you love with your whole heart, your mind is firing on all cylinders, and you aren't even really thinking about what you're doing or how? That was about how we made the next-generation NPC."

Yes, I knew that feeling well. I fairly often did

things without thinking, at times making decisions that looked strange and paradoxical while also somehow certain they were right. And that was exactly what I told him. So taking advantage of the opportunity, I clarified:

"Next-generation NPC? And what is supposed to make it unique?"

"It was supposed to be completely different. Not an NPC in the usual understanding of the word, not a program limited in its choices, where all possible moves are already proscribed. This was to be a nearly intelligent being, capable of analyzing the world around it, making conclusions and learning not only from its errors, but from any source. The work order came from the very top and went to me and a group of programmers. It wasn't even from President Thomas Heywood. It was straight from the owners of the corporation."

I whistled in surprise, but Alexandro Lavrius confirmed I had heard correctly:

"Yes, that's exactly right. You see, after the event with Fenrir 1.0 and his self-teaching Gray Pack, we have lots of valuable material in the form of algorithms, data and programming libraries. But at a certain stage in its development, the Gray Pack attained such a high level of intelligence that defeating it became a nearly impossible undertaking. Fenrir and his pack were the first digital consciousnesses to plan out many moves in advance like a grand master chess player. It would sacrifice individual members to gain advantages and avoid negative consequences. It wasn't quite enough for the digital entity to become something fundamentally new and better adapted for survival in *Boundless Realm* than a living player, but it was close. It is not a mind in the traditional understanding, but an agglomeration of lived experience combined with the ability to self-correct. Getting that agglomeration concentrated into one NPC rather than spread thin through a whole pack was our mission. And we beat ourselves up over it for a long time. We even achieved certain successes, but..." here he just splayed his arms in disappointment. "The NPC didn't recognize itself as a self-sufficient being, it didn't understand its own nature and still needed someone else to lead it."

I waited for the story to continue. I mean, I needed to know how this "agglomeration of experience," or whatever he wanted to call the next-generation NPC algorithms, ended up in Taisha, but he glossed over that particular detail. Either he didn't know, or didn't want to say. However he said the corporation had determined the location of my pretty thief wife after the Djinn Sultan helped her flee.

"In the Al-Pars province, which is located on a different continent of *Boundless Realm*, there has been some strange activity in the last few days. In a tract of hilly lands far from any city, where players seldom visit, something has been causing turmoil. NPC's are coming out of hibernation for no clear reason, leaving their assigned locations and interacting with one another. They've become so active that we even needed to allocate extra server resources to the area."

"Has anyone figured out what's happening?" I asked. The former director answered:

"Yes, of course. There's an NPC army gathering there to support the Dark Sovereign, and that army is led by your wife Taisha. There are currently eight thousand fanged and scaled monsters under her command. They are primarily desert nagas, which are half-human half-snake. But there are also manticores, chimeras and ankhs, which are half-human and half-bird. And none of that would be a huge deal, but recently Taisha charmed the Sphinx into her army. And that, you see, is a unique high-level creature connected with many game quests. It left its assigned location and followed Taisha into the desert."

I laughed and even gave a few sparing claps of approval:

"That Taisha really is a smart one! I just want to know how she managed to remove the program restrictions."

It was meant as a rhetorical question, so it was all the more surprising when he answered:

"About the same way you do it. She tweaked the world to her needs."

"But..." I knew this topic well and immediately caught on a discrepancy in Alexandro Lavrius's words: "To do that you need to become a superboss- or even demigod-level character. And you need Direct Intervention Points!"

I thought I had him backed into a corner, but the former Special Projects director twisted out of it with ease:

"Timothy, you must have forgotten that your NPC wife has the Leader's Shadow skill, so she is well within the bounds of the game mechanics to act as your official representative. Sure, Taisha doesn't get any extra experience from that because she's higher level than you now, but that doesn't stop the NPC from seeing her for exactly who she is, the legal spouse of the Dark Sovereign. So she is entitled to everything that goes with that. And as for the Direct Intervention Points... well, when has a lack of them ever stopped you?"

"What's that supposed to mean?" I didn't understand Alexandro's last question, but he eagerly explained in greater detail:

"Timothy, you have tweaked *Boundless Realm* to fit your needs a number of times! Like

~ Finding a Body ~

back when you broke into that Cursed House instead of completing the newbie missions in the normal order. That was originally a deadly quest location made for players over level fifty, but you just up and moved in! And the game was tweaked, changing a whole bunch of variables and even one constant. It actually marked the abandoned hut in the forest as a safe dwelling, where monsters weren't even allowed to enter! Or when you handed out quests to your companions, both NPC and player. Did you spend any Direct Intervention Points then? You didn't even know they existed! Or something very recent: you broke through the magic dome over the battlefield on your wyvern. Timothy, weren't you told that, in order to spend Direct Intervention Points, you had to be sitting on the throne?"

I felt embarrassed by his persistent and openly mocking gaze.

"I somehow forgot about that... The throne of the Dark Sovereign is uncomfortable. It's huge and it burns my skin. I only climbed onto it once, then I forgot and never used it again. I was just sure that it would work, then it did."

"Well, in that way you and Taisha are alike. Maybe that's why she's drawn to you."

I considered it an appropriate moment to ask a question that had held my attention for a while:

"Say, who worked on Taisha's appearance? I mean, she's so pretty. She can't be a randomly generated character. Some experienced artist must have spent days slaving over her. You should go find whoever that was. They might be able to tell you a lot about how she was created. And that might help you understand what makes her such a unique NPC."

"Bravo, Timothy. Very good question! But do you really think her doll-like appearance and body, which is attractive by human standards, didn't lead us to the idea she was made by hand? You bet your ass it did! We looked deep into it. Anyway, according to the system logs, the village of Tysh and its inhabitants, along with the entire surrounding area was generated as you and the mavka walked down the road toward it. Before that, the map just contained an empty undiscovered area. The whole location was just in the design stage. It was very crude and schematic with just basic characteristics. And because there were no players nearby, there was no reason to waste server resources to finish it."

"Does that mean Taisha wasn't there before?" I asked to gain a clearer understanding.

"That sounds about right. Taisha was 'born' just a few minutes before the Goblin Herbalist by the name Amra and his sister the Wood Nymph Valerianna Quickfoot entered the village of Tysh.

And based on the fact it created a female character of your goblin race with an unusual and attractive appearance, which you clearly were unable to ignore, I think we can assume this NPC girl was created especially for you."

"But... who made her? And for what purpose?"

Unfortunately, Alexandro Lavrius just shrugged his shoulders indefinitely:

"We don't know that yet. But I'm sure if we ever do, we can figure out all the rest. For now, this is your mission: meet back up with Taisha and lure her into your castle with whatever truths or untruths it takes. The fortress of the Dark Sovereign is still on its own special server, so we are very interested to see whether Taisha can truly function there. If Taisha hesitates and doesn't want to go into the castle, it's no big shame. We'll create another game location she won't be afraid of. No, Timothy, don't you worry. We aren't going to capture your NPC girlfriend. We're just going to observe her to better understand her essence."

But that didn't exactly calm me down. In fact, it only set me more on edge. Not going to capture Taisha my ass... Knowing how great a value my NPC wife represented to the corporation, I thought the opposite. They would try to catch her and study her as soon as they got the chance, and they were just giving me a song and dance to reassure me. But I didn't tell them my doubts. In fact, I decided to pretend that I believed all their tales and exploit that to get myself a little favor in the game:

"Alexandro, there is one problem. Taisha has a portal scroll in her inventory that she was given by the *Legion of Steel*. As soon as the Dark Sovereign, i.e. me, is in Taisha's visual range, it will open a portal and a squadron of extremely dangerous high-level players will come flooding out. And it cannot just be secretly taken from her. Taisha knows it exists and is on high alert."

"And what do you suggest?" he inquired.

"My suggestion is as follows: find a game location in a dangerous place — for example over the mouth of an active volcano, or in the middle of an endless ocean teeming with sea monsters. Create an illusion there of a peaceful meadow with sheep grazing or something else totally inoffensive, and make a magical platform in the air that will last a few seconds. I will also need two portal scrolls to the trap: one for me, and a second for Taisha. And I'll need another scroll to my wife's NPC army. From there it will all be easy: after dying I will respawn in my castle, and Taisha next to me. Then I won't even have to convince her to enter my castle."

Alexandro Lavrius gave an approving nod and a thumbs up to say he liked my plan. He told me everything I wanted was completely doable, and the preparations would be completed by tonight.

"And that's not all," I stopped the delighted man short. "Now let's talk about my compensation."

Alexandro Lavrius frowned. Seemingly my former boss naively thought that I would be willing to do this dangerous job for nothing but a thank you. But my former director quickly got himself in hand and asked how much I wanted in compensation.

"No, my reward won't be monetary, I want to be able to hurt my enemies as much as possible. I need you to increase the equipment drop chance as high as possible at the trap site. I know it can be done. In the underground city of the dwarves Dotur-Khawe, the leader of the *Goons* clan lost all his armor once because the drop chance was nearly one hundred percent. I want that same thing again! I want the most dangerous of my enemies to die and respawn with nothing but a loincloth, losing their unique weapons and armor for good. They spent so much time to get that stuff, and they're so proud of it. It would be amazing to see them lose it! Then, when the forums learn the most powerful clan of the Southern Continent is in a jam, all other players will think thrice before making war against the Dark Sovereign!"

"Well Timothy, you're quite the dangerous and cunning opponent," Alexandro Lavrius said with approval and even admiration. "You have a sick imagination and never forgive those who wronged you. Those are the exact qualities we want in a Dark Sovereign! Alright, we'll do it just as you wanted. Anyway Timothy, I've gotta run. I'm going to go give this assignment to the programmers so they'll have everything ready by tonight."

I walked the former director to the door and even shook his hand. But after the door closed, I allowed the happy smile to crawl out onto my face. Great! Let my employer work on the trap. I was going to try and escape this whole thing without me or Taisha losing even one item. I was certainly not going to lose my NPC wife's legendary emerald dragon-skin armor for good. I felt the same way about leading Taisha into a special server and putting my unique companion at risk.

* * *

LOADING... The abundance of game messages took me aback. I had leveled up... And twice... A Fame boost... I got some packages by magic messenger... My Player Killer achievement had gone up, and many times at that. I'd reached level one hundred, and could choose many new skills. Then, right at my feet, nearly crushing my toes, a heavy metal-bound chest plopped down with a thundering boom. The Steward bowed deeply to me and wanted to tell me something. And the Storekeeper. And the Keymaster. And next to my ghastly servants stood... a few unfamiliar bearded NPC dwarves, a group of living players with the clan tag *Amazons*, and a pair of warg children from my past. It was Darius and Darina, who I had allowed to leave the Gray Pack.

What was going on?

At the same time, I had a few chat windows flickering. There were messages from support_013, support_088, support_101 and support_104. But that didn't come as a huge surprise: corporate leadership must have been generous in handing out butt-kickings. Now tech support and the other departments had a fire lit under their asses and were striving to show their zeal and usefulness. The Keeper even came into the room. The glowing icy-white winged angel was hovering under the ceiling of the Throne Room, looking at the crowd gathered below and trying to find a place to land.

But all that instantly lost all meaning when my cell phone rang! Cell phone? Here in the game? My cell phone had been confiscated in the real world! But the game clearly still had my number, and the functionality of *Boundless Realm* allowed a player to make calls, though it was a bit pricy. I opened the game menu and, not believing my eyes, stared at the number and realized it was Kira.

"Hello. Hi!" I had no idea what to say or how to act, because for two weeks my girlfriend had been steadfastly ignoring me and she had suddenly decided to call.

"Timothy, just one question. And answer honestly, like you're at confession. In your video you said you were forbidden from leaving your room for ten days. Is that true? Or was that just some cute little story you thought up to raise a bit of hell?"

No, "hello," no "sorry I haven't called." Kira's voice was severe and tense, like a prosecutor or a judge. I confirmed that everything I said in the video clip was true from the first to the last word.

"I have to admit, it's hard to believe. Lots of it sounds like the ramblings of a madman. And the rest does not hold up to even rudimentary checking. If you hadn't said you weren't allowed to leave the room for ten days, I never would have believed it. It's just that exact part..." Kira went silent midsentence, not explaining what exactly had caught her interest or put her on guard. "Tell me everything."

I started with the assassination attempt and my desperate struggle with a technician named

~ Finding a Body ~

Arthur. I told her how I lost consciousness and woke up in a personal office on some high floor of the *Boundless Realm* skyscraper. I started telling her the president of the corporation had visited me personally when suddenly a familiar message ran before my eyes:

Poor signal quality
If connection problems persist, the Boundless Realm *client will be forced to close*

Someone was very displeased with this topic! But this time I didn't keep mum and just told Kira about the warning message. Her reaction was as unexpected as it was unforgettable. Kira raised her voice, and her already severe tone grew shrill enough to make metal ring:

"I am Kirena Tyle, co-owner of the Boundless Realm Corporation! If Amra's virtual reality capsule loses connection now, I swear that I will fire every employee responsible for signal quality from the lowest technician to the very highest director! I order all employees whose offices are located from floors minus sixteen to seven to stand up immediately, turn off their computers and go at least two steps back! If any of you do not obey, you will be immediately fired! Security service, make sure they comply!"

Woah! I guess my girlfriend *was* a co-owner

of the Boundless Realm Corporation! And clearly not low-down on the totem pole, as she had the right to order directors around!

I had to admit, I was in shock. And I had never seen Kira so worked-up before. She was like a mythical fury, but invested with total power and capable of doling out punishments or dispensing mercy. She was a real queen of the harpies! Just the impression made me shake!

I turned my attention to the flickering chat windows, which all disappeared almost at once. The tech support workers didn't dare disobey their highest boss's order. And the worrying message about poor signal quality also disappeared. Alright then, it worked! An interesting way of solving a technical issue!

In just a few seconds, Kira was back to her normal voice and asking me to continue the story about President Thomas Heywood's visit. I didn't hide anything, telling her what we talked about, my new office, the scars on my chest and how the president and I shared a beer.

When I was done, Kira asked pensively:

"Wait, Thomas drank beer? Woah! This is getting more and more interesting... I think I told you Timothy, but I know the president of the corporation well. Anyway, he's a real health nut. He's always working out and eating right. He's a vegetarian, he eats nothing fried or smoked, he's on a salt- and gluten-free diet, and his food intake is strictly measured down to the gram. And naturally he consumes no alcohol. Thomas Heywood downing a couple beers is about as hard to believe as a rabbi selling pork in a synagogue. Either you're flagrantly lying, or the situation is much more serious than I thought."

"Much more serious? Am I in danger?" I clarified, ignoring Kira's jab that I might be lying.

"You?" she considered it briefly. "Definitely not until the next board of directors meeting. In fact, if I understand what's happening, our employees will be pampering you and keeping you totally safe. It looks like there's been an information leak, and we need to find out where it's coming from. You see, Timothy, your name was mentioned in Inessa Tyle's will. But it has lots of conditions and variables. Many important people now have an interest in making sure nothing bad happens to you. The whole Boundless Realm Corporation has only one person who is financially interested in your death."

"And who might that be?" I asked, alarmed. "Kira, tell me! I have to know my enemy!"

Was it just me, or did my girlfriend give a soft giggle before answering?

"Timothy, just so you know, my grandmother was a big shit-stirrer... That person is me!"

Day Three

When the Sovereign is Angry

TO MY IMMENSE PITY, the conversation about Inessa Tyle's inheritance and my place in it ended there. Kira clearly thought she had already said too much, so she tried to end the conversation quickly. My girlfriend just asked one final question: which direction did my office face, and what could I see from the window? I answered that I could see a city park, a lake with catamarans and boats, several intertwined high-speed roadways and a multi-level exit ramp. I even tried to help with the approximate positioning of the windows:

"The windows are clearly higher than the Special Projects Director's office on floor forty-four and quite a bit to the right. You can also see the city park from his office, but it isn't this clear. There are skyscrapers blocking part of it. But from my windows, you can see the park clear as day."

"That's easily enough information, I'll find you. Expect me to come visit soon. I really hope my fears are misplaced and this isn't as messed up as it seems."

Kira signed off, and the frozen world around me came to life. Cripes, I only then noticed that all these minutes the players and even NPC's were standing motionless, afraid to interrupt an important conversation with the co-owner of the Boundless Realm Corporation. And I had lots of people waiting on me: my servants, the Keeper, some dwarves, and the *Digital Amazons*. But first of all I walked up to my sister, who was modestly shuffling from foot to foot behind the other visitors. I gallantly kissed her hand and led the sorceress out in front, trying to demonstrate my unique relationship with Valerianna Quickfoot.

"Thank you, Tim! I love you too!" my sister whispered with just her lips, after which she said, now loud enough for everyone else: "The Dark Sovereign and I need to have a talk one on one. It won't take long." After that Valerianna Quickfoot asked the Steward to bring us to the balcony of her room in the castle's central tower.

A moment later, we were standing on the

balcony. It was damp, cold and windy. And so high up! Woah! Dark shaggy clouds coursed no more than one arm's length above us, hiding the spires of their towers up in a dense mist. At that, only a short parapet divided me from a true chasm. We were six hundred feet up. And although the world around us was a virtual game, my heart froze in fear for a second. I looked down and noticed the new tents and pavilions on the square before the castle. What was more, there were many of these traveling tents. Very many, even. Noting my interest, the sorceress commented:

"The Dwarves have arrived to celebrate the marriage of Vanessa and Tondik. Two clans arrived today in full. Plus a bunch of supposed relatives, friends and friends of friends. But we can discuss that later. Now let's talk about more important things. I'm disappointed in you, Tim. You decided to go to such a dangerous event last night without me, and without any magical support at all. What body part were you thinking with when you took that risk, big-ears?!"

I could read judgement and doubt in my mental capacity in Valerianna Quickfoot's voice. I was always impressed by my little sister's ability to make her older brother feel like an idiot like this with just a couple words and a sour look. As a rule, she had good reason to talk to me like that, and Val was simply a master of putting me to shame.

~ Finding a Body ~

But today's lessons weren't over yet.

"Amra, were you even thinking with that big-eared head when you sent Dark Riders out to secretly scout the player camps and open portals? Did you forget that the coming of your emissaries is always accompanied by waves of unbearable horror that make both people and NPC's writhe on the ground? Dark Rider and 'unnoticed' are mutually exclusive concepts! But most of all, Timothy, I'm upset with how predictable you were. In one night you sent out Dark Riders to undying camps several times, then every time you followed up with an attack on the players. Why act surprised that you and your army were expected at the next one?"

Yes, my sister's reproaches were justified and well-deserved. I understood that and lowered my head.

"Yes, that was stupid... But in the end I escaped the trap!"

Valerianna shook her head judgmentally:

"The fact that you managed to escape is just a wonder! But Yunna wasn't so lucky..."

"Yunna? What are you talking about? What happened?"

I just had no idea. When I flew off on VIXEN, my goblin niece Yunna was still alive and fighting with the last soldiers covering my retreat. And after that, she was supposed to die and respawn.

Had something gone wrong? Valerianna shook her head with pity once again:

"I can tell right away that you haven't been on the forums today. Yunna was captured by players, brought to the city of Lars and harshly executed on the central square in front of a huge group of people. And the goblin girl had so many ghastly curses and death magic spells piled on her that she will never respawn again... Now the head of the niece of the Dark Sovereign is mounted on a pike for all to see next to the gallows on the central square of Lars. And it is right next to the head of the Dark Sovereign's general, Vaash the troll."

Yunna was dead once and for all? That simply could not be! I decided to use Direct Intervention Points to bring my dead niece back to life. My sister said before that NPC's could be respawned at a cost of two points per level. Yunna was level seventy-two. So I had more than enough points to bring her back.

"Yunna shall be reborn!" I said with the absolute inner confidence I had used to rip through the magical nets or change my servants' characteristics. However... nothing changed, and no points were expended. I tried again and again, but it was all in vain. Maybe I should sit on the throne first? Although inside I understood that was also no use. Then I tried to respawn Vaash, but the result was the same. Valerianna, silently watching my fruitless endeavors to break the rules, spoke up:

"Amra, accept it, Yunna cannot be brought back. She died a terrifying and torturous death. I saw a video of the execution of the niece of the Dark Sovereign on the *Boundless Realm* forum. Believe me, you'd better not watch it. Vaash the troll also met a long and torturous end. Turns out regeneration is not always a good thing. And there is another pike ready on the square. This evening, your First Mate Ziabash Hardy will be executed in Lars before a large crowd."

I let out a ghastly cry, more like that of a wounded animal than a goblin. The scoundrels! Animals! No, they were worse than animals. They were taking advantage of a total lack of higher authority do as they pleased without fear of punishment. But they would pay for this! No matter what it cost, I would avenge the death of my NPC companions and try to save my first mate! Oh, it would be ghastly and bloody vengeance! The people of the Lars province would shake just at the sound of my name for many years to come! Ah, and for now...

"I am the Dark Sovereign! With the power vested in me, I curse all players and NPC's present on the Lars central square during Yunna and Vaash's execution! Let a criminal marker appear next to their names in perpetuity and let their shameful game handles be appended with an indelible crimson tag: 'Child-killing scum!!!' And let all traders in all *Boundless Realm* refuse to do business with them even for all the money in the world. Let not a single inn feed them, nor give them shelter. And let not a single coachman nor ship captain agree to transport them anywhere. Not a single healer shall heal them, nor a single prostitute comfort their bodies! And let not even dying many times or praying in temples help these bastards be rid of this mark of shame! That is my word, let it be so!"

You have used 300 Direct Intervention Points
You have 106 points remaining

A blinding bright lightning bolt struck the spire of the tower over our heads, followed instantaneously by deafening thunder. The gods of *Boundless Realm* had heard my words! At the same time, the Keeper appeared on the balcony in midair. The glowing icy white figure spent two minutes hovering there, not at all worried about the huge altitude, and not even flapping his huge wings. He must have left the game and was consulting with colleagues on whether my use of Direct Intervention Points was lawful. After that, the Keeper gave a distinct nod and said he would

~ Finding a Body ~

wait in the Throne Room with my other visitors, then disappeared in a flash of light. The corporation confirmed that I acted within the rules and game mechanics. Great! But that wasn't all...

"Val, I need a ton of portal scrolls to Lars! And another rain or fog scroll... although you could just conjure up that weather with your water magic. But most importantly, I need one scroll with the forbidden spell Astral Explosion! No matter what it costs, you must get it!"

"A player who casts a forbidden spell in a city will be marked a criminal and sent to jail," my sister reminded me. But almost right away she added with a smirk that, given our position as antagonists to all *Boundless Realm*, it didn't matter. "What's more, Amra, you cannot read the scroll. It takes a very high Intelligence. I'll do it myself!"

I embraced my younger sister gratefully. She was so majestic and fearsome in her appearance as an all-powerful sorceress, but at that she was just as near, dear and reliable as ever. Valeria reacted decently at first and even hugged my short flap-eared goblin back, but eventually she grew embarrassed to show her feelings and backed away:

"Alright then, Tim. Enough sappy stuff! Let's go back to the Throne Room. I'll introduce you to our new allies from the *Digital Amazons*. They signed on to fight with us for the duration of the event for just three million credits no matter how the Dark Sovereign story ends."

"Three million?" I was reminded that I had only set aside two million coins for that. It wasn't that I couldn't find another million. I had the money, I was just surprised that Valerianna had outspent our agreed-upon budget without even asking me.

"No Amra, not like that! They're paying the three million, not us! For a clan of cyberathletes like the *Digital Amazons,* taking part in this bigtime event on the side of the Dark Sovereign is a unique and very powerful advertisement to the whole real world! The *Amazons* are hoping to restore their somewhat forgotten brand, and they have lots of plans: selling clothes, cosmetics and *Digital Amazon*-branded sports nutrition, video games, comics and 3-D movies. Even adult products like sex dolls and robot girlfriends with the bodies and faces of famous *Amazons*. So don't worry about wasting money, they're paying their own way, and in spades!"

~ Finding a Body ~

* * *

Iron Jeanette [AMAZON]
Human
Level-211 Amazon

ALL THE DARK-HAIRED amazon lady had on was a golden tiara, an armored G-string and an ultra-miniature bra made of two golden threads that just barely covered her ample breasts. I suspected her equipment was not actually as basic as it looked and provided excellent defense against physical and magical damage. But to my eye it covered at most three percent of her body. The muscular warrior woman had a striking mane of tar-colored hair and was not the least bit ashamed of her practically naked appearance. She eagerly extended her hand in greeting:

"It is a great honor to meet a *Boundless Realm* legend and someone who has taken part in such high-profile events as Goblin Herbalist Amra!"

Successful Strength check

Woah! Such an enthusiastic greeting would definitely have broken a normal person's hand. Continuing to smile happily, I returned the powerful warrior's handshake, which was more reminiscent of having my hand squeezed in a metal vice. Based on the tortured smile that appeared on Jeanette's face, she also found my Strength impressive. But I wasn't going to square off with this fortress of bones and unclenched my fingers.

"I welcome the legendary *Amazons* to my lands! The whole southern wing of my castle is at your disposal. Make yourselves at home! And honorable bearded dwarves of the subterranean city of Dotur-Khawe, I am glad to see you in my castle as well! My servants will provide you with everything you need. As it is the castle cellars are bursting with fine food and strong drink for Vanessa and Tondik's wedding!"

Seemingly, my new allies and dwarves had prepared a response and gifts for the Dark Sovereign. I could see muscular warrior women shifting from foot to foot in the back rows with the *Amazon* clan tag, plus some short subterranean natives trying to obscure chests and cages behind their broad backs. But I jumped out in front with an important message:

"Dear guests, the official celebrations shall come later. For now, I must leave you for a time. I have been gravely insulted by the undying in the city of Lars. They quartered my young niece on the central square just because she was my kin. And

~ Finding a Body ~

I could never forgive such a thing, even if I weren't the Dark Sovereign! So in one hour I will lead a raiding party to get revenge on everyone who was in any way involved with Yunna's death. And if the gods of *Boundless Realm* are favorably inclined, I'll return victorious by evening. After that, I will be happy to chat with all of you over a flagon of strong drink."

The dwarves exchanged glances and started whispering. A heavily-armored and beefy level-250 Royal Guard took a step forward. Perhaps this was Vanessa's brother from before, who she had pointed out to me in the subterranean city of Dotur-Khawe:

"Sovereign, you have been kind to my sister, and welcoming and generous to us all. So we consider it improper as guests to just sit around and feast while our host risks his life in battle! Amra, allow us to come with you! For the dwarves of all clans, it would be a great honor to embark on a military campaign under your banner!"

Dwarven and dark dwarven opinion of you increased by +10!

Diplomat skill increased to level 31!

Warchief skill increased to level 33!

"By the way, speaking of banners..." Valerianna Quickfoot whispered beside me. "The Dark Sovereign really does need some kind of flag or symbol to raise his soldiers' fighting spirit, and make them recognizable. We should figure that out..."

"We don't need to reinvent the wheel here," I answered my sister also in a whisper. "We'll use our old flag from the pirate galley: a fearsome white shark on a black background. The whole world watched the Great Hunt event and after the sea battle, all *Boundless Realm* associates that banner with Captain Amra and his band of pirates. Beyond that, I have certain plans for the *Brotherhood of the Coast*. With such a familiar banner, I'll have an easier time coaxing them onto my side."

But Valerianna was decidedly against my idea. The sorceress cringed in dismay and shook her head:

"Wrong choice. What does a shark have to do with anything here? What's the connection between a cartilaginous sea creature and the game boss the Dark Sovereign, whose castle is in a mountainous land a thousand miles from any sea? We'd be better off using a black banner with no emblem than that confusing thing."

The mavka and I quietly bickered, while Iron Jeanette's loud and dismayed voice rolled through the throne room:

"Hey, Amra. This isn't what we agreed on!" a flaming two-handed sword appeared in the muscular hands of the *Amazon* leader. I wondered where she was hiding that before. "No one can make me and the girls just sit around while the Dark Sovereign goes off to rip through undying flanks! We crave action, any way to prove ourselves! After all, what could be sweeter for a true *Amazon* than the ecstasy of battle, a river of blood and a bit of revenge to top it all of?! We're all coming with you!"

A battle cry rolled deafeningly through the room. "*Amazons* never lose!!!" came the chorus of warrior women, supporting their leader.

"And before you go anywhere," a calm voice came down from above. I only then remembered that I still hadn't spoken with the Keeper, "I need to finally have a talk with the Dark Sovereign and explain the changes to his abilities, skills and perks."

~ Dark herbalist Book Four ~

* * *

I LOOKED AT my character sheet and was baffled, not knowing how to react...

Name	Amra
Race	Goblin Vampire
Class	Dark Sovereign
Experience	12000000 of 12500000
Character level	100
Hitpoints (HP):	9999/9999
Endurance points	6231/6231
Statistics	
Strength (S)	310 (1134)
Agility (A)	300 (657)
Intelligence (I)	50 (82)
Constitution (C)	300 (1240)
Perception (P)	50 (96)
Charisma (Ch)	200 (200)
Unused points	0
Primary skills (8 of 8 chosen)	

Survivor (C S)	52 First specialization: double hitpoints bonus Second specialization: -10% damage taken
Heavy armor (C S)	45 First specialization: no penalty to Endurance Points
Athletics (C S)	35 First specialization: increased Endurance Point growth
Dodging (A P)	41 First specialization: 30% chance of avoiding AoE-effect spells
Stealth (A C)	49 First specialization: -20 discovery radius
Exotic Weapons (A P)	(25 + 18) First specialization: Flaming whip, additional fire damage, 5% chance of burning target
Riding (A C)	38

	First specialization: +15% movement speed
Regeneration (C S)	10

Secondary skills (8 of 8 chosen)

Veil	22 First specialization: shapeshifter (three times per day)
Acrobatics	26 First specialization: take no fall damage from any height
Alchemy	42 First specialization: make elixirs with more than one property
Foreman	82 First specialization: increased loyalty from underlings Second specialization: larger list of races to hire
Animal Control	69 First specialization: pet attacks improved Second specialization: pet

	defense improved
Warchief	33 First specialization: soldiers immune to recruitment
Diplomat	31 First specialization: fearmonger
Superboss	10

Why did my class change? What was this game profession "Dark Sovereign?" Was that really a job someone could train for? That made me think of a Dark Sovereign Preparatory University, where students would be taught to assemble a group of monsters and carry out raids on peaceful cities. Then, after graduation exams, they would go off to various continents and see who could conquer *Boundless Realm* first. But even if it was a profession, what were its main skills?

And where did my initial skill Herbalism go? Trading too had just gone up in smoke. Instead I had Heavy Armor and Survival, while Alchemy had been switched out of my primary skills for Athletics. None of the three skills even took advantage of the strong sides of the Goblin race, Agility and Perception, instead raising Constitution and Strength. No, I had no particular issue with Constitution but, for a Goblin, raising Strength came with a racial penalty of 50%... That was stupid to my eye. I'd taken the Alchemy skill long ago by accident, so I would have gladly traded that out for something more appropriate or at least have moved it into secondaries. But not for such a worthless replacement as Athletics! That alone lost my character thirty-two Agility, while giving very little in return.

And the Regeneration skill once again improved Constitution and Strength. But that was total crap. Why should I waste a skill slot, especially a primary when, as a vampire, I already had decent regeneration? With my present Taste Tester at 223, I got back 150 hitpoints per minute. On the one hand, it wasn't quite fast enough — restoring my health from zero to full took a whole hour. On the other hand, Taste Tester could still be leveled up a lot, and that would make my health regenerate all the quicker. Now onto that metal-bound chest lying next to the throne. I'd seen similar ones before, this was probably the brotherhood of vampires sending me a new collection of blood-sample vials. And I already had around one hundred untested samples left in the cold cellars of my castle, plus a couple dozen living creatures awaiting their fate in cages and aviaries. Given that, taking Regeneration as well as a skill was just wasteful.

~ Finding a Body ~

And now I had a mysterious new secondary ability, Superboss, which I could not find any description for. And as for some of my new specializations... here I just grabbed my head. I mean, who would have ever chosen those?! Even if I was drunk or half asleep, I would never have taken the Heavy Armor perk "no penalty to Endurance Points," nor the perk "increased Endurance Point growth" to the Athletics skill. Amra already had a ton of Constitution, and these new skills put it beyond sky-high. I had Endurance Points coming out my ears, why bother saving them?!

But as for the Flaming Whip perk, I liked that one. An excellent choice, really. It seemed created especially for the whip-wielding Dark Sovereign. I also liked the ability to shape-shift three times per day. Here, of course, I would have to take a closer look to make sure I wasn't mistaken. And for some reason I couldn't see what shapes I could take, but the ability to become, let's say, a big fish and escape underwater would have been a big help. As would the Acrobatics perk that let me fall from any height painlessly. In fact, I was totally fine with all the secondary-skill perks.

Nevertheless, I needed to have a serious talk with the Keeper and the corporate employees behind his winged back to correct the nonsense that had been wrought upon my Amra's skills and perks.

* * *

THE CONVERSATION with the Keeper was really drawing out. I made the seemingly logical and even obvious complaints that the Dark Sovereign had no need for Regeneration, and that the skills they chose for me did not take into account the pluses and minuses of my race. But still I had to chew it over for him and prove I was right several times with a calculator. How the hell could you call this an improvement?! They removed a few skills that leveled Agility, the strong side of goblins, given their +1.3 Agility per primary-skill level. But in return I got skills that improved Strength, which for goblins was penalized by fifty percent. And every time, the Keeper had the same objections:

"But the Dark Sovereign is a melee fighter! He needs Strength, not Agility! He has been using his Blowgun for a long time, and his main weapon is the Hair Whip, which does damage based on your Strength!"

"But the boost to Strength from those skills is minimal! All those changes did practically nothing to the Dark Sovereign's damage dealing ability. Damage per hit is up by less than seven percent! Plus I lost Agility, and that defines chance to dodge, parry, block projectiles and, most importantly, the chance and speed of a hit. That actually made my damage per minute fall! Is that an improvement?! And my hitpoints grew one and a half times: from six and a half thousand to ten thousand. But what good is that? The Dark Sovereign is just a punching bag now. He cannot dodge or parry, or strike back!"

The Keeper objected again, and the conversation was going in a circle... And it was the same story with the Regeneration skill. He said that restoring health was important for any fighter, and there can never be too much regeneration. My objections that it was better not to let yourself take damage, and that required high Agility, or that there were lots of healers in the Dark Sovereign's army ready to pitch in and restore their commander's health were not taken into consideration. And neither were my arguments about Taste Tester and restoring health via vampiric abilities.

The mysterious Superboss skill, as it turned out, governed regeneration speed for Direct Intervention Points, bringing that up one percent for every skill level. If the Dark Sovereign event were to last a few months, such a skill may have had a noticeable effect. But the decisive battles with the undying armies would be happening in the next few days, so the benefit of the fifty or sixty extra points I would probably end up getting was nowhere near obvious. I mean, it might kill one level-sixty enemy or respawn one level-thirty ally. That would have no impact on the outcome of the battle, and especially the war. There were no creatures that weak in either my army or that of my enemy. I asked to change the skill, and again hit upon some resistance.

Finally I'd had enough:

"Keeper, I don't give a crap how the directors of the corporation see the Dark Sovereign! I'm the one who's gonna have to play him, not some bosses sitting in luxurious offices who have never seen *Boundless Realm* firsthand and barely understand how any of it works! Do you want a strong monster that's gonna be hard to kill? Zero-out Amra's skills and perks, and let me rebuild them all from the ground up. By the end of the day I'll forge my Goblin Herbalist into a real superboss, the ideal Dark Sovereign!"

In response, silence. Seemingly, the upper leadership was conferring. A few minutes later, a clarification followed about whether I already had a plan in mind for the Dark Sovereign. Yes, I actually did know what I was talking about. I had a plan and an understanding of what I wanted in the end. But all these long disputes and negotiations were wasting precious time. I needed a character ready to do battle right now.

~ Finding a Body ~

My first mate's execution was supposed to take place in one hour, so I couldn't keep putting off the attack. My armies were lined up on the square before the castle and ready to invade the city of Lars. Magic scrolls were ready to go, the Amazons had been made centurions and assigned to a group of one hundred NPC monsters. The shamans and mages had blessed the warriors with positive bonuses, and even the cyclopes wanted to come join the fight. So I answered the Keeper that I wanted a reset of my skills. But not now, after this battle was over.

"Good. We await your changes, Amra. But for now..." the winged figure came down to the very earth and handed me three scrolls. "I don't know what this is, but I was asked to give it to you. They said you ordered these scrolls. And they also asked me to tell you 'the location is ready.'"

One of the scrolls had a ribbon tied around it with the words "To Taisha's army." The other two were unlabeled. Yes, I knew exactly what these were. I immediately summoned a magical messenger with a package and letter for my NPC wife saying to activate the portal scroll at exactly midnight Southern-Continent time. And that was, strangely, a relevant distinction. Although *Boundless Realm* had not implemented true time zones, each of the three continents had different times meant to better coincide with prime gaming hours in the most densely populated regions of the real world.

Alright, the final preparations were over. I walked over the Eye of the Sovereign and wished to see the city of Lars from a bird's eye view. The crystal ball showed just a gray fog, so I had to go below cloud level just to be able to see anything. It was raining, the narrow little cobble-stone streets of the medieval city were empty. The city dwellers were all taking shelter from the bad weather. Only on the central square did I notice some signs of life and I went over to investigate. There was a perimeter around the square. The city guard was chasing gapers away from a high scaffold where the executioner's assistants were dragging bundles of sticks and lumber. Seemingly, they were planning to burn my first mate Ziabash Hardy alive.

Opposite the dais, there was a grandstand with seats kept out of the rain by a canopy where the important spectators had already begun taking their seats. In the middle of the tribune were the most honorable boxes, based on the coats of arms on the shields of the elite guards looking after the King of Lars and his retinue. The ruler himself was still absent though. On the stage then, next to a pillar with chains, the huge fat red-hooded executioner was arguing with the commander of the city guard, pointing to the rain and wet timber. Seemingly, he was asking for more oil.

"Prisoners are held in the city jail," Valerianna Quickfoot's voice rang out behind me, also carefully observing the scene in the crystal ball. "It is located in the outer city, fairly far from the portal exit site. We might not be able to fight our way through to the prison before the undying come to and start flooding into Lars from every corner of *Boundless Realm.*"

"But won't the Astral Explosion scroll help stem the flow?"

The mavka shook her head:

"It won't, I already ran through the scenario in my head. The spell dome won't cover the whole huge city, it can only cut off a few regions. And there are too many players in Lars itself, more than two hundred thousand online on a typical day. And we aren't all combat characters of course. Also our average level is not high enough. Two hundred thousand is just too much for our army. So I suggest we cut off just the old town. That's where the palaces of the ruler and magnates are, plus the merchant guilds, fancy shops and a relatively small number of undying. What's more, the old city is walled off from the outlying parts of Lars. As soon as the prison convoy passes through the old city gates, we attack! We'll take Ziabash, capture the inner walls and gates and activate the

Astral Explosion scroll. After that, we'll only have to worry about the city guard. They have one hundred fighters at around level two fifty, and the king's guard contains fifty level-three-hundred veterans."

I took a closer look at the inner walls my sister just mentioned. They weren't too tall and clearly not intended to hold off a serious assault, but my fighters could hold them temporarily. After that I looked at the NPC enemies. The high-level elite soldiers, and especially king's guard inspired unwitting respect. They would be a problem... We would have a serious numbers advantage though, so I had no doubt in our victory.

I moved the image in the ball. There was the convoy. It had left the prison and was proceeding slowly down empty streets under the pouring rain. And it was surrounded by lots of watchful guards, pikemen, archers and mages. Among them I saw a few living players, too. In the center of the procession, beaten half to death and bound in heavy chains was a level-149 Orc Pirate standing on a caged-in cart. They really worked him over... My first mate's body was beaten and cut so badly there wasn't a single patch of intact skin on him. Nevertheless, Ziabash Hardy kept up his proud aura and was standing in the cage, looking contemptuously at his alarmed escorts. Alright, I had seen enough and wanted to get back to my castle.

I could see the even rows of my army of thirty-thousand standing ready for action. The *Amazons* were walking between the rows of monsters and undead, trying to get something through to their savage underlings. Orcs and minotaurs, giants and ghosts, all awaiting my command. I supposed that as their leader I should say something to send them off. And the right words just put themselves together:

"My warriors! The time has come for us to make our fearsome power known. From this day forth, all *Boundless Realm* will be forced to reckon with us! The government of Lars awaits. Their king is named Valeon the Thirteenth, and he dared to announce himself an enemy of the Dark Sovereign. He even officially declared war on me. But in this battle, you won't be fighting for the Dark Sovereign. You won't even be fighting for gold and riches, although we expect a huge amount of loot, and all of it to the last penny will be divided among you. No, you will fight for hope! The hope that, if any of you had the misfortune to fall captive, the rest would come save them from a gruesome death! And you also will be fighting for the future. A future in which the undying finally see you as equals worthy of consideration and sympathy, not merely walking fonts of experience and loot. A future in which any of you, regardless of race or skin color will have the right to life and freedom. A future in which orc and goblin cities won't be torched just for fun, elven women won't be kidnapped for harems, and the treasures and ancient burial mounds of the dwarves will not be plundered ever again. A future in which the undying will not also be unpunished, where they'll have to pay in full for each and every one of their foul crimes! If that is a future you want, CHAAAAARGE!!!"

Diplomat skill increased to level 32!

Diplomat skill increased to level 33!

Foreman skill increased to level 82!

Warchief skill increased to level 34!

Warchief skill increased to level 35!

In response, many throats roared back in exhilaration. It could even be heard from my position in the throne room through the many walls. Hundreds of portals were opened at once, and my army flowed through them like a raging river. Over all the soldiers, I saw positive effect symbols: immunity to fear, immunity to pain, increased attack, faster movement speed.

~ Finding a Body ~

Seemingly, my inspiring words had found a response in the hearts of the NPC soldiers and taken effect.

"Powerfully said," Valerianna Quickfoot confirmed, readjusting a sash of elixir vials on her magic robe. After that the mavka sharply changed topic. "Tim, admit it. Did you and Taisha... how to put it... did you ever hrm, consummate the marriage?"

"What?" I asked, simultaneously surprised and embarrassed at such a tactless question. "Why are you asking?"

"It's just that the seditious ideas you just voiced of a *Boundless Realm* without players farming NPC's is something I've heard your NPC girlfriend Taisha say a few times. And that's why I'm asking. I want to know how her idea infected you: was it airborne or sexually transmitted?"

Valerianna Quickfoot smiled, displaying her predatory teeth and simultaneously showing that she was making a joke. I knew that Val was very nervous before the battle, so she was somewhat choking up. But then my sister went totally serious:

"Amra, this battle is going to be tough. Do you need any magic scrolls, grenades or elixirs?"

I looked over the list of magical support items my sister had to offer and took a couple ice grenades, a darkness spell scroll (just in case the enemy tried to burn me with the sun) and a few strong healing elixirs. My own regeneration was already pretty good, but sometimes it wasn't enough.

Valerianna helped me sort out the vials and grenades in various slots on my belt and the pockets inside my armor, then she unexpectedly returned to the previous topic:

"Tim, I am still thinking about what you said about a future where players and NPC's will live in harmony. I'm not sure the leadership of the corporation will like that, even though to me the world you've described is inspiring. It may be utopian, but it is the kind of future I want to live in. Although... it would be a totally different game, not at all like *Boundless Realm.* But now we need to get back to reality. Your army has made it through, which means it's time for us to go, too. Grab your whip," my sister said, gesturing for our bodyguards to come closer. Then she unfurled a scroll and right in the throne room opened a huge oval-shaped flaming portal. "Onward, to fight for our future!"

Day Three
The Lars Massacre

THERE WAS NO organized resistance. The self-confident or perhaps foolhardy city-dwellers grabbed for their weapons when they saw the orcs and minotaurs, and were immediately wiped out. The undying nearby were just too relaxed by the calm happy reality of their surroundings so they weren't quick enough on their feet to log off before it was too late. My army skewered them on pikes or their monsters simply tore them to shreds in a matter of seconds. It was a harsh but necessary measure. Leaving witnesses alive just posed too great a risk. We needed to keep the Dark Sovereign's army composition, numbers and movements a secret. But if an NPC was peaceful and didn't put up any resistance, my soldiers wouldn't touch them. Well, except the ones with crimson red "Child-killing scum!!!" labels over their heads. We killed them on sight and without the slightest pity.

But we had a special fate in store for the living players with that indelible marker of shame. I had them disarmed, tied up and dragged onto the stage on the central square. I hadn't decided what to do with them, but I did know for certain that the revenge for killing Yunna and Vaash would be particularly gruesome. I needed to lay the smackdown so hard no player would even think of coming after my companions again.

"Merchant guild storehouses captured. There are a hundred carts worth of loot here. Shrekson Bastard."

"Sovereign, the western bell-tower of the temple of the sun has been taken. The priests did not resist, so we let them live. The main altar is here. I'll try to siphon its Direct Intervention Points over to your throne. Shaman Ghuu."

"Amra, the palace of the ruler of Lars has been double encircled. Not even a mouse could get out now. Part of the king's guard and city guard have been defeated, and the rest are barricaded inside. The king and his retinue tried to flee via underground tunnels, but local dwarves who once built those tunnels told us about them, and your cyclopes caved them in. We await your command to

assault. Iron Jeanette."

"I've placed archers and spearmen on the walls of the old city. For now it's quiet on the other side. Seemingly, the enemies were not expecting us to show up uninvited and still haven't really woken up. But that's no reason to relax. The Boundless Realm *forums are in a tizzy. There are groups of undying forming hurriedly to come to Lars. Any minute now a TOP clan might arrive. Valerianna Quickfoot."*

Messages were pouring in from all sides both standard, private, and those sent for money via messenger. I could hardly see and react to them all, but I more or less had the situation under control. Yeah, if anyone thought I was simply releasing savage monsters in a densely populated city, giving them total freedom and thus dooming Lars to destruction, they were deeply mistaken. My army had been training and drilling discipline for the last few days to prepare for this. And that was also why each hundred NPC monsters was assigned a living player to command them. There was no anarchy, nor any outbursts, senseless cruelty or disobedience. Even the extremely willful and stubborn cyclopes were being surprisingly obedient, breaking down locked palace doors on Shrekson Bastard's orders and smashing the hastily-constructed barricades of fine furniture.

I divided the army into three regiments, each with their own mission. Regiment one was supposed to take the walls and gates of the old city as quickly as possible, separating that wealthy area from the rest of the huge city of Lars. That was a mission of utmost importance, so I assigned it to Valerianna Quickfoot. I also gave her the most proficient Drow elves, dwarves and orcs. And just ten minutes after the invasion had begun, my sister wrote me a private message that the walls had been taken, the gates were locked up tight, and the black banner of the Dark Sovereign hung from all the guard towers of the old city, which was also capped with an Astral Explosion dome.

I already knew about the Astral Explosion from a game message saying the forbidden spell had been used in the city of Lars. But my little sister did not in fact risk prison, because the city guard had already been dispatched by regiment two, which was under the command of Iron Jeanette. At the time of the attack, most of the city guard was on the central square next to the scaffold, and that square was where the bloodiest battle of our invasion took place. Based on the replies in the chat and private messages from Iron Jeanette, the square and streets leading to it were drenched in blood. The hundred level-250 guards and the few level-300 royal NPC guards and fifty players who had come to watch the execution of

~ Finding a Body ~

Ziabash Hardy did not let their lives go cheap. In the five or seven minutes that conflict lasted, regiment two lost more than fifteen hundred NPC's, mostly undead and rougarou. Before the last defenders fell, thirty of my Amazons were also on their way to respawn.

Regiment three's mission then was to block off the center, catch the few players there and limit the NPC city-dwellers' ability to move about the streets. I was worried that King Valeon the Thirteenth would try to organize the scattered guard divisions under his command, both of undying and common citizens. But I overestimated my enemy. The King was just a big talker. With Yunna and Vaash tied up and helpless before their executions, he said he wanted to lead the war against the Dark Sovereign, reach my castle and execute me and all my companions. However, when the first battle horns sounded the king abandoned his subjects and tried to flee the old city like a coward via an underground passage. And now Valeon the Thirteenth was with his offspring, retinue and servants locked in the palace, where I was personally intending to have a chat with the rude fellow. The crowned head of the ruler of Lars would make a great addition to the back of my throne!

For the beginning of the assault, I was busy with another important matter. I was leading the strike brigade attacking the prison convoy. Unfortunately, we did not pull it off unexpected. It would have been quite the feat, given the audible screams, metal clanging and sounds of bloody battle already permeating the city. Fifty NPC prison guards and ten living players were bunched around the cage, keeping my warriors at bay and shouting they would kill Ziabash Hardy at once if my orcs and wolves took even one step further. However, I did not allow the prison guards to kill my first mate. All the healers at my disposal were ordered to heal the wounded Orc Pirate, restoring his life while I charged, slashing into the rows of armor-bound guardsmen, drawing their attention and striking down enemies left and right.

My hair whip proved itself brilliantly, especially now that it was reinforced with fire magic. The whip easily cut through the metal of the armor and shields, burning enemies as it did. But still my main strike force was the Gray Pack. Even I wasn't expecting such greatness out of my pets! Buffed up with blessings, my abilities, their own and my perks as well as bonuses from Fenrir's Cursed Regalia, the wolves, hounds and rougarou cut through the enemy ranks like a hot knife through butter, ruthlessly tearing the flesh of enemy players, their pets, and NPC's alike. In just one minute, all that was left of the prison convoy were bloodied scraps of viscera on the cobblestone causeway, while my orcs had already broken the lock off the cage and set their old friend free.

"Captain Amra!" exclaimed the brutally beaten yet huge and fearsome orc as he went down on one knee, gratefully kissing my hand and not ashamed at his tears of joy. "I was prepared to accept death on the pyre with honor and trusted that you would avenge me. But the idea that you would come here, to the very hive of the enemy and save me from certain death... I couldn't even dream of such a thing!" Ziabash Hardy grew embarrassed at the emotional outpouring and stood up to his massive height, roaring so loud the echo rolled down the narrow little streets of the old city. "Sovereign, you lead the way! I'll follow you to the edge of the earth! Even over the edge! You'll never find a more loyal first mate!"

Orc opinion of you has increased by +10!

Brotherhood of the Coast opinion of you has increased to +75 (loyalty)

Superboss skill increased to level 12!

Warchief skill increased to level 44!

And then Ziabash Hardy, now totally healed and decked out with new armor and weapons, helped me sort through messages from the couriers and lead my troops. In theory we could leave Lars now. The main goal of the invasion had been accomplished, and would already be leaving with plenty of loot. But I decided not to limit myself to half-measures. I was going to force the Kingdom of Lars and its ruler Valeon the Thirteenth to fully pay for his audacity.

So regiments two and three were given the mission of systematically clearing out the old town. The orcs and rougarou went scrupulously, building by building, suppressing any possible resistance, breaking into houses and searching for hidden undying. They also marked valuable loot and called my giants and minotaurs to drag the loot to the square just in case.

Just then, another swift-footed Drow elf messenger came to give me a message scroll. I tore the ribbon, unfurled it and gave it a quick scan:

"Amra, the dwarves of the Bank of Thorin the Ninth requests we not rob their building. They refer to some arrangement and a gift for the Dark Sovereign, which it looks like they all chipped in for. Are they lying, or are they really under your protection? I know that the Most Reliable Bank of Gremlins is not to be touched, but I heard nothing about the dwarven bank. What should I do? One of their workers is a distant relative of mine, I'd rather not make a mistake. Gnum Spiteful."

~ Finding a Body ~

I had to admit, I was also baffled. What arrangement, what gift? But still I was in no rush to accuse the bearded troglodytes of lying. Instead I whistled to VIXEN and scrambled onto the back of the Royal Forest Wyvern, who just barely fit between the buildings. I ordered her to fly to the surrounded palace. That was where most of the dwarven wedding guests were. With lizard-like speed, wriggling down a narrow street and scrambling up a wall onto a roof, VIXEN finally managed to spread her luxurious wings and take off.

I looked closely at the part of town we now controlled. From up here, I practically couldn't see any trace of war in the old city. There were just a few wisps of curling smoke and rain-quenched fires. On the central square, there was a towering mountain of chests visible even through the damp fog. And over my head there was a huge magic dome shimmering with all the colors of the rainbow, but obscured in places by dark rainclouds. I had to give the *Amazons* their due. They had a good handle on their fierce, savage underlings, and the invasion of Lars seemed likely to go down in history as the most well-managed and even delicate invasion of all time. Some may say this was the wrong way for the Dark Sovereign to act, given he was created by the corporation to be the ghastly bane of all *Boundless Realm*. But I didn't think so. I treated my enemies as harshly and even cruelly as possible, but I tried not to harm the neutral NPC city-dwellers too much. And it wasn't because of some sense of charity and kindness. No, I did it to play up that contrast.

The NPC's of *Boundless Realm* were, for the most part, fairly pragmatic and surprisingly well-informed even about events in distant lands. If they had a clear example of what happened to the enemies of the Dark Sovereign while neutral residents were left unmolested, many would think twice before helping my opponents. And if I layered that with the inevitable rumors that would spread about the Dark Sovereign's ability to appear in any city of *Boundless Realm* with his army, the NPC rulers and common citizens would lose their taste for fighting on the side of the Dark Sovereign's enemies and would try to distance themselves from them as much as possible.

But then, while flying on VIXEN, I got a phone call from an unknown number! That meant it wasn't Kira. After so many days of separation, I was growing impatient for her to call saying I should leave the virtual reality capsule and come see her in real life.

"Hi, Amra!" I instantly recognized the voice of my green-skinned companion Taisha. "As far as I can tell, your company's in a real mess. There are groups of armed guards combing every floor of the building. They're opening and checking every office! There's some red-headed director lady at their head. My vocal identification algorithms give a 97.4% chance she is your friend Kira, based on a voice sample I have on file. Has something happened?"

"They're looking for me," I guessed and immediately asked whether these search brigades were far from my office.

"I mean, I don't even know where your office is," Taisha answered with notes of abashment in her voice. But she immediately asked if I even wanted to be found.

When I said yes, Taisha gave a strange reply. She said she would "share all the information she had with Kira," then changed the topic:

"Just so you know, that isn't why I called. I just got a teleportation scroll from a messenger. It says it's from you. Did you send me something?"

I confirmed having sent the scroll and added that the note I sent with it contained very important information about exactly when to use thc portal so wc could rcach its destination at the same time. And we had to do that in order to lose our "tail" from the *Legion of Steel*.

"The note says, 'activate the portal immediately.' But I've been following the game forums closely and I know my husband is now in the city of Lars, and that there is a powerful spell over the city restricting the use of portals. So now I have my doubts about who sent the scroll..."

"Wait, Taisha, something isn't right! In my message I wrote to come at midnight Southern Continent time. But yours says to use it immediately? I didn't send that! And my magical messenger couldn't cross the ocean to another continent so fast! It's a trap! One of our foes wants to take you to a special server to find out whether you can exist there... Although, Taisha, you most likely don't understand what I'm talking about."

"I see, just as I thought. Then I'll see you at midnight." My virtual companion held a prolonged pause but she didn't end the conversation: " And yes, Amra-Timothy, I understand perfectly well what a special server isolated from the main cluster is. I could exist there, but I'm not exactly sure I'd like it." After these words, Taisha abruptly ended the call, leaving me in a state of very serious thought.

Had my employers really decided to try and get by without me? Seemingly yes. They got me to tell them a surefire way of luring the NPC thief girl to the proper location then decided not to waste time and immediately attempt to trap Taisha. But they underestimated her quick-thinking and cautiousness, as she could tell it was fake and decided to give me a call. But what a girl Taisha was! There was little left of the unintelligent naive goblin she was when I first met her. Now the NPC Taisha not only was perfectly capable of navigating *Boundless Realm,* she also had a decent understanding of many real-world issues.

The chat window flickered open. A corporate employee by the now painfully familiar nickname support_013 wanted to have a chat.

"Timothy! We have received a complaint that you have installed illegal modifications to your game client. In particular, a mod that allows voice messages in Boundless Realm *to be encrypted."*

What? I started to chortle. So that was why there were no faulty connections warnings while talking to Taisha. My stubborn observers seemingly had simply not understood! And that could easily be the case. I had run into this before when Kira didn't understand my phone conversation with the goblin girl. Then I had assumed we were speaking goblin, but I was laughed at and accused of lying. But how else could I interpret the fact that Taisha and I understood one another perfectly?

I answered this "support_013" that I was totally clean and the tech support could come check my virtual reality capsule for illegal software at any time. If of course they could find my office. As it was turning out, that was proving more than a bit problematic. I asked him to comment on that strange fact as well, but the chat window just closed: support_013 hurriedly cut off the conversation. And I was glad. With all these irrelevant conversations, I was totally ignoring the battle, and the Dark Sovereign needed to get back to controlling his troops.

* * *

VIXEN, flapping her large wings and raising a curtain of watery haze, landed in the midst of a well-maintained garden next to the royal palace. And it was quite lively there. Thousands of soldiers from regiments two and three were preparing to storm the palace. There were NPC's and living players darting here and there. Giants and cyclopes were hewing fallen trees into battering rams, while somewhat smaller beings were making large wooden shields, hooks and ladders. With all the hubbub, I didn't even notice my commanders at first, but Shrekson spotted me and hurried over.

Streaked with blood and soot, the level-124 Ogre Fortifier was holding a heavy spiked club in his powerful mitts, seated atop an even larger armor-bound level-140 moose. It was an impressive and fearsome sight. A true general of the Dark Sovereign! What was more, the crimson criminal marker over my friend's head bore witness to the fact that the commander of regiment three had not only given orders but personally crushed player heads.

You have used 2 Direct Intervention Points
You have 109 points remaining

The words over his head changed, too:

Shrekson Bastard
General of the Dark Sovereign
Level-124 Fortifier

The armor-bound titan raised the visor of his helmet, revealing a satisfied tusked face:

"Amra, everything is almost ready for the assault. Most enemies are concentrated around the central entrance and hall on the first floor. There are fifty NPC royal guards there at level three hundred, plus a couple hundred courtiers and common servants. The enemy also has mages and healers. Jeanette and I decided to attack simultaneously from two directions: through the central entrance and the windows on the third and second floors to stab them in the back. But no matter what we've got a hard battle ahead of us. There are so many high-level enemies. There will be no getting past this without losses. But beyond there, the corridors are basically empty. My scouts have been the palace and said that a few minutes ago they saw King Valeon the Thirteenth in the window of the western tower," said the Ogre Fortifier, pointing his big old hand at a tall angular tower with many balconies.

I turned and looked closely at the target, trying to picture if I could actually land on one of the little balconies from VIXEN's back. Hey, now there's an idea! If their ruler died, the high-level guardsmen might very well cease resistance, which would then allow us to avoid serious losses. While I looked over the tower, Leon drew my attention:

"By the way, Timothy, I haven't had the chance to say. I wanted to tell you that I went to our boss's office today on your request and apologized to Tina for you making her wait. But she looked extremely surprised and kept saying that this was the first she was hearing of it, she had never come to you and doesn't even have a clue where your office is."

Poor signal quality
If connection problems persist, the Boundless Realm *client will be forced to close*

A very predictable warning... This intrusive censorship was really getting on my nerves! I gritted my teeth in rage and, in order not to be kicked out of the game, hurried to give Leon a more or less plausible explanation:

"Probably Tina was just too embarrassed to discuss such delicate details of her personal life with a stranger."

But I didn't believe that, because it left a few other strange facts unexplained. Nevertheless, the warning disappeared, which was what I wanted. I pointed Leon to Iron Jeanette as she walked up to the soldiers preparing to attack. I asked my generals to hold off with the palace assault:

"Yes, there are many high-level enemies there and they can give experience, skill growth and all that. But we stand to lose too much if we sacrifice a few thousand of our soldiers just to clear a few tactically worthless rooms. Let's try to avoid pointless losses. Give me fifteen minutes and I'll handle the king. But first I need a highly ranked dwarf from their bank. They said something about a gift and protection."

Just a minute later, there were three short bearded chaps standing before me. I had a fuzzy understanding of ranks and distinguishing symbols of the subterranean natives, but still I appreciated the number of braids in their beards and the many vibrant ribbons woven into them, each of which had to be earned. Apparently, all three were very, very respectable members of dwarven society and could speak for their compatriots. I extended Gnum Spiteful's letter in silence.

"Yes, Sovereign," barely having familiarized themselves with the contents of the scroll, the grayest-haired of the three stepped forward. "We requested protection for the Subterranean Bank of Thorin the Ninth and brought chests to your castle with one million coins for your fearless soldiers and a special gift for the Sovereign himself: a new-born Mythical Hound by the name of Fjörm. Some dwarven prospectors found the unique creature deep below the earth in a cave carved by a subterranean river. The pup's eyes had never even seen the sun. Tondik and Vanessa informed us that the Sovereign collects rare puppies, and we were hoping the gift might be accepted with favor."

A unique creature as a gift? And it's a clear candidate for the Gray Pack? I found this reaction very surprising and, I won't hide it, pleasant. Such generous tribute was doubtless worth the Dark Sovereign taking the bank of the subterranean folk under his care. It was just a pity I hadn't received such a valuable gift before the attack on Lars. During combat, experience flowed like a river, and the level 100+ veterans accompanying me had gone up by ten or so levels. For a newborn pup, even a crumb of that experience would have been enough to hit thirty, or maybe even forty. Although... the battle was still ongoing, and I needed to take advantage of that!

I opened the Gray Pack control interface and threw out one of the rougarou archers I'd added back at Frigid Lake to free up a slot. As I was hoping, among the many and widely varied NPC's in the Gray Pack interface, mostly the rougarou and stray dogs nearby, there was one possibility of great interest to me:

Fjörm
Élivágar Guardian
Level-1 Mythical Hound (unique creature)

Great! I quickly took advantage of that and Fjörm appeared in the Gray Pack. However...

The Astral Explosion spell blocks the summoning of your pet

Damn! Apparently, the puppy was back in my castle and couldn't be brought to Lars for the fight. Although maybe that was for the best. The tiny Fjörm would be getting experience regardless, but this way he wouldn't die here in battle. I thanked the eminent dwarves for such a valuable gift and confirmed that, from here on out, no branches of the Subterranean Bank of Thorin the Ninth in all *Boundless Realm* would ever be targeted by my army. A swift-footed messenger was immediately sent to inform Vanessa, who had spent her wedding day waving a battle-axe and invading a city.

And then, when the issue of the gift from the dwarves was resolved, I scrambled back up onto VIXEN and ordered my sweet girl to climb. The time had come to pay a visit to the king of Lars!

YIKES! I TOOK off from massive height, unsuccessfully jumping off the back of the winged snake and underestimating the distance to the nearest balcony. I was still not used to my character's new lower Agility after the skill changes, which brought along worse jumping ability. My fingers passed a mere couple of inches from the balustrade.

Agility check failed!

Acrobatics skill increased to level 34!

I didn't even have time to feel any fear before my whole body slammed into the rough stone wall. Peeling the skin off my hands and face, I slid down and awkwardly plopped onto the balcony below. I was alive! And I took no serious injuries from the fall despite the respectable height. That must have been from the Acrobatics specialization. It just put a few wrinkles on my green face, but even they were quickly healed by my regeneration. I turned my head up and estimated the height I'd just eaten shit from. It was fifty feet, maybe even sixty!

I could have turned into a lizard and tried to crawl back up the vertical wall. And the forms Amra's new shapeshifter perk allowed included a huge lizard as well as a predatory fish and a giant spider. However, I had never used it before, so I wasn't sure it would all go smoothly. What was more, I was spooked by the half-hour reload time. Just think how hard it would be for me to fight as a lizard! So I didn't try to reinvent the wheel and with a crisscross of my fiery whip, I broke through the door, which was locked from the inside. Pieces of the heavy door thundered to the ground and I walked off the balcony into the western tower.

Three times around the spiral staircase, yet another door to break down and I flew into a small circular room, where I stopped sharply in surprise.

Valeon the Thirteenth
Ruler of the Kingdom of Lars
Level-315 Swordsman [Child-killing scum!!!]

The gray-haired king was wearing a cuirass and a leather traveling suit. He was standing in the opposite corner of the room from me kneading his hands and tracing figure eights with his long flickering blade. And standing next to him holding a loaded crossbow that glowed with overflowing magic was his wife Elvira, a level-230 Bowwoman. In front of the crown-bearing father and mother there were two dense rows of their sons the princes: nine fearsome knights wielding their weapons and hiding behind shields. The very weakest of them was level-255. The group of enemies was so scary and intimidating that, for a second, I considered taking the cowards way out, pretending I'd opened the wrong door and turning tail.

I had done so much to make sure the King of Lars didn't escape retribution, and tried so hard to meet him! My subjects and even sister Valerianna Quickfoot were consumed by the idea of how to stop the king from fleeing, and force him into an encounter with the Dark Sovereign. But none of us had even for one second considered what I should do if I actually did meet him. No one had ever tried to find his level, nor found out about his wife and children. But we should have...

"Is this the one you were so afraid of? This little shrimp? Is that all?" came one of the princes, not hiding his scorn for my short flap-eared goblin entering their room at level-112. He turned to his parents for an explanation.

~ Finding a Body ~

"Yes, that is the Dark Sovereign," the king confirmed, no longer fidgeting with his sword and seemingly himself surprised at his recent fears. "I was expecting someone a bit more imposing..."

I then gathered my thoughts and courage, speaking with as confident a voice as I could muster:

"The woman may leave, she does not bear the curse. And that boy there in the second row, he may go as well. Prince Edward was not involved in the execution of my niece. If he is wise and retreats, he will be made King of Lars later today. But the rest of you shall die here and now."

Fame check failed!

Fearmonger perk used successfully!

Diplomat skill increased to level 35!

Superboss skill increased to level 13!

The Queen looked at her husband and shook her head. She was in no mind to leave and opted to share her husband's fate. But a knight in silvery armor raised his helmet visor, looked to his brothers, then gave a gloomy chuckle, sheathing his sword and walking away with the words:

"And you said the eighth son would never

get the crown. We shall see. In any case, this is not my war!"

"Curse you, traitor!" screamed the enraged father, swinging with all his might. He brought his enchanted sword down on his retreating son, breaking through his armor and nearly cleaving the prince in two.

Messages about level growth flickered in. The game system thought Amra's actions had led to the death of the powerful NPC and shared the experience.

"Don't touch the child!" the queen quickly shot out at her husband's back, driving a crossbow bolt into his cuirass up to the fletching. But she was instantly knocked off her feet with a punch from one of her older sons.

What was going on here?! I stood and watched the bloody battle between the princes and their crown-bearing parents. Just in case, I opened my inventory and checked if I had accidentally activated my gong to summon the goddess of strife Eris. This just looked too much like her work. But no, the gong had nothing to do with this. Seemingly, the tension in this family was like an overfilled boil and this critical situation had popped it.

Woah... One of the princes lost his sword in a scuffle with his brother and bit off his ear. The stunned queen lying on the floor was slain with a dagger to the heart by her now animalistic husband at the same time as the eldest son was run through with a sword... I had never seen such abandon, such mutual hate even between wild animals... Jesus Christ... Messages flickered in about experience and leveling up. By the way, there was level one hundred twenty-five! Now I could put on the last item of Fenrir's Cursed Regalia without an Ifrit Heart.

"No, no. He's mine!" with a crack of my fiery lash I knocked back one of the princes as he tried to decapitate Valeon the Thirteenth, who was sitting on the floor strangling another of his sons.

Exotic Weapons skill increased to level 39!

And then, it was as if a delirium spell fell off the squabbling family. They abruptly stopped fighting and turned their bloodied blades on me. All that remained were maddened king, roaring like a beast with hardly a third of his life remaining and five princes spattered in the blood of their own kin. Quite a lot for one little goblin, but I was certainly not going to retreat.

Direct conflict with these six powerful enemies didn't bode particularly well for me, so I tried to alter the conditions. My fiery whip lashed at the walls, knocking off the flaming torches. I was hoping to immerse the room in darkness so I could use my Night Vision. It didn't work. The fallen torches stayed lit and the light from the loopholes was enough for my enemies anyhow. Then let's use a darkness scroll!

It instantly became so dark it looked like black ink had been dumped into the air. Even the bleakest moonless cloudy night wouldn't provide such thick and impenetrable darkness. This was more like the dark found in an underground storage room. I hurriedly activated my vampire abilities Search for Life and Night Vision. I even managed, contorting my whole body and dodging whistling swords, to silently slip past the six men approaching me as they blindly swung their weapons.

Stealth skill increased to level 46!

Stealth skill increased to level 47!

Acrobatics skill increased to level 35!

Dodge skill increased to level 50!
You may choose your second specialization in this skill

Now behind my enemies, I tossed two Ice Grenades at them one after the next. The three princes froze into grizzly ice sculptures, and I exploited that, pushing the nearest one out a window, sending the knight on a short flight onto the stones of the castle's internal courtyard. I saw some more lines run by about experience and levels. But I didn't care because the darkness suddenly lifted! All I could tell was that King Valeon the Thirteenth had used something to refill his health to maximum. And all the negative effects like his allies being frozen and blind instantly disappeared. Not good! Not good at all!

"VIXEN, spit poison through the window!" I shouted, and a second or so later the room was clouded with toxic smoke.

Successful check for Poison Resistance!

Aha! My big-eared goblin had excellent defense against poison, but my enemies all started choking. Two of the princes even dropped their weapons and fell to their knees, clutching at their throats and spitting up blood. I took advantage of that and gave a few lashes of my Hair Whip, bringing down their hitpoints even further.

Exotic Weapons skill increased to level 40!

However... King Valeon the Thirteenth

squeezed an amulet around his neck, and the room immediately aired out. The poison disappeared without a trace. Oh, what the hell! I shouted for VIXEN to breathe poison again, but nothing followed. Clearly, my winged snake needed time to bank away and turn around. And that was the very moment I was attacked by one of the princes. I dodged his falling sword, but a shield strike knocked my little goblin off his feet. I didn't have time to stand up, pressed down by two heavy bodies at once. I threw the whip away. It was worthless in close combat. Then I tried to reach an enemy's neck with my teeth, but it was no use. Next the other two swordsmen ran up and joined the fight, trying to get through me with their blades and even sometimes succeeding. But I managed to bite the king, healing my lost hitpoints. However, Valeon the Thirteenth also restored his health, again using his magical amulet. A fierce battle started on the blood-soaked stone floor.

"Don't hold back your anger! Let me out!"

Just like back on the island in the duel with Regent Uvari-Dor-Shu, I was hearing a voice in my head. But this time I didn't take too long thinking or doubting. I immediately let Fenrir out instead of having him stew away inside of me. A moment later, a wild and sharp pain started pulling out my joints and breaking my bones. I started yelling fearfully, not capable of withstanding these torments. My jaws grew longer, claws grew on my fingers, my green skin grew thick fur. My enemies began shouting in horror and stumbled back when the huge wolf shook the people off his hide and stood to all four legs. The room was too small for a beast as huge as me.

"Usually I don't eat people, just drink blood," I told the terrified king and his sons, who were frozen in horror. "But for you I'll make an exception. Yunna and Vaash must be avenged!"

It was no battle, it was a massacre. My fearsome bites crippled my enemies, removing their limbs with huge chunks of flesh. No armor or shields could stop my lupine teeth. Each bite, and each bit of flesh I swallowed restored the huge wolf's health, and no strikes or even swords stuck down the whole length of the beast's body could change the outcome of my bloody feast now. First I slurped down the princes one after the next, then it was King Valeon the Thirteenth's turn. I left just his head and amulet.

But I sensed I was not alone. I sharply turned and discovered a little curly-headed girl of three or four walking through a far door I hadn't yet checked. She was squeezing a ragdoll and watching the bloody animalistic feast in silence.

Anora

~ Dark herbalist Book Four ~

Princess of the Kingdom of Lars
Level-11 Aristocrat

The voice in my head obligingly explained:

"The last member of the old royal dynasty. All that remains is to devour her, and the Kingdom of Lars will be completely yours. The Dark Sovereign will be recognized as its new ruler. Plus she's doomed no matter what. Other aristocrats will kill her in the struggle for the throne. So better eat her yourself than leave her for the vultures."

But I didn't obey Fenrir's bloodthirsty advice. I don't know how I might have behaved if the little princess were there for the execution, and Anora was marked with the glowing words "Child-killing scum!!!" On the one hand, killing her would make me a child-killer. But on the other not doing so would mean breaking an oath to get revenge on everyone in Lars with that cursed label. Fortunately, the game hadn't provided me such a difficult choice. My rage passed, quickly being replaced with exhaustion and pain. My body started changing again, and a few seconds later I was back to the little big-eared goblin, now soaked head to toe in blood.

"Don't be afraid, girl. I won't hurt you," I said in the friendliest tone I could muster, and the little princess nodded eagerly.

In her place, I would have been terrified to

see the corpses of my relatives and a bloody goblin. But Anora was too little to realize what had happened. The girl just asked, pointing at Queen Elvira, who was lying in a puddle of blood:

"Why is mommy sleeping in the daytime?"

"Uhh... You see..." I faltered, not knowing what to say to the mewling little girl and looking down to avoid her gaze. Damn! Damn!! Damn!!! It would be easier for me to just die than explain to this NPC girl that I had just killed all of her relatives. Sure, I understood perfectly that Anora was just an NPC, basically just a chunk of code, but in this world that was the norm. I just couldn't wave off the little girl's problem.

But a decision came unexpectedly. What was the Queen's level? Two hundred thirty or something? That meant bringing her back would take four hundred sixty Direct Intervention Points. That was approximately how much I had left after Shaman Ghuu siphoned the points off the altar of the temple of the sun.

"I'll wake your mommy up right now."

You have used 460 Direct Intervention Points
You have 4 points remaining

The Queen's whole body writhed, she took a sharp breath with a scream and sat up on the floor, looking with mad eyes from me and back to her daughter. I didn't even have to explain; the Queen already knew what had just happened. The mother opened her arms for an embrace and squeezed her little girl tight.

"I did this for your daughter's sake," I told Queen Elvira the First. "I know all too well what it's like to lose your parents. I couldn't allow such a sweet curly-headed girl to grow up an orphan. You are now the sole ruler of Lars, and thus it is in your power to stop the violence."

"Yes, Dark Sovereign," the woman sitting on the bloody floor confirmed. "The Kingdom of Lars requests peace in my name. We shall pay the necessary contribution, and my subjects shall never again raise arms against the Dark Sovereign or his companions."

"That isn't all," I added a condition to the peace treaty. "The bodies of General Vaash and the Goblin girl Yunna must be surrendered so we can give them a decent funeral. All city-dwellers with the cursed mark must be declared criminals and executed at once. And as for the undying, very well, I'll handle them myself."

Diplomat skill increased to level 36!

Diplomat skill increased to level 37!

~ Finding a Body ~

Diplomat skill increased to level 38!

The queen nodded in silence, after which I saw a laundry list of identical experience growth messages scroll past. I suspected that was my new allies taking down the cursed soldiers of the Kingdom of Lars.

The soldiers and guardsmen of the state of Lars are no longer hostile toward you!

* * *

ALL MARKERS on the mini-map turned either blue or green, no hostile creatures remained nearby. I bid Queen Elvira the First goodbye, taking the head of her husband Valeon the Thirteenth in my inventory along with his mysterious amulet. After that I went down the spiral staircase to the very bottom, finding myself in a huge gala room. Here the royal guards were dismantling barricades, servants were picking up trash, and my healers and mages were healing their former enemies. Iron Jeanette, leader of the *Amazons* walked up. However, the warrior woman's face was very strained despite the fact we won:

"Amra, I need to speak with you alone."

We walked away from the groups of NPC and stopped in an alcove where no one would bother us. Nevertheless, the dark-skinned warrior woman did not think we had taken sufficient precautions and took out a scroll (I didn't know where from, considering her minimal clothing), then activated a dome of silence. We couldn't hear what was happening outside, and no one out there could hear us.

"Valerianna Quickfoot says the enemies have arrived and stand in the thousands at the walls of the old city. For now they're just standing, not making any attempts to assault, but I think I know what they're waiting for. For the last half hour my *Amazons* have all been reporting attempted bribery. Players from different clans are offering very large sums of money, inappropriately large even, for a portal to your castle. My opinion: we need to get out of here before anything unfortunate happens!"

Well, well... That really was a worrying factor. We had no way of stopping the *Amazons* from sending private messages to other players, or even knowing if they did so. And that meant there was no guarantee we were still safe. What if one of my *Amazons* had already agreed to sell the invaluable scroll to my enemies?! Maybe the sale had already taken place, just by throwing a scroll over the walls of the old city. I asked if that was possible, and Jeanette instantly flared up in indignation:

"I'm confident in my girls! As I am of the many fans and admirers in my clan. But the money they're offering keeps going up. And temptation goes with it. Any loyalty has its limits. We have to remove the portal-blocking dome and get out of here!"

I shook my head unhappily. If only it were all so easy... I didn't doubt for a second that, as soon as we removed the Astral Explosion dome, my enemies would just put up another one so we still couldn't leave. It might not cover the whole old town, which might buy us some time. Maybe some of my warriors could even go through a portal to safety, but they definitely wouldn't be letting us go unimpeded.

No, I had a different plan. First distract the enemy and give them bigger cares than us. For example, if someone went over the walls and summoned the goddess Eris. The goddess of strife, after three thousand years languishing in boredom, would just go hog wild on those undying. In an instant she would find every little rift between the players and clans and skillfully puff them up into an explosive conflict.

Or... I stopped Jeanette from trying to convince me to leave with a gesture, because she was interrupting my thoughts. Or show that the

Dark Sovereign already slipped away, so it was pointless to besiege us? What if we also made them think we were staying here because they already had a portal scroll to my Castle?! It was an interesting idea, but how could I pull it off?

"Jeanette, would you happen to have a person in your clan who cannot be bought with money, and whom you don't doubt in the slightest? It would be preferable if they were also a good actor."

The swarthy muscular warrior woman considered it briefly, then smiled and pointed at one of the few men in her lady clan. I had to admit, I had already noticed this muscular athlete of such unordinary appearance. He had a tall mohawk of green hair on his bare shaven head, innumerable piercings in his ears, nose and the nipples of his bare suntanned torso, a whimsical tattoo of Iron Jeanette on his chest and no clothing at all except a sequined silver G-string.

Titanium Joker [AMAZON]
Human
Level-245 Monk of the Wind School

I had yet to conclude whether I was looking at a professional stripper or a person from the dead semi-mythical subculture of the punks. Nevertheless, his respectable level of 245 and

~ Finding a Body ~

heavy two-handed staff forced me to treat Titanium Joker with respect. As did the nimble and deadly level-203 ermine running circles around his legs, which had been dyed a glamorous shade of pink.

Iron Jeanette, not hiding her happy smile, commented on her underling's appearance:

"Don't you mind his frivolous look. That's his way of letting go of real-world concerns in the game. In real life his name is Vladimir Toropov, a Russian oligarch who owns two thirds of all businesses in the world that are in any way connected with mining and processing titanium. He told me he has already survived seventeen assassination attempts by competitors and personal enemies, while he has sent so many foes to the other side that he can't even count. We've known each other since I was eighteen, maybe twenty. He used to be my biggest admirer. He never missed an online tournament if Iron Jeanette was going to be in it. He used to give me beautiful flowers and gifts..."

"And what docs your husband think about you having an admirer in your clan? Not jealous?" I asked cautiously. But Jeanette laughed uncontrollably:

"Amra, in the real world that half-naked muscular monk turned eighty-seven a while ago, so no. My husband is not jealous. What's more,

- 289 -

Vladimir has known Paul for a long time and they get along famously. Although in real life Vladimir Toropov is totally different. There he is cautious, predatory, and doesn't trust anyone. He has more bodyguards than I have *Amazons* in my clan! And no one on the whole planet knows where his virtual reality capsule is. But when he found out that my son Andre had a racing accident, Vladimir dropped everything and rushed to the scene. He was actually the one who paid for my son's treatment. So I'd put my head on the chopping block to say he would never betray me for any amount of money! But all that stays between us. All my girls think Titanium Joker is a young professional art model, a great lover of pretty ladies and virtual sex."

Day Four
A Piece of the Puzzle

"STOP RIGHT THERE, you rapscallion!" said my Amra in the form of a giant spider, jumping off the wall. I was chasing the practically naked monk as he very gracefully dodged the many arrows my archers fired.

In response Titanium Joker just gave me the middle finger, still running and not even thinking about stopping or slowing down.

The enemy players watching this were befuddled, not knowing what was happening, or who to attack in this situation: the enemy player from the *Amazons* clan, or the huge spider coming after him? Meanwhile, taking advantage of my fourfold advantage in leg count, I quickly closed the gap between us and broke out of the Astral Explosion dome. Now! Still racing on my four jointed legs, I took out the bronze gong with my two other limbs and clanged the hammer on the fragile, time-darkened plate.

BOOOOOOOOOOONG! Despite the small size of the divine artifact, I was momentarily deafened and stumbled, tripping over my own arms and legs. Seemingly everything around was ringing: the fortress walls, the houses in town, even the cloudy sky. While I got my legs sorted out, two or three arrows pierced my body, but I rolled behind a nearby building for cover.

"You summoned me, took me away from business, and didn't even have a gift ready..." next to me was a dark-haired lady of middling years in an antique tunic. "And that's at the fact that you spoiled my brother Charon with great presents. And you also brightened old Hel's day with some gifts as well. Not good, Amra..."

I didn't even have time to respond, much less read the stats of the unique creature I'd summoned before the screen went black. On the dark backdrop, some red text ran by:

Damage taken: 55777 HP (Divine magic)

You have died.
1430000 Exp. lost

~ Finding a Body ~

One level lost!
Current level: one hundred twenty-nine
You will respawn in 59 minutes, 52 seconds at the last respawn point you set

Now that was something... I simply didn't have the words to describe my state. Sure, I had read tales of genies who spent thousands of years cooped up in a lamp. It was highly recommended not to let them out because the long years of imprisonment in a cramped cell had almost certainly wreaked havoc on the mind of the all-powerful being. Seemingly, something similar had happened with Eris. The goddess of strife had never been known for her appeasing ways, but now she wouldn't even let me say one word. All I could do now was hope the goddess hadn't spent all the anger she'd pent up over those three thousand years on little old me and the enemies players would also take a hit.

I was not planning to wait a whole hour in the darkness of the virtual reality capsule, so I opened the lid, climbing out. I quickly got dressed, had a yogurt from the fridge and a hastily made sandwich, after which I took a seat at the computer and opened the *Boundless Realm* forum. I was extremely interested in what was happening in Lars after my forced disappearance.

Woah! There was a thread about that very

topic, and messages were piling in faster than I could read them. There was a real ass-kicking underway. The players weren't sharing the loot from the Dark Sovereign. That meant the legendary Amulet of the King of Lars had probably dropped along with a whole mountain of silver coins, probably just under three hundred thousand. The fight over my loot had now grown into a pitched inter-clan battle that threatened to spill over into a full-scale war. The dead already numbered in the hundreds, and that was seemingly just the beginning. No one had written a word about the goddess Eris, though. It was as if she wasn't even there. But there was already enough resentment between allies to fill a small pool.

The generals that commanded the players in Lars had refused to handle the loot issue as they had a personal stake. But they were looking high and low for who had caused the allies to fight amongst themselves at such an importune moment, allowing the Dark Sovereign's army to retreat from the old part of the city unpunished. I read some who thought it was bribery and betrayal. Accusations were piling up left and right. Former allies were looking at one another like wolves, not trusting anyone.

Information on Titanium Joker was extremely scant. Yes, a few players had seen the half-naked monk darting through the narrow alleys of Lars, or at least his red hostile marker. I even found a message that the runaway was killed eventually. But did Titanium Joker reach the respawn stone, which is where he was headed in our plan? I still didn't know. Although a lack of concrete information was probably a positive sign. It meant that my truly serious opponents still perceived one of the *Amazons* betraying the clan with extreme gravity and were trying not to spread that information.

Alright then, although I was not planning for my character to die, and wanted to just about catch the runaway, then use a portal scroll to run from the huge number of enemies nearby, everything else went according to plan. Titanium Joker had taken his portal scroll leading "right to the Dark Sovereign's fortress" and brought it to my enemies, while my army managed to leave the old city with all the loot and prisoners. Now it all depended on the acting and negotiating skills of that "poor young artist's model." Hopefully he could convince my enemies the scroll was the real deal, and they'd attempt to attack the Dark Sovereign's castle.

Iron Jeanette privately advised that he demand not game money, but real money to make it more plausible and to negotiate his way up to one hundred thousand before agreeing. To that the

Russian oligarch answered with a smirk that, when it came to negotiations and business, he knew more than one way to skin a cat. He would ascertain how to treat the buyers and when to stop negotiating to make everything look completely natural. Well, I had a lot of hope in Vladimir Toropov's professionalism and acting abilities.

If I considered it, the death of the Dark Sovereign was actually to our benefit here, making it more believable, which would allow Titanium Joker to ask for more money. There were also other minor details that lent the story credence. I waited to see a topic about it on the *Boundless Realm* forum and eventually it did come up! The players started discussing a message they'd all seen that the forbidden spell had been used once again, but in the lands of the Dark Sovereign. This time the Astral Explosion dome covered the Sovereign's castle itself and some nearby lands. It might have seemed minor, but the buyers of the portal scroll would be sure to notice it. If the Dark Sovereign feared invasion and was taking measures against it, he must have known he'd lost a portal scroll leading to his castle.

There was still some time left before respawn, so I sat down and started making the next daily video about the adventures of my big-eared goblin. No, I wouldn't have been able to make the whole video in thirty minutes, but I was planning to at least cut the many hours of gaming down into the parts that my viewers would enjoy. The *Amazons*, our visit to Lars, freeing the prisoners, the death of the King... There was more than enough interesting material. I was doing that editing when Tina silently slipped into my office.

"Hello, Timothy! It's hard to catch you in the real world, you're always in the game."

And again Tina looked different. Her hair was no longer purple but bright red. Instead of a form-fitting dress with a very deep neckline, she was now wearing a little top so short and nearly see-through that I was baffled as to how it even stayed on over her ample breasts. And add to that the jean shorts, which were very tiny and gave great emphasis to the length and fitness of the legs of "Miss Boundless Realm."

I answered her greeting, meanwhile unwittingly staring at the wall clock. It was six thirty. I remembered the note she left yesterday where she scheduled a meeting for eight. But then why come an hour and a half early? Was she watching my character in the game, saw me die and was expecting me to come into the real world? A seemingly logical explanation, but I had never seen any *Boundless Realm* streams on her monitor before. As far as I remembered, it was just social networks, pictures of cats, fashionable clothing, music and other stuff you might expect to see on the screen of a bored secretary. I also dismissed the theory that she might have been tracking my character with system commands. Tina wouldn't have had the technical knowledge for something like that, and she didn't have the access privileges. So then what explained her early arrival?

"The cameras in your room have been turned off." How could I believe that! It was the most obvious explanation. The people watching me had seen me leave the virtual reality capsule and given her a hand-wave, summoning the pretty girl before their elusive employee went back into the game. Or even... what was it Leon said today...? Tina told him she had no idea where my office was, and had never come here. An interesting fact that needed to be thought over. And the pretty lady's clothing... I found it extremely hard to imagine the assistant of the austere Special Projects Department director looking like that at work. Would she have had time to change? And then she walked through the whole building at peak time in such provocative attire? For some reason I had a very hard time believing that. At the end of the day, this was a serious organization with a dress code, not some red-light district. I felt I'd nearly guessed what was happening. I just needed one tiny detail, one little clue to make the pieces of the puzzle come together.

~ Finding a Body ~

"So, you wanted to tell me something?" I asked, politely inviting my guest to sit on the sofa as I opened the mini-bar in search of something light that she might enjoy.

Maybe the still-unopened bottle of champagne from yesterday? I remembered putting it in the cabinet last night, because it wouldn't fit in the fridge. The wine was of course now spoiling without an ice bucket, but it was better than some brutish can of beer from the fridge. Still, I offered both.

"You know, I think I'll have a beer," my guest made an unexpected choice. "And let's leave the serious talk for later. No, I'll open it myself! Whoops... That's what I get for being so clumsy... This is pretty awkward..."

Her already revealing light top was soaked through and totally transparent. I was still closing the refrigerator, so I couldn't say whether it was truly an accident or not. It was most likely on purpose, although I didn't have any evidence. But what nice tits... And between them on a very thin chain there dangled a pendant with an electronic key, most likely to my outside door.

Tina followed my gaze and gave a chuckle:

"Yes, they're my pride and joy. All-natural D's with no surgery or implants. Would you be opposed to me just taking off my wet top? It isn't hiding anything now, just clinging to my skin. It feels so gross."

I didn't answer the provocative question, but she took my silence as consent and, pulling her tight top over her head, raised both hands. And that was when I made up my mind. I don't know what serious business Tina was planning to discuss with me, if it even existed or was just an excuse to come see me, but I figured I might never get a better chance to escape my imprisonment. So, sharply extending a hand, I grabbed fitfully for the key and gave a hard tug, breaking the thin gold chain. Tina shouted in fear and tried to lower her arms but she was too late to stop me. In two bounding leaps, I made it to the front door, raised the electronic key to the lock and...

The world around me froze. I couldn't even lift a finger! Tina also froze, her mouth open in a wordless scream, trying to reach me with her hands but tangled up in her little top. But that wasn't the last of my surprises.

"Bravo, Timothy. You made the right decision! Probably the best decision you've ever made!"

The voice seemed to ring out from every direction at once. It was muted as if coming from underwater, and I couldn't see what it's source could be. And although the voice had a clearly female timbre, it definitely did not belong to Tina.

"It's gonna be dark for a little bit now," the

same voice warned. "And as soon as the light goes out, if you value your life, hold your breath as long as you can. We need two or two and a half minutes. And if you breathe in even once before we get you out, you'll die instantly! Get ready, we'll begin in a few seconds!"

"No, I'm not ready yet!" I shouted in fear, but no answer followed so I took a few rapid breaths in and out to enrich my blood with oxygen.

And then the world around me switched off. The sounds were gone and so was the light. Even tactile sensations were just missing. It was as if I was floating in total darkness. I took in a chest full of air and froze, trying to stay still and closed off from what was going on. After all, oxygen wasn't only used by the muscles in times of physical strain. The human brain could also use lots of it and other nutrients by working actively. What was more, increased brain activity required increased heart activity, which put more strain on the circulatory system as a whole.

Damn! I knew that instead of resigning myself and lying calmly, I was actively thinking and wasting invaluable oxygen. Meanwhile my air was already running out. Holding my breath just got harder and harder. How much did they say again? Two minutes, maybe two and a half... No, only trained divers could last that long. I was sure I could easily reach a minute and a half. I'd never tested it with a timer though... And seemingly this was my limit. Everything inside me was burning up. Another few seconds, and that would be it...

Wait, was that some kind of sound? I perked up my ears, having decided to hold out no matter what it cost. Then an unbearably bright light blasted into my vision! I exhaled loudly, blinked my teary eyes and even tried to turn my head away or cover my eyes with my arms. My arms... what was happening? Why couldn't I move them???

Several dark figures loomed over me in gas masks. A respirator and some kind of straps were torn off my face. One of the figures leaned in lower, unceremoniously grabbing me by the chin, turning my head and shining a light directly into my eyes. Without a word, the figure straightened up and walked away. But I did see a metal tool in the hands of another approaching stranger. it wasn't quite a bolt cutter or pliers, it almost looked like a huge pair of metal shears. A couple seconds later my wrists were released from a pair of metal cuffs. Then a pair of strong arms lifted me and helped me sit up. I took a look around.

I didn't recognize this room. The walls were metal, and the lighting was very bright. There were around ten people around me in rubberized jumpsuits, and all of them had on gas masks. Some were even armed. Where was I? And who were all these people?

~ Finding a Body ~

"Where should we bring him now?" the voice sounded vaguely familiar, and I turned toward it.

"To the medical center, the attendant doctor on the second floor. The doctor must examine Timothy," the tall man answered. His voice was distorted by the gas mask but also seemed familiar.

"No! It's too risky!" the shortest of all of them stepped forward. This new person had a feminine voice. Seemingly, this was the woman I'd been speaking with recently. "I'll take him with me. He's my responsibility."

Kira?! The voice was extremely distorted by the gas mask, but still recognizable. I couldn't see her face, but the powerful tone and body dimensions also gave away my girlfriend's identity. Seemingly, that suggestion was not to the liking of the "tall one." He was either cursing bombastically or shouting an emotional phrase in a language I didn't know. Behind him were two bulky guys holding snub-nosed machine guns as backup. Woah! It looked like there were at least two distinct groups here, and their interests and plans for me didn't exactly coincide. The "short one" (probably a woman, who I suspected was Kira) wasn't the least bit afraid to see her opponent's companions brandish their weapons and remained stubborn:

"Think for yourself, we still don't know who did the kidnapping, or who they might be working with. It's too risky to leave Timothy in the corporation building, or to allow anyone to perform medical procedures on him. I can provide the proper care, and a full examination. You know that I have the capabilities to do that. Please, at least now don't argue!"

I finally became convinced the lady was none other than Kira. Her harsh tone, and voice were too characteristic even despite the muffling. But who was her opponent? For a few seconds the two arguers looked right into one another's eyes, as if playing the staring game right in their gas masks. But the tall one relented:

"Alright. Take him. He'll be your responsibility. But tomorrow at exactly nine AM I expect you both at the meeting..." here he stumbled midsentence, tossed a quick gaze over me and slightly adjusted. "No, there's no reason for Timothy to attend a shareholder's meeting yet. That would cause idle chitchat and complications. Then I expect him in my office for a private conversation at ten thirty."

Half the people immediately left, leaving me with five. The largest of them picked up the metal shears again and freed my legs, which were held down with a steel wire so thick I couldn't even draw in my knees and cover my nakedness. Yes, I had already seen that, other than the wire-enmeshed sensor suit, I had no other clothing on.

~ Finding a Body ~

I was helped out, freed from the mesh and I turned around, finally able to see my prison from a different angle.

Beyond all doubt, this was a virtual reality capsule. But along with the usual set of wires coming out of it, there were also hoses leading to gas tanks and big semi-transparent tanks on the outside. One was full of water, the second with some kind of whitish porridge-like nutrient slurry. And there was no more than a third left in the food and water tank. What was more, from what I could see, the device was not made to take a second set of tanks. I felt a sense of doom after realizing what would have happened in a few days.

"Thank you Kira for finding me and getting me out of here."

Hearing my words and noting my interest in the clever device, the group leader walked up closer and commented:

"Yeah, Timothy, this isn't the first time I've saved your ass. But I couldn't have done it without your hints. Who could have thought a virtual reality capsule with a player inside could be brought into the sealed server floor, which is filled with toxic gas?! But let's save the talking for later. Right now we need to get you to a doctor. But before that we need to get you washed up."

She was right, too. Both about the doctor and the shower. I discovered with great surprise and dismay that there was an inflamed bright-red jagged scar on my chest. I couldn't even touch it because that made a sharp pulsating pain wash over my whole rib cage. And I definitely understood why I needed to get hosed down right away. In fact I could even smell the ghastly stench coming off my body. Although most modern virtual reality capsules had a UV cleaning function, which sanitized the device between gaming sessions, even the most advanced models had no functionality for prolonged stays, and no way of eliminating human waste.

KIRA WAS STANDING at a huge panorama window with a mug of hot coffee in her hands, staring down from sixteen hundred feet at the glimmering metropolis below. In a light track suit, I was sitting in a chair in silence, afraid to interrupt her thinking. Was she even still my girlfriend? The wall of alienation between us was now unmistakable. In all the time since she found me earlier today, Kira hadn't given single word, gesture or even tiny hint about the state of our relationship. What was more, the red-headed pretty lady was clearly ashamed and avoiding me.

But I could understand that. We hadn't seen

one another for two whole weeks. That was easily enough time to sober up from a fleeting crush. Maybe all her warm feelings for me were gone. It had been long enough to unravel her naïve illusions and take a rational look at things. She was of course the co-owner of the largest corporation on the planet, one of the richest women on Earth, and still young and insanely beautiful. She may have been the most envied and desirable woman on the planet. And who was I? Maybe I was no longer "nobody." I was after all a fairly famous *Boundless Realm* player, who had made a name for himself in some high-profile events and who had earned a decent amount of money. But even with all my achievements in the game, the chasm in our social status was practically insurmountable.

Also, today clearly wasn't doing me any favors. When Kira met me, I was athletic, pleasant and happy-looking. That's who she remembered. But the man who recently crawled out of the virtual reality capsule could barely stand, was horribly dirty and so sickly thin he was nearly dead. And I was in so much pain I needed immediate attention from a doctor. My stitches were inflamed, so I suspected I would need a massive dose of antibiotics, pain killers and stimulants. I couldn't see Kira's face yet, but I suspected my girlfriend wasn't even trying to hide her grimace of disgust. As soon as she got the chance, Kira handed me off to her underlings, then hurried to retreat. And it was hard for me to judge her for that. I truly was quite the indecent spectacle.

After seeing the doctor, armed people wearing badges from the Boundless Realm Corporation Security Service brought me straight here on a flier with tinted windows. I wasn't even close to appreciating what this place was. I only understood that I was not in Kira's normal home. The room was just too small, and the decor didn't match the palace of the richest young beauty on Earth. And this was not one of the modest apartments that belonged to Kira on floor-333 of the residential skyscraper the Castle, either. We were in a totally different neighborhood of the metropolis. And this also didn't have an elevated flier landing pad like the Castle. But no matter how I strained my memory, I couldn't remember any other residential skyscrapers in the metropolis that were this tall.

Then I asked for a telephone so I could get in touch with my sister. I was still not sure my troubles were all behind us. I was constantly expecting a hitch of some kind and didn't think she would let me have the phone. I was afraid that instead of the phone, she would just try to talk me out of it with empty promises. But no, one of Kira's bodyguards almost instantly gave me his cell phone, so I could finally talk with Val. My little sister was delighted to hear my voice and couldn't hide her tears of joy. I explained why I had suddenly disappeared from the game, told her about my misadventures in the real world and promised I would come see her tomorrow morning in the clinic. I also gave her my instructions for the Astral Explosion dome and the upcoming meeting with Taisha. The traps should work just as well without the Dark Sovereign having to actually be there.

"Timothy, I feel so guilty!"

I shuddered and turned in surprise. Kira broke the long, almost half-hour silence and not with the words I was afraid to hear. The redheaded lady looked me right in the eyes, and her face was damp with tears.

"You've always told me the truth, even though it sounded totally crazy. But I couldn't believe my own boyfriend! Instead I started imagining grievances, not answering phone calls and not noticing the obvious. Who could say what might have happened, if I believed what you said last time we were together? Maybe none of these horrible things would have happened!"

I didn't respond, allowing her to say her fill. It seemed like a rhetorical question anyway.

"But Timothy, I hope you understand it was

very hard for me as well! My grandmother passed away, and the world as I knew it fell apart right before my eyes! When Inessa Tyle died, everything just went topsy-turvy! The corporation's highly-ranked directors, who used to smile at me obsequiously every time we met, showed their true animal nature. Problems piled up all at once from every direction. I got the impression these seemingly unconnected events were being orchestrated by someone. At first most of my shares in the Boundless Realm Corporation were frozen because of some trumped-up lawsuit. Just a week ago no court would even have agreed to consider such a pathetic case! But everything changed, my stocks were frozen, and now the case won't be heard for a month. At the same time, my bank accounts were frozen for a totally different reason. After that, someone tried to murder me... you probably know that my Black Crystal was totaled, right?"

No, I didn't, which I told her. Kira gave a bitter chuckle:

"Lots of news channels talked about it without identifying the owner of the Black Crystal of course. There was a bomb planted under the engine right inside our building's guarded parking lot. A technician died when servicing my flier. I hadn't used the flying car for two days before that because I started hearing weird noises when it got up high, so I called an air-tech. Only that saved me!"

"So, what did the security cameras show?" I asked. And Kira just gave a good-natured smile:

"What do you think? Obviously nothing. No one even came near my car! But by then I had already seen a lot of issues with security camera footage. For example, there was no activity at all near your work cabin on your last day there. It was as if you didn't even come to work the day that guy tried to kill you. And of course, there was no footage of them moving your unconscious body through the building, either. Why did you think it took me so long to find you? If I hadn't gotten this video clip to my phone, which clearly shows a group of people pulling you from your cabin and carrying your bloodied body to the service elevator with the technician's corpse, we definitely would have stopped looking by now."

Well, well... I suggested aloud that the message must have come from Taisha.

"I don't know, it only said unknown number," Kira answered quietly. "I assigned a group of specialists to trace it, but that only revealed that it came from inside *Boundless Realm*. They were not able to determine an identity. But in one way or another, this guardian angel of yours had unedited footage from our security systems. After watching them we managed to determine that you were transported via the service elevator, which is usually disabled. It exits onto the tester floor, underground parking garages and a few floors that are isolated from the rest of the building. We found nothing in the garages, so I went to the president of the corporation for permission to open and look through the server floors. If you only knew how hard that was, Timothy! I had to get so many people to agree to unlock these toxic-gas-filled rooms! If not for Thomas Heywood personally taking part in the search, I'm afraid I never would have managed to force my way through the whole bureaucratic labyrinth."

"So, that tall man you were arguing with next to the virtual reality capsule was the President of the Boundless Realm Corporation?" I asked, just wanting to test a theory.

"Yes, it was him. You see, Timothy, in your last video you seriously wounded his ego with your biting expressions. And you aimed them not only at the corporation he leads but the man himself. So Thomas Heywood was looking for you and was eager to join my search party."

Any other day, that would have put me on guard or even scared me, but not today. What could the president do to me now? Officially reprimand me? Fine me? Fire me? I had just escaped a death trap alive, despite my kidnappers' clever tricks. In comparison with that, my work problems seemed laughably minor. If my highest superior was upset, that didn't bother me in the slightest. Especially because I had a way to respond to any hostility. I could put the corporation to shame before my millions of viewers by talking about my imprisonment and the mortal danger it put me in. And that would kick up so much shit, everything that came before would seem like roses!

"Don't worry, there's no reason for you to fear Thomas Heywood," Kira said, anxiously construing my thinking and trying to perk me up. "He of all people wants your story getting out the least. Especially in light of the upcoming board of directors meeting, where they will hear reports about the corporation's affairs and have the traditional presidential re-elections. The re-elections used to be a mere formality, but not this time..."

"Why?" I asked, because Kira fell silent before revealing the particularities of the upcoming vote.

"It's all very simple, Timothy. It's just math. Inessa Tyle's share of company stocks, plus mine and those of Thomas Heywood are enough to pass anything, in other words more than fifty percent plus one share. Everyone knows that perfectly well, both the other directors, and the very influential and somewhat mysterious co-owners behind them. They usually stay out of sticky situations and just go along with whatever we want. The Boundless Realm Corporation has always been basically a Tyle family business. Thomas Heywood respected my grandmother greatly and actively sought my hand in marriage. He was basically a member of the family."

Then my redheaded girlfriend fell silent, as if she wasn't sure she should share this information with me. But she still decided to continue:

"My grandmother held more than a few very old-fashioned viewpoints. She thought that for a strong marriage, both partners must be on the same rung of the social ladder. And so Inessa Tyle helped the ambitious and talented Thomas Heywood pile up a huge fortune with stock buybacks. And although Thomas and I dated very briefly, never even officially becoming a couple, the current president was very grateful and loyal to Inessa Tyle until the very last day of her life. But now all that has changed... My shares are frozen, so I'm temporarily locked out of the fight. Thomas Heywood is playing his own game, trying to get help from the other co-owners and thus retain his high position. Thomas is having a very hard time and can sense a huge resistance, so he needs some wins to show them right here and now. And that is exactly why the president is trying so hard to avoid getting the corporation into any scandals!"

I see... But Kira wasn't saying anything about what happened to the shares belonging to Vice-President Inessa Tyle. Also frozen? I asked that.

"Her will is in a sealed envelope, which is to be opened at the big yearly board of directors meeting. Officially no one knows anything. But a few days before dying, my grandmother told me what it says. And yes, Timothy, I can tell you now. Inessa Tyle really liked you, and she added you to her will! But your share can change significantly depending on a few factors. In any case we're talking about a colossal amount of money! Hundreds of millions or even billions, Timothy!"

Woah! Fantastic news! However, based on the alarm in Kira's voice, it was still too early to celebrate. My girlfriend took a long evaluating glance at me, studying my reaction to the important piece of news. She was clearly not satisfied with it, because from there she limited herself to just excuses and half-hints:

"Until recently I figured that I was the only one who knew what was in that will, as Inessa Tyle's only granddaughter who she loved so dearly. But the more I think about what happened to you, the more I feel certain that this could not have been random chance. You see, Timothy..." the redheaded beauty hesitated, choosing her words. "Inessa Tyle did not think she would die this soon and was planning for her machinations to be revealed at a much later board meeting. In a year, or maybe even two, but not just two short weeks. And because of that condensed time-frame, a few of the possibilities in her will are now totally implausible."

I didn't understand one bit of her vague explanation, but when I asked her to tell me more, she refused categorically. I had to come at it from a different angle:

"But then why kidnap me, and especially why set up this complicated virtual office system?"

Kira started smiling, set an empty coffee mug on the table and walked a step closer:

"That may not have been just for you. Perhaps you know this, but the game is nowhere near the only thing our corporation does. *Boundless Realm* is a huge testing ground for new technologies. I recently read some reports about how far we've come in the field of virtualization. And you just got to test out our new technology. Impressed?"

I decided not to deny the obvious. In all the days of my imprisonment, despite my periodic suspicions that my reality was false or digitized, I couldn't detect any evidence that I was in a virtual world. That was exactly what I told her. Kira smiled happily, as if that was her department and took another few steps in my direction.

"So then, Timothy, I can answer the question of 'how,' although I don't know the finer points. And the only thing I know about who is behind this is that it must be someone very high up and well-informed. But who exactly? I do not know. However, I do know why. You see, Inessa Tyle's will is clear about the fact that if you are alive and well when the envelope is opened, and you have allowed your real life to suffer in favor of burying your head in the game, your inheritance will go to the board of directors. My grandma wanted to see you active, alive and joyful in the real world and not... excuse the vulgar expression... some jackoff gamer."

The red-headed beauty walked another step closer. I then gathered my courage and, trying not to wince at the dull pain from my stitches, stood up from the sofa and walked toward her. I was not at all sure that Kira would take this positively. But all this lack of clarity in our relationship was getting to me, so let come what may! I decisively embraced my girlfriend and squeezed her tight. And Kira didn't object one bit! In fact, she squeezed herself up to me and our lips came together in a hot passionate kiss. When we finally unstuck our lips after a whole eternity, the most beautiful and desired woman on the planet whispered:

"Timothy, you can't even imagine how much I've missed you!"

Day Four

Talking with the President

"TIMOTHY, GET UP, you have to see this!" I was awoken by jabs to the shoulder that grew more insistent with every second. My groans of dismay did nothing to stop Kira and the beautiful redhead kept going until I got up.

I peeled my eyes open with huge effort, raised my sleepy head and tried to look around. It was three AM based on the glowing wall clock. Why the hell had Kira woken me up now?! I fell asleep just forty minutes ago. A semigloom reigned in the sleeping room, so at first I didn't even understand what my girlfriend wanted to show me. Her flawless body, barely covered with a semitransparent pair of underwear? An enticing offer, no argument there. I would be delighted to continue last night's playful romp... But it turned out to be something else.

"Not now," Kira said, slapping away my bold, outstretched hand. "Come into the living room. On the big wall screen, I put on a broadcast from a popular gaming channel about *Boundless Realm*. And they just so happen to be talking about the Dark Sovereign!"

Me? I was interested to see what they were saying. I just wanted to find my underwear... But my clothing had been flung God-knows-where while Kira and I were passionately kissing and undressing one another, and I hadn't found it yet in the darkness of the bedroom. So I wrapped myself in a bedsheet and walked into the living room, yawning and trying to wake myself up. There was an image frozen on the screen: some guy in huge earphones with a microphone, his eyes rolling and his mouth slightly open in a way that looked silly. With the remote, my girlfriend restarted the paused broadcast.

Based on his first words, I immediately guessed what the reporter was talking about with such glee and enthusiasm, all the more so because I assumed it would go something like this. As soon as the Astral Explosion spell dome went away, the players tried to attack the castle of the Dark Sovereign! They got ready, gathered a huge army and, a mere couple of hours after the battle in Lars, managed to multiply the "ill-begotten" portal scroll hundreds or even thousands of times. And that huge group of players, in their greed for a speedy victory — the hundreds of clans that came to the war, tens of thousands of fighters — ran through the open portals all at the same time, counting on the element of surprise, the late hour and the mass scale of the attack. Tsk, tsk... When exiting the portals, they were awaited by a ninety-foot drop into a raging ocean teeming with bloodthirsty creatures who seemed to be anticipating a feast. And reaching the nearest shore would have been a bit of an issue. It was over eighteen hundred miles away...

Most of the unfortunate players were badly hurt by the big fall or drowned immediately in their heavy armor. And those who knew how to swim were eaten up in a matter of minutes by ruthless sca monsters. None of the players survived, even members of underwater races like Naiads and Mermaids. What was more, some of the players had seen the Dark Sovereign walking atop the raging waves, and the sea monsters didn't touch him. The most resilient players even tried to attack their main enemy, but the superboss couldn't be damaged by any means. Not magic, not prayers, not weapons. And he just laughed offensively at their pitiful vain attempts to do him harm. Overall, the scheme to attack the Dark Sovereign's castle sunk in a matter of minutes in the literal and figurative senses.

On the forum, tens of thousands of players were mutually outraged. They had already begun believing they could win a speedy victory over the Dark Sovereign, but he played a dirty trick on them. And that wasn't even the worst part! That came an hour later, when all the players who died discovered that they were respawning basically naked! No weapons, no armor, no jewelry like magic rings, bracelets or amulets. All that remained on the undying were indestructible loincloths or chastity belts, depending on their initial race and gender settings.

The *Boundless Realm* forums hadn't seen such a deafening cry of dismay even during the Great Hunt for my Royal Forest Wyvern! However, the difference in how the players treated these global events was colossal. Here for every player who was outraged there came at least a dozen who were happy and left variously mocking comments about the "idiots who tricked the Dark Sovereign." Some who were "in the know" were even saying how much the dupes paid for the "invaluable portal scroll to the Dark Sovereign's castle" which had been multiplied so many times: two hundred forty-five thousand credits. That was a huge figure by any standards. It didn't seem possible to check, and more likely it was just invented out of whole cloth, but the outraged players demanded Titanium Joker be banned for fraud.

However, tech support reacted dispassionately to all the outrage and threats, saying it was all within the game mechanics. Yes, Titanium Joker never actually betrayed the Dark Sovereign. Yes, it was a trap all along. Yes, the only thing around the portal exit was an endless sea, and they had no chance of escaping without a ship. Yes, there was a very high drop chance for worn items in that location. Yes, the aquatic monsters were lured to that location on purpose. And all that was done in strict accordance with the game rules. What was more no one had forced the players to go to such an unwelcoming place, so any appeals about lost items and levels would not be considered. Adding to that, the army that died in full was not even the first to be tricked. One hour earlier, another group of guests had been caught in the clever trap. There was even a separate topic about it on the forums.

Kira stopped the recording and turned to me for an explanation:

"Timothy, I am not following this. What happened there? Who were these other guests?

And how could you have been there if you were with me the whole time? Did they let the bot replace you again?"

I laughed happily and explained, not hiding my pride:

"The *Legion of Steel* got tricked first before it was even midnight. To be more accurate, just their rapid-response force, which is always online and ready for combat. The issue is that the highest-level players of the Southern Continent were very dishonest, taking advantage of the trust of the naïve NPC Taisha to place an item in her inventory that would summon the *Legion of Steel* if she saw the Dark Sovereign at any point. And there was no way to throw the dangerous item away or get rid of it, so I had to set up a scenario that could trip the conditions."

Kira still didn't understand, so I had to explain in greater detail:

"Yes, I ordered that devious trap. It was made to look like a commonplace and absolutely safe location, but it was actually just illusions layered on illusions, all topped off with yet another illusion. At exactly midnight, Taisha met with another NPC who was disguised with illusion magic to look like the Dark Sovereign. The scroll triggered and the portal opened automatically, then the *Legion of Steel* squadron flooded out. Taisha was warned what would happen, so she had a few seconds to get away. From there it was all simple: while the players tried to take down the untouchable NPC, the air platform they were all standing on collapsed and the *Legion of Steel* forces tumbled into the ocean where all those hungry monsters awaited them. By the way, if I was the president of the corporation, I would look into who programmed that trap, because whoever it is must have something to do with my kidnapping."

"Wait, wait, wait! That is very important information!" Kira demanded I tell her more detail.

I had nothing to hide, and I told her about my understandings with the fictitious Andrei Soloviev, who in reality was director of the In-Game Security Service. Then I said the people who kidnapped me were obsessed with the idea of capturing Taisha on a special server. Kira got up from her armchair, walked over to her charging cell phone and went into the neighboring room, closing the door tight behind her.

Of course I could have come closer to the door to listen in on my girlfriend's conversation with her former lover, but I didn't. That would have been poor form, unworthy behavior. Instead I picked up the remote and pressed play.

The reporter finished the story of the unsuccessful attack and said that the players were planning to get back their lost equipment as soon as possible. To do that they were going to hire experienced water mages and some players from undersea races, buy underwater breathing scrolls and prepare for the monster-filled ocean and an encounter with the Dark Sovereign, who they believed would also be there.

Hrm, best of luck to them... The Dark Sovereign they had seen walking on water was actually my Demon of Avarice, the indestructible Storekeeper. Valerianna Quickfoot had placed an illusion on the demon to make it look like me and sent it out to meet Taisha at midnight. And it should have long since returned to my castle. The only explanation that came to mind to explain a possible delay was that there was too much valuable loot from the high-level *Legion of Steel* players. Only that could have made the Storekeeper hang back and witness the main attack. Knowing the Storekeeper's impossibly greedy character, I had no doubt that he gathered up all the most valuable and rare objects on the sea floor to take back to my castle. The exceptionally greedy demon had just one portal scroll, so it must have been hard to decide what to take with him.

Ugh, I hadn't thought to provide my servant with enough magic scrolls! The demon would have been very reluctant to abandon the remaining valuables. And if I had made him a few scrolls, my servant had no fear of the ocean depths nor sea monsters, so he could have gone back and forth bringing valuables up from the sea floor until he had it all to the last algae-covered coin.

Kira came back into the room and said she'd sent my information on to "the right people." The luxuriant redhead, insanely beautiful and sexy in her semitransparent negligee, shot a glance at the paused image on the screen, then turned her gaze to me. There were little hellfires now dancing in my girlfriend's eyes. The corners of her lips turned up into a slight smile. Kira clearly had an enticing and pleasant idea for the both of us... But we were interrupted.

The front door flew open without warning and the head of Kira's personal bodyguard who I now knew well walked or more like flew into the room. I didn't know his name yet, because he had never introduced himself, while Kira had never called him by name in my presence. Barely glancing at me, the bodyguard turned to my girlfriend:

"Kirena Tyle, we've noted suspicious activity on the external security perimeter. Some strange figures are observing the building from the windows of the neighboring skyscraper. We have spotted professional optics and comms, we have detected encoded messages being exchanged with unknown accomplices via radio. What's more, a semi-military flying vehicle has been circling this part of the metropolis for twenty minutes with its lights off. We were unable to find its plates in the aircraft database. That may be a simple coincidence and, if things were entirely calm, I wouldn't even have noticed. But these are hectic times, it couldn't just be nothing. I have taken the decision to evacuate!"

I was expecting Kira to object or argue, but nothing of the sort followed. In this moment of danger, the co-owner of the biggest corporation on the planet immediately became extremely concentrated and just asked her security chief where he suggested they go — to her well defended palace?

"That's out. Someone is keeping watch over the Land of Gloom, I have already seen pictures of the individuals apprehended on your property and the spy equipment they were carrying. What's more, yesterday evening we spotted an individual on the roof of the neighboring building with a portable homing-rocket system. Unfortunately he saw our strike team and got away. But there's no guarantee that he didn't just move to some other position, or that he came alone."

"Then what are your suggestions? As far as I understand, the Castle is also out, right?" Kira asked, probably less curious than just confirming a guess. Meanwhile, she was hurriedly getting dressed, not ashamed at the men in the room. I also got dressed, having found my stuff balled up in the corner.

"Of course the Castle is out. Ms. Tyle, the shelter on floor 333 has been insecure ever since you let that policeman scan the identification chip implanted in your palm. Everything the police know, our enemies also do because they have full access to the police database. And the radio-activated bomb in the Castle elevator shaft serves as clear confirmation of that, as do the quadcopters we've seen suspiciously flitting by floor-333. By the way..." the guardsman stopped short and turned to me for the first time, "Timothy it just slipped my mind. A week and a half ago, for safety purposes, I disabled all old keys to floor 333. I just kept waiting for you to come get a new one."

"What???" Kira started hissing like an enraged orange kitten. "So what does that mean? Timothy spent ten days without a roof over his head and you didn't even tell me?!"

"Ms. Kirena Tyle, you gave me an unambiguous order to stop tracking Timothy," the security head tried to justify himself and reminded his employer about the promise to stop tracking my every step. "So I had no idea why your boyfriend didn't come for new keys, or what was going on with him at all for that matter."

For a second it seemed that my enraged

girlfriend would throw herself on her bodyguard with fists or, even worse, scratch his eyes out. I had to intervene right away. I stood between Kira and her employee and said I was hiding from the Grave Worms gang and that I had spent the night in my gaming cabin twice. I had even brought groceries there so I wouldn't have to show my face in the breaks between gaming sessions. And then I got kidnapped, and couldn't even think about the keys...

Kira, now fully dressed, suddenly approached me, grabbed me with both hands and looked me right in the eyes. My girlfriend clearly had something important she wanted to tell me. But first she gave me the old song and dance about her shame:

"Timothy, I feel so guilty! I promised to give you a place to live. And you believed me, but I didn't keep it. A Tyle's word is just an empty sound, though! It has the power to found and merge corporations, purchase luxury yachts and tropical islands and make billions of other deals! So to compensate my guilt and not feel so uncomfortable, I'll give you one wish! And I'll do whatever you ask, as long as it's in my power, or my name isn't Kirena Tyle!"

The guard leader couldn't hold back and gave a quiet curse. Clearly he wasn't expecting his charge to do something so foolish. But I reacted with surprising calm. And it wasn't because I had already gotten such a generous gift from my redheaded girlfriend and wasted it on a promise to stop spying on me. This time was a totally different story. Now I had a fairly good idea of my smart and calculating girlfriend's character, so I understood that it all happened for a good reason.

Yes, Kira had just given me a fantastically expensive gift, and she had acted totally reasonably, not just on her emotions. But my girlfriend also knew me well and understood that I would not ask her for, let's say, a billion credits or a palace on a tropical island. So what was Kira hoping to hear from me, what wish? I didn't understand, so I told her that this time I would be more careful and think my wish over before I made it.

"So where are we going?" Kira turned to the bodyguard and repeated her question. "And let me remind you that, at nine in the morning, I need to be at a meeting with the president of the corporation, so going to a different hemisphere is simply out of the question!"

The security head had to think as well, so I decided to make a suggestion:

"If I understand correctly, we just have to spend a few hours here in the metropolis, right? Well what if we do something your pursuers are not expecting? Now they are keeping watch over all known homes and shelters belonging to Kira while tracking her security's fliers and vehicles. So let them track that! Have a convoy drive off with all safety precautions, then Kira and I use a normal guest telephone to call an average everyday taxi and, for example, head to a night club. Or just get on the underground and ride it to the final station on the seashore where we can meet the sunrise to the sounds of the surf."

Kira and her bodyguard's faces stretched out in surprise, so I figured I had just said something very stupid. But unexpectedly Kira supported my basically nonsensical idea:

"Well... that really would be unexpected! Everyone who's known me for a long time must be aware that I never ride city taxis or the metro, and I especially never visit restaurants or nightclubs. So long as some average security camera doesn't identify me on the way, I can just dissolve without a trace among the millions of normal people who live in the metropolis!"

The security chief started stroking the bald spot on the back of his head in thought:

"It isn't hard to block the facial recognition system. I personally know people in the police who can and will do so on my first call no questions asked. We could even get the cameras turned off temporarily for 'maintenance.' That said... I don't like this one bit..." he objected, shaking his head doubtfully. "It all sounds too haphazard, risky and ill-conceived. No. Definitely not. We can't risk it. We'll think up something else."

But Kira was stubborn and started insisting on my idea, refusing to even listen to other suggestions. It was obvious that the security chief was extremely surprised at her disobedience. This seemingly had never happened before. For some time the redheaded lady and her huge muscular hulk stared one another in the eye in strain and... the bodyguard relented!

"Alright, Ms. Tyle. But I cannot leave you two without protection, so I'll be coming with. I'll just call the police administration first and have them turn off the cameras in that area and give our guys an order to distract as many observers as possible."

IT WAS DESERTED in the metro. At the station, we didn't see a single person and the only people in our train were an amorous couple at the other end of the car, dozing off, embracing and nodding in exhaustion. I gathered my courage and sat Kira on my lap, wrapping her in my jacket because she was shivering in her light dress. And I squeezed her close. I did all that with the excuse that her red hair had to be covered with my jacket hood so no one would get curious about the glamorous lady riding public transportation and recognize her as Kirena Tyle. In fact though, I found it pleasant to feel her body near mine and just hug.

Kira's huge guardsman took a seat in the middle of the car and quite plausibly pretended to sleep, at times even giving very natural sounding snores. At first I admired his acting ability and even got surprised. I mean, who was he putting on such a masterful show for? But then I realized he really was just drifting off. Kira was also having a hard time fighting off sleep, her eyes closed and her head resting on my shoulder.

"This is just great!" she whispered right into my ear. "I almost forgot what it's like to feel this much peace and tranquility. I only felt this safe in early childhood when my parents held me."

I didn't flesh out the topic, which was painful both to me and Kira, because my parents died in a flying car crash. In fact, it was the same accident that took my sister Valeria's legs. And I knew practically nothing about her parents. I had just heard that long ago they lost custody of her for some reason, so she had been raised by her grandmother Inessa Tyle since her earliest years. Instead of responding, I just kissed Kira. She started smiling and opened her eyes. She glanced at her sleeping bodyguard and made a suggestion in a conspiratorial tone:

"Timothy, how about we run away? When else will we have the chance to just walk around the city at night and be free? I'm so sick of constantly being watched!"

It was a very adventuresome and even risky suggestion. There had recently been an attempt on Kira's life and she was being searched for by unknown assassins. But I could hear so much pleading in her voice it was almost a prayer. I just couldn't say no. Just then the train stopped at yet another empty station, so we quietly slipped out of the open door. A minute later, we were standing at the exit, just happy to be breathing in the chilly night air.

An unfamiliar neighborhood. Not the center, but also not the criminal slums on the outskirts. This was just a totally average street, like thousands of others in the metropolis. The office buildings were closed for the night, their windows all dark. I saw a many-story electric-car parking lot. Near it was a small park with well-groomed gravel paths. Street lamps turned on when we got near and went out behind us. It might seem strange and even stupid, but we didn't need anything more. We walked through the darkened city embracing, and we felt good. We would talk about nothing, but more often kept silent and enjoyed the rare moment of absolute freedom and happiness.

We met the sunrise at a viewpoint that looked out over the urban core of the metropolis with its unbelievably tall buildings and many-level highway tangles. Somewhere in that big mix of skyscrapers was the *Boundless Realm* building, but we couldn't see it. We weren't the only people there though. A few dozen intrepid photographers had their phone cameras at the ready, also awaiting the sunrise. And now the time had come and the tops of the tallest buildings started lighting up with orange sunlight. It was very pretty.

That was exactly when I decided to confess that I loved Kira more than life itself and couldn't keep going without her. I told her that I needed nothing more on this planet than my crazily beautiful ginger hothead, and asked Kira to be my wife. Listening with a happy smile, she suddenly went sullen and asked, now alarmed:

"Timothy, who told you? Answer me! It's important!"

"What are you talking about?" I didn't understand, but Kira wasn't listening anymore.

She wriggled out of my embrace and the beautiful redhead shouted angrily right in my face:

"I thought you liked me! But you... How could you?!"

Kira wound up and slapped me in the face

with all her might. After that, she sharply turned around and, drying her tears with her hands, ran to one of the flying taxis waiting next to the viewpoint. She gave a short command to the driver, jumped inside and slammed the door loudly. Thirty seconds later the taxi was out of view beyond a white cloud.

And I was just standing there with my cheek on fire, no phone to contact anyone and not a single coin in my pocket. But all those problems meant nothing in comparison with the fact that I felt as low as a person can feel. For a moment I totally forgot about the social gulf that divided Kira and I, and coming back down to the real world after that alluring fairy-tale life was very painful.

A NEW BUSINESS SUIT straight from the tailor's, a clean-cut visage, a nice haircut and expensive cologne. Nothing in my appearance spoke to the fact that, a mere six hours ago, I was abandoned in a random part of the city with no money or means of communication. An elderly lady helped me out, lending me her phone to make one call. Max Sochnier was a great help too because, thankfully, I remembered his phone number. After that I reached my apartment on floor-333 of the

Castle, and all the rest was just a matter of time.

At precisely eleven o'clock, I knocked at the door leading to the luxurious office of the President of the Boundless Realm Corporation. Thomas Heywood invited me in, greeted me drily and pointed me to the guest chair. After shaking hands, the president took a wet-nap from a desk drawer and started systematically wiping down his palm and fingers. If it weren't for Kira telling me about his pathological health obsession, I would have been surprised and even offended. I also saw on the desk before the president... yes, that's what it was, clear as day... It was my termination papers! I could clearly make out my name in the blank! And it even already had Thomas Heywood's employee number and signature. All it needed was my signature on an empty line. My heart simply stopped.

Finally, his hands once again pristine, the president threw the used napkin into the trash incinerator and got to the conversation:

"Timothy, I am extremely upset by what has happened in the last few days!"

"Well Thomas, imagine how I feel about it!" I answered him back tit for tat.

And really, what was the point of holding back or shrinking now?! The worst had already come to pass. I had been fired, so I wasn't in any mind to hold back. I had so many pent-up complaints about this company and I was prepared to voice them all now right to the face of its chief executive.

Thomas simply choked on air at my impudence, sitting frozen with his mouth wide open. For five seconds, we bored into one another with smoldering gazes. Then Thomas Heywood averted his eyes and spoke quietly, looking to the side:

"Hrm... Kirena Tyle has had a bad influence on you, Timothy."

I didn't respond to the thinly veiled insult, and Thomas suddenly raised his voice, starting to explain his theory:

"But no matter what Kirena says, I am not in quite so shaky a position as she assumes! I'm still the president of the corporation, after all! Yes, I have retracted my offer to make her Vice President. But there was a very good reason: her stocks have been frozen! Her bank accounts, too! Kira would be no use to me in the upcoming vote! What's surprising in the fact that I went looking for a more beneficial candidate?! I'm not mad at Kirena or anything, it's just pure pragmatism, plain and simple!"

I realized that the CEO was severely overestimating my knowledge of the corporation's affairs, and my closeness with Kirena Tyle. But why not take advantage of his confusion to try and tease out some information?

"Thomas, there's just one little thing I don't understand: why would someone be trying to kill Kira? Her stocks are frozen, her accounts too. Kirena has no way of influencing the vote at the board of directors. She's basically out of the game. But then why does someone want her dead?"

That really had been bothering me since this morning. Kirena Tyle was a famous and influential woman, and had a large security staff. If she wasn't bothering anyone, these dogged attempts to get her out of the picture looked utterly illogical. I was greatly hoping that the president of the corporation could explain that to me. Thomas Heywood did not refuse to answer the ticklish question:

"Ugh, Timothy, you've got it all wrong! See, that all makes sense. First off, Kira is a Tyle and there is a whole block of directors who will vote exactly the same as Kirena Tyle simply out of old habit. Second, there's a big difference between 'out of the game' and 'lacks the means to get back in it.' Kira needs around two and a half billion credits to pay bail on her case and get her stocks unfrozen. Now she does have that kind of money, but some extremely influential person has tried very hard to get all of Kira's accounts and whatnot frozen as well, so she can't touch them. I tried to help her, but I immediately took a smack to the nose and had to step back. It may sound offensive, but the Tyle family will not be able to retain control over the Boundless Realm Corporation. I was led to believe that there isn't a single bank on the planet that will give Kira a loan before the end of the board of director's meeting."

"Not one bank? Her opponent is that strong and influential?" I asked in surprise and — why hide it? — even fear.

"Timothy, did you really doubt that? Your kidnapping is obvious proof of what these people are capable of, and now they're trying to seize ownership of the Boundless Realm Corporation. Getting access to the sealed technical floors of the building is practically impossible without long and complicated discussions involving various departments. And doing it in a way the president doesn't notice is twice as hard. But they did! There is a large group of influential employees currently against Kira, including a few directors at the highest levels. Some of them could be seen in the video of your kidnapping. The commander of that group was head of In-Game Security, Andrei Soloviev. And I've called him into my office for a very serious talk."

Woah! So that meant that Andrei Soloviev was involved in the affair. But he was the personal assistant and right hand of the late Vice-President Inessa Tyle! Who would have thought?! Although...

I guess I did remember hearing his voice when I was fighting off the technician and passing out. I had always suspected that Andrei Soloviev was somehow involved in what was going on around me. But I wasn't entirely sure, so I didn't share my suspicions. As it turned out, that was the wrong move!

After all, Kira's grandmother trusted him fully! Andrei Soloviev was in the Vice-President's office for all our important discussions. He was probably also in the room when the richest woman on the planet spoke with her notary public and wrote her will! Yeah, that sounded right! So that was the reason my kidnappers knew such surprisingly fine details of Inessa Tyle's will!

And meanwhile, Thomas continued his monologue:

"We managed to uncover another group of conspirators this morning with your help. You see, adding the Dark Sovereign's trap to the game, which is all the players can talk about today, left a decent amount of program logs. Using them, we managed to determine which programmers worked on creating the trap, and that traced back to the directors who wrote the technical orders and gave the instructions. And we pulled at those threads and followed them even higher to some members of the board of directors. And I was planning to call them to task, but first I made some inquiries. And it was good I didn't rush laying the blame! Behind them are the largest financial corporations and investment funds on the planet. No one can go against such power! It would be pointless to go to war with them. I can only try to prove my worth so they think me a valuable ally and let me join them."

Aha... I realized that Thomas Heywood had basically turned against trying to simply further his own interests, and staying loyal to the former owners of the corporation. Now he was just looking for a way to suck up to the new owners and prove his worth. Could I really judge him for that though? Hardly. Pure pragmatism, as he just said. But I still couldn't overcome a feeling of disgust. I was clearly not cut out to be a politician, changing my position wherever the wind blows like a weathercock. I reached out to the desk and picked up my termination papers.

"Well apparently everything's already been decided. So where do I sign?"

"Don't get ahead of yourself," Thomas Heywood unexpectedly stopped me. "Yes, Timothy. After your biting video about me and the corporation, you must understand that there is no way out for you now but termination. But there's getting fired, and there's getting fired. I suggest we don't burn any bridges, just part ways on good terms. As you'll see, it's all written out in great detail."

I started lifting the paper to read it, but Thomas Heywood stopped me:

"How about I just tell you what's there so you don't have to fill your head with legal terms. I want to allow you to work a few more days for the corporation so the Dark Sovereign event gets a worthy ending with a decisive final battle against the player army. I would really like the final stroke of your work for the Boundless Realm Corporation to be an epic struggle. I want all the news channels on the planet to write about it, so it will be remembered for many years to come. And in that battle, the Dark Sovereign will die and never again respawn. Yes, Timothy, the corporation plans to make your character mortal like an NPC, which is what the Dark Sovereign was intended to be in the first place. But in return we'll make you level faster and get more experience so your Amra can be in good shape for the final battle and give the players a real run for their money."

I cringed in dismay. Hrm... Instead of an undying, I would become mortal. An unfortunate perspective. But if that was my "stick" for disobedience, there would have to be a "carrot," too. And it came next:

"Before the battle, you will have time to sell all your virtual property and convert your silver seven-sided coins into real-world money. And we will also remove the restriction against selling your most valuable possession: the Royal Forest Wyvern. I'm sure that will leave you with a tidy sum with seven or maybe even eight zeroes. Especially considering the large number of unique and legendary items your Storekeeper collected from the players today. By the way, the bug you found has already been fixed. Allowing indestructible NPC's to go through portals with an illusion enchantment was a crazy oversight. As a tester, you're even getting paid a bonus. So that's basically everything I wanted to tell you. Any questions?"

Yes, I had a question, which I immediately asked. What would happen if the Dark Sovereign won the epic battle?

Thomas Heywood sat back in his armchair and laughed uncontrollably, as if I'd just said something hilariously stupid:

"Timothy, don't fall for any naïve illusions, you aren't going to win! As soon as the front lines reach the Dark Sovereign's castle, and that news spreads to all *Boundless Realm,* hundreds of thousands and maybe even millions of users will want to come take part in the grand event, all for the corporation's benefit. What's more, our marketers have taken into account the negative experience of your curses and the mass refusal of NPC's to communicate with enemies of the Dark

Sovereign. All the curses and limitations you put on those players will terminate after your character dies. And everyone who took part in the war against the 'great and terrible Dark Sovereign' will get a special status marker next to their name. Players love those little souvenirs. So no matter what kind of army you get together in the next few days, it will not be able to withstand the invasion. What's more, your soldiers are 'single-use' NPC's unlike the living players fighting against them, so the outcome of the battle is a foregone conclusion!"

I tried to object, saying that losing one battle didn't necessarily mean the end of the whole war, that the Dark Sovereign could gather a new army in other distant lands of *Boundless Realm*. But I quickly figured out that the corporation was simply not going to allow an unending event:

"Timothy, after the beginning of the final battle, you won't be able to retreat. If the Dark Sovereign tries to run, it will be considered a technical defeat. He cannot emerge from a portal alive after that. And in any case, Amra will die just if the player army captures your castle."

Day Four

Becoming Mortal

BEFORE SIGNING, I read my termination papers in great detail. Nothing personal, let Thomas Heywood wheeze in dismay. After recent events, I just could not take anyone at their word anymore. But the president wasn't lying. Exactly what he said was written in a huge addendum though, to be honest, it was all laid out in these clever little legal terms. Also, I did find two important aspects that the president neglected to mention. First, the corporation would compensate all expenses incurred during the event, returning all the money I'd spent right after the final and irreversible death of my character. Good news! I was already curling my lip, planning to throw all available funds into game currency to build up the

Dark Sovereign's army, given the corporation was now promising to compensate all my investments. But then I saw a restriction just after it saying, "in an amount no greater than one and a half million credits." And that made me sad. It was about as much as I'd already invested.

"In your video when you referenced the 'big firm and the rented stapler,' you were absolutely correct," the president commented, having seen that I'd reached that paragraph. "Our budget really didn't have anything set aside to buy the Dark Sovereign an army. I knocked out some money from the leftovers of various projects. And that was despite the fact that, before the board of directors meeting, any off-the-books expense reflects poorly on accounting. A million and a half is the maximum we were able to squeeze out without seriously revamping our finance sheets."

The second important aspect was a point saying that, if I broke any of their rules, the payout would be cancelled and my ability to withdraw game currency into the real world would be immediately blocked. First and foremost that applied to public speeches or videos revealing commercial or technological secrets, or statements that might tarnish the reputation either of the Boundless Realm Corporation as a whole, or any of its employees. That paragraph was even specially marked in bold to draw my attention. So

~ Finding a Body ~

I was in fact being given an ultimatum. Either I held my tongue about being kidnapped and other unfavorable incidents, or I was out on my ass. And instead of my expenses being compensated, and being paid a tidy little exit bonus, I'd be getting zilch, nada, zero.

I didn't find any other unexpected points in the text. Thomas Heywood was sitting in agitation, awaiting arguments and objections. So he was unbelievably surprised when I simply signed and, without saying goodbye, left his office in silence. I was in no mind to try and justify myself, and I definitely wasn't going to beg. First of all, my pride wouldn't allow me to bow and scrape. Second, I understood that very little actually depended on Thomas Heywood here. The armchair he sat in was on very shaky ground. He couldn't give up anything that might not be to the liking of the future owners of the Boundless Realm Corporation.

Then the elevator opened and... I was shocked, shuddering in surprise and even taking a step back because out stepped Andrei Soloviev in the flesh! Ah yes. Thomas Heywood did say he had called him in for a serious talk. Noticing my reaction, the ghastly former spy gave a chuckle and condescendingly patted me on the shoulder:

"Timothy, you really had nothing to fear, I'm no enemy of yours! I have no problem with your work as a tester and living engine to move large events forward. As the most probable next President of the Boundless Realm Corporation, I would even like to promote you to lead the whole testing department!"

Now that would be a twist! Andrei Soloviev wasn't hiding the fact that, at the upcoming board of directors' meeting, he was planning to usurp Thomas Heywood and become president. Clearly he thought he had true power behind him given he was speaking so openly about his ambitions. But as far as I had seen, Thomas Heywood was not going to give up so easily. The upcoming meeting in the president's office was going to be interesting. Two presidents would be a bit much for one corporation, even one as huge as this, so their dispute was sure to be heated!

And meanwhile, Andrei Soloviev, holding the elevator door open with his leg, continued the conversation:

"Timothy, I have many grand plans for the future, and I'll need capable employees like you to carry them out. With me you'll shoot straight to the top and achieve many things! So I'm counting on your two percent of the stocks supporting us at the board of directors vote!"

While saying that, he was carefully gauging my reaction and laughing in satisfaction, having noticed a momentary flicker of surprise and

- Finding a Body -

confusion on my face:

"What, neither Kirena Tyle nor her former admirer and lover Thomas Heywood told you? Then let me be the first to break the pleasant news: you'll be fabulously wealthy soon! Vice-President Inessa Tyle was a big fan of your active gameplay style during the flying snake event, and of you as an ambitious man of action. That remarkable woman decided to take a hand in your fate and willed you two percent of stocks in the Boundless Realm Corporation! At present that's worth almost seven and a half billion credits! Congratulations, Timothy!"

My spirit faded at the earth-shattering news. Sure, I had heard veiled hints that my name was among Inessa Tyle's heirs. Nevertheless, this was the first time I was hearing a concrete figure: two percent of the stocks in the Boundless Realm Corporation. That was a lot. A ton, even. Such a colossal inheritance immediately made me not even a millionaire, which I potentially already was assuming I got compensation when losing my job. No, this could shoot me straight to billionaire! But that was if I could trust Andrei Soloviev and, as it happened, that man didn't inspire any trust in me. He was the one behind my kidnapping and, based on the design of my virtual reality capsule with the tanks, he was not planning to keep me alive after using me in his plans.

Nevertheless, despite the alarm and internal agitation, I was trying to smile and show the dangerous man a relaxed and satisfied demeanor. Andrei Soloviev took my smile for the genuine article and started smiling back in satisfaction:

"As you see, Timothy, I am being as open with you as I can. Now we are on the same side of the barricade and our goals coincide. And in the future I'll need your help, so I hope I can keep you close. I'll even tell you a little secret: the only person you should actually be afraid of is Kirena Tyle, the granddaughter of the Vice-President. You see, according to the will, if you die, your two percent goes to her. Kira is a flighty and emotionally unstable woman who ruins lives. She has been living beyond her means for a long time and has accrued so many debts her creditors sued and had her stocks frozen. So the temptation to get rid of you and thus her debts, might be too strong. By the way, you wouldn't happen to know where Kira is right now, would you? No one has been able to reach her since this morning."

Wow! Everything got turned inside out in Andrei Soloviev's words! The situation with the frozen bank accounts, which Kira had vigorously complained about, and which the president had commented on dejectedly, he described in a diametrically opposite way. And Kira Tyle didn't look like the victim of a corporate raiding scheme for her family business in this version, but a bankrupt spendthrift trying to dodge court orders, or someone pursued doggedly by creditors for outsized debts. And I didn't know whose version was more plausible. Perhaps the truth was somewhere in the middle but, deep down, I was still on my redheaded girlfriend's side. That said, when Andrei Soloviev asked a question, I answered with complete honesty, not bending the truth one bit:

"I have no idea where Kira is now. We went somewhere, her security mentioned a defended palace and a guy with a missile launcher discovered near it. It was all basically going fine but then Kira went nuts over something and abandoned me in an unfamiliar neighborhood, taking off in a flying taxi."

"That sounds just like her!" the former spy laughed. "Well, best of luck to you, Timothy. I suspect that you were actually being brought to a desolate location so she could secretly get you out of the picture. But either the conditions weren't right, or the spoiled brat hadn't steeled her nerves enough to commit cold-blooded murder and reconsidered at the last moment. In any case, in your place, I would not keep taking risks and stay as far away from Kirena as possible! Alright, I've gotta go. Leadership wants to chat. See you soon at the board of directors!"

Andrei Soloviev took his leg out, and the elevator doors finally closed, cutting me off from the fearsome man. I breathed a sigh of relief, only then having noticed how nervous I was. With Soloviev nearby, I felt helpless like a rabbit before a constrictor and didn't know what to do with myself. He just emanated death despite all the false friendship and promise of sweeping changes for the better. Also he was saying Kira wanted to kill me, and I didn't believe him one bit. Maybe the ex-agent wasn't even totally lying and, according to her grandmother's will, if I died Kira actually would get my two percent. But despite all my girlfriend's impulsivity and all her current financial problems, I didn't even slightly believe the beautiful redhead might stab me in the back.

In any case, I would have to think very carefully over all of this squabbling around Inessa Tyle's inheritance. The conspirators' obstinate desire to isolate Kira from the battle or even physically eliminate her had to have some kind of rational explanation. As did the baffling attempt to keep me locked in a virtual reality capsule until the board of directors' meeting. Why limit my freedom if I would never get my two percent of the stocks anyway? Getting me into that virtual office must have been risky and complicated. There was a huge risk that my imprisonment would leak or spill out yet, on first glance, there was no benefit whatsoever. Those kinds of things didn't happen. There had to be some kind of logical explanation, but I just couldn't find it.

* * *

I WAS ALREADY at the clinic and heading to see my sister when my cell phone rang. It was a new phone that I bought today and wasn't used to. It had a different ringtone, so at first I didn't even realize I was getting a call. But I had the number in my contacts and it was saved as "Boss." That meant it was coming from the office of the Director of the Special Projects Division. But despite my expectations, the person calling was not Max Tohner, but his assistant Tina:

"Timothy, I'm calling to say that your gaming cabin 4-16A is ready. The equipment has been installed and set-up, and it's ready to go. Mr. Tohner asked when you'd be coming into *Boundless Realm*, too. It's just that lots of stuff is happening, and lots of people are waiting for the Dark Sovereign to return."

I glanced at the clock and answered I couldn't be there any earlier than one thirty, because I had an important meeting.

"Alright, I'll send that on. And before you load up the game, Max Tohner wanted you to drop by his office. There are a couple papers here for you to sign, plus he wanted to brighten your day with two pieces of good news."

Good news? And what about the fact that I had at most three or four more days left to work here? Strange. I wondered what could even happen over such a short time. The issue was that I had gone to see Max just an hour ago and we had a long and substantive conversation. We discussed my termination, the end of the Dark Sovereign event and various aspects of the game. Most of all, we decided to reset and redo my character's skills. We also thought over how to turn the upcoming final battle into a big show so the viewers on the gaming channels would be humming in delight when seeing the enthralling pictures of the big "meat grinder."

I also discussed the future of my NPC friends: Taisha, Irek, my adopted daughter Chai-nee Shu and other companions. Yes, they were just mobs, essentially a chunk of programming, but I insisted that, after the Dark Sovereign's death, they would all be saved and brought to some far-away location in the huge *Boundless Realm*. One where players hadn't been before. It would be easy enough to come up with an explanation for my companions disappearing. For example, they could say it was the last wish of the Dark Sovereign, which took the last of the game superboss's Direct Intervention Points. The moment Amra's companions disappeared could even be played up elegantly and made into a beautiful video. The corporation's specialists had that down pat. But I was worried and my speech was occasionally disjointed or lacked decent argumentation. I was afraid the director wouldn't agree to take a hand in the fate of some mere NPC's. But much to my surprise, Max Tohner didn't object and even promised to help solve this issue and speak with programmers and marketers.

So, was this good news? In these worrying times, good news was like water in the desert. I wondered what Max Tohner wanted to tell me. I had to admit, Tina had me intrigued. Had the issue of rescuing Amra's companions really been approved? Or was I being allowed to gain experience even faster? Not especially counting on success, I asked Tina to tell me the secret. What did he want to say? And the director's assistant agreed with surprising pliability:

"Only if you never say I told you!" Tina warned me. "And it means you owe me at least one chocolate! So then, the first piece of news: the boss just agreed with other directors on how experience would be divided for killing the whole army of the Dark Sovereign's enemies. We should have given the players some kind of explanation about who put it all together. The forums still won't shut up about the deadly trap in the middle of the sea. The experience will be split equally between Titanium Joker, Valerianna Quickfoot and Amra. And it will be enough to bring all of you over level four hundred! Congratulations, Timothy. The three of you are now the highest-level players in *Boundless Realm!*"

Woah! Apparently, the corporation had found a simple and elegant way to both respond to the players and make the Dark Sovereign more powerful. Now as the president said today, by the time of the final battle, the Dark Sovereign would be in good shape. I thanked Tina for the information and asked about the second piece of news.

"Alright, second: our boss managed to push one of your suggestions through leadership. Now, players who fight on the Dark Sovereign's side will also get a souvenir marker so everything is fair. Now they're just discussing whether the enemies and allies of the Dark Sovereign should be able to fight throughout *Boundless Realm* until the end of the event, including in defended locations. If so, they don't want the city guards interfering. I don't know what the directors will decide, but in any case it will help you get plenty of allies. I'm sure there are players who will want the unique souvenir marker of an ally of the Dark Sovereign!"

~ Finding a Body ~

I considered it. Yes, I had indeed suggested adding souvenir rewards for all taking part in the event regardless of which side they chose. After all, we needed to encourage participation for the *Amazons,* Max Sochnier, Shrekson and Valerianna. I hadn't considered the possibility of spontaneous fights between my supporters and detractors, although... that would be just great! If players were allowed to fight right in the cities, that would be quite the happy hunting ground for all kinds of PK'ers. Just get the Dark Sovereign's ally badge and you can attack players unpunished so long as they participated in the corporation's global event! I already had a few hundred thousand enemies and, in the last few days of the event, their numbers would grow sharply into the millions, if the president was right. All these hordes of undying were strong together, attacking my holdings in organized squadrons. But all alone in cities, not expecting attack, these players were easy targets for PK'ers. I imagined the chaos that might ensue if the directors eventually did allow players to fight in protected locations!

"TIM, YOU'RE back!!!" Valeria stopped talking with a tall curly-haired boy and hurried down the hallway to meet me, flailing her crutches and making every step a silly little hop.

I had brought her some fruits as a gift, but threw the bag right on the floor and ran out to meet her. I hugged my little sister tight, lifted her in my arms and spun her around. Val laughed sonorously in glee and squealed just like a little girl playing a game with her older brother. I couldn't even hold back my tears of compassion and joy. How nice it was to see my dear little sister!

"Tim, this is Andre!" Valeria said, now a bit calmer and pointing at the curly-haired boy as he walked up closer.

Carefully setting my sister on the floor, I picked up her fallen crutches and gave them to her to lean on. After that, I gave a big smile and extended a hand to greet the athletically-built six-foot-six boy. But he just stood there with his arms hanging limp and a strange grimace of embarrassment and confusion frozen on his face. Only then did I realize my mistake and quickly become ghastly embarrassed. What an ass I was! Valeria told me about him. And I read about Andre online as well. How could I forget?! He just had an operation to implant bionic arms! He was probably barely able to control his limbs yet, even if the operation was a success!

"Glad to meet you," he said with clear strain on his face, his lips squeezed tight and his teeth clenched to the point of crunching. He looked like a man trying to lift an overloaded barbell in the gym. But after all that he did eventually manage to slightly raise his right arm.

I took over from there, grabbing his hand and giving it a slight squeeze. Andre breathed a heavy sigh and lowered his hand as soon as I released my grip. I must have guessed right and the new bionic arm was still a challenge to control. Seemingly, Andre wouldn't have any use for that guitar for quite some time. Nevertheless, the elated gazes Val and Andre were exchanging didn't escape me. Seemingly, even that slight lift was a huge breakthrough in Andre's recovery and Valeria, having been in a similar situation, appreciated just how hard it was to achieve.

"My parents should be coming soon. A few minutes ago, they called to say they'd already left home, so I'll go meet them," Andre said and tactfully walked away from our private conversation.

"So, what do you think?" my sister asked, making sure Andre had walked out of earshot.

I shrugged my shoulders indefinitely. Just another boy. Tall, athletic. Probably from a woman's perspective he was pretty cute. Polite, sensitive, proud and goal-oriented. That's basically what I told my sister.

"Yeah, he's great!" Of all my words, Val

seemingly had taken only the positive. "Andre came out of his coma just yesterday, and he's been going to the doctor since this morning demanding to be released. The doctor refused, of course. He said he needed at least another two weeks of observation and treatments, and that's in the best case. But Andre didn't give up and is already making plans to run away. He has so many ideas after these months of forced inactivity that he doesn't want to wait even one more day! But alright, that's enough about Andre, that isn't why you came. Let's talk about us and our stuff."

Yes, Val and I really did have a lot to talk about. So much had happened, both good and bad since the last time we'd seen one another in real life! It was as if a whole lifetime had passed! I didn't hide anything from my sister. I told her about my wounds, even lifted my shirt and showed her the scars. I told her about my fabulous office, which was actually a virtual reality capsule in the middle of a room filled with toxic gas. I told her I would soon be out of a job, but that they promised me a big payday. I told her the Dark Sovereign event would be over soon, and my Amra would be dying permanently. Valeria reacted with surprising calm to the last piece of news:

"Maybe that's for the best... I don't want to play *Boundless Realm* alone. And I've actually been looking at my life and realizing that, other than computer games, it has been totally empty for the last few years. Talking to Andre actually makes me feel awkward. He is full of energy, has been to every continent on Earth and is just a fountain of ideas about new travels and adventures. Just imagine, Andre even applied to join the space fleet. He wants to go on the third expedition to the rings of Neptune and help build a base for humanity on Triton. Or he's considering applying to crew the first starships going to Alpha Centauri and Barnard's Star. By the way, Tim, will you let me go with him? I also want to get out of my wheelchair and start living, not just existing!"

I was not used to hearing such bold plans from my normally clammed-up and unconfident sister. Sure, the plans about space voyages, to my eye, looked childishly naïve. Even a healthy person had an extremely hard time being approved for space travel. For someone with bionic appendages, passing all the tests and high G-loads would be twice as hard. But I could only be glad that Valeria finally had some interests outside of virtual worlds. So I answered that I would support her in any endeavor. Most likely, after finishing work as a videogame plotline tester, I would also start doing something different. What was more, soon enough our money problems would be gone for good.

I told my sister about talking with Kira and

what I knew about Inessa Tyle's will. I told her about the attempt on Kira's life, her difficult financial position and the conspiratorial scheme that bordered on a maniacal obsession to cut Inessa Tyle's granddaughter out of the upcoming board of directors vote. At a certain point I let slip the phrase: "It's too bad we don't know how much stock Kira has. That might clear up a lot." My sister answered that by simply taking out her cellphone, calling up a search engine and saying:

"Boundless Realm Corporation. Main shareholders."

After that she showed me the results. It was that easy?! How hadn't I thought to try that? My sister always had a unique talent for making her brother feel like an ass, but this really was the apotheosis of my idiocy, even compared to all my past confusions. I thanked Val for the simple solution and picked up her phone.

Among the many useless links, I found results from last year's board of directors vote to once again elect Thomas Heywood president. And that had the exact information I was after: Inessa Tyle — 33.33% of voting shares, Kirena Tyle — 10.40%, Thomas Heywood — 6.28%... This article led me to believe that a year ago Kira was in possession of more than ten percent. Well, I'd take that into consideration and think it over...

I had only heard tell that Kirena was a

spendthrift and lived too high on the horse. And that was from Andrei Soloviev, so it was hard to believe. I mean, he was an insanely biased source. Also, no matter how luxurious my girlfriend's life was, no matter the Black Crystals and tropical islands she bought, she would never have been able to spend thirty billion credits and change.

That meant Kira still had a very respectable amount of stocks, even if they were frozen at the moment. If she still had, let's say, ten percent, then... I quickly imagined it... ten percent was out of the picture, just the remaining ninety percent were voting. Given Andrei Soloviev was so confident he could win the vote, he must have already had forty-five percent or more, or he could see a way of getting that soon. But he definitely did not have fifty percent of the shares, otherwise there would have been no sense in tracking Kirena Tyle or attempting to knock her off.

That meant that, no matter how confident he was in winning the vote, Andrei Soloviev's accomplices were actually in a fairly tight spot. With the new powers so obviously wanting to replace the president with their own loyal candidate, they would never get an alliance with Thomas Heywood, so the conspirators wouldn't have more than fifty percent. Also, with that outcome, one option of upending their whole game became obvious: I just had to get Kirena Tyle's shares unfrozen before the board of directors' meeting. Then Andrei Soloviev and his mucky-muck backers would simply not have enough shares to take the vote and their candidate wouldn't go through. I had no idea what would happen after that, though. Perhaps the current president of the corporation would retain his post, but maybe the new president would be someone else.

According to Thomas Heywood, she would need to pay a bond of two and a half billion credits to get the shares unfrozen. At first glance such a huge sum was impossible. But with control over the richest corporation on the planet at stake, with a value of one hundred billion credits, finding a two-and-a-half-billion-credit loan didn't seem totally impossible.

Then I had to stop thinking because a big group of people came up. One was Andre, two others must have been his parents and there was also a short balding geezer wearing a white hospital gown over an expensive suit. The old man was accompanied by a large contingent of security, although they didn't have any obvious weapons. Still they shot cautious gazes at all the people in the hallway and even scanned the walls and ceiling with a device that looked like glowing frame. I had never seen Titanium Joker in real life, but I immediately realized this must have been him, the

~ Finding a Body ~

Russian Billionaire Vladimir Toropov, who Iron Jeanette had described as a great friend and admirer. But what was he doing here? Ah ha! I remembered that this Russian oligarch had paid for Andre's treatment. He was probably coming to check up on him.

"What an auspicious occasion! We've got the three highest-level players of all *Boundless Realm* in one room!" came the geezer, extending a hand in greeting. He was surprisingly well informed, too. He must have heard this news from Tina no more than fifteen minutes ago. "You really brightened my day, Amra! I love big publicized projects and operations, but recently I haven't had the chance to take part in any for a long time. I hope you have plenty other enemies to keep delighting this old man for weeks to come, Dark Sovereign!"

I answered that I had more than enough enemies and, in the next few days, there would be plenty of large and small battles. After that, the decisive battle would surely be coming when my subjects would have to stand up against an unheard-of number of players, over a million and maybe even several million. I also told him that the corporation hoped the Dark Sovereign and his allies put up worthy resistance and the final battle would be epic.

"And yet I don't hear any enthusiasm in your voice," the oligarch retorted. "I get the impression that you aren't hoping for much more than 'worthy resistance.' It's bad when soldiers don't believe they can win a battle. But it's much worse when their commander doesn't either!"

"But how can anything stand up against an army that cannot be wiped out?" Valeria shot out. "There are many times more of them and they're undying, unlike the Dark Sovereign's NPC fighters! Also the Dark Sovereign himself was made mortal, so when he dies the whole structure Amra created will fall apart!"

The old man shifted his dim gaze to my sister. Val grew embarrassed and, shuffling her crutches, hurriedly retreated behind my back. Vladimir Toropov shook his head in reproach and said thoughtfully:

"The morale situation is much worse than I thought, if even Valerianna Quickfoot allows herself to doubt. You are the most powerful enchantress in *Boundless Realm,* girl. Your praises are sung on the forum and your very name makes our enemies freeze in horror. My girl, this is not some sporting competition where everything is trite and obeys the rules. Here, the stronger team does not always emerge victorious. This is a true fight without any rules or referee. And in a battle like that, there are many factors beyond brute strength. It comes down to whoever has the most confident mindset and who is willing to fight to the end!"

Iron Jeanette, who had been standing in silence and listening to our debate, also joined the conversation, supporting her old friend:

"That's exactly right! Amra, I have seen the mood of the players of *Boundless Realm*. The vast majority of them do not want to stand against the Dark Sovereign no matter what. They think you're dangerous! You've already demonstrated a number of times what happens to those who oppose you! Some poor fools had a ghost suck their level down to one, others were chased down city streets shamefully by NPC villagers who wouldn't even do them the honor of killing them. Others drowned in the sea, stripped to their clothing and losing all their valuables. Or the prisoners on the deck of the galley that you executed and had your wyvern eat alive. Or the *Legion of Steel*'s strongest players, who spent days moaning on the forum that they were unable to log into the game! Also the shameful and indelible curse you put on your enemies! The Dark Sovereign hits very hard, everyone knows that by now. There are many examples, so there are extremely few left who want to see what it's like to experience Amra's rage first hand. Just keep going like that and there will be much less than 'millions of players' opposing you!"

"What's more, you could try to get more players on your side!" Valeria said, once again confident and stepping out in front. "Tim, offer the players something interesting: something they'll get only for playing in your faction. After all, no matter what they say in the advertisement about an open world for all to discover, there are actually millions of people in the game who don't know what to do with themselves, or how to differentiate themselves from thousands of cookie-cutter characters. If you can provide a way to stand out from the crowd, a huge amount of players will come join your side."

"Girl, you simply delight me. Your acumen is beyond your years!" the Russian oligarch praised my sister. "And if that doesn't give you enough, there are mercenaries after all. And there are a huge number of such clans in *Boundless Realm*. You could also quietly, or maybe even not so quietly lure your most dangerous enemies to your side along with some particularly experienced commanders. An army without commanders turns into an uncontrollable pack of cowards. There aren't so many players in *Boundless Realm* with experience leading troops. We could compile a list pretty quickly then try and bribe them all to our side. Yes, it will cost a lot. But as experienced businessmen say, if a problem can be solved with money, it isn't really a problem, just an expense."

~ Finding a Body ~

Luckily, Iron Jeanette and her old friend managed to restore my fighting spirit, which was all the way down in the dumps after my chat with the president. In fact, the situation didn't look quite as hopeless as Thomas Heywood was trying to convince me. I smiled a predatory smile and answered:

"Yes, I am bubbling with ideas, so it's still too early to bury the Dark Sovereign. The enemy will cry in pity a thousand times because he dared take up arms against me. But it might cost a lot. It might even cost a ton."

"Money is isn't hard to get, I can help you with that," the oligarch light-mindedly waved his hand as if talking about empty things that didn't merit his attention. "Just tell me, what kind of money are we talking about?"

I took some air into my lungs and spoke loud and clear, attentively watching to see how everyone reacted.

"Two and a half billion credits!"

The lightminded smile instantly crawled off the old man's face. The others sharply fell silent and just stared at me, batting their eyes in astonishment and not knowing what to say.

"Yes, two and a half billion. Just for two weeks," I repeated in case someone didn't get it the first time. "Plus we'll need another couple million credits for the thing we were just discussing: to buy up commanders, clan leaders and plenty of mercenaries."

"That might be a bit steep... But I wouldn't say impossible..." Vladimir Toropov said in a raspy voice, slightly coming to his senses. "All I understand is that you cannot need that much money just to put into the game. But I'll allow it. What do I get for risking my two and a half billion, though?"

I held a long pause for greater effect and spoke decisively and clearly:

"You can be Vice-President of the Boundless Realm Corporation, or appoint a representative!"

Day Four
Calm before the Storm

THE TESTER FLOOR. I hadn't been here in the daytime for a long while. I even managed to avoid the crowds of newbies, who were milling about and standing in line for vending machines or bragging to their equally green colleagues about their first successes in *Boundless Realm.* For some reason, there were a lot of them today. Was this their lunch break or something? I glanced at the time. Yeah, that was it. One thirty. Then I could see why there were so many people crowded up here in the hallway.

When I first came to work as a tester I was surprised and even annoyed at my colleagues' habit of leaving the game on a schedule and going to get lunch and chat. But eventually I got used to it and my attitude softened. In the end, they just wanted to share their joys about gaining levels, skills and completing their first quests. And who better to tell than their equally green new colleagues?

"Timothy, we're over here!" Max Sochnier's familiar voice drew my attention, and I started staring through the crowd.

Predictably, Max Sochnier was at the table with our friend Leon and another person I really wasn't expecting, Veronica. She was the lady who played the Dryad Dancer. I didn't know that she and Leon had made up. However, due to my virtual imprisonment, I had fallen behind on life and missed a lot in the last few days.

"The two of us are trying to get Veronica to bring her pirate fleet to Frigid Lake," Max Sochnier told me and I just totally lost the thread.

Excuse me, what? What business did Veronica, or more accurately her character Angelica Wayward and her pirates, have with my plight? The last time I asked about the Dryad Dancer, she was on a huge slave ship on its way to the Eastern Continent. And although Angelica Wayward was no longer chained up in a box as a prisoner, and was now free and had used her charms to take the captain under control, my calculations showed that her ship would still take quite some time to reach its destination.

~ Finding a Body ~

That said, the idea of a pirate brigade on Frigid Lake was very promising, and I actually had proposed it as an aside to my friends. We had a mission to somehow secure my eastern borders, given the undying had taken down the Dark Sovereign's warband on the far bank and founded a stockade town there. I had my rider Darkness periodically scouting around their fortification, and I had also seen the enemy-controlled shore through the Sovereign's Eye. So I knew the players had dug in hard there and had a strong garrison. And beyond that fortress with several levels of defensive ditches and walls they had already built docks with launch slips and were busy building large transport ships. Apparently, in a few days, we could expect an attempted landing on the other side of Frigid Lake. I knew all that and yesterday I told Max Sochnier the idea of hiring the *Brotherhood of the Coast* and teleporting them and their galleys and frigates to the lake. My French friend, whose trade galley plied the native waters of these dangerous pirates, promised to ask around in the ports and find out what he could. But where did Veronica enter into this?

Hearing my question, Leon couldn't even hold back and exclaimed in surprise:

"Timothy, do you really not know?! Veronica defeated all the leaders of the *Brotherhood of the Coast* in duels, and now she wields sole authority over the pirate fleet!"

"Well, it's hard to call them duels in the traditional sense of the word," Veronica laughed happily, clearly very pleased with herself. "Feminine wiles, guile, lots of magic, dances and potions. And all the fearsome scar-covered captains bowed before the small naked dryad who had never in her life even held a weapon, recognizing her unquestioned authority!"

"Lots of people wrote about it on the forum and the corporation even released an entertaining clip about her unusual gameplay style," Max Sochnier confirmed. Veronica started laughing again:

"To be honest, the ad did have a few parts blurred out, but still it turned out great. I really, really liked it! And yes, I've been a senior corporate tester for a few days now! My fleet has seventy-eight ships ready to do battle. There are another six big triremes under repair after a boarding, but they'll be fixed in two or three days. With no false modestly I can say that there is no force on the Southern Continent that can stand up against my pirates!"

Well, well. That changed everything and, like it or not, I would have to come to an agreement with Veronica. I asked her price directly.

"Look at you, Timothy. But still that is boring..." the girl cringed in dismay and put on a dejected face. "Does this issue really have to be settled monetarily? I've already got cash. I earn plenty on my 18+ streams. And in the game, pirate captains, both NPC and living player give me all kinds of rare gifts. It's honestly beyond what I can handle. They simply shower me in coins and precious stones."

"What do you want then?" I had no idea what she was hinting at and couldn't hide my confusion.

Instead of answering, Veronica smiled just with the corners of her lips then, looking bored, she stared at her well-groomed nails for a long time as if proving a point. A minute later, she raised her eyes:

"I mean, I don't even know... Try and convince me, I guess. Just compliment me or something. Or offer me something interesting that will make my pirates think it's worth going off to die in a cold snowy land."

"What makes you say die?" I hooked into the last bit and Veronica's voice immediately turned cold and calculating.

"Well what do you think will happen, Timothy? And don't lie. The Dark Sovereign has a few days left to rule, a week at most. Then you and all your mobs will be swept away by an army of undying, all of your territory will be captured by your enemies. So tell me, why should I bring my pirates to a hopeless battle if you won't win no matter what?"

That was biting and extremely frank, without any attempt at humility or diplomacy. I noticed that Leon and Max had perked their ears in expectation of my reply. Just this morning I would have started burbling away that the outcome was "still unclear," and how "maybe we can fight them off," or "at least we'll give them a good fight." But now I was in a totally different mood.

I sat back in the armchair and, my hands folded on my stomach, began to speak with the look of a man who knows all the secrets of existence stooping to explain elementary truths to an ignoramus:

"That's the whole point. I'm trying to look weak to trick the players! I'm trying to attract as many players as possible into the army against me. You see, the event is stalling out, but the corporation and I want it to finally grow to mass scale!"

"And what's the truth?" Leon immediately asked, impatient.

"Well actually... do you know what a pack of fifteen level 400+ predators can do in the game with significant buffs from items, skills and perks? No? Not surprising. I don't even know myself, though I am at the head of just such a pack. Or what a Royal Forest Wyvern also at level 400+ could do? Her mother Kayervina was fifty levels weaker and she still gave the players a run for their money. But there is one important difference: Kayervina was mortal. The Gray Pack and VIXEN respawn after every time they die, so they're never out of the battle for long."

They went silent, digesting what they'd just heard. I hurried to continue, building on their impression and staring stubbornly at Veronica:

"Other than that, I have Valerianna Quickfoot on my side. She's the most powerful Beastmaster in *Boundless Realm.* She is now at level four hundred twenty. It's scary to even imagine what her pets could do now. I think that deadly flying snake Kayervina would be stung to death in a matter of seconds by my sister's hornets. Plus the level-four-hundred-eleven Titanium Joker. He alone could stop a whole army. Also consider the mercenaries. And I'll have a lot of them. After all, you aren't the only one with money! And that is disregarding the main army which now has more than thirty-eight thousand of the most fearsome monsters who have been receiving training from experienced specialists around the clock!"

"Alright, alright, you've convinced me," Veronica stopped me. "Losing isn't a sure thing. I admit the Dark Sovereign actually might stop the player army. What remains is the question of my price. So can you offer me something unusual that might catch my fancy?"

I understood perfectly that money or other valuables would not do the trick. Even if I promised Veronica an apple-sized flawless diamond in the game (if I could even get such a thing), that offer would most likely just scare her off rather than draw her to my side. No, I had to try something totally different... So what if... It was such an idiotic idea that it just might work:

"What if I could make you a unique creature in *Boundless Realm*? Just imagine: a golden marker on the mini-map and any character description you want. You want to be Angelica Wayward, Pirate Queen? Or maybe you want Angelica Wayward, Admiral of the Dark Sovereign?"

"Ha, an admiral in a skirt," Max Sochnier sidled in with a poorly timed barb. But Veronica answered with complete seriousness:

"More like an admiral with no skirt. But I prefer the title 'Pirate Queen.' Alright, Timothy. Can you really make that happen in the game?"

I gave a slow distinct nod, afraid to scare off my luck. Veronica then lit up and, extending a hand in a sign of a deal sealed, said:

"Alright Amra, I'm in! I'll need a few portals to bring my ships from New Tortuga harbor. And from me you'll get round-the-clock surveillance of... what was it called again...? Frigid Lake. I'll make sure not one enemy ship can slip through to your shores."

I squeezed her outstretched hand, confirming our understanding. Alright then, it worked! I'd just have to spend three Direct Intervention Points and the strongest fleet of the Southern Continent would come join my side! If I were in the game, I'd already be reading lines of text about increased Trading and Diplomacy skills! Yes, pirates were not the most reliable allies, just about like Veronica herself. But the authority and ghastly fame of the Dark Sovereign would keep them from making rash decisions for a time and, with this big time-crunch, that was plenty.

I TALKED with Leon and Max though somewhat filtering myself in Veronica's presence to avoid sensitive details. The Ogre Fortifier told me that he had spent whole days building fortifications in the Icy Mountains, and the passes and slopes most ripe for incursion were already covered, while border garrisons of Drow elves and orcs were stationed at the forts. Giants, minotaurs and cyclopes were very hard workers when it came to building and, after the successful operation in Lars, the Dark Sovereign's authority had grown significantly in their eye. And that increased their enthusiasm and building speed as well.

They also started working harder because they just got paid for the first time. Strictly on schedule, the Storekeeper had paid everyone who took part in the big construction projects exactly what they were owed. What was more, and here I couldn't believe my ears, the cheapskate demon agreed with Shrekson and paid bonuses to the hardest workers. That had me so intrigued I asked about it in greater detail. And Leon was eager to explain:

"Your Storekeeper just isn't himself today. Usually he's incredibly cheap. If you really need something that costs pennies, you practically have to beat it out of him. But the demon just isn't himself today. He was fairly easy to convince. I just said construction speed and worker enthusiasm was the best security our coffers could have. He constantly asked when the Sovereign would be back in *Boundless Realm*, too. I think he has something to tell you."

I suspected I knew exactly what the Storekeeper was so desperate to tell me. The demon was just not physically capable of dragging all the valuables up from the sea floor, but his natural greed didn't allow him to just leave them so the Storekeeper had probably hidden all the most valuable loot. And now that the patch made it impossible to send indestructible creatures through portals, he was kicking himself because he couldn't get back to his massive secret treasure. This story was partially confirmed by the fact that the players who went off after the sunken loot had taken down the underwater monsters, but didn't find anything of interest on the sea floor. On the forums, there was a story going around that someone managed to get there before the treasure hunters. And I thought I knew exactly who that might be.

Max Sochnier in his turn not hiding his pride at a job well done reported that the trade system in my lands was already built up and quite stable. Orcs, rougarou and even forest monsters were spending the money they earned and selling their loot from Lars in market pavilions to buy food and drink. Blacksmiths and armorers were also working nonstop on weapon and armor orders from my subjects. Just in the last twenty-four hours, four ships loaded with fish had been sent to the Dark Sovereign's lands, and they all came back full of antiaris wood, rare herbs, unique rose pearls from Frigid Lake and mithril.

"Mithril?" I stopped my friend.

"Yes! The dwarves are as happy as pigs in shit! Almost directly below your palace they discovered rich veins of iron, silver, and 'true silver.' Two thirds of the bearded chaps got their picks out as soon as they heard and left straight from the wedding!" After seeing my disturbed expression, Max Sochnier hurried to add. "Don't worry Timothy. We've been keeping track of what's mined and the Dark Sovereign will get coins and a share of the ore."

That was very interesting and informative, and there was lots I still wanted to discuss with my friends, but I had to twist out of it. The problem was that lots of testers had started gathering around our table, clearly having overheard our conversation. A few had their phones out and were taking pictures with me in the background, some even selfies. I heard muted voices from all sides: "That's the Dark Sovereign!" "Yeah, that's Amra himself!" It was becoming harder and harder to ignore the buzzing crowd which grew by leaps and bounds with every minute. What was more, a few especially rude beggar types had started edging into our conversation and asking my friends and I for money to "grow their characters." So I got up from the table showing that the conversation was over and suggested we all get back to the game.

~ Finding a Body ~

* * *

SO THEN, loading. And the first thing I noticed was a big bright full-screen message congratulating me on setting a record. Level four hundred and forty-two!!! I was the first and for now only *Boundless Realm* player ever to reach such dizzying heights! But I hadn't actually spent my many stat points, or selected new specializations and perks yet. I just didn't have it in me now, and this important issue would need to be thought over long and hard, all the while holding in mind that I might be able to reset and redistribute all my stats later.

I found myself deep in the dungeons under the palace, where I had placed a respawn stone. It was behind many locked doors, impenetrable to other players and thus safe. A second later, the Storekeeper appeared nearby and gave me a deep bow. The NPC demon couldn't come any closer to the humming stone, but was acting impatient with his whole appearance, so I hurried to walk over to my servant. But before I'd taken five steps, the Storekeeper was suddenly hidden behind a furry block that took up half the room. Where the heck did that come from? I shuddered in surprise and only then realized I was seeing the Gray Pack rammed into a room that was too small for them like a can of sardines.

But oh how my pets had grown! I could only recognize Fimbulthul by the words over his fanged head. The unique Mythical Hound was at level 420. Now he wasn't so much a hound as an elephant or a woolly mammoth covered in thick white fur. And the gray Akella, now an Ancient Alpha Forest Wolf, was no smaller than the icy white Fimbulthul. Woah! He had now changed classification from normal to rare and his stats had grown to match. Lobo, White Fang and Blanca also became rare "ancient wolves." The level-421 Guard Dog had also become rare, but still remained nameless. The Ancient Alpha Swamp Wolf Baron was at level-421 and had even entered the ranks of the unique creatures.

Gjöll couldn't be called a little girl anymore either. The unique piercing black she-wolf was just two levels behind Fimbulthul, while at shoulder height she was no smaller. And I was seeing Fjörm in the flesh for the first time. The pup I'd received yesterday from the dwarves had grown in one day from level 1 to 418 and was an exact copy of Fimbulthul, but bright red and his fur was not quite so matted. The animals whimpered for joy and ran over to me but they couldn't get past the invisible boundary. It was as if the area around the respawn stone was blocked by transparent glass.

I then walked over to the huge beasts and,

caressing the pets who rushed out to greet me, sent the Gray Pack out to hunt in an endless glade of magically-warped centuries-old trees inhabited by ghastly monsters. Even the scouts I sent out to explore the Dark Sovereign's lands didn't risk going too deep in there, impressed by the power and danger of the creatures that lived in the murky forest. But now I'd let the eternally hungry giants of the Gray Pack hunt for monsters in that distant forest. Better than having them lick their lips while staring at my subjects. What was more, no matter how fearsome the huge monsters in that dangerous glade were, my pretties could take them down in one bite. And that would make the forest less dangerous.

"Well Storekeeper, I trust that you managed to hide the underwater treasure," I started, getting straight to business as soon as the giant predators were out of the room.

I was expecting a long story from the Storekeeper about what was hidden where but the demon unexpectedly fell to his knees and went into a frenzy, tearing at the already sparse hair on his head and chest:

"Master, I couldn't carry it all! I only took one trunk of the most valuable weapons, and some luxurious rings and jewelry. I hid the rest of the treasure in an underwater cave guarded by a huge kraken. There is enough treasure down there to make Aladdin's cave look like a dump! I thought I'd go get it all in another few trips. But for some reason I couldn't go back to that magical place! So much has been lost! Forgive me, master..."

The demon had done much more than I had hoped. He not only acted as live bait which the *Legion of Steel* took hook line and sinker, he'd done the same trick to a whole army of undying, scrupulously gathered the most valuable loot and brought it to my treasure chamber. However, seeing the greedy demon lament about the rest of the lost treasure, it would have been fundamentally wrong to try and calm him down and tell him everything was fine and we already had plenty. Doing that would only damage my authority in the eyes of my servant. So I whipped up a fearsome dressing-down:

"How could you?! We've lost a whole cave of treasure! And right now every coin is important to reinforce my army before the final battle! You dolt, do you even understand how my foes will laugh at me? Could you at least put together a map of the location?"

The demon gave a very rapid nod of his horned head and extended me a rumpled yellow sheet of rough paper with some partially-erased numbers and half-smeared scrawling. These must have been the approximate coordinates of the hidden treasure and a sketch of the cave entrance drawn by the Storekeeper himself. So let's see what we have here...

A depth of twenty-three thousand feet??? And thirty miles away from the ocean trap? I looked at my servant in surprise and even unwitting admiration. He must have made hundreds of trips in complete darkness at such a monstrous depth to get it all there in the first place.

Mission received: Don't drown, Aladdin!

Mission class: unique, group, time-limited

Description: Explore the underwater cave within 2 days, 23 hours, and 59 minutes. Watch out for sea monsters!

Reward: variable

I hadn't received a quest in a good long while! And this one was unique and time-limited! In any other situation I would jump for joy and immediately start hunting treasure. But this was such bad timing! And if I approached the issue from a purely technical standpoint, how could I even haul the treasure up from underwater???

Anyhow, it was a unique quest and, as Kira had once advised me, it could always be sold to others at a profit. Or... I bared my teeth in satisfaction, revealing my sharp fangs... I could use it to have a bit of fun! When else would I get such a great chance to play on the greed and vanity of the players!

"You are forgiven!" I told the Storekeeper and the demon instantly relaxed, got off his knees and straightened his shoulders. "I'll be keeping this paper, though. You go show Valerianna Quickfoot the loot you did get. My sister might see something she likes in there. The rest you should seal up tight under lock and key! Ah yeah, I almost forgot. Also show Valerianna the unopenable case the Gremlin Banker gave me. If even the highest-level enchantress in *Boundless Realm* doesn't have the Intelligence to unravel its mystery, I'll have to regift it. Let the mystery occupy someone else's mind!"

As soon as the demon of avarice disappeared, I demanded my Steward bring me to the Dark Sovereign's personal chambers. I needed to spend some time alone concentrating to gain inspiration. I understood that, in the next few days, I wouldn't have the strength or time to deal with the underwater treasure. In a different situation, without a Sword of Damocles hanging over my neck with the risk of invasion, I might have done it. Even still there would have been a whole bunch of technical issues on the path to victory. But now was not the time for that.

~ Finding a Body ~

I could, however, use that unreachable treasure another way. What did Iron Jeanette say today? Amra was known for his unexpected gifts, which often made his enemies look like fools. And the players knew that so they were in no rush to get into a war against the Dark Sovereign. The last thing they wanted was to join the sad list of losers with blackened reputation. So I needed to ramp up the psychological war and stem the flow of volunteers joining my enemies!

So, in ten minutes, all *Boundless Realm* saw a new message from the Dark Sovereign:

"Today, I'll be celebrating a glorious victory over a grand army of jackasses who forgot they were land animals with hooves and thought they were dolphins. And jackasses, as you know, don't need any clothes or weapons, so I took all their valuables and hid them in a secret location. That means somewhere there is a buried treasure worth tens and maybe even hundreds of millions of game coins. But the Dark Sovereign will simply give the coordinates of that treasure to whoever can write the most acrid, pointed and memorable poem about my enemies and posts it on the **Boundless Realm** *forums. I will be tallying the results in exactly twenty-four hours and will personally name the winner. And they will become a millionaire that very instant! Of*

course, that is if they can take the treasure in the next forty-eight hours. But that will all depend on the moxie of the victor and their team.

P.S. My enemies who want their things back can also take part in this literary competition. Self-criticism will be looked on with special favor.

P.P.S. I am aware the items are exceptional, so the winner will be free to remain anonymous."

* * *

I DIDN'T EVEN have time to leave my chambers before two huge iron-bound chests plunked down on the luxurious carpet right at my feet one after the next. The magical winged demon messengers, wiping the sweat from their brows and grumbling in dismay about the long road and massive weight, both disappeared at once, leaving a palpable stench of sulfur in the air. Without opening the chests, I already knew what was in them. New shipments of blood. And just in the nick of time! I had just finished the last one. My alchemy laboratory was running low on samples, and I'd even already eaten half of the caged beasts. And meanwhile, I was levelling Taste Tester double-time.

A high Taste Tester score was vitally necessary, because it gave me increased defense against sunlight and holy magic. Those types of damage were well known to be a vampire's critical weakness, so that was exactly the way they would want to take down creatures like me. I had to prepare for the inevitable sunlight attack, so I was just downing one vial of blood after the next. And what was more, Regeneration improved in parallel with Taste Tester, which was also pretty vital.

So, what did I have here? It came with a description of the contents as usual. This time it was the "Complete Collection of Blood Samples from the Pearly Sea" and the "Complete Collection of Blood Samples from the Gloomy Swamps." But there was also a letter attached. I immediately unfurled it and read:

"Dear junior brother of the night!

We have heard your call and will come to your aid. All seventeen of the elder vampires of Boundless Realm *voted unanimously that it was time to emerge from the shadows and announce our existence. We come from various races and classes, but the thing that binds us all is that we're each worth a dozen soldiers in battle. And Sovereign, you need not doubt our loyalty because there is too much at stake and we cannot go back. Expect us to come by tomorrow. We would like to make a new home in the ancient ruins of Acheron, which is rumored to be in your lands. We are not afraid of the undead that live there, while the ancient mysteries of the city are worth enough to leave our past lives behind.*

P.S. Amra, if you can, please put together a list of blood samples your collection is missing and send it in a private message. My game name is: Rick Jolly. Human. Level-249 Jester. We'll all try to get some together before going off to see you."

Very interesting! To be honest, I did not understand how the group of vampires was planning to get to my castle. Maybe, when they thought they were ready they'd ask me to send a portal scroll. Or did the elder vampires have modes of transportation normal players couldn't use? Too bad I was such a blockhead and hadn't thought to record all the blood samples I'd already tried. Now, having drunk more than three hundred different samples, it would be quite an undertaking to get that information in one place. And obviously that made it all the harder to know what was missing. I also hadn't ever seen any place that listed all creatures in the game with unique blood for leveling Taste Tester.

Alright, I'd handle the dangerous bloodsuckers on my own. I'd find them a place in my army and something to do in peacetime. What was more, the old ruins of the ancient city, located half day's walk to the south of my castle and teeming with ghosts was not a place claimed by the rougarou clans or any other settlers and refugees. Why not have it become the place for all vampires?

Now I'd have to get to other business. For appearances I at least had to attend Tondik Exuberant's wedding to Vanessa Hamfist. At the same time I'd have to talk with the dwarves about moving to my lands long-term. I had to figure out why the warg werebeasts Darius and Darina had come back to me after asking to be set free. And most importantly, I had to finally see my beautiful goblin bride Taisha. We had so much to discuss.

DESPITE MY high Resistance to Poison and Constitution of well over fifteen hundred, I left the dwarven wedding a bit tipsy and on shaky legs. Heady meads and strong liqueurs flowed like a river, toasts to my health came one after the next and the zombie servants couldn't pick up the empty dishes and bring new ones from the kitchen fast enough. And although half the dwarves were sawing logs under the tables, there were also a good number in a soberer state. My long-awaited coming was met with a howl of joy. I was then quickly assigned a half-bowl "penalty drinking" for the almost one day I had come late. So, popping the cork out of an ancient barrel, they poured some aromatic ruby red wine into a bowl.

"We waited to open it until you came, Sovereign. This is mandrake wine, it's been in an oak barrel for three hundred years and infused with Blue Agave pollen and dragon's blood," Tondik's mother Pirona Zealous explained. "No drink in *Boundless Realm* is rarer or dearer! The legends say dwarven King Balin the Third cut down eight of his own brothers for the pleasure of drinking a bottle of this stuff all on his own!"

Well then... Sounded intriguing. I raised the bowl, wished health to the young couple who were not there at the time, and to all the wedding guests, then I drank the impressive-sounding beverage.

Woah... The floor shuddered under my feet. It felt like I had swallowed liquid fire. But at the same time the drink had a luxurious sweetness and a bitter foretaste that kept my throat from catching flame.

Seemingly, despite the centuries since corking, this wine still had an appreciable quantity of dragon's blood.

Achievement unlocked: Taste tester (328/1000)

~ Finding a Body ~

Blessing received: for the next two weeks your Resistance to Fire is increased by 30%!

I didn't want a repeat of the drunken shitshow I started on the Isle of the Wanton Widow, so I refused a second swallow and returned the bowl to Pirona Zealous, who in her turn also drank a bit of the fiery liquid and let the precious wine make its way further down the room. The gloomy dwarven woman, also barely having caught her breath, dug in her endless jacket pockets and extended me the promised vial of blood:

"Here is the rare item I promised you. Please let me express my gratitude to you, Amra! My son Tondik is now the most respected dwarf in our clan. Our minstrels have even written a ballad about his ghostly hand and all-seeing eye. Now my son will go down in the ages! And look at the bride you found for him, she's just a delight! And she has character, which is very important. She told me off as soon as I came to give advice about their first night. And the expressions she used! I hadn't even heard half of them before! Still I am sure that my son will be well looked after!"

Mission completed: Marrying off a son
Experience received: 40000 Exp., vial of Horror of the Depths blood
Bonus condition completed

Experience received: 80000 Exp. +10 to the opinion of all Dwarves in Boundless Realm

At my level of 442, I was neither hot or cold toward an extra one hundred twenty thousand experience points, but the rare unique creature blood came in very handy. And what timing, improving dwarven opinion of me right before a round of serious negotiations! Now I had no doubt I could entice the underground folk to permanently settle in my lands and get their unsurpassed master smiths to make weaponry for my army. And the capable bearded engineers were very useful in building fortifications both in the Icy Mountains and the other sections of the border.

And that's exactly how it went. Whether the dwarves should remain in the lands of the Dark Sovereign wasn't even up for discussion. Of course they would! All the clans of underground natives were now confident they wanted to move closer to my barely explored but extremely rich ore veins. So we were just ironing out the details, timeframe and their share of the ore. They needed space for workshops, furnaces and smithies, somewhere to keep ore and finished goods and land to build first temporary then permanent housing. We would also need to plan where each clan would make what things, and where to put the underground passages. And they would also be using ore dumps for fortification dikes, and needed to know how much weaponry and armor my army needed and so on and so on...

The dwarves had a perfect idea of all these issues and came with their own suggestions. I could only confirm my agreement, and the Steward behind me added more and more new lines to his thick record book, immediately getting permission for a building project. We agreed on many important issues. The deserted spaces to the west of the castle would soon be turning into a production center for metallurgy and forging. I didn't argue about the little stuff, allowing temporary tax indulgences where needed, and even agreeing to close my eyes to the fact that some of the underground buildings would be placed in areas already settled by orcs and rougarou. Those were minor issues I could solve later, if the undying army didn't wipe me and all these buildings off the face of *Boundless Realm*.

Now in my understanding, this was all supposed to provide for making as much metal, weaponry, tools and armor as necessary in the next few days. I didn't even delve too far into the understanding between the dwarves and leader of the Thief's Guild, someone by the name of Gray

Raven[2]. It said that a tenth of the mithril mined would go to the thief's guild in exchange for a guarantee that none of the thieves would target my storage, the traders, or caravans of valuable metal.

I even signed a special edict saying the most recognized smiths and craftsdwarves, would be freed from serving in the Dark Sovereign's army in perpetuity. After all, it was smarter and more beneficial to place a hundred more experienced soldiers and monsters in formation than one bearded hammerdwarf, only to lose an experienced craftsman if they were wounded or killed.

The negotiations took place right in the big banquet hall on the backdrop of the ongoing boisterous wedding with periodic interruptions for yet another toast.

Dwarven traditions didn't allow us to skip a toast either. That would be a direct insult to the toastmaster, and I didn't want to insult my guests with lack of attention. Wine and strong liqueurs flowed like a river, and I periodically saw messages about failed Poison Resistance checks. Somewhere in the process of the negotiations I also saw that the mission to bring the bearded miners to my side was finished:

---

[2] *Gray Raven is a character from the YA fantasy novel series of the same name by Michael Atamanov.*

~ Finding a Body ~

Mission completed: The only thing better than a mountain is a mountain range
Experience received: 800 Exp.

Eight hundred experience points was an unnoticeable drip to the Dark Sovereign now, cause only for laughter and yet another toast. The dwarves were normal NPC's and didn't understand a thing I was saying, but they didn't refuse to drink. Fortunately, the negotiations with the dwarven leaders ended before my big-eared goblin fell truly drunk. So although Amra was sloshing around as he left the wedding, he still did so on his own two feet.

* * *

"DARIUS, DARINA. I EXPECT you both in the throne room in one minute!" The voice of the Dark Sovereign boomed throughout the castle and surrounding countryside, amplified by the Eye.

I didn't know where the pair of young werebeasts were but, in just one minute, the brother and sister ran into the hall and, stopping two steps from me, fell to one knee and bowed respectfully in tandem. It looked elegant and even beautiful. I didn't know where they'd learned this act. I had already grown used to these young wargs either in the form of man-eating fanged predators or as humans wearing simple street clothes. Now before me were aristocratic children, based both on their stylish clothing of identical coloring and cut and their fine and proper behavior.

I kept silent, not knowing the proper way to formulate the question. "Why the hell did you come back after begging me to let you go? I had to seriously weaken the Gray Pack to fulfill your request!" That's what I wanted to say. But not having found decent words, I simply pointed a clawed glove to Darius and barked an order: "Speak!"

"Sovereign, we were sent to you by a mysterious werebeast society. When you set little Daria and I free, the werebeasts of *Boundless Realm* deeply appreciated the gesture of good will. And now we were sent with a message that your call has been heard and the time has come to pay back like with like. Wargs and werewolves, kitsune and all other shapeshifting beasts are prepared to swear loyalty to you and become your subjects. And we have brought you a summoning medallion." With these words Darius stood up and, with a respectful bow, extended me a round heavy bronze wolf-print medallion, darkened by the passage of time. "Activate it, Sovereign, and hundreds of werebeasts from all *Boundless Realm* will come to you at once!"

Alright then, that changed things, though I still wasn't sure I was getting more than I gave up. When Darius and Darina left, I lost two slots in the Gray Pack. The predators that could have been in those spots now would be deadly creatures over level 400, and would also have given extra bonuses to the strength and survival of my other fifteen pets. And what was I getting in return? I had the urge to instantly activate the medallion and see who came. All that was stopping me was the size of the throne room. What if the hundreds of creatures didn't fit in here and crushed one another to death?

I wanted to order the Steward to take me to the palace exit or simply walk there on foot and take a look at my new first floor after the remodel. But I stopped, seeing Darius frozen in fear and staring stubbornly at the same spot. I followed his gaze and figured it out.

"Yes, that really is the head of your good friend Yunna in the back of my throne. And there a bit higher is the head of Vaash the troll, who you should also remember. They both died fighting for me. And when the new Queen of Lars gave their bodies back to my soldiers and they were burned on a funeral pyre with full honors, the heads of my companions appeared in the back of the Dark Sovereign's throne."

Darius took a slight step back in shock and nodded. I understood his horror perfectly. I still shuddered every time I saw the squirming heads of my dead friends. It was just a sickening sight. I even tried to pull them out, despite the fact they strengthened the artifact just like the other heads, speeding up the flow of Direct Influence Points. But it didn't work. My hands went through the ghostly heads, not feeling any sort of resistance.

And I wasn't the only one who felt grossed out seeing these not-fully-dead heads. My guards said that my goblin nephew Irek just about lost his mind when he first saw his dead sister's head. Irek talked to her for a long time, made promises and begged his sister to forgive him for letting her die. Meanwhile Yunna's head nodded in reply and smiled, sometimes even winking... Irek had to be dragged away by force because the guards saw that the goblin boy was going to climb up the leg of the huge throne and was about to touch the deadly antiaris wood. Sure, Irek would have respawned after dying as he had many times, but the guards still decided to escort the goblin youth out and away from this ghastly artifact.

I used the Steward anyway and, in a moment, found myself at the gates of the large palace square. I went a bit away from all the buildings and other obstacles, then activated the medallion, just clicking the nail of my pointer finger on it. I didn't know why, but I was sure it would work. And indeed, before the shrill ringing died down, a whole zoo of animals appeared on the square. Wolves of all shades and patterns, brown and polar bears, lynxes and pumas, gray and red foxes. I even saw one incredibly large moose. There were no living players among them, just NPC's, but there really were a lot. Fifteen hundred, maybe even two thousand. So I was wrong after all. This number of reinforcements, and I saw quite a few high-level creatures among the new arrivals, was more than enough to compensate the loss of two Gray Pack members.

I just wanted to know why all the werebeasts were in animal form, not human. I glanced at the sky and, seeing the sparse clouds and full moon peeking through them, instantly understood. Yes, there was a full moon over the Southern Continent today, the very peak of werebeast activity. They were unable to control themselves and had turned into wild animals. Too bad, I really would have liked to talk with my new subjects — greet them, inspire them, explain all the most-important rules of my lands. But now it was totally useless. Before me were animals. They couldn't speak or even understand when spoken to.

By the way... it occurred to me what a massive striptease there would be on the square tomorrow when the lycanthropy charms expired.

The werebeasts, insofar as I understood, came to me in their animal forms, leaving all their items and clothing very far away. And after all, among them were almost certainly respected citizens and well-to-do courtly ladies who would be very upset to awaken nude in public. Damn, this had not turned out for the best! I wouldn't want to be here when these thousands of animals transformed back. I'd have to hand those concerns off to my Steward. Let him sort out the newcomers in the morning, issue them some clothing and give them everything else they needed for a new life. And thankfully, the Steward was invulnerable, so even the most enraged werebeasts wouldn't be able to hurt him.

I myself would have to handle the very last important task I had planned for this game session. I was going to use a portal scroll and go to another continent where my beautiful wife Taisha's army was camped.

Day Five and Six
Final Preparations

I WAS WORRIED as a schoolboy to finally see Taisha again. That surprised me, but at least I honestly admitted that I seriously missed my redheaded goblin lady. She was contentious and obstinate, but I still needed her. And in my thoughts I didn't consider Taisha an NPC, even an advanced one. I considered her a real pretty woman. I hadn't seen my virtual bride for five long days and our last time together was the same day I became Dark Sovereign. I didn't really get the chance to have a good talk with Taisha then. When was the last time her and I had really spoken our minds?

I tried to remember and was horrified. It was at the very beginning of the voyage through the scorching desert, before my orcish squadron had even reached the Styx! Then after talking with the *Legion of Steel,* Taisha was very high-strung and challenged me to a duel. We let off our steam then had a decent talk and, after that, we had the truest possible night of love. Insanely passionate and sincere, in real life I had never had that with any woman, even Kira. And after that night, Taisha and I finally came to a mutual understanding. I trusted her absolutely and loved her, and I now could not live without my virtual bride.

But reminiscing just made me want to get right underway. What would the weather be like there now? The issue was that here on the Southern Continent it was a moon-filled night, but on the Eastern it should already have been early morning and I did not want to find myself under the direct rays of the sun. Sure, my Goblin Vampire would no longer just turn to ashes on the spot. My Taste Tester had finally leveled enough for that, and I would be safe for five seconds, which was enough to use a teleportation scroll and get back to my castle. But there was nothing pleasant in feeling your skin burn. What was more, I had only one portal scroll to Taisha's camp. I had plenty going back home. Valerianna Quickfoot had put together hundreds to provide for my subjects and level her skills but, to Taisha's camp, I did in fact have only one.

~ Finding a Body ~

So then, how to find out about the weather? The Eye of the Sovereign was no good for that because I didn't have a map of the location. Should I risk jumping over without scouting? The risk of a mistake was too great. Or... here I face-palmed. I was such a dumbass! I was forgetting about my Dark Sovereign abilities!

"Let thick dark clouds gather over the camp of my wife Taisha!"

You have used 1 Direct Interference Point
You have 424 points remaining

With just one point, the weather problem was solved. Wait just a second! I realized I had enough Direct Intervention Points to respawn a creature I had been saving up for. The issue was that my sister and I hadn't found any information about Ravenous Curs either in the *Boundless Realm* bestiary or on the forums. And yet I had the living skeleton of one in a cage in my dungeons after Hel goddess of death gifted it to me. And when I asked my immediate superior Max Tohner, he opened the service database and dug around for a long time. Then he... just refused to answer, claiming it was top secret. He limited himself to basic words, saying it was created during the beta version of the game before the official release and had existed only on test servers but, in the end, was not added to the game.

I had some idea of how glitchy and unbalanced the beta version was. My vampirism was a holdover from those distant times as was my short name. But the goddess Hel wouldn't have sent me such an unusual gift if there wasn't some possible use. What was more, I needed time for the winds to gather clouds over Taisha's camp. They couldn't just fly in in an instant. So I ordered the Steward to bring me to the dungeon, right to the cage containing Faithful's skeleton.

The level-210 Modified Chimeroid skeleton was lying on the bare stone floor and staring indifferently past me with the red fires burning away in his eye sockets. I was not wrong. My four hundred twenty Direct Intervention Points were plenty, two points per level of the dead creature.

You have used 420 Direct Intervention Points
You have 4 points remaining

All of the caged beast's calm evaporated in that instant! No longer a skeleton, it was now a fur-covered lanky and ghastly canine with unnaturally long paws and elongated jaws like an alligator. And it was thrashing around inside its cage. It was a bit strange, but it was afraid of me! When I took a step closer, Faithful huddled in the opposite corner and started wailing hysterically. No words or commands could do anything.

"Hey dummy, don't be afraid of me! I'm a friend!"

Hoping to calm the terrified canid, I extended a hand through the grate. What happened next came as a complete surprise: the shivering and terrified beast... disappeared!

> **Mission received: The Horror of Beloria**
> **Mission class: Rare, group**
> **Description: hunt down and eliminate the invisible man-eating monster terrorizing the peaceful villages**
> **Reward: 800.000 Exp., Tracking +3, Hunter +3**
> **ATTENTION!**
> **Recommended level: 180+**

Would you look at that! A quest! And they had been so rare recently! But I had no idea where to find this mysterious Beloria, which had once been terrorized by Ravenous Curs. And I thought I knew all the provinces of *Boundless Realm.* Perhaps it was left on the test server and it hadn't ever been added to the game. In any case, I was not planning to complete the mission and kill such an unusual beast, nor was I going to track down some invisible monster. Why look for something that can easily escape a locked cage?! I activated Night Vision and Search for Life one after the next, then met gazes with the creature. It was still huddled in the opposite corner of the cage:

"So then, you must be the horror? But why are you shaking like that? I already said I'm not going to hurt you!"

Animal Control skill increased to level 89!

This time Faithful let me pet him and even gave his tail a couple scant wags. That was more like it! I opened the Gray Pack control interface. The invisible monster had my attention, and I wanted to make him my pet. But where could I put the Ravenous Cur? All fifteen slots were occupied. Who could I remove from the pack?

The four Ancient Forest Wolves, who had been with me since my first days in the game? I had to keep them, and it wasn't just sentimentality. I had long since come up with an explanation for why the corporate programmers just couldn't put all of Fenrir's Pack's abilities into one creature after it proved itself essentially equal to human intelligence at the last stage of its existence.

It was all because a few creatures from Fenrir's Pack had survived and disappeared in

Boundless Realm, so their knowledge and behavior algorithms were not added to the main database. And those were Akella, Lobo, White Fang and Blanca. Way back when we first met I noticed how differently they behaved from normal NPC's, how much they stood out. They were different, and *Boundless Realm* abhorred them, trying to eliminate them time and again. But my four Ancient Forest Wolves managed to survive all the tracking as they had survived the defeat of Fenrir's pack before that. And as a matter of fact, the wolves had been interested in Taisha since our first meeting and were drawn to her, seemingly having recognized they were cut of the same cloth. After all, she was based on the Fenrir's pack algorithms!

I wanted to keep the wargs Darius and Darina in the Gray Pack for the same reason. Sure they may have been tiny puppies back then, but they were also once in Fenrir's pack, so they might have carried some pieces of the puzzle in their code. Today I had suggested that the werebeast teens return to my pack and Darius and Darina immediately agreed. Yes, they were much weaker than the other members of the Gray Pack in level, but levels were easy to get. I was now much more interested in making sure the wargs stayed alive.

So then, who to remove? The three unique Mythical Hounds? No, of course I needed them! In fact, I liked their combat qualities and brutish looks so much that I set myself a goal to collect all twelve Mythical Hounds. After the war, of course. I couldn't worry about that now.

The unique Baron was also out. I wouldn't part with him for anything! The proud and self-confident Alpha Swamp Wolf was now demonstrating such advanced combat characteristics and survival abilities that he could take on ten enemies over level 300 without even losing any hitpoints.

The Gray Pack also had my adopted daughter Chai-nee Shu in it. But that was what made her respawn after death, so I could not let my daughter go until the war was over, no way. The Gray Pack also had the Chieftain of the Clan of the Laughing Otter See-Uhn-Rhu and the Regent of the Clan of the White Lily Uvari-Dor-Shu. With time I planned to move them both out of the Gray Pack, but for now I wanted a guarantee that the sweet rougarou girl Chai-nee Shu wouldn't die in the upcoming war.

The rare Guard Dog which I had stolen from the giantess Modgud's yard? Our relationship just wasn't working out. He still wouldn't accept any name, and wouldn't carry anyone on his back. Sure he was aggressive, fast and bloodthirsty, but no more than that. I figured I could let him go, even though it would be a shame to lose such a strong creature.

But in the end I settled on the rougarou archer Ama-Rohd, who had been in the Gray Pack since the night battle at Frigid Lake, simply to bring my pet number to the max and get higher bonuses from the Pack Hunter perk. I added her at random, and I had just left the quiet girl there. During the battle in Lars she worked wonders, putting one arrow through two and sometimes even three enemies. After recent events and the experience that rained down on everyone, Ama-Rohd had leveled up to four hundred and was now one of the strongest Rougarou in *Boundless Realm*. To my eye, she'd had enough! Especially given that she wouldn't just run away and would remain in my army. With such a high level, she could easily become chieftess of a rougarou clan!

Right after I deleted Ama-Rohd from the Gray Pack, a new creature popped up in the list: a Level-210 Ravenous Cur. I immediately confirmed. The yellow neutral marker on the mini-map instantly turned to blue, meaning ally. At the same time I saw a message saying I'd failed a quest:

The Horror of Beloria mission not completed!

But the lost experience, and especially the two points for leveling two of Amra's skills didn't bother me one bit. I was looking at something else. Now, when the respawned creature became my pet, I could see its perks and abilities. I already knew the Ravenous Cur had the Invisibility ability. And I could easily have guessed it had Quick Run by its lean body and long paws. But as for the Loyalty perk, what good was that?

Loyalty: no circumstances, mind-control spells or enemy abilities can make this creature abandon its allies and change sides in a conflict

Strange perk. What was it even for? A pet was already extremely hard to take from its master, and even harder to lure to another side in battle. So why waste a perk on such nonsense? I looked at the description of the fourth and final perk and my eyes rolled into my forehead. Talent for division. What the heck was this???

Talent for division: unique Modified Chimeroid ability. Each time this creature kills twenty enemies, it will divide into two creatures half its level

Instead of one strong level-210 predator, I'd get two fairly average level-105 fighters? Come on, what the crap? Why would I even want this? I could understand putting a perk like that on, let's say, VIXEN. If the flying snake flew one time over an enemy army and spat poison, I could get rich selling little Royal Forest Wyverns at auction. But in the Ravenous Cur's case, what was the point?

Actually, how crap was this? Having the Ravenous Cur kill twenty enemies would be easy. Let's say I fed Faithful a pack of a thousand field mice. Then I wouldn't have just one canid crocodile that could turn invisible, I'd have fifty-one! Sure, at first they would have quite a low level. But levels, as I said, were easy to get. The first few levels were just a cake walk. Seemingly, I understood why this creature wasn't added to the game. Under certain circumstances, even without a master it could turn into a real menace, emptying entire provinces and even governments. But with an experienced player controlling it... That reminded me!

"Valerianna! Come over here, I've got something you should see."

I didn't manage to finish the private message, because my sister was already standing next to me, transported by the Steward.

"I was already thinking of coming to see you," said the sorceress, extending me the open bone tube. "What a job! I busted my brains over this thing. Well, here you go!"

With these words, Valerianna Quickfoot handed me a golden sphere the size of a pool ball.

It was perfectly smooth and polished to a shine.

Insufficient Intelligence to identify object
Required minimum Intelligence to identify:
1200

"This is the Egg of New Life," my sister eagerly informed me, showing plainly that the Wood Nymph did have that much Intelligence. "It's a very rare item which allows a player to change character in *Boundless Realm*. It's the only way to start the game over from level one. Take it, Tim. As for me, no matter how this war with the undying army ends, I have decided to quit computer games for good. We live in such an interesting world, I'm done spending my days cooped up in a virtual reality capsule!"

I accepted the rare Egg and stuck it in my inventory:

"Thanks for the gift, Val. But while you're in the game, look at this big-toothed guy."

I didn't have to explain a thing to the Beastmaster. Valerianna needed five seconds to familiarize herself with Faithful's description, after which she couldn't hold back and broke out swearing. Then she looked at me with her eyes wide in surprise:

"That's what I'm talking about! What an awesome combination of abilities. Loyalty goes especially well with the rest. With one of these under your control, all the copies that split off will obey unquestioningly and attack your enemy! I've never even seen that perk before. But it's a way to get around the maximum pet number. I wonder if this is even legal?"

I just shrugged my shoulders unconfidently, because I had no idea how the corporation would react if the Gray Pack had, let's say, seventy pets instead of the fifteen it was supposed to allow. Or if Valerianna Quickfoot replaced one of her hornets with a pack of fifty Ravenous Curs.

"On first glance it doesn't look fit to live with that set of perks," I said, voicing my own observations. "In battle, it will quickly turn from a few strong beasts into a swarm of harmless little shrimp. But if you give the first one the Pack Hunter perk instead of the speed one, which is pretty worthless for an invisible creature, the picture changes drastically!"

"Yes, Tim. If you let it all go on autopilot, in a prolonged battle the Ravenous Cur really will quickly lose effectiveness and drop severely in level, multiplying into a large number of weak copies. But if you keep an eye on all these clones and don't let the highest-level ones land finishing blows... It would be hard but possible... In any case this creature isn't made for a prolonged battle because it will always eventually turn it into a pack of little cockroaches. But it can be fun at the very beginning of battle! You could cobble together and level a whole army of invisible crocodiles who could instantly attack enemy support and mages, cutting down everything alive before the enemy's main forces get back, then have them return to invisibility. Due to the extremely high number in the pack, the main high-level fighters would have such great damage multipliers that those Ravenous Curs could eat their way through any army!"

"You deal with that then, Val. And you only have a day and a half before the enemy army is within view of my castle."

WHY WAS IT so dark? That was the first thing I thought after going through the portal to the Eastern Continent. Was it still night here? Or was there a solar eclipse today? No, that wasn't it. Seemingly, I had overdone the thickness of the dark clouds a bit and now they were so thick no light could get through. The sky was drawn-over with such black impenetrable gloom that I even had to turn on Night Vision.

The world grew more contrasting and I looked around. So, where was I? And what direction was Taisha's camp? All around I saw only tall dark cliffs and the odd flash of distant lightning. I was getting the impression that I was at the bottom of a deep stone well. The mini-map wasn't helping change my mind, either. It showed a gold marker right on my position. Weird, was that me now? But then... one of the nearby rocks moved and turned toward me! From seventy feet up, two huge red eyes were staring down at me!

> *Sphinx*
> *Wise and Eternal*
> *Unique indestructible creature*

"Well, well. If it isn't the Sphinx!" I must have said that out loud because the lion-man answered me with a booming echo:

"Well, well. If it isn't the Dark Sovereign!"

An awkward silence followed. I was fitfully trying to remember everything I knew about the Sphinx. Predatory, immortal, tried to confuse people in the desert. I also knew that it acted with a certain nobility, never attacking a victim unannounced. It always offered travelers a chance at salvation by answering its clever riddles correctly.

Here in *Boundless Realm,* it belonged to the realm of demigods or maybe even higher, also having the Indestructible quality and a beastly appetite. As far as I knew, the Sphinx was the only indestructible creature in the game that could attack and eat a player. As a rule, indestructible creatures were plentiful in *Boundless Realm*. For example NPC guards in locations for beginner players were invincible. But those NPC's either never attacked first or, like my Steward and Storekeeper, were fundamentally incapable of hostility. But the Sphinx's imbalance was compensated by the fact that this legendary creature always stayed in the same place, which was very hard to reach, making it nearly impossible to encounter by accident. But by some wonder, my wife Taisha had convinced the Sphinx to leave that place and follow her.

Good girl, Taisha. But what should I do now, where to look for my green-skinned companion? Was I really just going to ask this red-eyed walking mountain?

"Oh great Sphinx! Could you please tell me where to find Taisha?"

The mountain leaned in closer and bellowed in reply, pressing me with a column of hot air:

"For that you'll need to get past me! If you answer my riddle correctly, I'll allow you to pass peacefully. If you cannot, you have only yourself to blame! Tell me, Dark Sovereign, which creature has one voice and yet becomes four-footed and two-footed and three-footed? No creature on the planet changes the way it does. When four-footed, it has the least strength and moves the slowest!"

At first, I was afraid I'd have to respawn, and I didn't have a second portal scroll. But after the first words of this very famous riddle, I quickly remembered and could hardly wait for the huge being to unhurriedly finish its rather drawn-out retelling.

"Sphinx! After King Oedipus answered that riddle correctly three thousand years ago, everyone knows the answer! It is: a human! Think of something harder, this is child's play..."

"Well it used to work," the Sphinx replied, somewhat abashed. "And that is not going to count, Amra! You didn't figure out my riddle, you just knew the answer! So here is my second riddle. It's a bit harder, as you wanted. What's red and green and goes round and round and round?"

"Sphinx, are you actually like a child?! This is the exact riddle Merlin asked you[3]!"

"You're no fun!" the huge monster objected, just like a child. "Just like your wife Taisha, you know all the answers already. I wasted a whole day on her and have nothing to show for it. I must have asked her a thousand riddles, but she'd already

---

[3] Translator's note: In the Rodger Zelazny series *Chronicles of Amber*, this section in particular is famed in Russia for a humorous mistranslation of the answer, "a frog in a Cuisinart."

heard them all! Just go. What's the point...?"

The huge creature moved aside, opening a passage in the stone wall. Just then, the Gray Pack appeared next to me, slightly late. And a few of the rougarou and wargs were somewhat shaken up by the sudden transportation. Chai-nee Shu appeared in just her nighty. She must have been pulled right out of bed. And the huge half-man half-lion greeted them with great interest:

"What an interesting retinue you have! So many unique canines! Does that mean you like big dogs? Well then why don't you have the strongest hound in all *Boundless Realm*? I'm talking of course about the three-headed Cerberus!"

Good question. And it was right. What was stopping me from taking Cerberus? Or at least trying.

Sure, I didn't know for sure where the large fierce beast lived. But that was not really a problem. My Dark Riders could move throughout the cloudy reaches of the Styx, and the entrance to the kingdom of the dead was somewhere around there. Even if my emissaries couldn't bring me, I could ask Charon. That old geezer definitely knew. Every day he ferried dead souls there. And Cerberus couldn't attack me, because Amra had an ability that guaranteed no legendary or mythical canine would ever come at him unprovoked. And Cerberus couldn't use his renowned aura of terror, either because I had complete immunity to fear. Fair enough, I'd have to try!

I thanked the Sphinx for the valuable advice and entered the narrow rock passage. It looped around for a quarter mile before leading me and my companions out into a brightly lit camp, located in a valley surrounded by mountains on all sides. There were hundreds of large and small tents. Lots of very unusual creatures. The majority of my wife's army was made up of nagas, which were half-human and half-snake but there were also plenty of goblins, kobolds, and giants. When we walked up close they all stopped their weapons training and led long studious gazes over my group. At any rate, none of them ever tried to stop me, so I walked into the middle of camp over to the largest tent.

The first surprise awaited me there. The entrance to the leader's tent was guarded by someone I knew very well — Djinn Sultan Al-Hassan Godsbane. Once upon a time, this deadly creature had escaped confinement and killed my Amra in an instant along with half of the strongest players in the *Legion of Steel*. But now I could see a red-skull marker over the Djinn Sultan. He was over twenty levels higher than me, but less than fifty. A strong enemy, but no longer quite so insurmountable. With the Gray Pack, I could most likely take down this so-called godsbane.

And the Djinn Sultan understood that. There was a look of confusion and insecurity frozen on his grayish-blue ghostly face. Finally having made up his mind how to treat me, Al-Hassan gave a bow of respect:

"Sovereign, your wife Taisha is asleep. Many desert clans came to join her army today. She was accepting their chiefs until late and only got to bed around sunrise."

I gave a short nod to the uncanny doorman and, leaving the Gray Pack on the step, threw back the tent flaps and walked inside. Taisha's room was dark and smelled of sandal wood. And my goblin wife was asleep on a black warg pelt, her arms splayed and her fiery hair spread out on the pillows. I was surprised to see the goblin beauty using the black thief's clothes I'd once gifted her as pajamas. The thin fabric didn't hide a thing, in fact it emphasized the shapes of her feminine body. I looked over my sleeping bride with polite interest until suddenly one detail drew my attention. Taisha's stomach looked round. Was my wife pregnant? Could players impregnate NPC's? As far as I knew, *Boundless Realm* didn't have such a feature. The other way around yes, I had once met a player named Belle Sweetypie who was playing a quest to bear Fenrir's son, but that was different.

~ Finding a Body ~

Just then, Taisha opened her eyes and caught my gaze. Her eyes instantly went wide in surprise, and her lips started quavering. She just couldn't believe she wasn't dreaming. I smiled and sat down on the pelt of the predator my wife and I had once killed:

"Why hello Taisha Spark. You asked me to come find you after I'd sorted out all the weird stuff going on around me. Well now I have and, as you can see, I came to find you."

The green-skinned beauty finally believed this was real, looked carefully at me and, not hiding her surprise and admiration, said:

"My husband look how powerful you've become! I'm taken aback! The goblin race has never been blessed with such a powerful leader before."

Taisha sat up, extended her hands, and I embraced my beautiful companion firmly. The few minutes that followed we just sat there, hugging in silence. Then I pulled the Egg of New Life from my inventory:

"A gift for you! I'm no longer immortal and, if anything happens to me, there will be no one to protect you. I don't want my enemies to find you after, because I will slaughter them all many times. Many, many undying will be trying to find you. Even worse, a group of people in the other world have a strange obsession with you. Using this artifact you can change into whatever creature you desire! No one will ever find the connection between the new you and the beautiful Taisha."

My wife held the heavy golden egg in her hands for a long time staring at the extremely rare item in thought. Then she gave me back the artifact and stroked her bulging belly with tenderness:

"This is your son! So I cannot die no matter what, nor respawn. Because I would respawn, but not him. And don't you dare think of dying and losing this war. You and I have a long time left to live, and so does our child!"

"CHARON! CHARON!" my voice carried a long way in the night, frightening the creatures that lived along the river.

My big-eared goblin was up to his knees in dark stagnant water and holding a bottle of wine. All around me was impenetrable fog, and it was pitch dark. Where this place was I had no idea. But Night the Dark Rider responsible for the western border and the River Styx brought me right here when I asked to be brought to Charon. And that meant the immortal geezer must have been somewhere nearby.

Finally I heard a familiar rhythmic splashing and a dark figure emerged from the fog. The ferryman of souls was piloting his ancient vessel with pole in hand.

"What are you screaming about? You scared away all my fish!"

I extended the bottle to the old grumbling man:

"Mandrake wine! This is the best stuff made by mortals on the planet!"

The ghastly old man's brusque demeanor immediately turned to intrigue. Charon extended his pole and helped me up on his boat. He spent a long time twirling the bottle in his hands and looking it over, clicking his tongue in approval. But he didn't open it and stashed it beneath the bench.

"What do you need then? Shall I bring you somewhere?"

"That is one thing. I need to get somewhere that's hard to reach and you know the way. But that's for later. First I wanted to talk business. I've got a big war with the undying on the horizon and I wanted to ask you a question. How hard would it be to get your divine relatives to come help me? And how much might that run me?"

Charon thought for a long time. And when he spoke, I could sense a lack of confidence in the old man's voice, actually more like veiled refusal:

"They'll never agree, Amra. I mean, you know us gods. Before they do you a favor, they make you run around the world on some wild goose chase. One day its 'perform twelve feats,' another it's 'go get the Golden Fleece.' After that it's something else. And it would be fine if they really needed those things. But they never do. The gods are just bored after a thousand years of life. And we mock the people who pray to us, sending them to every corner of the globe with ridiculous tasks."

I understood that I needed to fundamentally change tactics. I couldn't be asking the gods for things, I needed to approach this differently. If the millennia had bored them so, maybe I could have them beg me to join in and have some fun.

"Yes, that's what I'm talking about! There will be a massive *battle royale* soon! Even the Trojan War will pale in comparison both in number of fighters and diversity. And I'm offering the gods the chance to take part. Hundreds of thousands of soldiers, overwhelming hordes of monsters! Mythical creatures, djinns, humans, orcs and elves, combat magic and all kinds of blessings on every side. And the most unbelievable pets. You won't see that kind of variety in the best zoo! Even the Sphinx, who's legendary for always staying in one place, couldn't hold resist the temptation and will be there!"

~ Finding a Body ~

"The Sphinx is coming?" Charon was surprised and didn't hide it. "I know that old cat. He hasn't moved an inch in fifteen thousand years. And you're saying he's going to take part? That means this really will be a sight to see. But Amra, just so you know, the gods can't just up and come to someone else's party uninvited. It isn't right. It just feels somehow like we're punching below our weight..."

"Well that won't be how this goes at all! As Dark Sovereign, I invite them officially! I have the full right to do so! So no one will be surprised if all your relatives show up. And I can say for sure that no one will think it's beneath them! The price for entry to the whole grand show is just one little vial of their blood each! Then they can muck about to their hearts' content!"

"Is that it? Just a bit of blood? Then count me in!" the ghastly old man took an old bronze knife from a gap in the boards and slit his arm. "Will this be enough?"

I hurried to place an open flask to it, collecting a few of the thick dark droplets.

Blood of Charon (unique alchemy ingredient)

"That's plenty!" I said, hurrying to stuff the rare divine blood into my inventory.

What a treat this was for a vampire! Divine

blood raised Taste Tester by fifty points in one go! And if any of Charon's kin decided to show up, well... I was afraid to even guess. Meanwhile Charon, whose wound was already healed, started speaking:

"My sister little Eris dropped by a couple days ago. She was very upset that I gave the ancient gong away. And she's mad at you, Amra. She says you summoned her to do a job and didn't pay her for it, not even as much as a simple thank you! Eris meanwhile turned all your enemies against one another in Lars. More than three thousand undying died in that little dustup! Many of them were so mad they refused to stay in the war against the Dark Sovereign! You should apologize to Eris or something, at least send her a gift..."

I promised to fix it and curry the favor of the easily offended and capricious goddess of strife. Finally, it was time to discuss the main reason I'd come to these marshy riverbanks, and ask Charon to bring me to see Cerberus.

"I really don't recommend it, Amra!" the immortal geezer tried to talk me out of it. "You have just one life left, and Cerberus is a ferocious monster, the very strongest beast in *Boundless Realm*! And his temperament..." Charon turned around for some reason and started looking over his old ratty chlamys. Only then did I notice that, at butt level, it had a new patch sewn in.

"I need to go there regardless!" I kept insisting. But the ferryman of souls just waved a hand gloomily:

"It's your life, it's up to you. For what it's worth, the kingdom of the dead is just two steps from here. You can get there on your own without my help. But let me warn you, no one can keep Cerberus for long! Even Hercules," Charon said, distastefully spitting out the hated name of the man who once bested him. "He had to let the three-headed hound go eventually. And let me warn you right now, I will not transport Cerberus in the boat! He won't fit, and he doesn't like me for some reason. So you'll have to use a strong chain of some kind to lead him up the river on your own. Well, that's if you can actually handle the fanged titan, of course."

Wait! I actually could get a strong enchanted chain. I got the idea to rush to my castle and have my dwarves forge me a mithril chain. It would be strong, and there was no better metal for enchanting. But I remembered the legend of another ferocious beast, Fenrir. He had broken several such chains, even those forged by the best smiths in the land. And yet that powerful wolf, who struck fear into the hearts of even the gods, was powerless against a hair rope. But I had something better. A whip made from a hair of Hel, goddess of death. That would make a fine leash! So I asked Charon to get underway.

* * *

THE CURSED CERBERUS was quite awe-inspiring, both his colossal dimensions and ghastly appearance. His three heads each had a set of jaws that could easily fit a sedan. His teeth were each a foot and a half long! Instead of hair he had poisonous snakes. His bark knocked me off my feet and shook me to the bone. If not for my absolute immunity to fear — a property I gained from the Fenrir's Paws gloves — I would have just forgotten about his and run far away without looking for a road. And what a stench emanated from all three of Cerberus's jaws! My eighty percent Poison Resistance and respectable Regeneration wasn't enough. I constantly had to drink alchemical elixirs to restore my health and raise my resists.

And although Cerberus was not trying to attack my Goblin Herbalist, our massive level gap was too much for me to take him under control even very briefly. VIXEN came at this importune moment to gift her master some rare prey, but the ghastly hound knocked her out of the air with a roar, then tore the one-hundred-thirty-foot-long level-430 winged snake to shreds in less than a minute together with her bounty. I didn't even manage to see what my stunning emerald pet had brought, nor could I help her in any way.

And the huge carcass of the winged snake wasn't even enough for Cerberus! Seemingly there was no sating his thousand-year hunger. Whatever food I brought, the hound just snapped it up and demanded more. And although I brought A LOT of food, in the end I used it all up. I even had to feed him the Mythical Hound guard dog, may Modgud and all dog lovers forgive me. It just hadn't found a place in the Gray Pack. It was a great shame, but the alternative was to turn around and leave empty handed.

Time passed and nothing changed. The only thing that consoled me was that my Animal Control, Regeneration and Superboss skills were going up at least once a minute, if not faster. I actually found a way to level these abilities very rapidly. I just sat calmly next to Cerberus as he drooled profusely and fed the fearsome beast by hand all while making sure he didn't bite off my arm and that his poison-snake hair didn't bite me. I was really hoping that my rapidly-improving Animal Control skill would eventually be enough. To increasing my chances, I also took all my remaining stat points — and by level 442 I had 936 of them piled up — and placed them into

Charisma.

And then, after seven hours of sitting around bored, when I was just about to doze off in exhaustion, it happened. A line in the Gray Pack control interface flickered past saying a new creature was available: *Level-999 Legendary Hound.* Unfortunately I didn't react in time, and missed that little nibble. But it gave me renewed strength and, an hour and a half later, I didn't miss my second chance!!!

Cerberus
Modified Chimeroid
Level-999 Legendary Hound (unique creature)

Hurriedly, my hands shaking in agitation, I tied the indestructible hair-whip around the middle neck.

The marker on the mini-map flickered and the red became green. Not even blue, meaning ally, simply green: friendly.

ATTENTION!!!
You may only control this creature for a limited time
Cerberus will break free in 71 hours 59 minutes 56 seconds

Three days? More than enough because my

enemies had already crossed the Upper Styx and mountain passes. All they had left was a day and a half or so to reach my castle.

I didn't take Cerberus anywhere, leaving him in his usual place to guard the entrance to the kingdom of the dead. There was no reason for my enemies to know about this little goblin's new weapon. Cerberus should come as a great little surprise! But still, I was not allowed to leave so easily.

Black whirlwinds gathered, and next to me appeared a ghastly old man in a black chlamys just as raggedy as Charon's but wearing a crown of bone over his matted gray hair. He had a heavy staff raised in his bony hands.

Hades
God of the Kingdom of the Dead (unique creature)

Would you look at that! Here was one of the most powerful gods of the ancient pantheon! The brother of Zeus and Poseidon! I gave an immediate deep bow and greeted the deity with all the politeness I could muster.

"Come now, Dark Sovereign. That's no way to behave..." grumbled Hades, lowering his staff and leaning on it.

Seemingly this was an irritated master

coming to the news that his guard dog was being stolen from his yard. But he quickly realized it was all temporary and in full accordance with the game rules, so he didn't argue. "Just don't make my little dog mad and try to keep him out of the light. Cerberus's right head has conjunctivitis, so bright light hurts him. And feed Cerberus well before releasing him back. Even I sometimes forget."

Judging by the three-headed hound's insatiable hunger, "sometimes" meant at least the last few millennia. But I of course didn't say that out loud: Quite the opposite, I answered that I was a vampire and also couldn't stand light. And so I said would be just as cautious with this astonishing creature.

"Ah Amra, it's good you reminded me about vampires and blood. There's a rumor going around that you're inviting people to a rare spectacle of combat. I myself am not a great lover of shows and wouldn't go, but my wife Persephone has been nagging because we haven't been out in three thousand years. She keeps saying we're gonna grow mold down in my kingdom. So we will be coming. Here, take our payment for the ticket!"

Blood of Hades (unique alchemy ingredient)

Blood of Persephone (unique alchemy ingredient)

~ Finding a Body ~

I then trying not to reveal my extreme excitement, accepted and stashed both vials of divine blood. Cool! Another +100 to Taste Tester!!! The old man then started making excuses:

"Persephone and I of course are no warriors. So I wouldn't count on us doing any fighting. We're just coming to watch and do some relaxing. But I heard that Ares and Athena are planning to have a grand old time, just like in the olden days. They're supposedly already sharpening their swords and polishing their armor. So expect us all to drop by! See you soon, Amra!"

I MORE FELL than walked out of the elevator on floor 333 of the Castle. My legs were quavering and not obeying me, there were dark spots floating before my eyes. I was simply so exhausted I was in a stupor. It wasn't enough that I had hardly slept for two nights, my next day was also just packed to the brim with events. And my game session turned out longer than ever. My only desire was to crawl into bed and collapse, dead to the world. But that was not in the stars. Kira was inside waiting for me.

"Timothy, apologies for what happened

yesterday. I just didn't expect it to turn out that way, I wasn't ready. But if you haven't changed your mind, let's go!"

"Where?" I didn't understand, my mind stalled in exhaustion.

"What do you mean where? Let's just sign the thing quick without all the pomp and circumstance. It will be safer for you if no one knows about our marriage. Let's just have couple trusty quiet witnesses and your sister Valeria. We don't need to invite anyone else. Your suit is on a hanger in the next room, there are a pair of rings on the table, too. The witnesses are waiting in flying cars in the parking lot, so get dressed and let's go!"

It was all so unexpected and spontaneous that I couldn't find any objections. Then, just an hour later my ring finger was adorned with a prim little gold band. And Kira had the same decorating her finger, though to be honest a bit smaller.

"Timothy, did I make your wish come true?" my glamorous wife asked cunningly on the ride home. She looked utterly incomparable in her white wedding dress.

"Wish? When I asked you yesterday, that was an outpouring of the soul. That was sincere, not some wish. But considering the significance of what's happened of course my wish has come true! I could never have even dreamed I'd marry a woman this pretty!"

But for some reason that answer didn't satisfy Kira and she looked at me in astonishment:

"Wait, wait, Timothy. Are you trying to say that was authentic? You just spontaneously offered me your hand and heart? It wasn't about Inessa Tyle's will?"

"Kira, I have no idea what's in that will! More accurately, Andrei Soloviev mentioned that your grandma willed me two percent of the corporation's stocks. But I don't get what that has to do with our wedding."

"Two percent?!" My young wife started laughing sonorously. "You don't want thirty-three and three tenths of a percent? My grandmother's adherence to old-fashioned viewpoints was not limited to family matters. She was also a bigtime schemer. Clearly, she wanted to test my feelings for you. The will says that if we get married before the next board meeting, you get all of Inessa Tyle's shares. And that is no more and no less than one third of all stocks in the Boundless Realm Corporation! It includes the eleven percent I would have gotten and everything that was going to all other potential heirs. To be honest, the will also said that if you died, my share would increase from eleven to thirteen percent. I assume that was my grandmother testing my feelings as well, just a bit on the grimmer side. But I have turned down the twenty-five and thirty billion credits in exchange for a great husband!"

Val, sitting next to us in the flying car, was listening to Kira's speech. Once again she couldn't hold back her emotions and swore out loud. How many times had I told my sister off for that! But this time Kira and I both wagged our fingers, then exchanged glances and started laughing. And I answered about her losing billions:

"All those losses are more than compensated by the fact that our family will now retain control over the richest corporation on the planet."

"How do you mean, Timothy? Your share isn't enough, and even if you manage to get mine unfrozen, our combined total still wouldn't constitute a majority at the meeting!"

"That's my concern now, Kira. Believe you me, we easily can win that vote. But first I have another battle that will be no less heated! And I'm counting on you to help. I need an item I asked you to get for me a long time ago."

Two Battles
Two Peaces

THE BATTLE WAS already entering its eighth hour, and there was still no end in sight. It all began when thirty large enemy ships had tried to cross Frigid Lake in the early morning under thick fog. Despite their best efforts, the incursion did not go unnoticed, and the attackers were met by a pirate fleet of eighty galleys and triremes. And that started a pitched battle. Pirate Queen Angelica Wayward had more than twice as many ships, but the two forces were approximately evenly matched. At the end of the day, living players were just more intelligent than NPC's and made decisions faster.

The sea monsters loyal to the Dark Sovereign were a big help, though. They were commanded by the thirty-foot-long Oceanid Olilissa, Max Sochnier's longtime companion. I had her brought from the ocean to Frigid Lake well in advance so she could get used to the fresh water and bring the local creatures over to my side. And the mermaids, naiads and tritons really did help, puncturing the bottom of the enemy ships from underwater, tangling their nets in the rudders, breaking oars and killing oarsmen.

But in the end, it wasn't the rage of the pirates or the aquatic monsters that tipped the scales of victory, it was the unexpected arrival of Hades' brother Poseidon, king of the sea. I didn't know how the marine god, who was thought to live at the bottom of the deepest oceans, got into the icy and freshwater mountain lake. He couldn't have come up rivers. That path was blocked by the dam my giants and cyclopes built. And that slippery rapscallion hadn't paid for his ticket with a drop of blood. When I cautiously mentioned that Max Sochnier, who had a better understanding of the sea god's nature, explained that Poseidon hadn't come for the Dark Sovereign. Instead he was answering the call of his children and grandchildren: the cyclopes.

Poseidon fundamentally changed the balance of forces with his devastating trident and all that remained of the enemy fleet, just two tattered ships, fled in shame. However Pirate

~ Finding a Body ~

Queen Angelica Wayward only had eleven of eighty ships in fighting shape herself.

At the same time, twenty thousand undying were attempting to break through in the Icy Mountains. But there my defenses were strong. There were many strategically placed fortifications covering the whole route. Ballistae and catapults were mounted on all guard towers, and my many orc crossbowmen and Drow archers knew exactly what to do when the time came. What was more, we set off a couple of avalanches to quench the enemy ardor and bury their hopes of getting through the Icy Mountains both literally and figuratively.

But the west was more problematic, nothing was going right there. No matter how my brave soldiers tried to hold back the enemy, no matter how they rained down arrows, stones and spells on the attackers, there were just too many undying jostling across the Styx. No less than three hundred thousand based on my scouts' reports, and maybe even half a million. The Boundless Realm Corporation's correspondents, who were broadcasting the epic battle live, were choking with elation and giving ever-larger numbers. In their words, there were now one or even one and a half million players, but everyone who had a rough idea how these things worked knew that wasn't exactly true. Sure, the

Boundless Realm Corporation wanted to trumpet their grand success and claim huge player interest in the event, but there were many times less participants than President Thomas Heywood was hoping.

And my actions were what killed the demand. First and foremost, my spontaneous poetry contest was wildly popular, surpassing even my boldest expectations. Of course, I wouldn't have had time to actually read the several million paltry rhymes posted on the forum, so I called for help. Hundreds of *Boundless Realm* bards responded eagerly to my call, alongside some very famous and respected real-world poets. They sifted through that mound of cockle-shells, leaving me with only the most brilliant and biting works. I didn't even have to pay my volunteer assistants, because there was just too much demand to judge this contest.

The biggest zinger was that all the poets who had passed the selection stages were invited to one of the biggest news channels on earth, where they made a real show of choosing the winner live on air. The CEO of the channel got in touch with me in advance to ask my permission. And dressed as their characters, the players recited their poems, answered questions from the audience, talked about what made their gameplay in *Boundless Realm* interesting and took part in all kinds of contests. He really tried to get me to come into the studio myself too, offering eight-figure sums for the hour-and-a-half-long program, but I refused outright. I didn't have the time to fly half way around the world and record a show. I needed every precious minute to prepare to repel the undying attack.

Nevertheless, I did agree to give a speech on camera to the winner. It was a very famous Japanese poetess, a level-115 Brigand in the game. I couldn't speak Japanese but I was told that, in translation, her haiku sounded approximately like this:

The Dark Sovereign stared
As the hordes approached his castle
What naïve losers!

More than two hundred fifty million people watched that show, the ratings were off the charts and the whole audience wore identical black t-shirts with a white shark, the emblem of the Dark Sovereign! The victor received the coordinates and the remaining poets also got a prize: a random object from the Dark Sovereign's treasure chest. Funny how things work out. I didn't even manipulate the results one bit. It was entirely and truly at random. But the prize was the very same legendary necklace from the Elven Amazon set which Kristina Mozzi, the TOP warrior queen of the *Legion of Steel* had lost. I honestly thought my sister Valerianna had put the invaluable object up for auction, but apparently she told the Storekeeper to fritter it away.

Even a bomb going off in the studio would have caused less uproar. The audience shot to their feet and began screaming and applauding. The victor then jumped onto a table and wailed into a microphone in exhilaration, even losing the ability to speak for a time and making disjointed sounds. The host of the show even lost control of the situation, while the millions of viewers most likely started thinking all the Dark Sovereign's chests were filled with stuff just like that. And that would have meant he also had the funds to hire any number of mercenaries. After that broadcast, many players must have lost confidence that they could ever defeat the Dark Sovereign.

Another reason the players had little appetite for war was my last video clip, in which I showed the thousands and thousands of NPC warriors training to repel the attack, as well as the many player mercenaries who had come to fight on my side. I also showed my smithies, which worked day and night and my dungeons and torture chamber just waiting for their chance to shine. I also showed the master of the torture chamber, the fearsome level-325 Grave Curse, who loved nothing more than sucking levels and stat points down to zero. I showed my huge alchemy laboratories and the NPC laborers plugging away. There were also some Alchemist players busy preparing medicinal elixirs, magical bombs and poisons for the Dark Sovereign's army day and night.

What was more, not all the poisons were made to kill players or sap their strength. I purposely demonstrated one of the poisons of a different variety for the camera. It was an advanced and significantly improved version of the clever elixir I used at the Goblin Wedding competition in the village of Tysh. This time, the extremely strong attack of diarrhea was accompanied by skin blackening, hair falling out and an array of other effects, which were extremely unpleasant both to look at and smell. Respawning wouldn't save them either, it would take a whole week of real time before the negative effects began to fade. As far as I heard from Taisha, who was watching the situation in the enemy camp carefully, after my video, tens of thousands of players, especially the handsome elf men and pretty elven ladies chickened out. Further, my remaining opponents had been dubbed the "fail army" on the forum, which of course did not add any popularity to the already flagging event.

And everyone at the corporation understood that. Today, at four o'clock AM I jumped up after an alarming call from Iron Jeanette and hurried to work in a taxi because my enemies were on the attack. But another call followed. It was Tina, my boss's secretary. Tina was at work at this ungodly hour, as were many other Boundless Realm employees:

"Timothy the president of the corporation just called the Special Projects Department himself. He was asking for you. He sounded very upset. I told him you were on the way to work. Thomas Heywood said that, when you get to the building, he wants you to come straight to his office. He wants to discuss your plans for the upcoming battle from the very first shots to the culmination and finally the fall of the Dark Sovereign. In his words, 'despite the low number of participants, everything must look epic so the audience is entertained.'"

Low number of participants? Very upset? And that was not all! Today it finally became clear that there were many fewer participants in the event than he was hoping. So, did the president want me to just lie down in a certain round and let them win?! No doubt he was hoping to place some bets at a casino for a quick buck, huh? That was not gonna fly! To hell with him, I'd never surrender! If the Dark Sovereign did fall today then, before dying, I would strive with all my might, not sparing any effort and certainly not sparing any enemies!

~ Finding a Body ~

"So then, Tina..." I tried very hard to hold back and talk normally. "Please give President Heywood a message from me: 'Suck on my little green pee-pee!'"

Based on the gasp of fear, she just about fainted.

"Yes Tina, you heard right. I want you to say that word for word. And don't worry. If Thomas fires you I promise to pay compensation of one million credits. Also tell him this: 'I'll see you at the board of directors meeting!'"

There was no way back now. Even if the Dark Sovereign won today's battle, the president would never forgive the insult and, by the end of the day, I'd certainly lose my job. But still I was satisfied that I had told this slippery asshole exactly what I thought about him.

THE BIG BATTLE was now in a lull. We'd blown the dam, releasing a flood which split the undying army and swept away their front lines. Unfortunately, nowhere near all my enemies were sent to respawn. It was hard to say how many players died, I hadn't seen any numbers. Maybe eight thousand, maybe twenty. In any case I was greatly hoping for Hel and Hades, who had the power to temporarily trap players in the kingdom of the dead and delay respawn.

So now I could tally up my first results. And to my immense pity, they were not comforting. Of my eighty thousand initial soldiers, I had no more than fifty thousand left in formation. And that was at the fact that my generals were trying to place respawned mercenaries from the clans *Mercs*, *Amazons*, *Bregan D'Aerthe* and around ten other smaller clans on my front lines. The enemy force had also suffered deaths in the tens of thousands but they all respawned and were still pressing in, occupying the narrow pass leading to the flat plain foot by foot.

The level-402 rougarou archer Ama-Rohd was dead. The nameless dark elf who was the last survivor of the night battle at Frigid Lake had also passed, having been made commander of my archers. After a severe wound, the god of war Ares was also forced to leave the battle and return to Mount Olympus. I personally considered him a hotshot, too self-confident in battle, with no real knowledge of tactics. He just ran alone into the ranks of undying, which didn't exactly work out. I was even forced to recall Cerberus after his life bar sagged into the red. I handed him off to some healers, but the three-headed hound's pride had clearly somewhat diminished. He just bared his teeth sluggishly when they treated his wounds, healed him with magic and pulled the deeply-embedded harpoons, spears and massive ballista bolts from his body.

The Ravenous Cur was also basically used up. While saving the dying Cerberus, I got distracted and stopped watching Faithful and his many clones. And that horde, now without attention, attacked the enemy rear guard of support players, craftsmen and healers. The invisible monsters flew through the noncombat characters in an avalanche of blood, eating them up and dividing uncontrollably. When I came back, instead of the menacing Ravenous Curs I started with, I had a pack of low-level bugs, which the undying were stomping left and right. I saved ten of the invisible monsters, but with their level at twenty or thirty, they posed no threat to anyone.

But the Sphinx was like a duck in water. Both invincible and dangerous, he was just frolicking and bringing wanton death. Unfortunately the Sphinx was alone, and also very slow. The attackers just went around him at a good distance and kept going. The gods were more use, but they eventually threw up the white flag after a concentrated attack of thousands of players. The psychological effect of their presence was still palpable, though. My scouts, and the vampires and werebeasts embedded in the enemy ranks were reporting that the morale of the attackers had taken a big step back.

Eris also played her role brilliantly. The goddess of strife had completely forgiven me for a few strips of vibrantly colored fabric and a collection of women's fashion magazines from the last two hundred years. After that, the leaders of the *Keepers* and the *Lords of Chaos* declared that they'd had it up to their necks with the worthless commanders, and pulled their clans out of the war.

Overall, the situation was still up in the air. On the one hand, my army had taken serious losses and was falling back gradually step by step. Now in the fairly narrow crevasse, neither side could fully deploy and the battle was being fought by just one and a half thousand soldiers per side, leaving the others back in reserve. But once the undying broke through to the plains, the situation would become critical. Unfortunately, the enemy army was still five times as large as mine and, out in the open, they could finally take advantage of that. Everyone understood that, so the enemy was desperately pressing forward, not particularly worried about losses.

On the other hand, the enemy was seriously trailing their expectations as well, and had shed the illusion that they might win this quickly. The arrival of the invisible Ravenous Curs, the indestructible Sphinx, the fearsome Cerberus and the large number of divine beings, as well as the unexpectedly huge size of the Dark Sovereign's army were all unpleasant surprises. The enemy was just not ready for such a fierce battle. I was even forming the impression that one big push might be all it took to make them flee. Actually, the first little birdies had already taken flight. Now I would have to make their retreat grow into an uncontrollable rush for the hills.

I had been in my throne room since morning observing the situation through the Eye of the Sovereign and accepting reports from my commanders. I hadn't joined the battle myself yet, not wanting to risk it for so little. But every time a sector threatened to go out of control, my Gray Pack was there to replace normal NPC soldiers with respawning predators. All my generals were tired, but I could still see in their eyes that they still believed we would win. And that was what mattered.

Just then, in the silence after my generals finished their reports, Taisha's words sounded out softly:

"When defending one of the stone towers at the third defensive echelon, the entire catapult team led by Tarek Bigfoot died."

I didn't realize at first why my goblin lady was drawing my attention to that episode in the battle. After all, I'd lost a number of defensive towers since morning while dead goblins, as with other creatures, numbered in the thousands. But then I realized. Tarek Bigfoot was Taisha's father!!! I didn't even know he had come to this fight. When I offered my condolences, the beautiful goblin lady just waved her hand:

"It's nothing, Amra. After all, I already know that my whole family and all my memories were just a story invented by some programmers for atmosphere. None of it existed before and was created along with me. And yes Amra, I free you from the oath to hunt down and take revenge on my sisters' killers..."

Taisha said one thing but her deadened face immediately told me that the impressionable girl was just trying to reassure herself and that her father's death really had shook her to the core. So I was categorical:

"It was the gods of *Boundless Realm* who accepted my oath. You have no power over them. I will only stop avenging the deaths of your sisters after I bring them both back to life. And I can bring your father back too. It's all a matter of time and Direct Intervention Points."

All of Taisha's distance and lethargy blew away like the wind:

"So do it, Amra! Do it as fast as you can! And I'll help you! Including in the real world!"

At that very moment Gloom the Dark Rider

rode into my throne room:

"Sovereign, invasion again! I have detected five *Legion of Steel* players flying over Frigid Lake on silver pegasuses! They're coming straight here!"

Iron Jeanette was first to react, saying what we were all thinking:

"We proved too much for them. Now they're trying to send troops behind our back and open a second front! We cannot allow them to cross the lake!"

But how? Angelica Wayward's ships took severe damage in this morning's battle, and her pirates could not stop the winged pegasuses. They just flew too high. Only a player on a flying mount could stop this. To the attentive gazes of everyone in the room, my flap-eared Goblin Herbalist hopped down off his huge throne:

"The time has now come for me to enter the battle! Valerianna, attach your hornets to me. Friends, wish me luck. I just might need it!"

I ordered the Steward to transport me to my front door and whistled for VIXEN. The Royal Forest Wyvern was now as large as an airplane at level 440 and, flapping her wings noisily, plopped down next to me. I walked up and looked my love right in her big intelligent eyes:

"You've done a great job today spraying acid and poison on my enemies. You know the undying even gave you nicknames: Winged Death or F**ksup-Armor. That's because your acid has destroyed many of the best weapons and armor in the game today. But now we have another battle. It will be most important battle of either of our lives. There will be many enemies and they're very strong and experienced. But we cannot afford to lose!"

I took a heavy sigh and opened my stat sheet, showing what I had to work with in what very well might have been my final battle:

Name	Amra
Race	Goblin Vampire
Class	Dark Sovereign
Experience	#overflow error
Character level	442
Hitpoints (HP):	25271/25271
Endurance points	15826/15826
Statistics	
Strength (S)	652 (1751)
Agility (A)	630 (3642)
Intelligence (I)	50 (554)
Constitution (C)	642 (3159)
Perception (P)	50 (1251)

~ Finding a Body ~

Charisma (Ch)	896 (1650)
Unused points	**0**
Primary skills (10 of 10 chosen)	
Survivor (C S)	552 First specialization: double hitpoints bonus Second specialization: -10% damage taken Third Specialization: 30% defense against magic Fourth specialization: tripled Regeneration speed
Heavy armor (C S)	555 First specialization: resistant to acid. Second specialization: reduce all damage taken by 20%. Third Specialization: no penalty to movement speed. Fourth Specialization: all armor set bonuses increased by 25%
Foreman (Ch P)	210 First specialization: workers immune to recruitment Second specialization:

	doubled number of workers Third specialization: increased speed of all works Fourth specialization: tripled number of workers
Dodging (A P)	1000 First specialization: 30% chance of avoiding AoE-effect spells Second specialization: 50% chance of dodging arrows Third specialization: 30% chance of second Agility check, if first fails Fourth specialization: chance of dodging heavy weapons increased by 90%
Stealth (A C)	55 First specialization: -20 discovery radius. Second specialization: -50% discovery radius in the dark
Exotic Weapons (A P)	(440 + 18) First specialization: Flaming whip, additional fire damage, 5% chance of burning target Second specialization:

	Throwing nets, +300% throwing range Third specialization: Melee weapons, +20% chance of causing bleeding Fourth specialization: Blowguns, +1500% to Blowgun range
Riding (A C)	160 First specialization: +15% movement speed Second specialization: +20% movement speed Third specialization: +30% movement speed Fourth specialization: +40% movement speed
Acrobatics (Ch P)	89 First specialization: take no fall damage from any height Second specialization: +20% chance of dodging in close combat Third specialization: no penalty for using weapons from an unstable position
Warchief (Ch P)	199

	First specialization: soldiers immune to recruitment Second specialization: blessing effect doubled Third specialization: 50% defense against fear for all soldiers Fourth specialization: number of soldiers receiving positive effects tripled
Animal Control (Ch P)	690 First specialization: pet attacks improved Second specialization: pet defense improved Third specialization: pets receive stat bonuses from master Fourth specialization: pet speed increased

Secondary skills (5 of 10 chosen)

Veil	25 First specialization: shapeshifter (three times per day)
Diplomat	47 First specialization:

~ Finding a Body ~

	fearmonger
Alchemy	42 First specialization: make elixirs with more than one property
Herbalism	8
Superboss	66 First specialization: Direct Intervention Points regenerate 25% faster Second specialization: increased influence on NPC's

So obviously, I spent practically all available points on my main skills, improving Amra's stats and consciously sacrificing secondaries. I even left some of my secondaries empty for a time. There was no use for them in battle. Plus if I survived this day, in my new life I could take whatever I needed. At the same time I removed all the garbage like Regeneration or the Heavy Armor perks giving Endurance point bonuses.

The Dark Sovereign was now a strong buffer for his soldiers, workers and pets. But still he was not opposed to fighting up close. That just was not my character's main forte in combat. No, my strong suit was that it was very hard to find any way to damage the Dark Sovereign if you didn't already know one.

And that was confirmed in the beginning of the midair battle with the *Legion of Steel*'s five strongest warriors. As soon as I saw the white dots of the silver pegasuses approaching over the waves of the lake, the thick clouds above me dispersed, and the gloomy sky cleared. Light? How predictable, attacking a vampire with light. Apparently they hadn't gotten the memo! When I reached Taste Tester level 1000 (thanks to the packages from my vampire friends, and more importantly the gods) my vampire was no longer vulnerable to either light or holy magic!

Seemingly the enemy was expecting something radically different, because they spent some time just flying straight at me, clearly were hoping Amra would just burn to ashes. I even managed to take advantage of their confusion and got off a blowgun shot, stitching right through the Pegasus beneath Violetta Bestia [LEGION]. I considered the mage woman the most dangerous of the five enemy players and sent her on a short flight into a whirlpool in the lake. After that, the flying vee of icy white pegasuses made a line. Magical defense shields lit up around the players and whole swarms of insects began buzzing. Well, well. These flying players even had flying pets! It would be intriguing to compare them with my sister's hornets... by the way, where were they?

I looked around for the insects and was disappointed to find that VIXEN had flown here too fast. Of course, the Royal Forest Wyvern was the second fastest creature in *Boundless Realm* after the Phoenix plus she had bonuses and four speed-related perks. Seemingly the hornets just got too far behind and returned to their master. Too bad, I'd have to somehow twist out of this without them. And I'd have to twist out literally. Only by entering a spiral could I get my flying snake to dodge the first barrage of throwing nets. Still, one arrow shot by Kristina Mozzi [LEGION] did hit my VIXEN.

No matter, my pet's life bar was practically unaffected. I turned the flying snake around, but... nothing happened! VIXEN wasn't obeying me! What was more, I could hear my pet shrieking in terror. Something was wrong. And not exactly just "wrong." My mount's hitpoints should not have been falling so fast from one lone arrow. Meanwhile a portal opened behind me and a whole group of undying came out to join the four on pegasuses: one on a silver dragonfly, one on a griffon, a few on eagles, one on a manticore, and one on a normal wyvern... Had they made a team of everyone with a flying mount?! Seemingly yes.

And meanwhile, VIXEN just kept getting worse. She could barely stay in the air. Her life bar was going down faster and faster with every second. What had they used against her? I bent down, barely holding onto the flying snake's spines with my finger tips and trying to pull the arrow out of VIXEN's throat. But I jerked my hand away as soon as I saw what was there. A cursed arrow! They shot us with a cursed arrow! Most likely this was the very same one that my emissary Murk used to destroy the undying in the Upper Fort on the Styx. I'd never get it out now. And that meant there was no saving my VIXEN. My sweetie would soon be replaced by a Midnight Wraith.

I steeled my nerves and got ready to jump into the freezing water, giving my beloved pet one last order:

"As soon as I jump off, fly as fast as you can to the enemy stockade on the opposite shore. And do not let your death be in vain! Take the whole enemy garrison with you. When you respawn, wait for me in the castle!"

I couldn't say whether VIXEN understood me or not, as she was being eaten alive from the inside by the ghastly wraith, but my winged beauty seemed to take the proper course. I then went shooting downward from that massive height. And no, I wasn't afraid to go splat on the water. Amra had a perk from Acrobatics that eliminated all fall damage. And I was also not especially afraid to be taken captive, because at any moment I could turn into a fish and take a deep dive. What was tormenting me was the fact that the midair battle was now lost and everyone knew it. And even worse the enemy would now reach the shore unimpeded and open portals, which would bring a flood of enemy troops.

"That's for selling my necklace," came a message in the local chat from Kristina Mozzi.

"And for what you said about your 'pee-pee' this morning."

The second message came from the leader of the *Legion of Steel* and immediately made me think. It actually had me so intrigued I temporarily forgot what was happening. So that meant that the leader of *Boundless Realm*'s strongest clan Till Quick_Fingers [LEGION] was also the President of the Boundless Realm Corporation Thomas Heywood! Well, I'll be damned!

I floated on top of the water. Many enemy players were circling in the sky above me. Mockery and insults rained down from every direction, but I was in no rush to dive to the bottom. I was purposely trying to look pitiful and helpless so my enemies would forget their mission and fly lower to watch the Dark Sovereign die with their own eyes. That was my last chance to stop them from reaching the shore and opening a portal. If I pulled it off exactly right, I could eliminate the whole flock at once, but they all had to be close. Closer. Closer. Just a little more. Now!

My enemies weren't the only ones who knew how to open portals for winged allies. And my portal was somewhat more effective. First of all, the portal itself was larger as were the creatures that came out of it! Out flew hundreds of harpies led by their Queen, Kirra'ellita Huntress of the Night. And after them came gargoyles, manticores and most importantly deadly dragons!!! And what was this leviathan??? I didn't even know how such a colossal creature managed to come through the portal:

Tiamat
Mother of dragons (unique creature)

The huge red dragon loosed a stream of fire almost a quarter mile long, turning the fleeing undying into flaming torches. The large harpy herself then, heavily and loudly flapping her huge wings, hovered over the water and extended me a clawed hand:

"Grab hold. How many times am I gonna save your ass, Timothy?!"

I thanked my wife for the timely aid and immediately asked whether she had brought the package I asked for.

"It's in my inventory. But maybe we should get to the shore before you put it on? Fenrir is supposed to be pretty huge, I'm not sure I can hold him in my claws!"

* * *

KIRRA'ELLITA LANDED right at the gates of my castle and was finally able to firmly embrace me. Her arms merged with her wings, which prevented her from doing so in flight. Taisha ran out of the palace to meet me but stopped sharply when she saw us. The Harpy Queen answered with a smirk:

"I make no claim on your husband in *Boundless Realm*. Here he is entirely yours!"

And meanwhile the Dark Sovereign's troops were all in formation for a counterattack. I saw perfectly straight lines of orcs, elves, rougarou and undead with various glowing symbols over their heads for buffs. And my troops were full of vim and vigor, ready to drive the undying back beyond the crevasse and mountain passes. They were only awaiting my command.

And then I started to speak, doubling it in the local public chat for my nearby enemies:

"Soldiers! Enough retreating! I'm sick of playing a losing game. The corporation told me to entertain these undying and I have done that. Now the time has come to show the enemy our true power!"

With these words I donned the fur high-boots, the final piece of Fenrir's Cursed Regalia. And a superpowered wolf howl rolled over the plains to the very mountains, reinforced by my troops who were shaking their weapons and greeting the enormous Fenrir's return to the mortal plane.

> *Mission completed: Fenrir's Legacy (4/4)*
>
> *Reward: Animal Control +10, Strength +50, Agility +50, Constitution +50, Gray Pack member limit now depends only on your Charisma and skills*
>
> *Current Gray Pack member limit: 550*
>
> *ATTENTION!!!*
>
> *Your character will have the Criminal tag to all* **Boundless Realm** *until all items of Fenrir's Cursed Regalia are removed. Character death will not remove Criminal tag*

I ignored what it said about the "Criminal" tag because I'd been constantly killing players for a while now and was used to having it most of the time anyway. Plus the Dark Sovereign was essentially a criminal and antagonist to most players even without that. But as for the Gray Pack being able to have 550 members... my heart sped up... that could spell the end of everything

~ Finding a Body ~

alive!

"Brother, you've returned!" Hel goddess of death appeared before me, now equal to me both in power and height. Behind the old crone came two huge heavenly wargs at level 600, Sköll and Hati. They were the hounds of the Eternal Hunt and Fenrir's children. My children.

From my enormous height, I could see the square packed with soldiers. I greeted the ancient gods with a deep bow of respect. With a nod of my fanged head I separately greeted the god of trickery and Fenrir's father Loki, here to watch his reborn son in action. Cerberus pressed himself to the ground and gave a bark of submission, admitting my superiority. Well then, time to teach my enemies some respect! Let the word "Amra" make the knees of all undying quake!

Although, I supposed that all I wouldn't even need all my troops to defeat this pitiful enemy, which was now hunkered down in the mountains. I needed just a few hundred rougarou or wild animals. As it was, the bonuses would be enough and the power of my fighters would be so unlimited that even the gods couldn't stop my warband!

* * *

CURRENT PRESIDENT Thomas Heywood was first to present his program. His well-formulated speech and confident tone brilliantly conveyed a story about the company's incredible financial figures in the last year along with record payouts to corporate shareholders. Finally, he showed some beautiful massive holograms of new game locations, and talked about future events and ways to attract new players.

And although I personally liked the speech Kira, sitting next to me, could only cringe:

"No, that's not gonna cut it. Thomas has been told before that the inflow of new players has basically stopped. Now it's impossible to ignore. And no crazy fantasy locations can solve that. To maintain a positive dynamic, we need a tectonic shift."

And the next speaker and candidate for President, Andrei Soloviev, just so happened to mention a drastic change in strategy. No, the popular online game *Boundless Realm* wouldn't be disappearing once and for all. We would keep it alive as a stable source of income, but the corporation was going to use all their available income on other projects which, with time, would replace this one universal game with a vast array of narrowly specialized ones. We would make virtual entertainment for every kind of person — from erotic adventures for horny young people to extremely realistic postapocalyptic worlds for those who liked to test their nerves. But his capstone idea was virtual worlds for the disabled and elderly where they could be surrounded by warmth and care in a way the real world could never provide. And beyond that they would polish the NPC algorithms and even, why the hell not, search for artificial intelligence algorithms. The way he explained it, we already had a head start there, which gave him a timid but growing confidence that we might one day achieve success.

And although the second presentation was clearly outshined by the first, Kira thought Andrei Soloviev's ideas had more potential to garner interest from the owners of the corporation.

"Your turn, Timothy. Don't let me down, boy!" came titanium oligarch Vladimir Toropov, cheering me on from our box.

I walked out on stage but there was a slight hitch. Although I had announced my speech very far in advance, most people in the room had only two speeches in their program. I wasn't even given the floor right away because some directors wanted to skip right to the next stage of today's meeting — reading Inessa Tyle's will and then, of course, get straight to a vote. But the issue was decided in my favor and they let me go to the podium. And my very first words instantly drew the attention of all the directors and co-owners of the corporation:

"Ladies and gentlemen, perhaps some of you have heard of me before. I play a character named Amra. For those who have, there's no need to mention my leadership qualities. But for the rest of you, in a short time, I was able to assemble an army that surpassed all the rest of *Boundless Realm* combined. You may also know me as the corporate tester who got a few directors fired after they messed with him, including some very influential ones. I ask you to hold that particularly in mind, because we will certainly be returning to it. But most importantly, I'd like you to know me as Timothy Tyle, new head of the Tyle family, which has historically owned the Boundless Realm Corporation."

Fervent chatter broke out in the room. My words resonated and sparked a few arguments and discussions. And that abruptly grew stronger when I declared myself the lone true heir of Inessa Tyle and even asked them to open her will to check.

Three minutes later, after everyone was familiar with the will, they listened to me with even greater attention, hanging on my every word.

"So then, ladies and gentlemen, first my

personal thoughts on the last two speeches. Thomas Heywood — all clear, standard, worn out so bad it has a hole in it. I'm not interested. Thomas is an experienced manager who has unfortunately been left to stagnate. Still, the corporation needs him for his vast knowledge. He and I had a little scrap recently, but that does nothing to diminish Thomas's dignity and experience. So the first thing I'll do when I become President of the Corporation is to appoint him to a different part of the company that is no less important than *Boundless Realm* itself. I'll talk about that a bit later. But for now let me give my thoughts on Andrei Soloviev's speech, especially his 'worlds for the elderly.' I have seen and even been imprisoned in just such a world for a decent length of time. One might call it a painless sort of euthanasia, but it is in fact a kind of murder. If we take Andrei Soloviev's suggestion, sooner or later the corporation will see its day in court for mass murder of the elderly and disabled, and every last one of us will get the electric chair. So I am fundamentally opposed!"

Andrei Soloviev tried to pick up the microphone, but I sharply demanded he return to his seat because I hadn't finished.

"Now on to something else the previous speaker mentioned: studying artificial intelligence. I assure you, ladies and gentlemen, that would be a complete waste of time. Andrei Soloviev's team will not be able to make any inroads there. But it isn't be because I don't believe artificial intelligence exists. It's actually the opposite. I am all too familiar with it. Allow me to introduce my companion." I asked them to bring out the android girl we said was a simple robot secretary at the entrance. "This is Taisha, the same consciousness that first Alexandro Lavrius's team, then Andrei Soloviev's team were unable to capture in *Boundless Realm*."

The clamor in the hall became deafening. I heard people exclaim that it had to be checked, while others just shouted about fakery and manipulation. But I tried to reassure all the unbelievers:

"Naturally you may perform a Turing test, or whatever else you like to confirm her identity. Well, no copying her data or any other method that could put the corporation's intellectual property at risk. But still I request that you treat Taisha as the exact same kind of independent intelligent entity as you or I. Everything you do to her must be with her consent. Taisha has the best understanding of artificial intelligence perhaps on earth, so she will be made responsible for that new division of the company. And I would ask current President Thomas Heywood to handle financial issues for this high-potential division because it is the very kind of ambitious project he needs to realize his tremendous abilities. Taisha has opened a door to a future where the Boundless Realm Corporation is at the very forefront of many if not all innovative fields! Spaceflight, autonomous science stations and new ways of keeping government and its judiciary impartial. Our corporation will be making and developing all that! That isn't just billions of credits, that's trillions at least, maybe more!

And now that I've explained my program briefly and with minor digressions, let's get back to the issue of fired directors. I don't want any traitors or anyone else who'd put a stick in our spokes in my corporation. So first of all, the post of Vice-President will be given to the experienced, strict manager Vladimir Toropov. Vladimir owns a large metallurgical business, but he's already agreed to hand it down to his children and grandchildren so he can fully concentrate on whipping the Boundless Realm Corporation into shape. Second, I propose we hold an open vote for our next president. Any objections?"

ON A SANDY beach, Val and her boyfriend Andre were playing volleyball against Leon and Taisha.

Leon's children, three teen girls, were making sand castles with Max Sochnier's help. Simply idyllic.

I had spent the morning swimming in the cold water until I got muscle cramps. And now I was relaxing on a lounger with a glass of nonalcoholic cocktail, simply enjoying the rare moment of peace alongside Kira, who was doing the same.

"I still can't believe it all ended so well! Just imagine, ninety-seven percent of the votes were for you! I mean, that sounds like fiction! And the finale... who could have guessed that Andrei Soloviev would bring a pistol to the board of directors meeting and shoot himself in the temple!"

"Yes, the end of the meeting came as a surprise," I agreed, remembering the bloody scene. "Although he knew he'd lost everything and the investors behind him would be sure to demand he return the funds they invested in his candidacy. And I never would have been able to forgive the attempt on my life. And I'm not talking about placing the virtual reality capsule on the utility floor. I can just tell Andrei Soloviev was behind the technician's attack as well. He wanted to kill two birds with one stone — both isolate the two of us and make it look like Taisha paid for it. But I knew my NPC companion too well to believe his insinuations.

~ Finding a Body ~

And as for the vote, that was all bold self-assurance. The directors weren't used to being pressured like that. In their minds, the stronger and more self-confident one usually does the pressuring, so many of them instinctively lined up behind me. What's more, I understand Thomas Heywood's mentality. He will always follow whoever has the power. But the greatest impact on the vote of course was Taisha. If she hadn't come to the board meeting it would all have been much harder. By the way, it took me lots of work to convince the fickle NPC. You won't believe it, but she didn't want to come to our world at first, because here you are my wife."

"Wait, is that right? Well, I did tell her I made no claim to her position in the game. She simply answered me in kind. We both 'marked our territory,' you might say," Kira laughed happily.

"Taisha understands people well, so she's very, very cautious. She left her main body in *Boundless Realm* and the android body is just an interface for communicating with us. If the connection with *Boundless Realm* were to somehow break, this robot would be little different from the millions of others just like it. Taisha didn't agree to have her mind copied fully or partially because she was afraid to be made obsolete. But I think, after the child is born, she should calm down somewhat. And that will have a double effect, because she has already admitted she's looking for a way to get a child from the game into the real world. And not as a program in a robot's brain even the most advanced, but as a real baby made of flesh and blood."

"Sounds like fiction," said Kira, shaking her head in disbelief.

I had to be honest. I didn't much believe it could be done either. But Taisha said it was possible to write data into a human brain in theory, something of a "reverse digitization." And she was prepared to put forth all her effort and even bring in basically unlimited computing resources to create a biological body for our new baby and give it a mind. And if that worked... I was even afraid to think about what a leap forward that would be and how much our normal lives would change. After all, if the memory and nature of a human could be copied and transferred into a younger body made with a DNA sample... that was basically immortality!

We kept silent. Then Kira dropped down to a whisper and asked:

"Do you have any more wishes to ask me?"

I had already thought this through. I had a son, or more accurately would soon. The Egg of New Life would allow me to make him into a boy of any race, not necessarily just a goblin. And if Taisha's experiments bore fruit, my son would not be restricted to the game. What more did I need to be totally content? So I looked at Kira and whispered:

"I want a daughter!"

The End

About the Author

Michael Atamanov was born in 1975 in Grozny, Chechnia. He excelled at school, winning numerous national science and writing competitions. Having graduated with honors, he entered Moscow University to study material engineering. Soon, however, he had no home to return to: their house was destroyed during the first Chechen campaign. Michael's family fled the war, taking shelter with some relatives in Stavropol Territory in the South of Russia.

Having graduated from the University, Michael was forced to accept whatever work was available. He moonlighted in chemical labs, loaded trucks, translated technical articles, worked as a software installer and scene shifter for local artists and events. At the same time he never stopped writing, even when squatting in some seedy Moscow hostels. Writing became an urgent need for Michael. He submitted articles to science publications, penned news fillers for a variety of web sites and completed a plethora of technical and copywriting gigs.

Then one day unexpectedly for himself he started writing fairy tales and science fiction novels. For several years, his audience consisted of only one person: Michael's elder son. Then, at the end of 2014 he decided to upload one of his manuscripts to a free online writers resource. Readers liked it and demanded a sequel. Michael uploaded another book, and yet another, his audience growing as did his list. It was his readers who helped Michael hone his writing style. He finally had the breakthrough he deserved when the Moscow-based EKSMO - the biggest publishing house in Europe - offered him a contract for his first and consequent books.

Want to be the first to know about our latest LitRPG, sci fi and fantasy titles from your favorite authors?

Subscribe to our NEW RELEASES newsletter: http://eepurl.com/b7niIL

Thank you for reading *Finding a Body!* If you like what you've read, check out other sci fi, fantasy and LitRPG novels published by Magic Dome Books:

Reality Benders LitRPG series by Michael Atamanov:
Countdown
External Threat
Game Changer
Web of Worlds
A Jump into the Unknown
Aces High

The Dark Herbalist LitRPG series by Michael Atamanov:
Video Game Plotline Tester
Stay on the Wing
A Trap for the Potentate
Finding a Body

Perimeter Defense LitRPG series by Michael Atamanov:
Sector Eight
Beyond Death
New Contract
A Game with No Rules

League of Losers LitRPG Series by Michael Atamanov:
A Cat and his Human

The Way of the Shaman LitRPG series by Vasily Mahanenko:
Survival Quest
The Kartoss Gambit
The Secret of the Dark Forest
The Phantom Castle
The Karmadont Chess Set
Shaman's Revenge
Clans War

The Alchemist LitRPG series by Vasily Mahanenko:
City of the Dead
Forest of Desire
Tears of Alron

El Diablo by G.Zotov
(a supernatural thriller)

Mirror World LitRPG series by Alexey Osadchuk:
Project Daily Grind
The Citadel
The Way of the Outcast
The Twilight Obelisk

Underdog LitRPG series by Alexey Osadchuk:
Dungeons of the Crooked Mountains
The Wastes
The Dark Continent
The Otherworld

An NPC's Path LitRPG series by Pavel Kornev:
The Dead Rogue
Kingdom of the Dead
Deadman's Retinue

The Sublime Electricity series by Pavel Kornev:
The Illustrious
The Heartless
The Fallen
The Dormant

Citadel World series by Kir Lukovkin:
The URANUS Code
The Secret of Atlantis

You're in Game!
(LitRPG Stories from Bestselling Authors)

You're in Game-2!
(More LitRPG stories set in your favorite worlds)

The Fairy Code by Kaitlyn Weiss:
Captive of the Shadows
Chosen of the Shadows

More books and series are coming out soon!

In order to have new books of the series translated faster, we need your help and support! Please consider leaving a review or spread the word by recommending *Finding a Body* to your friends and posting the link on social media. The more people buy the book, the sooner we'll be able to make new translations available.

Thank you!

Till next time!

www.ingramcontent.com/pod-product-compliance
Lightning Source LLC
Chambersburg PA
CBHW060756030726
47503CB00002B/265